SACRED GAMES

ALSO BY GARY CORBY

The Pericles Commission
The Ionia Sanction

SACRED GAMES

Gary Corby

SOHO
CRIME

First published in the United States in 2013
Soho Press, Inc.
853 Broadway
New York, NY 10003

Library of Congress Cataloging-in-Publication Data
Corby, Gary.
Sacred games / by Gary Corby.
p cm
Includes bibliographical references and index.
ISBN 978-1-61695-227-3
eISBN 978-1-61695-228-0
1. Nicolaos (Fictitious character)—Fiction. 2. Private investiga-
tors—Fiction. 3. Diotima (Legendary character)—Fiction. 4. Olympic
games (Ancient)—Fiction. 5. Pancratium—Fiction. 6. Murder—
Investigation—Fiction. 7. Athens (Greece)—Fiction. 8. Greece—
History—Athenian supremacy, 479–431 B.C.—Fiction. I. Title.
PR9619.4.C665S23 2013
823'.92—dc23   2012046373

Interior design by Janine Agro, Soho Press, Inc.
Map illustration by Katherine Grames

Printed in the United States of America

10 9 8 7 6 5 4 3 2 1

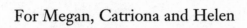

For Megan, Catriona and Helen

In Praise of Timodemus

So as the bards begin their verse
With hymns to the Olympian Zeus,
So has this hero laid the claim
To conquest in the Sacred Games.

The Second Nemean Ode of Pindar, dedicated to
Timodemus, son of Timonous, of the deme Archarnae of Athens

A Note on Names

MOST MODERN WESTERN names come from the Bible, a book which had yet to be written when my hero Nico walked the muddy paths of Olympia. Quite a few people have asked me what's the "right" way to say the ancient names in these stories. There is no right way! I hope you'll pick whatever sounds happiest to you, and have fun reading the story.

For those who'd like a little more guidance, I've suggested a way to say each name in the character list. My suggestions do not match ancient pronunciation. They're how I think the names will sound best in an English sentence.

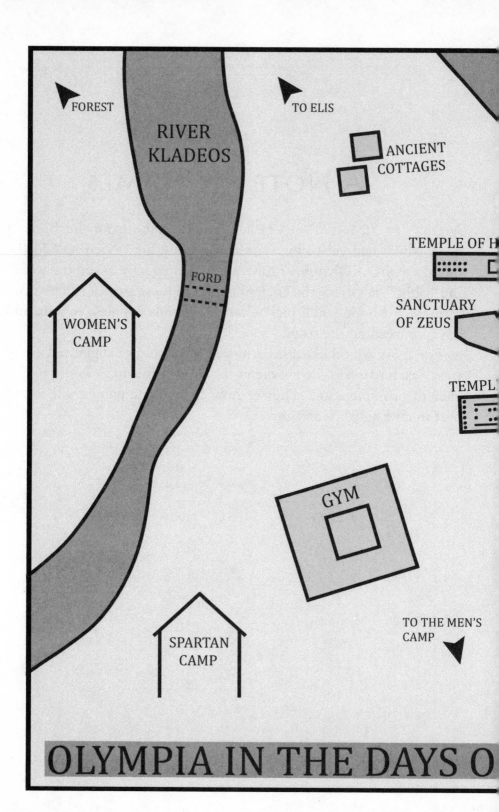

FOREST

TO ELIS

RIVER
KLADEOS

ANCIENT
COTTAGES

TEMPLE OF H

FORD

SANCTUARY
OF ZEUS

WOMEN'S
CAMP

TEMPL

GYM

TO THE MEN'S
CAMP

SPARTAN
CAMP

OLYMPIA IN THE DAYS O

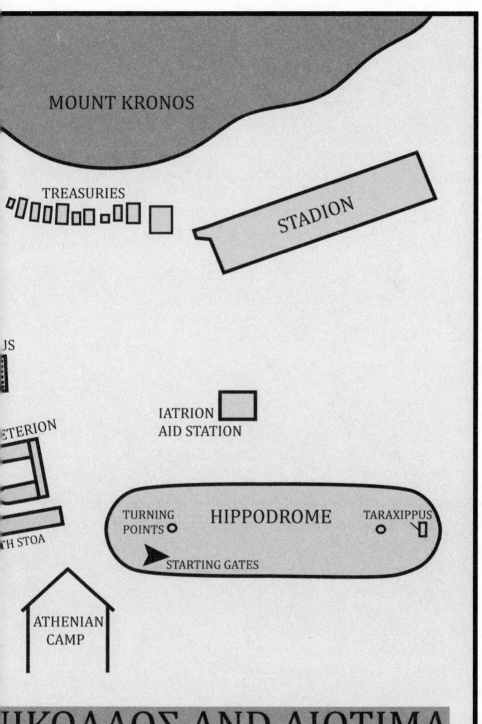

MOUNT KRONOS

TREASURIES

STADION

JS

ERION

IATRION
AID STATION

TH STOA

TURNING
POINTS ○

HIPPODROME

TARAXIPPUS
○

STARTING GATES

ATHENIAN
CAMP

ΝΙΚΟΛΑΟΣ AND ΔΙΟΤΙΜΑ

THE ACTORS

Characters with an asterisk by their name were real historical people.

Nicolaos NEE-CO-LAY-OS (Nicholas)	Our Protagonist	"I am Nicolaos son of Sophroniscus, of Athens."
Socrates* SOCK-RA-TEEZ	An irritant	"Will we get to see someone die?"
Diotima* DIO-TEEMA	A priestess of Artemis	"Have you any idea how deadly it is in here?"
Timodemus* TIM-O-DEEM-US (Timo)	Athenian athlete, a friend of Nicolaos	"This is embarrassing."
Arakos AR-AK-OS	Spartan athlete	He's the big, silent type.
Markos MARK-OS (Mark)	A Spartan	"We seem to have a problem here."
Exelon EX-EL-ON	Chief of the Ten Judges of the Games	"I blame Athens for this disaster."
Pericles* PERRY-CLEEZ	A politician	"Nicolaos, I want an Athenian victory. We need a victory."
Gorgo* GOR-GO	The dowager Queen of Sparta	"So you're the ones they say are causing so much trouble."

Klymene KLY-MEN-EE	Priestess of Demeter	"I woke up, and there he was, naked."
Pindar* PIN-DAR	A famous poet	"I could teach you tricks of sycophancy that would make your eyes water."
Pleistarchus* PLY-STARK-OS	King of Sparta	"Why are you still alive?"
Festianos FEST-EE-AHN-OS	Uncle of Timodemus	"I was a trifle worse the wear for drink."
Niallos NEAL-OS	Team manager	"I killed my friend."
Timonous* TIM-O-NOOS (One Eye)	Father of Timodemus	"A father is not always the most objective when it comes to his own son."
Heraclides* HERA-CLEED-EEZ	A doctor	"I'm a doctor. The idea is to not be with a corpse."
Iphicles IF-E-CLEEZ	A charioteer	"This is my lucky whip."
Petale PETAL-EE	A hooker	"I told you we girls were full up, so to speak."
Pythax PIE-THAX	Chief of the city guard of Athens. Sports fan.	"You look like you ain't got a muscle in your body."
Sophroniscus* SOFF-RON-ISK-US	Father of Nicolaos	"Don't add lying to your father to your crimes."

Empedocles* EMP-E-DOKE-LEEZ	Philosopher	"My plan is simple, yet brilliant. I was once a fish, you know."
Libon* LEE-BON	An architect	"The next three days will decide whether my life has been worthwhile."
Xenia ZEN-E-AH	A slave	"Are you hitting on me?"
The Fake Heracles	A weakling	"We do it for fun."
Xenares ZEN-AR-EEZ	An ephor of Sparta	"None of your wit, please. You can see this is a crisis."
Aggelion, Megathenes & Korillos	Athletes from Keos, Megara and Corinth	"How can someone who doesn't understand sport solve a sporting crime?"
Dromeus* DRO-MAY-US	An Olympic champion	"Murdering don't mean a thing, kid."

The Chorus

Assorted athletes, judges, heralds, slaves, donkeys and crazed, drunken sports fans.

DAY 1 OF THE 80ᵀᴴ OLYMPIAD OF THE SACRED GAMES

THE PROCESSION WOUND past the Sanctuary of Zeus. They'd been walking two days, from Elis to Olympia.

"Will we get to see someone die?" Socrates asked. Like any boy, he looked forward to the violence of the struggle more than the beauty of the sport. Unlike me, Socrates had never seen death. To him, it was still a game.

"How should I know?" I said. "You can only hope."

We stood in the crowd to watch the long line file past: the athletes, their fathers and uncles and brothers, the trainers, and the Ten Judges of the Games. Socrates jumped up and down to see over the shoulders of the spectators in front. That's what he got for being a twelve-year-old in a crowd of mostly men.

The team from Sparta passed by, one of the few teams I could recognize without having to ask, because Spartans march in step where others walk. At the rear of the Spartans came one of the largest men I had ever seen, a towering hulk—he was half as tall again as me, with shoulders that could have hefted an ox. The chiton he wore had enough material to double as the sail for a small boat. The blacksmith who'd made his armor must have wept for joy at the challenge, then died of exhaustion trying to cover such a chest. Despite the two-day march, the large man's stride was brisk; he looked neither left nor right, and he swung his well-muscled arms in much the same style as the Titans once had done when they strode the earth.

The Athenians came next. Leading them, almost in the shadow of the huge Spartan, was Timodemus, son of Timonous, of the deme Archarnae. I waved at once and shouted, "*Chaire*, Timodemus! Hail, Timodemus!"

He smiled broadly and waved back. "*Chaire*, Nicolaos!"

I raised my arms in a victory salute, meaning he would win his event. Other men, all Athenians, cheered for Timodemus, too. Everyone knew he was one of the stars of this Olympics, a likely winner of the pankration, and Athens's best hope of a victory.

The large Spartan, who had ignored everyone around him up to now, turned and said something to Timodemus. Timo's smile disappeared in an instant. Perhaps the Spartan had complained of too much levity on what was supposed to be a solemn occasion.

Beside Timo walked a man who looked so like my friend I could have sworn the two were brothers, had I not known better. They were both short men and wore their hair cut almost to the scalp, but by his weathered skin and destroyed left eye, I knew the other to be Timo's father. A third man, stockier and noticeably taller, walked with them a half-pace behind. He looked like an older brother, and one more tired by the long march. This could be no one but Timo's uncle, and the eldest of the three. The men of Timo's family were all former athletes, and though they were too old to compete, the father at least had kept himself in decent condition.

Timodemus and the rest of the Athenians were followed by the Corinthians, then the Thebans, the men of Argos and Thessaly, and Rhodes and all the other cities with athletes whose excellence permitted them to compete at the eightieth Games sacred to Zeus, king of the gods.

The last of the contestants passed by, the forlorn and grimy men from Megara, who every step of the way had eaten the dust raised by those who'd gone before. We spectators waited for the tail to pass, then followed as one large, milling crowd.

Though it was still early morning, already I sweated freely. The close mass of spectators added to the heat of this already hot midsummer day. There must have been ten thousand of us, from every part of Hellas, all at this one place called Olympia, here to bring glory to Zeus in the form of the greatest sport in the world.

We skirted the Sanctuary of Zeus, passed the newly raised temple—so new in fact I'd yet to look inside—and stopped at the Bouleterion, the council house of Olympia. Men elbowed one another for the best positions to see and hear the ceremony to come. Those at the back would struggle to hear. Socrates and I were small enough to weave our way toward the front.

The *hellanodikai*—the Judges of the Hellenes—took the steps up the Bouleterion. They were dressed in formal chitons of bright colors, with long sleeves that covered their arms and hems that went all the way down to their ankles. All ten wore expressions to match the gravity of their task. The judges were citizens of the city of Elis, within whose land Olympia lies. For the next five days, the word of these men was law, and no man, not Pericles nor a king of Sparta, could gainsay them. All were chosen for their honesty and integrity.

Before the council house stood a bronze statue of Zeus Herkios, who is Zeus of the Oaths. He was twice the height of any man, and he held in each hand a deadly thunderbolt, his right arm raised and ready to throw, a promise of retribution to any man who broke an oath made before him.

An enormous tripod stood to one side of the Zeus. It held aloft a wide brazier that had been polished till it gleamed and from which orange flames leaped up in a futile attempt to touch Apollo's sun. I could feel the heat of the fire upon my face, even from a distance.

On the other side of Zeus lay a thick altar stone, where a boar squealed and struggled, its legs held down by two assistants whose chitons were soaked with sweat.

The Chief of the Judges stepped away from his fellows to stand before Zeus and address the crowd. He delivered a prayer—a loud one over the squeals of the waiting sacrifice—then recited the oath of the judges, in which he promised to be fair and honest in all his decisions, to take no bribes, and to respect the rules of the Games.

An assistant handed a knife to the Chief Judge, who took two steps to the writhing boar. He pushed back its head with his left hand to expose the neck to the sharp blade in his right. As he did, the animal twisted so much its hind legs came free; the body rotated and almost fell. The men swore, and their knees sagged under the weight as they struggled to prevent the squirming, screeching sacrifice from hitting the ground.

Men about me drew in their breath; if the animal escaped, it would be a disaster. The assistant who'd presented the knife jumped in and got his arms underneath at the last moment, and together they hauled the sacrifice back up. The Chief Judge didn't wait for anything else to go wrong. He plunged his knife into the boar's throat at once and sawed across the flesh. The blood spurted over everyone clustered about the altar. As sacrifices go, it had been as bad as you could get, but it was a death offered to Zeus, and that was the most important thing.

The crowd resumed breathing.

A man beside me said, "The sacrifice didn't go willingly. It's an ill omen." Men around him nodded, and I could only agree.

"Not so," said another man. "The boar struggled to live as the competitors will struggle to win. Zeus favors us with a tough contest this Olympiad." It was a middle-aged man who spoke, and balding, but his voice held authority and a melodious tone that carried well. Many heard him, and the crowd settled at his words.

The way the man had controlled us with his voice reminded me of Pericles. Curious, I studied this stranger from aside. He had the look of a priest about him. But no priest I'd ever seen had such a piercing way with his eyes or such intensity of expression. His head turned at that moment, and our eyes locked. He must have known I'd been staring, but he didn't seem upset so much as resigned, as if he was used to such rudeness. I was embarrassed and turned back to the action before I felt forced to say something.

The Butcher of the Games stepped forward with his meat cleaver. He dismembered the thighs of the still-quivering boar and cut the meat into thin slices. The Chief Judge took the first slice, and with bloody fingers tossed it into the brazier, where the offering could be heard to sizzle as the meat roasted to charcoal. They were not cooking the flesh but giving it to Zeus, because meat on which an oath has been made may not be eaten by mortal man.

Each Judge in his turn repeated the actions of the Chief until all ten had made their oaths and reinforced them with the blood and meat of the sacrifice.

Next it was the turn of the athletes. They stepped forward, one by one, and made their oath—a different one than that of the judges—to obey the rules, to neither cheat nor bribe, and in addition they swore they had trained for at least ten months. To the men who would compete in the boxing and the pankration, after each made his oath, the Chief Judge added, "Mighty Zeus absolves you, athlete, from the charge of murder if you kill your opponent in the contest." Each athlete to whom the Chief Judge said this thanked him and stepped away.

The trainers and the fathers, brothers, and uncles of the athletes, too, were required to make their oaths, but without the need to affirm they had trained. For them, the oath was required merely to ensure they did not cheat in favor of their relative.

As they waited their turn in line, I saw the Spartan turn once more to Timodemus and say something. It must have been an insult, because Timo scowled and started forward. As one, Timo's father and uncle grabbed Timodemus by the shoulders and dragged him back. The Spartan laughed and turned his back on them.

Timo's father spoke to Timo, and even at a distance I could see they were harsh words. He'd probably ordered Timo not to let the man provoke him. What was going on? It was an act of utmost arrogance for the Spartan to insult a man and then expose his back.

I nudged the man next to me. "The big man to the side over there, the one among the Spartans. Do you know who he is?"

He looked where I pointed and nodded. "That's Arakos. He fights for the Spartans in the pankration. They say to face him is like fighting a rock."

The pankration was Timo's own event.

Dear Gods, Timo would have to fight that monster? Timo was a dead man.

Arakos the Spartan stepped forward to take his turn at the altar, along with his trainer but no father or family. Arakos made his oath, and the Chief Judge absolved him of murder in the coming contest.

Then it was Timo's turn to take the oath, to promise not to cheat, and to sacrifice a thin slice of the boar.

Arakos of Sparta spoke once more as Timodemus came down the steps. Timodemus froze, then snarled in rage. Every man present heard that snarl. Every head snapped in their direction. My friend Timodemus, in full view of the judges and the crowd, launched himself off the steps, hands stretching to strangle the Spartan.

THE FIRST EVENT of the Olympics is always the competition for the heralds. It begins straight after the opening ceremony. Each contestant in turn stands in the Colonnade of the Echoes—a narrow passage lined with columns—where he makes a practice announcement that echoes back and forth seven times. The judges decide which hopefuls have the loudest, clearest voices, and they become the Heralds of the Games, their job to start each event and announce the winners.

I didn't need to hear a lot of men shout at the tops of their voices. If I wanted to be shouted at, all I had to do was find my father; he was with his friends somewhere in this crowd.

This was my first Olympics. Father had always refused to take us when I was a child. He had no interest in sport, only in sculpture. Yet all of a sudden, he'd taken an interest in the Games. I wondered why but not enough to risk the question. It seemed every time Sophroniscus and I spoke these days, it turned into an argument.

So instead I went in search of my friend Timodemus, who'd been dragged off the Spartan and led away by his trainer and his father in utmost disgrace. They might have taken him to the temple to sacrifice and pray to Zeus—for surely Timo had breached his oath the moment he'd spoken it, when he attacked another competitor—or perhaps they'd taken him to the river to throw him in to cool down, or back to the Athenian camp where he'd be safe from angry Spartan fans, or to the temporary gymnasium reserved for the athletes.

He wasn't at the temple, which surprised me a little. If I were in his position, I'd have been praying as hard as I could, because Zeus is not a forgiving God, and the thunderbolts in his hands are hard to forget. Instead I found Timo, with his father and uncle and trainer, at the second place I looked: the gymnasium. When I walked in and saw them there, I was taken aback for a moment. Some men might have thought it a trifle callous, or at least arrogant, to repair to the revered place of athletes straight after such an unsportsmanlike incident.

But I should not have been surprised. Sport is the one true god for the men of the genos Timonidae. Timo's family had a long tradition of pankration. His father, Timonous One-Eye, and his uncle Festianos and his grandfather had all been experts. Among them, they claimed four victories at the Pythian Games, eight at the Isthmian Games, and seven at the Nemean Games, one of which Timo had collected himself. It was an extraordinary tally for any family, but none of them had ever claimed the greatest prize on earth: an olive wreath at the Sacred Games in Olympia. Timo's father was desperate to see his son crowned a victor.

I watched unnoticed from the doorway. Timodemus paced back and forth, swinging his arms and jumping about on the training patch.

The gymnasium at Olympia was a temporary affair made of new-painted wood. There's no point in a permanent structure when it'll only be used once every four years. Instead, they use rough planks that are strong enough to last the few days that it will see use and don't bother with the finishing touches, such as decorative woodwork and frescoes, that you'd see in a city gym.

The design was the same as you'd find at any gym in any city in Hellas: four walls enclosing a square. The square on the inside formed four porticoes, well-roofed to keep off the sun, with alcoves set aside for masseur tables and places to sit where a friend might rub down an athlete with olive oil. I noticed there were even spaces built into the walls to hold the oil flasks, and hung from hooks were bronze strigils with which to scrape away old oil and dead, dirty skin from the sweaty athletes. Like all gyms, the center was open to the sky, and it was in the sunny middle that Timo paced. The middle ground was dotted with nine training patches of sand, each the right size for an Olympic contest, where the boxers, wrestlers, and pankratists could practice their martial skills. I wondered how the athletes could stand the new-paint smell of red ocher and lime. The builders must have finished mere days before the Games began.

Timo's trainer and uncle sat to the side on a bench and watched him pace off his agitation. His father, One-Eye, stood beside the practice ground. The grim expression on his face said it all, but if I needed any confirmation there were his words, repeated in an endless stream. "Idiot. Moron. What were you thinking? No, you weren't thinking, were you? Idiot. Moron . . ."

One-Eye stopped when he saw me at the entrance. This was the father of my oldest friend. He'd seen Timo and me play together when we were children.

"Nicolaos," he said. "We haven't seen you in months."

"Hello, sir. You and Timo have been busy with training for the Games, and I've been busy, too. I came to see how Timo was."

"As you see. As stupid as ever. We will keep him here until this matter is resolved. I leave you now. I must plead with the judges not to disqualify my idiot son."

"Could that happen?" I asked in alarm. Timodemus had spent his life preparing for these Games. More than his life: he was born to be here. To be excluded now would be worse than disaster.

One-Eye turned his single, searing eye on me. It was like facing an angry Cyclops. "What do you think? Timodemus broke the Sacred Oath where thousands of men could see him. I'll beg, but even so, to dissuade them would probably require the honeyed tongue of Apollo . . ." He trailed off and stared at me. "Here now, you know this man Pericles, don't you?"

"Yes, One-Eye, I do." In recent times, Pericles had risen to great prominence as the most influential statesman in Athens, largely on account of his honeyed tongue. It was he who had commissioned my first job as an investigator. We had something of an uneasy relationship.

"You're a friend. You have influence with him."

"Not exactly—"

"Pericles will help me, won't he, if I mention your name? Yes, of course he'll help."

"I'm more like an acquaintance," I said, suddenly worried. Somehow this had gotten out of hand. "One-Eye, with the best will in the world I can't ask Pericles—"

"You want to help Timodemus, don't you?" He said it as if I'd suggested otherwise. I would have been offended if I weren't worried for Timo's future.

"Of course I do, One-Eye," I hurried to assure him.

"Then you can have no possible objection to recommending me to Pericles." His tone was commanding.

If I demurred, it would sound as if I was scared to help. If I said yes, it would look to Pericles as if I'd claimed the power to command his support.

Pericles would ignore any reference of mine anyway. He knew my true value for political influence. It came to about half an obol.

On the other hand, it couldn't hurt if One-Eye mentioned that he knew me. I could explain to Pericles later what had happened.

I said, "No, but . . . well, certainly if it will help Timo."

"Good. I'll tell him that." One-Eye strode out of the gymnasium without a thank-you or a backward glance. I'd never known a man more difficult to refuse.

Timo walked across to where I stood and said quietly, "Nicolaos." He hung his head in shame.

"Timo. What happened back there? What in Hades was that all about?"

"You saw. That bastard Arakos kept baiting me until I reacted. He did it the whole time we walked in the procession from Elis."

"You know him?"

"We fought last year for the crown at the Nemean Games. I won; he didn't."

"What did he say to anger you so?" For all he was a master of the martial art of pankration, my friend Timodemus was the mildest of men—unless he was angered, at which point he became one of the Furies.

Timodemus hesitated. "I'd rather not say."

It must have been something very embarrassing to Timodemus, because it could hardly be a secret; the men around them would have heard every word.

"So you might face him again. Are you worried he'll tear you apart? The man's built like a boulder."

"Timodemus has nothing to fear from Arakos," a voice beyond us said. This was Dromeus, from the city of Mantinea, Timo's trainer, who himself had won the crown for the pankration at the seventy-fifth Olympiad, and now was hired by One-Eye at enormous expense to ensure his son won it at the eightieth. He was a big man, but more than that, he was a wide one. What you noticed most about Dromeus was the way the muscles bulged across his arms and shoulders. I made a mental note not to annoy him.

"As the young idiot says, he faced Arakos at the Nemean Games and won handily," Dromeus said.

"But Arakos must be twice his size," I objected.

Dromeus and Timo had a good laugh at my expense.

"Big means slow, Nico," my friend explained. "Arakos can flail about all he likes. If I dodge the blows, all he does is tire himself out."

"Quite right. The trick against Arakos is don't let him close on you. Avoid the grapple." Dromeus glared at Timo. "This idiot has much more to fear from himself. Timodemus is the only man who can beat Timodemus."

"It wasn't Timo's fault," I said. "The Spartan provoked him."

"Rubbish. The first lesson of any serious fighter is self-control. The moment you react to taunts, you hand control to your opponent, and then you lose. I see you're not a pankratist," he said, looking me up and down. "Pity."

"Me?" I said, surprised. "No. Why?"

"Timodemus needs to fight out his anger. We'll have to wait until the contest for the heralds is over and then see if anyone who can fight is willing to spar with a man who's on the verge of being banned from the Games." Dromeus glared at Timodemus again. "I doubt anyone will take the risk."

I said, "Let me do it." Anything to help my friend.

Dromeus laughed. "You just admitted you can't fight."

"I can fight."

"Not the way you have to if you want to match an expert."

"Timodemus and I used to spar when we were boys."

Dromeus blinked. "You did, did you?" He glanced at Timo, who nodded.

Timodemus said, "Nico, are you all right with this?"

"Sure I am."

Dromeus the trainer considered me like a horse for sale. "You'd be doing him a favor, and it's only for exercise, not even a real fight."

I wore an *exomis*, the short tunic favored by artisans because it leaves the arms and legs free. But even that's more than a pankration fighter wears. I pulled the exomis over my head and dropped it to the ground. Timodemus was already naked. He was smaller than me and thinner, but what there was of him was all muscle and speed. He stood at the edge of the ring, his face a polite, unsmiling mask, seemingly bored, perhaps even arrogant. I'd seen him wear the same face many times before, whenever a fight was to begin and he was about to demolish someone.

Then it occurred to me Timo was not merely my friend but also a highly trained machine for hurting people. All of a sudden I was nervous. I told myself it was a friendly fight and jumped from spot to spot, flexing my arms as if that would somehow help me.

A few men had trickled in as we spoke, like me not interested in the heralds. They'd come to the gymnasium to watch the athletes exercise, to compare the form of this one versus that, and no doubt to lay a few side wagers. More than one of these spectators glanced at Timo with obvious curiosity. They were bursting to ask him what had happened on the steps of the Bouleterion. None dared approach him, but when they saw a practice fight about to begin, they quickly crowded around the border of the training patch to watch.

Two of these men offered to act as referees. They seemed to know what they were about, so Dromeus nodded. Each picked up a short whip, walked around us, and called, "Start."

Timodemus and I advanced to the middle of the ring, crouched low, knees bent. He pushed one straight hand forward for attack and kept the other behind for defense. His left foot was forward and his right behind; from that position he could advance quickly. I kept both hands in line, hoping to deflect a blow and riposte.

I knew Timo liked to attack, and it came almost immediately: a blade-like hand slashed at my face. It was almost perfect for my plan. I blocked the attack with my open left palm and grabbed his wrist with my right. I exulted; his attacking hand was out of action already, and I had the better of a top pankratist. All I had to do was hit him with my left, and I had plenty of options. I could punch his nose or his throat, or grab his balls and twist.

This was the pankration: the roughest, toughest, most brutal, and frequently the most fatal of the Olympic sports. There are no rules in the pankration, except it's illegal to gouge eyes or bite, and many a desperate pankratist has broken even those few strictures. The only punishment for an offender is a whipping from the referees. A match ends when one man is unconscious or dead or raises his arm in defeat. At Olympic level, to raise an arm is considered shameful.

Pain sheared down my right shin. He'd kicked me. I realized too late his attack had been a feint to keep my hands occupied while he came in low. I looked down in time to see him lift his foot again and in a lightning movement slam it into my kneecap. It didn't crack, but the pain was searing. My right leg collapsed.

There was nothing for it but to make the best of a bad situation. I held on tight to his wrist and let myself go down, landing flat on my back. His kick meant he'd been leaning slightly, so when I twisted his arm down and to his left, he overbalanced. Normally it's very bad for an opponent to fall on top of you, but I was ready. The knee of my good left leg shot up into his groin precisely as he fell, for some satisfying revenge. He grunted, and I felt his hot breath.

Feet stepped around my head as we grappled in the dirt, the referees watching to see we did nothing illegal.

His right hand was still caught by mine, so I tried pushing back on his fingers. He was far too smart to let me do that. He pulled back his right hand to protect the fingers while snaking his left up underneath my armpit, over my shoulder, and across my throat. That was bad; if he got a firm grip on my throat, I was done for.

I rolled us over to get on top, then pushed myself up to an unsteady crouch, putting all the weight I could on my left leg. The right was in agony.

I wanted to kick him while he was down, but he jumped up in the blink of an eye. He held his fists before him, knees bent, head down, and punched me hard—one, two, three—in the diaphragm. I bent over and coughed all the air from my lungs. He aimed a flat, open palm straight at my nose. I panicked and swerved my head. His palm glanced off my cheek, but in a trice he kicked my feet out from under me. I went down once more, face-first, and he threw himself on my back. His forearm locked around my throat. I couldn't breathe. Both my hands scrabbled upward. I had to prize off his arm, but it was like trying to bend an iron bar. I could feel my carotid artery throbbing. I flailed about, hoping for a miracle that wouldn't come. Little black dots appeared in my vision. They grew larger. The lack of air could kill me at any moment.

In desperation and despair I raised my arm high as I could.

The pressure on my throat eased at once. Timodemus rolled away, leaving me to flop over on the ground. He breathed hard, and there was a sheen of oily perspiration on his sandy body, but otherwise he looked at ease when he sprang to his feet. I felt like I might die at any moment. Had the fight broken anything inside me?

Lying still took the least effort. I opted for that and stared up at the sky.

The crowd dispersed now that the fun was over.

After a while a face appeared, upside down, blotting out the blue. I didn't recognize the face but had no doubt he needed to wipe his nose.

"Are you Nicolaos, son of Sophroniscus?"

My diaphragm hurt too much to speak.

The face studied me in mild curiosity. "His eyes are open, but he's not moving. Is he dead?"

A voice replied, "Nah, he went a pankration round with Timodemus." It was Dromeus the trainer.

"Ahh." That was explanation enough. The face with the nose thought about it, then asked, "How come he ain't dead then?"

"Only a practice round, it wasn't a serious fight."

"Ahh." He prodded me with his foot. "Can you hear me?" The nose dripped on me.

This was one indignity too many. I nodded slightly, tried to speak, and instead gasped at the fire in my throat. It felt like acid had been poured in. "What do you want?" I rasped, pushing myself off the ground.

"Here, let me help you." Timodemus grabbed my arm and hauled me up.

I winced for a moment when I put pressure on the injured knee, but it took my weight. I tried a few practice steps, limping with Timo's support, that took us away from the group of spectators. I said, "At least the kneecap isn't broken."

"I deliberately hit you slightly to the side so it wouldn't break." Timo shrugged. He seemed embarrassed.

And there I was thinking I'd been lucky.

He slapped me heartily on the back, and I almost went down again. "Good fight, Nico. It's lucky you never trained, or I might be facing you at these Olympics."

"The Gods spare me that," I said hoarsely but with a grin. I rubbed my throat. "I pity any man you face in a real fight."

Timodemus suddenly looked serious. "They all practice the way I do. Even if they let me stay in, it's going to be rough."

"Not too rough for you," I assured him. "All of Athens says you're the best pankratist in a generation."

"They would," he replied, glum. "They expect me to win for them."

"Hey!" The man with the dripping nose begged our attention. Timo and I both turned to look at him.

"I got a message for Nicolaos. My master, Pericles, son of Xanthippus, requests a meeting at your earliest convenience. He says to emphasize 'earliest.'"

"What does he want?"

"How should I know? I'm only a slave." He turned to go but halted for a moment and said to my friend, "Good luck, Timodemus. I hope they let you fight. All of Athens is behind you."

"That's just it," Timo muttered as the slave departed. "They're all behind me."

I hobbled over to a bench where we sat down.

"Feeling lonely?" I asked.

"Yes." He put his head in his hands. "I've trained all my life for the Olympics, Nico. It was fine when I was doing it for myself; I enjoyed the challenge. If I failed, the only person I'd disappoint would be myself. Now that I'm here, I feel I'm fighting for everyone, and if I fail, I fail for everyone, not only my family but all of Athens."

"Is that why you attacked the Spartan? Looking for a way out?"

"No. That was my anger speaking. Maybe a touch of nervousness too. But here we are talking only of me, when I've barely seen you these many months. How have you been, Nico? What's been happening to you?"

I grinned. "That's my big news. I can't wait to introduce you to Diotima!"

Timo looked puzzled. "Who's Diotima?"

"My wife," I said.

"Your what?"

"My wife. Well, fiancée, I suppose, I'm not sure. It's not official yet; there are still one or two little details to sort out, but as far as Diotima and I are concerned, we think—why are you laughing?"

"Who is this lucky girl?"

"She's the stepdaughter of Pythax, chief of the city guard of Athens."

"Perfect. He can help you with your work as an investigator, or an agent, or whatever it is you do these days."

"No, he can't. Pythax probably wants to kill me."

"That's ridiculous, Nico, you've only just married his daughter. What could you have done to upset him so quickly?"

"I married Diotima without his permission. That's the little detail I mentioned."

Timo's laughing halted abruptly. "You're a dead man."

We both nodded glumly.

"Couldn't you have run off with the daughter of someone less likely to hurt you?"

"It had to be this girl."

"When in Hades did this happen? Why didn't you invite me to the wedding?"

"It was last month, while you were in training at Elis, and Diotima and I were in Ionia on the other side of the Aegean Sea."

Besides which, I didn't add, we'd only married because we were in a tight spot where neither of us had expected to live long enough to suffer the consequences. We'd survived by the will of the Gods and some outright trickery, only to face the wrath of our fathers when we returned.

Timo looked down at his hands and said, "Do you want my help with this? What if Pythax seeks to punish you?"

"I don't think he will. Pythax likes me, sort of. I hope. Anyway, you're in enough trouble over violence, Timo."

"Yes, you're right," he said, and sighed sadly. But then he looked up at me. "Hey, you're a married man!" He clapped me on the back. "I can't believe it. What drove you to do something crazy like that? Did you get her pregnant?"

"No. I love her, Timo, seriously love her."

Timo winced. "No dowry?"

"None. No contract either. No one's happy."

"Couldn't your fathers work it out now between them?"

"They could, except mine refuses to acknowledge the marriage."

"Why?"

"Because Diotima's mother is a . . . er . . . she was a *hetaera*."

"A courtesan?" Timo guffawed.

"At least she was an expensive one!"

"Oh, well, that's all right then!" He laughed.

"Anyway," I said, slightly miffed. "Diotima's mom is retired now and married to Pythax."

"So your girlfriend's mother is an ex-prostitute, her stepfather is a former slave, and your father isn't impressed? I can't imagine why," said Timo. "You know your father's never going to agree, don't you? Mine certainly wouldn't. One-Eye would probably beat me senseless if I did anything like that. Can you give her back?"

"Never! Besides, in the words of Diotima's stepfather, I've soiled her."

"Er . . . how soiled is she?"

"Very," I said with a broad grin.

Timo whistled. "Pythax isn't only going to kill you. He's going to tear your limbs off first. But I still can't believe it. My friend Nicolaos is married."

"Your turn will come, Timo."

"Not so long as I can help it. I'll do what any normal man does: hold out until I'm thirty and then ask my father to find me a fourteen-year-old virgin from a good family."

"Fair enough."

The masseur slave stepped forward and reminded Timo he must submit to massage immediately—if he didn't, his muscles would lock, and his groin might be permanently damaged. Timo departed with good grace, stopping only to ask, "Nico, if they let me stay in, will I see you at the contest?"

"Of course, Timo! I wouldn't miss seeing you crowned for anything."

THE ATHENIANS HAD been allocated camp space well to the south of the central Sanctuary of Zeus, where stood all the buildings. To the north of the Sanctuary was Mount Kronos, some ancient ruins, the agora, and the road to Elis. To the Sanctuary's east was the stadion and the hippodrome. To the west was the river Klodeos and, across it, the women's camp. It was to the south, then, where most of the city camps went. They nestled where the Klodeos met the Alfeios River. The flat ground was well suited for tents, but unfortunately less so for drainage.

The Athenian camp was a confused, raucous mêlée of tents and campfires; men drank and laughed and sang, and tethered donkeys brayed. It was only the first day of five, yet already the air blowing past the tent flaps was a trifle rank with the aroma of donkey droppings, sweat, stale wine, and the urine of men who couldn't wait. The scene would be the same in every direction about the stadion. Every city was allocated its own grounds, and only the brave or the truly drunk would walk into another city's camp and declare support for their own.

A new spirit of enthusiasm, pride in our city, and optimism for the future had infected the Athenians ever since the new democracy had begun the year before. We were at Olympia to cheer on our city, which we knew to be the greatest in the world.

I found Pericles in the middle of this chaos, in his tent, located in a prime position on the main thoroughfare through the camp. He read a scroll and scratched notes upon a wax tablet with a stylus. He looked at me in surprise when I entered and raised an eyebrow. "What happened to you?" he asked.

I was bruised all over. I limped from my damaged knee, which was visibly the size of a melon below the material of my short-hemmed tunic. Timo's trainer had worked it over and assured me the swelling would soon disappear, but it still hurt like Hades.

My left eye was black and swollen—I didn't even remember Timodemus hitting me there—and my neck was bruised from side to side. Everything above my diaphragm hurt, so I couldn't quite stand straight.

"I was sparring partner for Timodemus," I said modestly.

"Oh, is that all." Pericles dismissed my injuries. He had no interest in sport of any kind. It was a wonder he'd come to the Games at all, though every Athenian of importance had made the trek this year, as well as many obscure families such as my own.

"It's Timodemus I want to talk to you about. The judges have decided your friend is to be expelled. The father has been to see me. What's his name?"

"The father? Timonous. People call him One-Eye."

"Timonous, yes. How did he lose the eye?"

"Fighting in the pankration, in his youth."

"I thought gouging was forbidden."

"Sometimes people cheat."

That took Pericles aback. "So it seems. Well, Timonous One-Eye has been to see me. He's asked for my help with the judges."

"You're not a member of the family," I said. "You have no standing."

"No, but I can be . . . persuasive . . . on their behalf."

So true. Pericles could persuade a fish to try rock climbing, a lamb to try lion hunting, a man to try criminal investigation.

I asked him, "Will you help?"

"These are the first Games since we instituted the democracy." Pericles avoided the question and continued to play with the stylus between his fingers. "A victory would be good for Athens. It would show the world we are still the first city in Hellas." Pericles smacked the bronze stylus down onto the folding table. "The experts tell me the only event an Athenian is likely to win this Olympiad is the pankration."

I nodded. I'd heard the same opinions.

"Our enemies would be pleased to see us humbled," Pericles

continued. "If we won nothing, they would say the democracy had sapped the will of the people or claim the Gods have abandoned us because our way of government is unnatural."

He was probably right. Powerful men all across Hellas already feared that the democracy might spread to their own cities.

Pericles walked to the entrance of the tent and raised the flap to look out upon the chaos. At that moment an unwashed donkey passed by. It stopped right outside the tent and turned its head to stare at Pericles. Pericles stared back. The donkey excreted a large quantity of diarrheic poo, then walked on.

Pericles grimaced in disgust, flung down the tent flap, and turned back to me. "If I intervene, it will cost political capital. Capital I don't want to spend, unless this Timodemus will win. Tell me, Nicolaos, he's your friend, what do you think?"

I said, "Timodemus is good, very good." I rubbed my throat and winced. "But so are the other competitors. At this level, anything could happen."

"Particularly if the Gods take a hand," Pericles added.

"Yes, but no one has a better chance of winning than Timodemus," I said, careful with my choice of words but determined that Pericles should support Timo.

"Not even this Arakos from Sparta, to whom your friend took such a dislike?"

"Timodemus defeated Arakos at the Nemean Games last year. He has nothing to fear from the Spartan." I repeated the words Dromeus the trainer had said to me.

"Nicolaos, I want an Athenian victory. We need a victory."

I said, disturbed, "Pericles, why do you tell me? It's Zeus who grants the victory. No one else."

"But Timodemus is our only hope. Let us give Zeus every opportunity to decide the outcome our way. I will go to the judges and convince them that this has been a tussle between two young men worked up by the emotions of the ceremony, and no different from the hundreds of squabbles we all know will occur

over the next five days. No one expels the young men in the
camps for high spirits and rough play. I will persuade the judges
to see this unfortunate incident in the same light."

"Thank you, Pericles."

"Don't thank me. I haven't finished yet. The Spartans will
want our man out of the Games, especially since he beat their
man last time they met. They will argue that Timodemus has
committed a clear breach and must be expelled. If I convince the
judges otherwise, the Spartans will feel there's bias against them,
and tension will rise between Athens and Sparta."

"Will anyone notice? The Spartans already hate us."

"It could be a lot worse than it is. We know Corinth has asked
Sparta to help them in their war against us. We also know Sparta
hasn't said yes, at least not yet. We don't want to encourage that."

Athens and Corinth had been at war for some time, the issue
being control of Megara, a weak city that lay halfway between
us. Megara controlled access in and out of the Peloponnese. If
Athens won that war, we could block any Spartan army from
reaching Athens, and we'd be safe at last.

Pericles was right. We definitely didn't want Sparta involved
in that fight.

Pericles picked up the stylus once more and slapped it against
his palm. "Your job, Nicolaos, is to keep your friend out of
trouble. No more incidents. Assault can work both ways. You
understand me? The same people who'd like to see us humbled
might not be averse to helping Zeus with his decision."

I hadn't thought of that.

"Don't worry, Pericles, I'll watch like a hungry eagle."

I RETURNED TO the gymnasium to find Timodemus still
there with his uncle and trainer. He was safe enough, which left
me free to visit the person I wanted most in the world to see.

The women's camp serves two purposes: it's where the men
who've brought their families can leave them so they don't get

in the way, and it's also where the prostitutes—the cheap *pornoi* and the expensive hetaerae—set up for business. The women's camp is on the west side of the river. On the east side are the men's camps, the sports grounds, and the temples.

Two soldiers of Elis guarded the ford across the river. They were dressed in formal armor of polished bronze to befit the occasion, their helmets tilted back on their heads for a quick pull-down if required, but they leaned on their spears while they argued over which team would win the chariot race the next morning. They ignored me completely as I passed by. There was considerable traffic back and forth, which they also ignored; I guessed the guards were more to ensure drunks didn't trip and drown on the way across than for any pretense of security.

The women's camp was smaller than the men's and tidier and smelled better. Unlike the men's, it wasn't divided into city camps, I suppose because there were fewer tents or because the women were less likely to riot. I had no trouble finding Diotima's tent, because I had helped set it up.

A knife flew past me as I entered. It almost went into my eye but missed to embed itself in the tent pole beside me.

"Dear Gods! Do you want to kill me?"

"Oh! I'm sorry, Nicolaos! I didn't hear you coming."

She sat on a travel chest, dressed in a bland and well-worn chiton, and looking very, very beautiful. My wife. At least as far as I was concerned. Opinion was divided on our relationship. Diotima and I believed we were married. The rest of the world was sure we weren't. We had carried out an ersatz version of the Athenian marriage rites in the midst of a bad situation, one in which neither of us had expected to survive. But we had, and now it looked like a quick trip to Hades might have been the better alternative.

"Do you usually practice knife throwing in a tent?"

Diotima grimaced. "Only when I'm bored out of my mind. Have you any idea how deadly it is in here?"

I put out a finger to stop the knife's quivering in the wooden pole. "I think I have some idea."

"No, you don't. You're not a woman."

"But I'm glad you are."

It had come as a shock to both our families when I arrived with Diotima on my arm. We'd come to Olympia direct from Asia Minor, because I knew Pericles would be here, and I needed to report on the outcome of our last mission, a delicate matter that had required a certain amount of discretion. I hadn't expected to find my father, and we certainly hadn't expected to find Diotima's stepfather.

My father was furious with me. He had twice before refused to negotiate for Diotima. By Athenian law he had every right to refuse, and as long as he did, by Athenian law the marriage had never happened.

My girl had always been known as Diotima of Mantinea—the town of her mother's birth—rather than by the name of her father, because she was the illegitimate child of a prostitute by a prominent citizen. Diotima had risen to become a priestess of Artemis, but the miasma of illegitimacy still clung to her. That had changed when Diotima's mother finally married—not Diotima's father, who had died, but a newly made citizen: the barbarian Pythax.

Pythax was, if possible, even more angry with me for marrying Diotima than my own father was. He'd become responsible for Diotima the moment he married her mother. Now he faced the prospect of a daughter for whom he could never hope to find a good husband, because I had, in his words, "soiled" the love of my life. No Athenian father would accept Diotima as wife for his son in her new and entirely irreversible condition.

Now she sat in a tent, waiting to learn her fate while our fathers squabbled.

Diotima balanced a knife on one finger and said, "Would you believe Pythax—Father—took away my bow and quiver?"

"I should hope so. The Sacred Truce forbids arms at the Games."

"I don't even have my mother here to talk to and . . . oh Gods, how desperate do I have to be to have said that?" Diotima grimaced. She and her mother were not exactly close friends.

"I think I can relieve the boredom for you." I told Diotima how Timodemus had broken his oath, and the fallout from it, finishing, "No one knows what's to happen. Timodemus may or may not be banned."

"Interesting." Diotima had paid close attention to my story. I knew if I asked her, she could repeat everything I'd said almost verbatim. "Why did your friend attack the Spartan?"

"He wouldn't tell me."

"That's worrying."

"It's irrelevant, unless they let him back in."

"It's certainly irrelevant to me while I'm stuck in this tent."

"What happened with Pythax?" I asked her. After we'd arrived, and my father had disowned the marriage, Pythax had taken control of Diotima and rented this tent to install her.

Diotima shrugged unhappily. "Pythax says I'm not to leave the camp without a responsible adult. By which he meant himself. I'm not sure it means you."

"Oh. I thought about taking you to visit the agora."

She pushed herself off the travel chest. "Good, let's go."

"You just said your stepfather wouldn't allow it."

"Yes, he will. Pythax is desperate to win me over, and besides, he isn't all that bad, you know. Beneath that callous, gruff exterior there's a . . . a . . . ." She was lost for words.

"A callous, gruff interior?"

"Well, all right, yes. But he's besotted with my mother, and if he wants me to call him Daddy, he'd better not stop me."

I wondered if Pythax had met his match in his new stepdaughter, and what that might mean for me and whether there was something I should do about it, but I wasn't about to stand in the middle of any fight between Pythax and Diotima. There are easier ways to die.

I led her across the ford, and we walked through the Sanctuary of Zeus and out the other side to see the famous festival agora of Olympia, which for forty-nine months out of fifty is an empty field of weeds and for the remaining one month is the most exciting place in Hellas.

The festival agora lies to the north of the sports grounds, on the east side of Mount Kronos, where the market catches the sun in the morning. We heard the sound of the people before we saw the market itself, just around the bend.

"Yaah!"

A man in a lion's skin jumped out in front of us. He swung a gnarled club at our heads. Diotima and I leaned back instinctively. The madman missed us by a wide margin.

I stepped forward into the swing, hooked my leg behind our assailant's, and pushed him to the ground. I snatched the club from his hands as he fell.

"What do you think you're doing!" I shouted at him.

He picked himself up. I expected another attack and gripped the club in both hands to use on its owner. But when he only stood there, head hung low, I asked, "Who in Hades are you?"

"I'm Heracles," he said.

"Wasn't Heracles larger and"—I looked him up and down—"slightly better muscled?"

The man before us was dark-haired, small and weedy. A faded and somewhat patchy lion skin draped over his left shoulder fitted him like a tent. Now that he no longer swung the club, I saw he had the muscle tone of a dead chicken.

The weedy character said, "You've never heard of the Heracles imitators?"

Diotima and I both shook our heads.

"Milo of Croton did it first. Men at the Games have been

dressed as Heracles ever since. We do it for fun. Playacting, you know? And to impress the crowd."

"Who's Milo of Croton?" Diotima asked.

"He was the strongest man who ever lived, barring Heracles himself. You've never heard of Milo?" said the fake Heracles.

"This is our first Olympics," I said.

"This is my fifth." He smiled. He'd scored a point over us. "I'm from Elis. I come to every Games."

I inspected the club. It really was a solid piece of twisted wood. I handed it back.

"You should be careful with that; you might hurt someone."

The club hung limply from his hands. "It's just a game. I'll be more careful. So, what do you think of the festival agora?"

"I don't know," said Diotima. "You're standing in my way."

"Oh. Sorry." Fake Heracles stepped back to reveal a vista of the festival ground of Olympia.

Men and women in gaudy festival clothes moved like a flowing rainbow among the stalls and displays. Jugglers wandered among the crowd, tossing and catching balls with blinding speed. Flute girls swayed and played their lilting tunes.

"Oh, Nico," Diotima breathed. She took my hand and stepped into the swirling crowd.

We wandered from stall to stall. Vendors had come from all over Hellas to sell every imaginable thing: fine jewelry, beautiful cloths of many colors and patterns; bronze ware that shone in the sun, plus fine food. A man stirred a large kettle of sizzling spiced lentils. His wife handed out steaming bowls to those with coin. Every second stall sold wine.

I bought silver earrings for Diotima, because they matched her headband, and a bronze mirror because I knew she didn't have one with her. The earrings were in the shape of bears, the animal sacred to the goddess Artemis, whom my Diotima serves as priestess.

We came across three more Heracleses. One of them lifted a

vast block of stone, his every muscle straining to burst through his skin, before he tossed it over his shoulder to the applause of the onlookers.

"This is what I imagine it must be like every day for the Gods on Mount Olympus," Diotima said. "Can you imagine walking through such a crowd and coming face-to-face with a goddess?"

"I already have," I told her, and she blushed.

Naked acrobats tumbled and somersaulted past us.

I put my arm around Diotima's waist and squeezed tight. It wouldn't have been proper to kiss my wife in full public view, but the temptation was almost overwhelming.

"Why don't we go back to your tent for some tumbling of our own?" I whispered into her ear.

"What will you do if Pythax catches us? He's already furious with you."

"I'll point out you can only break a pot once," I told her.

Diotima smiled, but she hesitated. "I'd love to, Nico, but . . . let's use your tent. I wouldn't want the other women to think you were a custom . . . er, that is, not my . . ."

Diotima had a horror of anything that could possibly be mis-construed to suggest she was a professional woman, as her mother once had been. Her background, paradoxically, had made her more prim and proper than the most natural-born of citizen women.

I said, "Wouldn't it look even worse if you were seen walking into a tent in the men's camp?"

"Men don't notice. The women have nothing better to do than spy on one another and gossip."

When we returned to my tent, a message awaited me, scrawled untidily into a wax tablet and left to lie on the ground. It read:

Pericles says this to Nicolaos: Timodemus has been reinstated. The Spartans are furious. Keep a close eye on your friend.

Diotima had rested her chin on my arm and read along with me.

"I'll have to go at once." I sighed.

"How long do you think this tablet has been here?" Diotima asked.

"Could be as long as half the afternoon."

"Then he can wait a little longer," said Diotima. She pressed her body against me, put her arms about my neck, and raised her face to be kissed. I was instantly aroused. I pulled the shoulder pins from her dress, and it fell to the floor.

"NOW TIMO, DO you promise me you'll go into that tent and not come out until morning?"

Timo laughed. "What are you, Nico, my mother?"

A mother wouldn't have trailed as close to Timodemus as I had that afternoon. I'd caught up with him at the gym, where he was being congratulated by friends. The friends had been strangely absent in the morning, when Timo was in trouble, but were exceedingly visible after the judges announced his rehabilitation. Man after man said that Timo was sure to win, for he must have the favor of the Gods, and all of Athens was behind him.

I knew how uncomfortable such talk made him feel. I waved from the back of the crowd and said in a loud voice that Timo was wanted at the Bouleterion. Timo edged away, and we made our escape. When we were out of sight, we diverted to the agora, where I bought a few wineskins to celebrate, and we found a quiet spot by the river.

We were both in a more relaxed state than we had been in the morning. We stayed there until it was well and truly dark, after which we meandered back to the campsite. An athlete needs his sleep.

When we came to Timo's tent, I insisted he stay there and not go wandering about. "I promised Pericles I'd keep an eye on you. I can't do that if you go partying across Olympia in the middle of the night. What if some Spartan tries to get revenge?"

"You are protecting me?" Timodemus was too polite to point

out that he had beaten me to a pulp that morning. Instead his eyes
lingered on my bruised neck and my aching knee—Diotima had
wrapped a wet rag around it to reduce the swelling—and he smiled.

"I thought you were sticking with me to make sure I didn't do
anything stupid again."

"Perhaps a little of both," I conceded. "I know you could
destroy me with your little finger, Timo. But has it occurred to
you that even the weakest man could knife you as you sleep? Or
attack you from behind as you walk through the crowds? I can
watch your back. Pericles said he spent political capital on you,
and he doesn't like his property damaged."

Timodemus laughed. "All right, Nico. I'll stay in the tent."

"Promise?"

"I promise."

"Good night, then."

Timodemus stepped into his tent and closed the flap.

I settled down outside and listened to the night. All over
Olympia, men partied. Bonfires lit up the night in every direction. Sweet smoke drifted in the light breeze. Men sang. Women
laughed. Somewhere close by, music played, growing louder.

A *komos* line appeared, happy shouting men and intoxicated
women. Aulos players danced alongside and fingered their
V-shaped flutes with both hands. The revelers kicked in time to
the music and snaked their way down the street. They waved at
me to join them, one a lovely redheaded woman, but I shook my
head and smiled. The line passed around the corner and out of
the camp, leaving me alone once more.

I was missing the biggest party in the world, all because my
best friend couldn't be trusted not to strangle people. I hoped
my sacrifice was worth it. I made a mental note to remind
Timodemus of this every day for the rest of his life.

What was Diotima doing while I sat here in the dark? She
was probably stuck in her tent, reading a scroll or throwing knives, or—a sudden thought struck me, and my breath

tightened—maybe she'd met some handsome man and gone off to a party. Diotima liked men's chests. It was a particular thing for her, and this was the sort of place where she'd see plenty of them.

I put my hands under my exomis and checked my chest. I had to admit, there were men with broader, better muscled chests, especially around here. Maybe I should ask Timo's coach Dromeus for some exercises to make my own chest more manly.

But that would have to wait until tomorrow. It was getting late. Even the parties in the distance had quietened as the drunks fell by the wayside.

I yawned and lay back to relax.

"Are you all right?" a voice said in my ear.

I sat bolt upright. A man stood beside me. It was Festianos, Timo's uncle. His cheeks were flushed enough that it showed in the bright moonlight. A garland of flowers sat askew atop his thinning hair.

"Oh, it's you," he said when he recognized me. "You're Timo's friend, aren't you? I thought you must be a drunk who'd passed out beside our tents. You were asleep."

"I wasn't asleep. I merely rested my eyes."

Festianos laughed. "Then you're one of the few men who snores when he's awake."

I never snore. But Festianos had worried me. I lifted Timo's tent flap quietly to peer inside. There was Timodemus, on his camp bed. The blanket that covered him rose and fell softly. I let the flap fall back.

"It's good news about the lad, isn't it?" Festianos said.

"Yes, it is."

"We're very proud of him, my brother and I."

I yawned. I couldn't stop myself.

"Why don't you go get some sleep?" Festianos said.

"I have to keep an eye on Timodemus."

"I can do that. Old men like me don't need as much sleep as you young ones."

I hesitated. My head ached. My eyes felt like someone had rubbed grit in them. I could indeed use some sleep, and wouldn't I be a better guard for Timodemus in the morning if I was rested? He was safe enough with his uncle.

"I'll do that. Thanks, Festianos."

I left him sitting outside their tents, with his head back, the garland circlet crooked on his head, watching the moon and stars.

I STAGGERED INTO the small tent I shared with my brother Socrates. Our father snored in an even smaller one beside us. Socrates was already asleep. It was chilly. I pulled my traveling cloak over me and edged close enough to my brother to steal some of his warmth. I was so tired I don't remember falling asleep.

"Wake up! Wake up, Nico!" That was Socrates, his voice anxious.

"Huh. What?" I rolled over. "Go to sleep, Socrates."

"Get up!" Someone swore mightily and kicked me in the back. Hard. Not Socrates.

I sat bolt upright while my hand scrabbled around for a knife it couldn't find. "Who is it?"

My eyes focused. Two men stood in our tent. Both wore light armor but held no weapons in hand. The one leaned over me, and I wished he hadn't because he'd been eating garlic. "Get up. You're wanted."

I struggled not to gag. "By whom?"

I expected him to say Pericles.

"Timodemus asked for you. Better hurry if you want to be there for the death."

I moved.

I grabbed my exomis and pulled it over my head as we marched. The almost-full moon was high, the sky cloudless. It was easy to step among the tents and equipment left lying on the ground. A few men were still awake, clustered around fires drinking, talking, singing, and arguing. They watched us pass, the two guards and me, with Socrates trailing behind. I let him come; there wasn't time to stop to argue with him.

To my surprise we left the Athenian camp altogether and followed the path that snaked past the camp of the Spartans, and I choked with fear. Had they dragged Timodemus within?

Apparently not, because we hurried by the entrance without pause.

The Sacred Truce meant even mortal enemies could pitch their tents side by side in perfect safety, but still the Spartans arranged their own tents in regular clusters, and they left nothing loose on the ground for men to trip over if there were a sudden call to arms. I suppose they knew no other way.

The guards led me to the river Kladeos, which flows north to south along the western edge of Olympia. We crossed the ford without a word to the sentries, who in silence watched us pass by. The water was chilled and moved with relative speed, enough that a hurrying man might slip, but the people of Elis had long ago placed strong stepping-stones; it was easy to cross with only damp feet.

The path on the other side forked. To the left was the women's camp, to the right a forest that had been there in the days of Heracles. We went right.

I could see our destination now. A group of men clustered among the trees, easy to spot because two or three carried torches despite the moonlight.

I discerned a lump on the ground. The lump became a man, the man a body, lying all too still.

A body large enough to look like a mound.

A man with his back to us turned as we stepped into what I now realized was a small clearing.

"You're too late," said the Chief Judge of the Games. "Arakos has died."

———

THE FLICKER OF the torchlight across his face made the Chief Judge look like one of the Furies, and he was approximately as angry. He held in his right hand the badge of his office: a long staff, which forked into a Y, and this he stamped into the ground.

"Who are you?" he demanded of me.

"I am Nicolaos son of Sophroniscus, of Athens," I said.

"This is the man Timodemus requested, Exelon," said one the guards. "You said to bring him."

"Oh. So I did." Exelon the Chief Judge studied me for a long moment. "You're a young man. Why?"

"I'm sorry, sir. I'll grow out of it."

"I mean, why did Timodemus call for you? Why not a responsible older man?"

"Is Timodemus also dead, sir?" I asked, anxious for my friend. "Is he hurt? Where is he?"

I looked around. I counted at least thirteen men within the clearing, in various states of visibility, depending on their proximity to the torches and their obscurity behind the thick vegetation. The moon was bright above us, so that the clearing itself was well lit. Yet the coverage of leaves upon the surrounding trees was such that in some parts of the perimeter I couldn't see if anyone was there. The body lay in one of those shadows.

The Chief Judge of the Games said, "You are here at the request of the accused. It seems only fair to give him a chance to explain, if he can."

"Timodemus is accused?"

At that moment Pericles bustled into the clearing, accompanied by One-Eye, and I breathed a sigh of relief. I agreed with Exelon the Chief Judge on one point: this was no place for a young man to represent Athens.

"One-Eye's told me what happened." The usually elegant Pericles was unkempt by his high standards. His hair was uncombed. He wore no himation—Pericles owned one made of the finest Milesian wool, and he normally would not be seen dead out of doors without it. He did wear a formal chiton, but it was smudged and crumpled. Was it possible that Pericles, like any normal man, dropped his clothes on the floor when he went to bed? He'd forgotten to put on sandals.

Exelon banged his forked staff on the ground again and said, "I blame Athens for this disaster, Pericles. Your man attacked Arakos this morning, and now Arakos is murdered."

"A scuffle in the morning does not necessarily mean murder in the evening," Pericles said.

"There's more," said the Chief Judge. He moved a step to the side.

Over the shoulder of the Judge I saw Timodemus with his head bowed and a guard to either side of him. The guards held his arms tight. It was the second relief for me for that night. I'd been afraid that Timodemus too lay dead or dying.

Timodemus looked up at that moment, and our eyes met. His were unreadable. The expression on his face was identical to the one he wore in the pankration, the same expression I'd seen right before we'd fought that very morning.

Pericles said, "What do you have to say about this, Timodemus?"

"There's nothing I can say," Timodemus said. "I didn't kill him. I haven't even seen Arakos since this morning."

I said to the Chief Judge, "Did you find Timodemus here?"

"Close by, in the women's camp. Hiding."

"Hiding?" That didn't sound like Timodemus.

"Guards found him in the tent of Klymene, the High Priestess of Demeter," the Chief Judge said grimly.

Uh-oh. The Priestess of Demeter was an integral part of the Sacred Games; the contests could not be held without her. If Timodemus had hurt or polluted the priestess by his presence, then the Games would be delayed, and ten thousand angry sports fans would butcher Timo before the day was out. I decided not to ask the obvious question.

"What he was doing in the women's camp is irrelevant," said Exelon. The Chief Judge seemed equally reluctant to follow that line of thought. "The fact is the women's camp is the shortest of runs from where we stand, and that is meaningful in the extreme."

"The implication is obvious," Pericles said. "But that's all it is: an implication. How many other men were in the women's camp tonight? Hundreds, at least, probably thousands. No court would convict a man for that."

"You're not in Athens now, with your courts and your rhetorical tricks," said Exelon. "This is Olympia, where the Ten Judges decide. It's in our power to ban Athens from the next Olympics."

Pericles said at once, "I apologize, Exelon. I didn't mean to imply otherwise."

Pericles contrite was a sight to behold, but not at the cost of Timodemus, which was the way this was headed. Something had to be done. I asked, "How did Arakos die?"

"See for yourself." The Chief Judge stepped back to let me pass.

The body lay in half darkness. I knelt down. It was impossible to see detail.

"Can I have some light here?"

One of the torchbearers stepped over beside me, and suddenly the scene was revealed. The flame was fresh and still smoked considerably and burned with a strong yellow light that was hot and eerie in how it revealed the ghastly corpse.

Arakos had been laid out straight, a scarlet cloak placed under his head. It was the standard-issue cloak beloved of the Spartans. Blood had dribbled from his crushed nose and mouth and now dried on his cheek. His jaw hung slack, and there were bloody gaps where teeth had been. But the worst was his eyes had been gouged out, both of them. The sockets were bloody holes.

I looked behind me at once, to where Socrates stood. He'd never seen violent death before. Well, now he had. I worried what effect the ugly sight had on my little brother.

"What happened to his eyes?" Socrates asked in the same casually clinical tone he used for all his questions.

So much for worrying about my little brother's mental health.

But it was a good question. Where were Arakos's eyes?

Something small and sharp jabbed under my knee. There were some front teeth, in a small pool of blood. But not enough teeth. I opened his mouth and felt about inside, with a finger. Yes, I felt a few more teeth lying loose. Whoever had hit Arakos had done a thorough job.

"Who found him?"

A man stepped forward. "I did."

He spoke with a Spartan accent. Terrific.

"What were you doing in these woods so late at night?"

Another man said stepped forward and said, "I was with him." He took hold of the first man's hand.

"Er . . . right. Nice night for a walk, I guess. Is this how you found him?"

"No, he was alive. We tried to save him."

"How did he lie?"

"Curled in on himself, knees drawn up, arms wrapped about his torso, facedown in the dirt."

It was the position of a man being beaten who has no way to fight back.

Arakos couldn't fight back?

I inspected his wrists and his ankles. There were no tie marks, no indents into the skin that might have been caused by the pressure of a tight thong. His arms and legs were also clear of all but the bruises any fighter carries.

There was a large clot of blood in his hair. I pressed on it, gently at first, then harder. The scalp, and the bone beneath, moved inward under the pressure. In fact it wobbled. This was probably what had killed him.

I asked the group in general, "Did Arakos say anything before he died?"

"He was unconscious most of the time." A man in the outer shadows spoke up. "He breathed in a funny way. Really labored, you know? And he blew bubbles of blood."

Everyone knew what that meant. Arakos had been struck in the chest, and the ribs had pierced his lungs. I lifted his chiton and probed. There were no open wounds, but there was movement beneath the skin where there should not have been.

By all appearances, Arakos, one of the finest bare-handed fighters in all Hellas, had been beaten to death.

I stood up and dusted off my knees. "This is impossible."

The man who stood next to the Chief Judge said, "It seems obvious enough to me. The Athenian surprised Arakos, perhaps in an ambush, and hit him from behind. There are many trees and other places from which to leap. He knocked out Arakos with the first blow and then proceeded to beat an unconscious man to death." The man who spoke was middle-aged, perhaps fifteen years older than me, but his shoulders were broad, and he looked fit. He had a rich, dark beard and black, curly hair that was well kept. He stood straight and wore a cloak of the deepest scarlet.

I said to him, "With no weapon, not even a knife? Why wouldn't the killer wait until Arakos had passed and stab him in the back?"

"It wouldn't be the first time things didn't go to plan in an ambush," he replied. "Especially in a night attack."

"In my experience it's unlikely," I said, doing my best for Timodemus. "And I have some expertise in these matters; I've examined more than one crime scene."

He said, "In my judgment it makes perfect sense, and I know something about ambushes."

"Who are you to be making judgments?" I demanded.

He said mildly, "I am Pleistarchus, son of Leonidas, of Sparta."

My stomach lurched. Dear Gods, I had challenged a King of Sparta, one of the most powerful men in Hellas. This man's father was the Leonidas who had led the Three Hundred at

Thermopylae and died the most revered warrior of our times. With a word, Pleistarchus could have an army of Spartans at his back—there was one available in their camp—and the dead man before us was one of his own. I swallowed.

"I'm sorry, King Pleistarchus," I said, as apologetic as I could be. "I didn't recognize you. But I don't think your idea can be right."

"Why not?" He didn't seem offended.

I touched the body's head. "See this wound? It's toward the front, almost on the forehead, and slightly on the left-hand side. This wound could not have been made from behind. It was almost certainly made by a right-handed man from in front."

King Pleistarchus leaned over and examined the body with an air of genuine curiosity. "You're right. Is there any wound behind?"

I was already running my hands around the back of the head. "Nothing there."

"What of his back?" Pleistarchus waved to two soldiers, who together rolled over the heavy, awkward corpse. We all three felt about.

Nothing. No wounds. In the combined torchlight and strong moonlight we could see bruises, but with death there would be bruising in any case.

Another Spartan stepped forward. "Pleistarchus, I remind you this man who examines the body of our comrade is an Athenian. He will say or do anything to get another Athenian off the charge."

The man spoke as if to a difficult and slow child. I waited for the King of Sparta to explode, but all he said was, "I know this, Xenares. Trust me, I will keep it in mind."

The man named Xenares was dressed in the style of formal chiton that covered him from neck to ankles in one long, flowing robe. He had a small, pinched mouth that looked like it was set in a permanent expression of distaste. Or perhaps it was the cares of office, for he seemed to be an official of some sort. He turned to one of the Spartan soldiers and said, "Send for Markos." The soldier scampered off as if he'd received a command from Zeus.

"This whole question of the guilt of Timodemus can be put away at once," Pericles declared. "Nicolaos has watched over Timodemus like a hungry eagle, every moment since he was reinstated to the competition. He can certainly swear that Timodemus was nowhere near Arakos."

Every eye turned to me.

Suddenly I was very nervous. I felt myself blush.

"Er . . . Pericles, that might not be entirely true." I had to admit it; there might be a witness to prove otherwise if I lied. "After Timodemus went to bed I handed over the watch to someone else."

"What!" Pericles fairly screeched.

"Well, Timodemus was asleep. It wasn't like there was much to do, and it was someone reliable," I said in my defense. "His uncle, Festianos."

"So reliable we found the killer in the women's camp," Xenares pointed out.

Pericles turned to me and said, "Watching like a hungry eagle, were you?" His voice dripped with sarcasm.

Pericles was being grossly unfair. But nor could I provide Timo with an alibi, so I obviously hadn't been watching him closely enough. Pericles had spent his precious political capital for nothing, and it was I who had advised him to do so. I had no choice but to accept his withering stare.

"Where is this uncle now?" Exelon the Chief Judge asked.

"Asleep before our tents," said One-Eye, his first contribution. "Chief Judge, I swear before Zeus my son had nothing to do with this. You mustn't let this incident interfere with the Games—"

I think my jaw hit the dirt. The Chief Judge stared at One-Eye as if he were some strange creature suddenly in our midst, and so did everyone else.

"Interfere with the Games? Incident?" the Chief Judge repeated in shock. "One-Eye, do you understand what's at stake here?"

"Is Timodemus permitted to compete in the pankration on the fourth day?" One-Eye asked.

How could he ask about such a thing with the life of his son forfeit?

"A man with blood guilt upon him? Not only that, an oath breaker before Zeus Herkios? Don't be ridiculous." The Chief Judge stamped his staff hard upon the earth.

"This is terrible," One-Eye wailed. The death of a man didn't affect him. The thought of sacrilege at the Sacred Games moved him not at all, but the thought of his son unable to compete caused him to cry.

Everyone stood speechless, embarrassed by his behavior.

"You're looking for a friend of the dead man," said Socrates into the suddenly frosty silence.

I'd forgotten he was even there. "Be quiet, Socrates. This is a business for men."

"Who is this boy?" said the Chief Judge. "And what is he doing here? Is this disaster some sort of show for children?"

"He's my little brother. I'm sorry, he was in the tent when your men came to fetch me. I'll send him home at once. Socrates, disappear."

Pleistarchus raised his hand. "No, let the boy speak."

"Very well, what do you mean, Socrates?" I demanded.

"You said it yourself, Nico. The dead man was attacked from the front."

"So?"

Socrates looked at us quizzically. "It's just that if you met a man in the woods at night, and if he'd attacked you that same day, would you stand still to be hit again? It doesn't seem likely, does it?"

"I was about to say the same thing," I lied.

"Your brother makes a good point," said Pleistarchus. "If Arakos had seen Timodemus, he would certainly have expected another attack. He would have been ready to defend himself."

"Yes, it's very confusing, isn't it?" Socrates shrugged. "Because on the face of it, only Timodemus could have killed Arakos."

"Whose side are you on here?" I demanded.

Socrates looked puzzled. "But Nico, isn't the idea to work out the truth?"

I ground my teeth and managed not to shout at him.

"Sorry, Nico," he said meekly.

"The boy makes sense again," said Pleistarchus. "The only man ever to best Arakos in the pankration was Timodemus of Athens. Who else could have taken him on without a weapon and killed him?"

Unfortunately the King of Sparta was right: what Socrates said made sense.

"Would you all excuse me for a moment?" I marched over to Timodemus, grabbed him by the arm. The guards watched me drag him out of their earshot.

"Did you kill him?" I hissed in the lowest voice.

"Nico!" he said, obviously hurt. "How can you ask such a thing?"

"I'm asking," I said through gritted teeth, "because when I defend you, I need to know what I have to deal with. Are they going to find any evidence against you? Tell me true, Timo, and swear by Zeus."

"I didn't kill Arakos. I swear this by Zeus, may he destroy me if I lie."

"All right." I let go of his arm and walked back to the body, stood over it, turned around. I wanted to see what Arakos saw, the moment before he was attacked.

Another man strode into the clearing; he pushed his way into the inner ring. The new arrival stood opposite me over the freshly murdered corpse. He glanced down, and said, "It looks like the pankration started early this year."

Xenares said, "None of your wit please, Markos. You can see this is a crisis."

The man Xenares had named Markos was slightly taller than me, which meant neither tall nor short. He stood with a straight back, his face by torchlight pleasant but unremarkable. Our gazes met, and he smiled. His intelligent eyes were so deeply blue as to be almost black.

"We seem to have a problem here," he said to me, as if he'd walked into a room where someone had spilled the wine.

I didn't know who this Markos was, but Xenares had called for him, and that made him an enemy. For that matter, I didn't know who Xenares was, except that he hated Athens, and a king of Sparta treated him with respect.

"There is another issue," said King Pleistarchus. "It's important to determine whether Arakos died fighting."

"Why do you care?" Pericles said. "It doesn't make him any less murdered."

"It is the custom of our people. If my fellow Spartan died in combat then he is entitled to a headstone with his name upon it, so he will be remembered. But if he died without a fight, then his name is to be forgotten."

I said, "He was beaten, as you see, but there are signs of a long struggle. Look at these bruises, here and here and here." I touched different places on Arakos's arms and neck. "All we have to do is look for a man who's been in a fight."

Markos said, "Of course there are signs of a struggle on him, he's a pankratist! He's been doing nothing but practice fighting for the last ten months."

"Oh yes, of course." I had no choice but to admit it; Markos was right and looked alert, while I had just made myself look like an idiot in front of these men.

"The same will go for Timodemus and every other contestant," Markos continued. "There's no point searching for evidence of a fight on any of our suspects."

"What about looking for recent, fresh bruises?" a voice in the darkness asked.

"Was there anyone who didn't train this morning?" Markos asked reasonably.

That was true. Why, even Timodemus, who had been thrown out of the contest, had picked a fight this morning. With me.

I wiped my hands, though there was very little blood on them—the wounds of Arakos had not bled much and were already quite dry—but there was another problem. "I've touched a dead body. I'm ritually unclean. Is there seawater?"

Exelon the Chief Judge said, "The water of the Kladeos is considered cleansing. You can wash on the way back to camp."

During this conversation the other nine judges of the Games had trickled into the clearing, in varying states of wakefulness, and been apprised of what had happened. Now the Chief Judge turned to them, and they muttered together for an interminable time while some of the most powerful men in Hellas waited in silence.

"Here is our judgment," said the Chief Judge, turning back to the main group. "The evidence against Timodemus, son of Timonous, is strong. For the murder of Arakos he is to be imprisoned in one of the ancient disused buildings, and after the closing ceremony he is to be tied hand and foot and thrown to his death from Mount Typaeum."

Mount Typaeum is a place of high cliffs along the road from Elis. To be thrown from it is the punishment reserved for women who sneak into the Games. It is a particularly shameful death.

Pericles turned to the judges and said, in a voice trained to oratory, "This is not according to the law, which states there may be no executions during the Truce."

"That is so," the Chief Judge said. "But this is Day One, and the Sacred Games end on Day Five. Soon thereafter the Truce ends, when the Hellenes have had enough time to return to their homes. We'll give ourselves dispensation to act

early, while everyone's still here to witness the consequences
for sacrilege."

Pericles said, "The men who compete in the pankration are
issued a blanket pardon for murder. This is the law."

Xenares spoke up. "The law provides immunity if one athlete
kills another during the competition."

Pericles opened his mouth to protest, but the Chief Judge held
up his hand. "Wait, I've not finished. The Athenians raise seeds
of doubt regarding the guilt of Timodemus. Perhaps they will
grow to bear fruit, perhaps not. The Athenians may nominate
a man to investigate this crime and, if they can, clear the name
of their athlete. They have until the end of the Games to prove
Timodemus innocent."

"Four days is not enough time," Pericles said.

"It's all the time you have," the Chief Judge said without sympathy. "After that, the people return to their own cities, and every
witness and any suspects will be gone."

Pericles could only nod at the truth of that.

Xenares scoffed, "Such an investigation can have only one outcome. Of course the Athenians will whitewash their own man."

"You're right, Xenares." Pleistarchus turned to the Chief
Judge. "Xenares, who is an ephor of Sparta, makes a good point.
Sparta cannot accept this."

I wondered if the Chief Judge would threaten Pleistarchus the
way he had Pericles, but instead he held up his hand in a placat-
ing gesture and turned back to his fellow judges. They conferred
once more, in low voices. I strained to hear what they said but
to no avail, until Exelon the Chief Judge announced, "We, the
Judges of the Games, will appoint a third city to investigate this
crime."

Pericles and Pleistarchus both snorted at that.

"Every important city in Hellas is either for Athens or against
her or allied with Sparta or allied against!" Pericles exclaimed.

Pleistarchus nodded. "For once I must agree with Pericles.

There are no neutral cities of any importance. Moreover, if you appoint some minor city to oversee the investigation, the Athenians will immediately put pressure on them. The Athenians will offer generous trade agreements to save their man, or threaten to impose extra import taxes on the city's merchant ships if they find against. That's the way of Athenians, to cheat with their money."

I nodded to myself. Yes, that was exactly what Pericles would do.

Pericles said, face-to-face with Pleistarchus, "And I suppose if the judges selected a minor city, you Spartans wouldn't threaten to attack them if they don't see things your way? The only cities free from Spartan bullying are the powerful ones or the ones far from Sparta on the islands in the Aegean Sea. The judges must select one of them to investigate."

Pleistarchus objected, "That's no good. They're all pro-Athenian."

"Because we protect them from the Persians," said Pericles, "while you Spartans refuse to venture so far from your homes."

"You have the ships, we don't," said Pleistarchus. "I don't recall Athens whining so much when you needed us to defeat the Persians for you. If you protect the islands with your ships, it's because we protected you on land with our army."

"We fought the Persians together," said Pericles. "And so did every other Hellene city. There was nothing special about Sparta."

"Except that without us you would certainly have been conquered. My father died in that war, Athenian."

"So did many fathers."

"Enough. Silence, both of you." The Chief Judge looked from Pericles to Pleistarchus, scowling. "This squabble between the Athenians and Spartans is irrelevant. You will wait while the judges confer. Again."

The Chief Judge and his fellow judges stepped apart and spoke in low tones to one another in the semidarkness. The rest of us waited in silence.

Pericles caught my eye. As usual I had no idea what he thought. Pericles could hide his true thoughts as easily as most men hide their dagger. What Pericles saw in me I don't know, but what I felt was confusion for the contradictory evidence and fear for my friend Timodemus.

The Chief Judge returned. He stamped his staff to get our attention. "This is our final judgment. Athens and Sparta both speak truth. There is no city to investigate this crime that is beyond the influence of either one of you. Therefore here is our decision. Let the Spartans assign their own investigator. Let the Athenians, too, have their own man investigate the crime. The Spartan and the Athenian shall see the same evidence and hear the same witnesses. Both will swear before Zeus Herkios to show no prejudice to their own city, to accept no bribes, and to do their best to discover the truth. Both will swear the oath of the Olympic contestants, at first light, on the steps of the Bouleterion."

Pericles nodded with visible reluctance.

Pleistarchus considered for a moment. Xenares the ephor grabbed the arm of his King. There was furious whispering between them. Xenares was obviously unhappy and wouldn't let go. Pleistarchus shook him off. The King of Sparta nodded agreement to the judges.

The Chief Judge said, "Name your men."

Xenares the ephor spoke for Sparta. He said, "Sparta nominates Markos, son of Glaukippos."

"Very well. Pericles?" the Chief Judge prompted.

"Athens nominates Nicolaos, son of Sophroniscus."

"Then it is decided. We grant you until the end of the Games. You will convene before us to argue your cases after the closing ceremony. If you cannot prove his innocence, Timodemus of Athens will be thrown from the mountain."

I REMAINED TO examine the scene. So did Markos. I said nothing to him; he said nothing to me. In the absence of outraged Olympic officials, the forest was eerily silent.

Markos and I both wandered about the perimeter of the clearing, looking high and low. I had no idea what I was searching for, and I doubt he did either, but I was cursed if I'd be the first to leave the scene of the crime. If Markos felt the same way, it was going to be a long night.

He whistled cheerful hymns, which quickly became irritating.

Just when I thought I couldn't stand it any longer, my eye caught on something. Ten steps down the track to Olympia was the longest snake I'd ever seen. I halted and stared.

The snake didn't move.

Maybe it wasn't a snake, maybe it was something else. A dark rope?

I walked down the way to touch whatever it was. When it didn't leap at me, I picked it up. It was thin leather, and as I pulled on it, something longer and heavier emerged from beneath the bushes.

"What's this?" Markos had seen me.

Now I knew what I had. "It's a whip." I held it by the wooden handle, about which a leather grip had been wound.

"Were there any whiplashings on Arakos?" Markos asked.

The Spartans had removed their fallen comrade. Fortunately I had examined the body carefully. I cast my mind back over what I'd seen. I said there'd been plenty of beating marks, but none that were long lacerations, nothing that looked like a whip mark.

Markos took the whip from my hands and flicked his wrist. The thong entangled among leaves and branches no matter what direction he faced. "It's long."

So it was. The referees in the pankration use whips to control the contestants, but a referee's whip is shorter and less flexible.

"What's a whip doing here?" I wondered.

He shrugged. "I suppose someone must have dropped it."

"Yes, but who carries a whip around Olympia?"

The Spartan shrugged. "It might have nothing to do with the murder. I'll show it around, see if anyone recognizes it."

I snatched back the whip. "I'll keep it, if you don't mind."

"What if I mind?"

"Finders keepers."

"THANKS A LOT, Pericles," I said, after I'd tramped back to the main grounds. I'd caught up with Pericles at the Bouleterion. The moon was on the way down. Soon Apollo would rise upon his chariot of fire. "But I must warn you, I'm not sure I can do this."

"Yes, you can," he said. "You've done it twice before." He turned and began a quick step south, toward the Athenian camp and, presumably, his tent.

Indeed I had. My first investigation had been such a success that I'd made it my trade. But this time there was an important difference.

"That's not the point," I told him. "Timodemus is my friend. I can't possibly do this and remain objective."

"Objectivity isn't the requirement. You're supposed to get him off."

"But what if he did it?"

Pericles stopped his fast, angry walk and turned on me. "Listen, Nicolaos, I don't give a curse if—" He broke off to see who of the men staggering back and forth in the cold early morning might be listening in. He dragged me into an alcove of the nearby gymnasium, where we wouldn't be overheard.

"I don't give a witch's curse if one of our people murdered some Spartan. If your friend's innocent he deserves justice, and if he's guilty I don't want the rest of the world to know it. If you feel strongly about it, we can punish him in the privacy of our own city, but not here at Olympia. There are political

considerations, and I'll point out we wouldn't have this problem if you'd watched that overmuscled, underbrained friend of
yours like I told you."

"You didn't say to watch him every moment. You said to make
sure the Spartans didn't eliminate him. Well, they didn't."

"He looks pretty eliminated to me!"

I had to concede Pericles was right. Pericles saw he'd won, as
he'd surely known he would. He stalked off with his final words:
"Stop arguing. Get out there and save Timodemus."

THERE WERE TOO many things to do and, as Pericles had
pointed out to the Chief Judge, not enough time to do them.
Day Two of the Sacred Games was about to begin; four days,
then, to find the man who killed Arakos, or at least prove it was
not Timodemus. Or—and I had to be honest, though I wanted
to believe him—perhaps prove my friend was a murderer; for
Socrates and the Chief Judge were right; on the face of it,
Timodemus looked as guilty as any man could be.

Two actions were pressing: I needed to talk to Timo, who
had been led away, and I needed to interview that priestess of
Demeter in whose tent Timo had been discovered. The testimony of a woman of her stature would hold great weight at
judgment time.

The Priestess of Demeter from Elis was the only woman permitted to observe the Games. Indeed, she was required, and once
the Games began at dawn, she would be ensconced in her box,
in full view of the crowd, and unapproachable until the night—a
whole day lost.

But a strange man could hardly expect to be admitted to her
tent. I needed help, and luckily for me I knew just the person. I
went to pay a call on my Diotima.

I'D LEARNED MY lesson. I wasn't rash enough to poke my
head through the tent flap without warning. Instead I stood

outside Diotima's tent, where flying knives couldn't hit me, and called, "Diotima, it's me. Is it safe to come in?"

Not a word in reply.

Of course. Normal people were still asleep at this time. It was only slaves and investigators who tramped the cold, damp ground of Olympia before the sun was up.

I crept into Diotima's tent, so as not to wake her, then realized how silly that was, since the entire point was to wake her. There she lay, curled up fast asleep, as innocent as a small child. In sleep she was lovely. Her red lips were slightly parted, her dark tresses fell across her face, and her chest rose and fell as she breathed softly.

I wondered how I'd been so lucky as to get her. An awful lot had gone wrong in my life, but Diotima was my one victory. At least, I hoped she was; there were still some parents to overcome.

I reached out an arm and shook her gently.

"Diotima, honey, wake up. It's me—aaarrggh!"

"Oh, I'm sorry, Nico!"

Diotima had turned and plunged a short, sharp knife straight into my arm: her priestess knife, which she used for sacrifices and always kept in a pouch about her. She'd only stopped her stab as the curved point sliced my skin. Blood trickled down my forearm.

"I'm so sorry," she said again. "I thought you were a man creeping into my tent." She paused. "Well, actually, come to think of it, you were."

But it was the first part of her statement that grabbed my attention. "Diotima, have men been creeping into your tent?"

She grimaced. "There've been one or two incidents. The drunks who stagger into the women's camp seem to think every tent has a *porné* in it. They don't bother to look for hanging sandals."

Sandals hung up outside a tent mean the occupant is open for business. Sandals, because porné means "walker," as in a woman who walks the streets. At Olympia there are no streets to walk, so the women for hire hang their sandals beside their tent entrances. I could see how a drunk man in the dark could make a mistake, but that wasn't going to save anyone who threatened Diotima.

Diotima read my thoughts. "It's all right, Nico. I dealt with them."

"Are they still alive?" I asked, wondering if we'd need to hide any bodies.

"Mostly," she said.

I decided not to pursue that.

"I'm in no danger, Nico," Diotima tried to reassure me.

"Keeping you safe is my job." Merely saying it made me feel good. I liked the idea of protecting Diotima.

"Stop worrying about me, Nico. You didn't used to behave like this."

"We didn't used to be married."

"We aren't married now either. We still have our fathers to convince."

I sighed. "I know."

"And even if they do let us marry, it doesn't mean I'm suddenly helpless."

I could see life with Diotima was destined to be unusual. "We have a problem," I said, using the same words the Spartan Markos had said to me over the body.

I told her what had happened while she slept and/or knifed intruders. I only got a few words in before she sat up, excited, and wrapped the blanket around her for warmth.

I ended by saying, "We need the evidence of Klymene, the Priestess of the Games, as soon as possible. Once the Games begin, she'll be locked into her box at the stadion, and she won't be free to tell her story until tonight. A whole day's delay for her evidence might be a killing problem."

"Literally killing, for Timodemus," Diotima added.

"A fellow priestess like you could give me an entrée."

"Good, let's go." She hopped off her bed and tossed aside the blanket to reveal her outstanding body in all its glory.

"Diotima, you sexy woman, why don't we stay here for a while and—"

"I have to decide what to wear for this priestess." She began to rummage through the wooden trunk that she'd brought with her from Asia Minor. She pulled out clothing and tossed it on the camp bed.

On our last mission, before we'd left Magnesia, Diotima had been given a whole new wardrobe as a gift from the people we'd helped. A slave who specialized in Persian fashion had sniffed noisily when asked to make simple Hellene chitons, but after lavish flattery and some physical threats, the dressmaker had measured Diotima and, in the space of a only a few days, had cut and embroidered ten new chitons from a large range of exotic, brightly patterned fabrics. Some were of a shiny new material called silk, fabulously expensive stuff the Persians imported from a country so distant no one even knew its name. When we got back to Athens, Diotima would be the envy of every woman.

Diotima liked wearing the silk, and I liked it when she did, because when I held her against me the effect was intense.

"Wear the red silk," I encouraged her.

"No. I know what will happen, and we have work to do." Diotima stopped to consider. "I think I'll wear the blue chiton. And some jewelry." She rummaged through her travel chest. "Help me put on this chiton, will you?" She wrapped the large rectangle of material around herself and turned her back to me to fix the brooches that held the dress over her shoulders. Last of all, she carefully hooked in the silver bear earrings I'd bought her the day before.

Then she said, "Let's go. I'll do the talking."

"She might respond better to me, Diotima."

"I doubt it. She's probably some withered prune with no interest in men. They always pick the old, ugly ones for the top jobs."

"I WOKE UP, and there he was, naked."

Klymene spoke to us while a red-haired slave girl fussed about arranging her hair. She turned her lovely neck so the slave girl could pin up the dark tresses. Another slave washed Klymene's feet. A slave apiece attended to her hands, which she was holding out for them to clean her nails.

"Then the guards ran in and tackled him. They took him away." She spoke as if Timodemus had been a stray dog.

The slaves stepped back, and Klymene examined herself in a polished bronze mirror. She gave herself a smile.

Klymene was about to be the only woman present among thousands of excited men at the stadion, and there would be times when she was the center of attention. She knew it, and knew exactly what effect she would have on all those men. She stood and smoothed down her chiton.

I was glad Diotima had stopped to put on her fine clothes and her necklace and silver earrings. Klymene was a stunner, no doubt about it, but my girl was her match.

"You didn't hear him enter?" Diotima asked.

"What? Oh no, of course not. I would have called or something."

"You seem to have a relaxed attitude to naked men staring at you in the middle of the night," Diotima remarked. "Does this sort of thing happen often?"

"First time. Of course, if I hadn't woken, I wouldn't know, would I?"

"Hmm."

It was clear Klymene wouldn't blame a man for breaking in to see her. Come to that, I wouldn't blame a man either.

"You're not married?" I asked.

"No."

Diotima said, "What about your mother? Shouldn't she be here with you?"

"She died when I was young."

"I'm sorry," Diotima said.

"So am I. I miss her. It would have been nice to have a mother."

"How did you come to be a priestess?" Diotima asked. "You don't seem like the usual sort."

Klymene looked my wife up and down. "I could say the same for you, honey. Artemis, I think you said?"

"I served at the Temple of Artemis Agroptera in Athens and the Artemision in Ephesus."

Klymene looked impressed. These were serious credentials. The two haughty priestesses faced each other eye to eye and, I noticed in appreciation, breast to breast.

What Diotima had neglected to mention was that she'd been barely tolerated as a junior priestess in Athens and had been cold-shouldered at the Artemision after fighting with the other priestesses.

Diotima returned to the subject at hand. "You find a strange man in your bedroom, and this is your total reaction?"

"Well, I may have screamed a little. That's what brought the guards running. Everyone's looked after me so well."

I said, "What's your function, Klymene, here at the Games?"

Klymene glanced over the assembly of rings, necklaces, and headbands that littered the table before her. She pointed at several items, all of which looked elegantly expensive.

As the slave girl decorated her with jewelry, Klymene said, "The Priestess of Demeter oversees the Sacred Games. She's had this role since time immemorial."

"Yes, but why Demeter? Why not Zeus, or even his queen Hera? There's no temple to Demeter at Olympia, is there?"

"None. The ancient temple is the Heraion, the temple to Hera that also housed her husband Zeus until this Olympiad. Have you seen inside the new Temple of Zeus?"

"Not yet."

"It's amazing. They left space to erect a huge Zeus." She frowned into the mirror. "Xenia, the tresses aren't quite right."

The redheaded slave girl stifled a sigh, picked up a comb made of fine bone, and began reworking the hair. Klymene watched the girl's progress in the mirror as she spoke. "They say that in ages past, my goddess Demeter ate the shoulder of King Pelops, and that's why her priestess must attend the Games, but if you ask me it's a load of old wash water. A goddess eats better than that. All I can tell you is Demeter opens each day, blesses each contest, and closes every day with a prayer, and this Olympiad, it's me who represents the Goddess."

Klymene studied herself in the bronze mirror with much complacency. Then she stood. "I must go."

Diotima said, "But for most of the time, you have to sit alone in a box upon an altar. What do you do all day? It must be mind-numbing."

Klymene laughed. "With all those superfit naked young men running back and forth in front of me? Oh, I have a way to amuse myself!"

Klymene brushed past Diotima's stunned silence, and a slave raised the tent flap. "If you'll excuse me, I have some naked men to watch." She waggled her fingers at us. "Ta ta."

"WOW," WAS ALL Diotima could say. "What do you think, Nico?"

"I think I want to be in the box with her when she amuses her—oof!" My wife delivered a swift elbow to the stomach.

"What did you think of her story?"

"Unfortunately, it all makes sense," I said, rubbing my stomach. "I can imagine how the Spartan Markos will reconstruct it. Timo waylays Arakos in the forest and beats him close to death. He hears men approach. Timo takes off down the narrow track that runs through the woods to the women's camp. Meanwhile the men discover Arakos and raise the alarm while trying to save the victim. Timo looks for a place to hide. There are plenty of tents, but he doesn't know which ones are safe; many of the tents house pornoi, and they're probably entertaining men. In the middle of the ground is a tent larger than all the others; he doesn't know what it is, but it looks official, maybe no one's in there at night. In he goes and stumbles right into Klymene. She sees him and screams."

"What about him being naked?"

"Perfectly normal. The athletes are required to compete naked, and many don't bother with clothes for the duration of the Games. Everyone knows that."

Diotima looked dubious. "There's a lot of supposition in what you said."

"It's almost all guess, but it fits exactly with what we know, and it sounds convincing."

"What was Timodemus doing, if not escaping the crime scene?"

"Good question."

"For that matter, what was Arakos doing in the woods?"

"Another fine question."

"We need to trace his movement on this side of the river."

"No, you need to trace his movements."

Diotima looked at me quizzically.

"I need to take the Olympic Oath."

DAY 2 OF THE 80TH OLYMPIAD OF THE SACRED GAMES

A POLLO'S LIGHT SHONE cold and distant over the horizon. I stood, shivering, in a place I'd never expected to be: on the steps of the Bouleterion of Olympia, before the statue of Zeus Herkios, about to take the Olympic Oath.

Markos the Spartan stood beside me. His blond hair hung to shoulder length, in the manner of the Spartans, and like the Spartans he wore a scarlet cloak of fine wool, which kept him warm in the chilly dawn. He looked relaxed but serious, the very picture of a responsible young man about to assume an important burden. I on the other hand nervously sprang from one foot to the other, my arms wrapped about to stop me from shivering too visibly. I knew I made a poor impression compared with the Spartan.

A crowd milled about before us. The men of Sparta and Athens were up in force to watch the unprecedented oath. News of the murder and the investigation had spread faster than plague.

The men of Sparta clustered together in the center of the crowd, easy to spot because, like Markos, they'd assumed their vermilion cloaks. The Spartans normally forswore their famous cloak at the Games, to blend into the crowd and be less divisive, but now they wore them as a badge of honor.

The Athenians, too, were easy to recognize. They were the nervous ones. They stood in clusters with their backs to one another. A few seemed angry.

Pericles stood at the fore of the crowd. He looked tired. He hadn't slept any more than had I.

One belligerent fool among the Athenians waved a wineskin and declared loudly that no one cared about a dead Spartan; in fact, those were the best kind. Pericles turned quick as lightning to push his way through the crowd. I saw him speak to the drunk fool, not with harsh words, but soft ones, and I saw him gently remove the wineskin from the man's grasp. That was a riot averted.

I could see King Pleistarchus, and beside him Xenares, hanging about like a bad case of the gripes. A knot of younger men surrounded these two; there was no doubt what they were: Spartan bodyguards.

At the back I saw the weedy fake Heracles who'd attacked Diotima and me. He still wore his ill-fitting lion skin, but at least he wasn't carrying his club. He stared at Markos and me, his jaw hanging. He probably hadn't expected to see me again, let alone standing where I was.

My father, Sophroniscus, pushed his way to the front of the crowd. I'd had no chance to speak to him since the murder; I hoped Socrates had brought him up to date. What he thought of this I couldn't tell. Father had permitted me against his better judgment to pursue my career as agent for Pericles for a period of two years, a period that now was more than half gone, under the condition that if at the end I could not make it pay, then I was to return to the family trade of sculpting. Now he saw his son standing at the Olympic altar. It occurred to me I'd come a long way in a very short time from that first, perilous mission, which had almost ended in my death and his ruin. Our eyes met for a moment and he nodded. Socrates stood beside him and for once he didn't fidget. My little brother looked up at me in wonder.

Pythax, the huge barbarian from the north, chief of the Scythian Guard of Athens, former slave and now a new-made citizen, stood in the throng. As a barbarian he was forbidden to compete—not that he wanted to, he was too old—but as a citizen of Athens he had every right to be here. I stood to attention at the sight of him, desperate to make a good impression.

Timo's uncle Festianos looked up at me from the crowd with a quizzical expression; beside him, One-Eye scowled.

The old man with the bright face was there, too, the man whom I'd noticed yesterday at the first swearing in. He held a long walking staff, and I saw him look from me to Markos and back to me again. I wondered who he was. Other men seemed to know him, for they made way for the old man wherever he chose to go. Or perhaps they were merely being polite to an elder.

The giant brazier had been rekindled. I took a step closer to it to try to catch some of its warmth. No one else seemed to be cold, but I shivered.

Exelon, the Chief Judge of the Games, emerged from the Bouleterion behind me. As he walked past the Spartan Markos and me, he muttered, "Look confident and put on a decent show, you two."

We both nodded that we understood.

Exelon stood with his back to Markos and me. He banged his Y-forked staff on the steps until he had the attention of the crowd. "Hellenes! I know you've heard what passed during the night. A competitor has been murdered. I know that feelings will run high because of this, it's only natural, and I remind you all, here and now, that the Sacred Truce remains in force. Anyone who transgresses will be punished."

The Chief Judge was tense. I saw it in the set of his shoulder muscles and the knuckles that stood out on the hand that gripped his staff.

"That's all very well, but what of the killer Timodemus?" a faceless voice in the crowd shouted. "Will you punish him?"

"Timodemus is innocent!" another man yelled. "You just have it in for us Athenians."

"Hold!" Exelon shouted into the argument and banged his staff once more. "If Timodemus is guilty, he will pay the debt of blood as custom demands, under the laws of Elis in whose domain we stand. To that end, two men will investigate the crime:

one an Athenian, the other a Spartan. The Judges of the Games will make the final decision based on their reports."

The crowd quieted at his words. They sensed this was a fair judgment.

"They report to me and the other judges, not to their cities. I call upon them to take their oath." Exelon nodded to me. "You first."

Suddenly I felt nervous again. I stepped forward and spoke my words. Whether anyone heard me I don't know, because I spoke quickly to get it over with, and I fear I mumbled.

"I swear by mighty Zeus that I, Nicolaos, son of Sophroniscus, shall contest the Sacred Games fairly and with honor, when I compete in the event of—" I staggered over the next words. In a sudden panic, I realized nobody had told me what to call this strange new event. "In the Olympic event of . . . murder investigation."

The crowd stirred and murmured. It is the right of the judges to create any event they like, but this was a new one for everyone present.

Exelon gave me a stern look. I continued in a louder voice over the hubbub of the crowd. "I shall obey the orders of the Judges of the Games. I shall do everything in a way that is right. May mighty Zeus of the Oaths destroy me if I do not."

I saw Pericles wince as I spoke and wondered what his problem was.

The sacrifice wasn't the traditional giant boar but a small piglet. There were only two of us, and anything larger would have been a waste. The animal had probably been picked up from the festival agora and was destined for a meal in any case. The man with the piglet laid it on the altar and stroked the little animal gently but firmly. It squealed as the knife went in and struggled for the briefest instant but relaxed for a last time as its lifeblood flowed away.

"The sacrifice went willingly," I heard someone in the front row say. "It's a good sign. Unlike what happened yesterday."

I took a slice of piglet from the altar—the Butcher of the Games had begun his bloody work—and with thumb and forefinger threw the dripping meat into the burning brazier. The meat sizzled at once, and I smelled burned flesh. My oath to Zeus was complete.

Markos stepped forward and proceeded to make the same oath I had. He spoke slowly in a clear, carrying voice and didn't stumble at all.

The oath was complete. Criminal investigation was an Olympic event for the first time in history.

I had thought, when the Chief Judge set the requirement in the night, the oath would be a mere administrative detail that would keep me from my work for a short time and then could be forgotten. Now that I was upon the steps, I was overcome by the importance of what I had sworn, and understood his wisdom. The Olympic Oath is a sacred dedication, and by speaking it before the Hellenes my investigation was removed from the realm of politics and became a part of the Games themselves. I was no longer Nicolaos of Athens; I had become Nicolaos of Olympia.

The heralds, their voices so loud they could be heard across all Olympia, announced the first event of the day: the chariot race at the hippodrome.

The crowd before us instantly broke. Thousands of men elbowed to be first to the best vantage points. It was like a mob of particularly vicious goats on their way to the feed bin. As I stood and watched the chaos, it occurred to me that whoever had killed Arakos had done it in a remarkably confined space. All my life I'd heard men speak of Olympia—after the sacred sanctuary at Delphi, it was the most famous place in all of Hellas—now I was here for the first time, and I saw it was much smaller than its enormous reputation. The permanent buildings covered a tiny area; the tent city was larger, but still no larger than a village. Crowded into this space were more men than you would find in a medium-sized city. To kill Arakos must have been for the murderer like trying to scratch his nose in a closet full of men.

One would have thought that would make catching the killer easier, but I had no idea who might have done it. Unless of course, it really was my friend.

Timodemus had exactly four days left to live.

I STOOD AND considered what to do next until everyone was gone.

Well, almost everyone.

"It's not fair," Socrates whined. "How come you get to be an Olympic contestant and I don't?"

"It wasn't my idea. The Chief Judge insisted."

"Why?"

"I don't know, but we should consider ourselves lucky. Exelon didn't have to permit an investigation, you know. He could have condemned Timo out of hand."

As I spoke, I caught sight of the fake Heracles. He took the steps up the Bouleterion, I suppose for a shortcut though to the hippodrome. He swerved away when Socrates turned and I stared at him. He probably remembered how easily I'd disarmed him.

"Nicolaos of Athens?" It was the Spartan Markos. He'd wandered up to me from behind. It occurred to me Markos could be very quiet when he chose.

"What do you want?" I said, more abrupt than I intended because he'd startled me.

He said, "Now that we've sworn the oath, we're required to share our witnesses. I only wanted to know, do you have any plans? Shall I come with you?"

The polite inquiry wasn't fooling anyone. I had no more wish to work with Markos than he did with me. I particularly didn't want Markos in the room when I interviewed Timodemus. I said, "Why don't we follow our own paths, then share notes. If we don't trust each other, we can always check by talking to the same people."

"As you wish." He smiled thinly, turned on his heel and walked away.

I wondered if I'd been rude, but I wasn't sure.

The old man with the look of a priest approached me and Socrates. "Your voice is a disaster," he told me.

"What?"

"I witnessed your oath. Who taught you rhetoric?"

"No one."

The old man nodded. "It shows."

Pericles had once promised to teach me to speak before the people, but he'd never gotten around to giving lessons.

To change the subject, I said, "I am Nicolaos, son of Sophroniscus, of the deme Alopece of Athens."

"*Kalimera* Nicolaos," he said. "Good morning. I wish to know if Timodemus, son of Timonous One-Eye, is a murderer."

"Don't we all," I muttered.

He raised an eloquent and somewhat-bushy eyebrow. "You haven't formed a view? Surely you cannot have long to investigate this dreadful crime, a few days at most."

"Have you talked to the judges?" I demanded.

"No, but your deadline is obvious. In a few days the Games will be over, and everyone will depart. You must be swift as the stadion runner if you wish to catch this killer."

Whoever this old man was, he was sharp. "Who are you, sir?"

He smiled. "Ahh. When you stared at me during the sacrifice I suspected you didn't recognize me. I am Pindar the praise singer."

Merely the greatest living poet of the Hellenes.

"It's an honor to meet you, Pindar," I said, and meant it. Everyone knew the songs of Pindar. To be praised by him was to be immortalized. "But I must ask, sir, do you have an interest in this?"

"After the Nemean Games, the father of the accused, One-Eye, commissioned me to praise the young man Timodemus in song. I took the money of One-Eye and praised Timodemus. So I ask myself, did I waste my words on a cheat? I hate to think it." He put a hand to his head, like a tragic actor who hears bad news.

"Thank you, Pindar. At least there are two of us who don't believe he's guilty." Pindar was an influential man. His support would be invaluable to save Timo.

"No, young man, you misunderstand my words. I said I hope he's not a killer, not that I believe it."

"Oh." I felt deflated.

Pindar didn't seem to notice my disappointment. "I must be neutral in this matter. The victim and the accused are both known to me."

"Then you know Timodemus hasn't the personality of a murderer," I said.

Pindar raised an eyebrow, and that one expressive movement told me I'd said something stupid. "On the contrary. Both these young men are highly aggressive. Both are capable of the greatest violence."

I hadn't thought of it like that, but Pindar was right. By definition, a top pankratist was a potential killer.

Pindar went on, "And yet I flatter myself as a fair judge of men—it's an occupational skill, you know—and that's the funny thing. If one of them was to kill the other, I would have expected Arakos to murder Timodemus."

"Pindar," I said, "let me buy you a drink."

In most places, to buy a man a drink at dawn is tricky. In Olympia, you need only stretch out your hand to grab one of the passing fast-food merchants. I did that and noticed that Pindar wasn't averse to drinking under the rosy-fingered dawn. We sat on the steps of the Bouleterion.

"So you were there at Nemea," I said to him.

"I attend all four of the major Games: the Nemean, the Isthmian, the Pythian, and, greatest of them all, the Sacred

Games here at Olympia. At Nemea I saw Timodemus fight for the first time. I predicted then that he would win these Sacred Games. Do you want to hear my verse?" Before I could decline with thanks, he launched into this:

So as the bards begin their verse
With hymns to the Olympian Zeus,
So has this hero laid the claim
To conquest in the Sacred Games.

"THOSE WERE MY words at Nemea, the first stanza anyway, that I wrote about your friend Timodemus. What do you think?"

Pindar stared at me, his left and right legs jittering in turn. If he'd been anyone but a world-famous poet, I'd have said he was nervous for my reaction. The only problem was I'd lost attention after the first few words.

"I thought it was, er . . . very nice," I said, desperately trying to remember anything he'd said.

He pounced. "Nice? What were the nice bits?"

"Well, er . . . I liked your choice of words, and—"

"Was there anything you didn't like? Don't be afraid to critique! I'm very good at taking criticism."

"No! No! I loved it. I'd definitely buy a scroll with this—"

"Does the allusion work? I was pleased with it myself."

"It's terrific!"

He gave me a stare. "You have no idea what I'm talking about, do you?"

"Er . . ."

He sighed. "We praise singers always open our songs with a few words in praise of Zeus. Because it would be impious to praise a man before a God, you see."

"Yes?" I wondered how I could politely excuse myself.

"Just as the words addressed to Zeus presage the hero who is our real subject, so does the victory of Timodemus at Nemea presage his ultimate destiny here at Olympia. Your friend is good. Very good. I've rarely seen better, and believe me, I've seen them all."

A small party of Spartans passed us by, recognizable by the scarlet cloaks. Pindar drank deep of his wine. When the Spartans had passed, he said, "But I've rarely seen such antagonism between contestants."

"At Nemea?" Thanks be to the Gods, he'd returned to something important.

"Nemea had its own problems, there was some unpleasantness, but there was no special antagonism between Arakos and Timodemus. Not that I noticed, in any case. No, Nicolaos, I refer to the march from Elis to Olympia, not two days ago. Arakos baited Timodemus every step of the way. It went beyond the usual athletic rivalry. There seemed to be real hatred on the part of Arakos. I wondered why, and until we reached Olympia, I wondered whether Arakos would attack Timodemus."

I blinked at that.

"Did Timodemus return the feeling?" Since Pindar was a fine judge of men—it being an occupational skill—I thought he must have all the answers when it came to motive.

"Timodemus seemed to me both knowing and confused."

"That's a contradiction."

"Welcome to human nature. Conflict, young man—the passions of great men in opposition, in sport as in war—it's the stuff of great poetry."

"But truth is what we need here."

Pindar snorted. "What is truth? I seek something more important: inspiration for my art. I've been in the thick of every war, attended every great sporting contest. So when Exelon announced this contest between Athens and Sparta, one in which the life of a man hangs in the balance, I was instantly intrigued. My plan is to observe this battle of wits between you and the Spartan." He looked me up and down.

"Are you sure you're prepared? Someone who's never heard of allusion is hardly in a position to be solving crimes. Perhaps I can help you."

"I doubt it."

"That's what your opponent said when I made him the same offer, but he changed his mind quickly enough."

"What?"

Pindar did the eyebrow raise again. It was obviously a stock theatrical move for him, and it put me in mind that this man was accustomed to performance before thousands of men. "As you and Markos took the oath—I must say in passing his voice projection was better than yours—you should work on that . . ."

I felt myself about to explode.

"Where was I? Oh yes, as I say, I told him it was odd you should carry the whip of a racing chariot."

Of course. It was so obvious now that Pindar said it. What other long whip would you find at the Olympics?

"I don't suppose you know who owns this whip, do you great Pindar?"

"A driver, of course. May I?"

Pindar took the whip from me. He held it lengthways before him. "It's a lucky thing for you I have observed hundreds of chariot races." He ran his finger along the handle. "Observe the threads woven into the leather. This declares the team," he said. "All the teams have their own racing colors, so the spectators can discern who is who in the thick dust of battle. See the distinctive checkered pattern in reds and greens? This is typical of teams from Thebes."

"And you've already told Markos?"

"Yes."

I seethed. That bastard Markos had tricked me. He'd asked me about witnesses, knowing I'd say what I had, so he could interview the chariot driver on his own in perfect innocence.

"Why didn't you tell me the important part at once?" I said.

"I like you; I was enjoying our conversation. My dear lad, if poets got to the point immediately, then it wouldn't be poetry, would it? The important thing is to savor the words along the way."

I said through gritted teeth, "I must speak with the driver of the Theban team."

"Then perhaps you should hurry. If I do not mistake, that trumpet we both hear is the summons to the hippodrome to observe the chariot race. The teams must be in the final stages of preparation."

I HAD TO find that driver. I had to find out if he was the killer; if he wasn't, I had to find out if he knew anything.

Pindar beside me strode along at a good clip for such an old man. He needed to be at the race, he explained, in case the winner commissioned a praise song. "It helps if I've seen what I'm paid to describe," he said. I left him at the gates and hurried to the stables behind the hippodrome.

"I'm looking for the chariot team from Thebes," I said to one man after another amid the frantic preparations. They pointed me from one box to the next, until I came to the one that housed the Megarans, at the end of the line.

Markos was already there, next to a man in a pure-white chiton, which marked him as a chariot driver. They stood alongside the chariot, decorated in the same colors as the whip handle I carried. I silently cursed Pindar for telling my competitor first, but refused to let Markos see I was upset.

"Does this belong to you?" I asked, and proffered the whip.

"That it does." The driver cast aside the whip he held and grabbed mine. He said, "This is my lucky whip; I've never run a race without it, so thanks. Where did you find it?"

"I wondered when you'd arrive," Markos said to me.

"What did you get from my witness?" I demanded.

"*Your* witness?" Markos smiled the superior smile of a man

who'd won a race to the man who'd come in second. "I found him first. What do the little boys say? Oh yes. Finders keepers."

I grated. "We'll interview this witness *together*."

"Didn't we just agree to compare notes later?" he said, in all apparent innocence. He even managed a slightly hurt tone.

"I'll save you the trouble in this case. He might have vital information, and it'd be a pity if any of it unintentionally slipped your mind in the debrief."

The Spartan gave me an evil grin. "Very well, we can question him together."

The driver's head had swiveled between Markos and me as we argued. He opened his mouth to speak, but an angry voice behind us got in first.

"No, you can't. Not now." A short, dark man who sweated freely and wore a harried frown stepped between us and the driver. The stress oozed from his voice. This had to be the team manager. He pointed to the hippodrome. "Iphicles is about to risk life and limb out there in a race that requires the utmost concentration, and you idiots want to bother him? Right when he needs to focus?"

"These are important questions," Markos said. "King Pleistarchus commands they be asked."

The manager snorted. "You think I care about kings now? You could be bum-boy to Zeus himself, and I wouldn't halt the team for you."

Iphicles said, "They found my lucky whip, Niallos. Look, they returned it."

He held up the whip to be seen.

That stopped the manager. "They did, did they?" Niallos looked from one of us to the other. "In that case, I thank you. Chariot drivers are the most superstitious men alive. Well, you can see why; their lives depend on luck as much as skill. Iphicles was convinced he'd die in this race unless someone found that whip."

Iphicles said, "Niallos, there's nothing for me to do yet but stand here. I may as well speak to them. I owe them. I might win the Olympics because of these two."

Niallos turned to Markos and me and said, "You have until the trumpets sound again." He marched off to bellow orders at the crew.

I said, "Thanks, Iphicles." The driver was as short as his team manager, but his shoulders were massive, and the muscles in his upper arms were like ropes. I glanced down. The middle two fingers of his left hand were missing. "What happened to your fingers?"

"Racing accident, years ago when I was young and reckless."

"Now you're older and wiser?"

"Just older."

"Dangerous for you."

"That's where the luck comes in. I'm one of the veterans of this race. It's the youngsters more likely to make mistakes, but we all have to watch out."

Iphicles could not have been much older than me.

It was hard to think among the barely controlled chaos of the race preparations. The crew swarmed all over the chariot and the horses. Two grooms stood at the front to hold the bridles and prevent the team from bolting. Men checked leather straps, made minute adjustments, and checked again. A slave rubbed oil into the harness. Another slapped pig fat and oil about the axle. One man checked the coupling between the harness and the chariot, and another man checked the work of the first. If that coupling failed, it would be disaster. One man, his eyes closed, ran his fingers along every part of the reins to ensure there was not the slightest nick, nothing to snap under the intense pressure of the race.

The roar of the crowd rose steadily over the noise of the race crews as they put the vehicles through final prep. Nervous horses neighed and danced in excitement, held barely in place by struggling grooms.

Against the noise I said, "Do you know a man named Arakos?"

Iphicles bent close to say, "Isn't he the dead man? Heard of him but never met him. I'm a race driver, not one of those fighting thugs."

Unfortunately, that made sense. "Where were you last night?"

"Across the river, screwing as many women as possible and guzzling the best wine."

I blinked. Iphicles was a straight talker.

"I puked twice already this morning. I'm still nursing a massive hangover."

"Do you always drink and wench yourself senseless before a major race? The preparations don't seem entirely adequate."

Iphicles laughed. "Look about you." Across the boxes, attendants and crews everywhere made last-moment preparations the same as the men next to us. In many boxes the driver had already stepped up to his vehicle. "See those men taking the reins? Some of them will die today. What man doesn't make the most of his last day on earth?"

"Last night, did you see—"

Iphicles said something I couldn't hear over the rising noise.

I leaned close to his ear and shouted, "What did you say?"

He leaned close to my ear and shouted back, "I said, *What did you say?* You'll have to speak up; I can't hear you over the crowd."

The next box along housed Team Megara. Their chariot had a problem of some sort; the wheels screeched fit to tear out my teeth. Men with buckets smeared fat as fast as they could ladle.

I cupped my hands together and shouted into Iphicles's ear, "How did you lose your whip?"

"This is hopeless," Markos shouted. "We'll have to wait till after the race." He abandoned the struggling conversation and stepped back to watch the crew prepare the chariot. I silently agreed with Markos that there was no hope of getting any useful information, but I wasn't willing to give up.

Iphicles had watched my mouth as I spoke, and he nodded to

show he understood. He shouted something back, but though I heard fragments, I couldn't make sense of what he'd said. I wanted to drag Iphicles away from the noisy place, but I knew he couldn't go.

The noise level suddenly dropped.

"Quick, tell me how you lost the whip."

"I already told your friend that. I took a wrong turn while I staggered home, went left into those woods instead of right across the river. Sounds dumb, I know, but my head wasn't working too well, so I followed the guy in front of me."

"What guy?"

"I dunno. There was a man ahead of me. Obviously I thought he was going back to camp, too. I just staggered along behind."

"Obviously. What happened then?"

"The man turned around and said I was going the wrong way. He pointed me toward the ford. I said thanks—at least I think I did—and then I must have tripped, 'cause next thing I knew I was flat on my face. When I came to, I went in the right direction. I don't remember much else."

"You carried a horsewhip to meet women?" My imagination ran wild.

"It's a *lucky* whip. When I woke this morning without it in my hands, I almost died." He shuddered. "I realized I must have dropped it when I fell, and like a fool I was so wasted I hadn't noticed. I went back for it, but it was gone."

Because Markos and I had taken it for evidence.

"Would you recognize this man if you saw him again?"

"I dunno. Maybe. Ask me later. Right now I'm all nerves."

And there I'd been expecting the owner of the whip to solve the case for me. He knew almost nothing. But who was it he'd followed? The murderer? Or Arakos?

As we spoke, a crewman beside us scooped out a large handful of grease from a bucket, slopped it onto the chariot's right axle where it joined the wheel, and spread it around. When he was satisfied, the crewman raised his arm and called. "Right wheel. Check!"

At almost the same moment a man on the other side raised his arm and called, "Left wheel. Check!"

Markos had crouched down to admire the chariot. "It's a remarkable piece of machinery," he said, rising and wiping the pig fat of the axle grease from his hands onto his tunic. "So small, so light."

"The horse team barely knows I'm there," Iphicles said. "As long as I've somewhere to put my feet and a leading panel to brace myself against the pull of the reins—that's all I need."

All along the line, race crews were doing the same as Team Thebes. Men stepped back from the chariots with raised arms to show they were ready, an action easily seen and understood no matter the noise and chaos of the race start.

I had only moments. Iphicles must have seen more than he'd said, something he probably didn't even know was important. I said to Iphicles, "Quickly, what I really want to know is—"

Trumpets drowned me out. The herald called the contestants to the starting line.

Iphicles stepped up to his chariot. "If you want to talk to me, it'll have to be after the race."

Markos said, "By the orders of my king, you must tell us—"

Iphicles grabbed the reins of the two leftmost of his horses in his left hand and the reins for the others in his right. I wondered what happened if a driver dropped his reins, but this didn't seem a good time to ask.

Iphicles flicked his lucky whip. "I have a race to win. Poseidon preserve me and bring my team home first."

"Step back there!" The team manager pushed Markos and me out of the way.

Iphicles flicked the reins, and his eager team started forward. We watched him depart without a backward glance, shoulders braced to control the uncontrollable: four peak racing horses that ached to run.

Markos shook his head. "We never had a chance. Bad luck. I hope the rest of the investigation doesn't go like this."

"What do we do now?" I said.

"The only thing we can. We watch the race." Markos took off without a backward glance to see if I followed. "There might still be time to find a good spot." I hurried to catch up with him. And that is how I came to see the first event of the Olympics in the company of a Spartan.

Most of the crowd was clustered about the two turning posts, particularly the one at the east end, which had a reputation for producing the most spectacular crashes. There was no room at either end, so we elbowed our way to the front at the middle of the field, where we would have a good view of the sprints between posts. There was plenty of room for anyone who wanted to watch; the hippodrome is three times larger than the stadion where the running races and the fights are held.

The judges were already seated, ten abreast in their special box on the opposite side of the field.

I nudged Markos. "There's Klymene." She stood alone in a box beside the judges. I told Markos about the interview Diotima and I had held with her. His eyes brightened at Klymene's parting words, and he studied her from afar. "Now there's a girl I'd like to meet. Do you think she's doing it now?"

"Control yourself until after the Games," I told him. "Have you any idea what would happen to the man who polluted the Priestess? They'd have to suspend the Games while they replaced her." I thought about it. "I wonder if it's ever happened?"

"Not that I've heard of," Markos said.

I looked at the sports-crazed Hellenes all about us. "Imagine telling this lot they have to wait because some guy had it off with the Priestess of the Games. They'd impale him."

"If he was lucky. Maybe they'd remove the offending organ first. All right, you've made your point."

The trumpets sounded again. Each chariot made a single turn

around the track, stopping before the judges, where the driver reached into a jar held up by attendants and withdrew a lot.

The drivers took their places according to their lots in the stalls of the hippaphesis, the horse-starter, which ensured every team had a fair start even though not everyone could begin at the center line. The hippaphesis was a huge V-shaped frame, with stalls built into it to hold the teams; the apex of the V pointed at the start of the course. Teams of horses four abreast, massive beasts bred for power and speed and aggression, stamped and snorted and pawed the ground in their eagerness. The beasts had been born and lived their whole lives for this moment when they would run this race. Each team of four pulled a chariot so small and light that one man on his own could lift it. Drivers braced themselves in the flimsy vehicles and waited for the hippaphesis to release them.

In the center of the V was an altar to Poseidon, into which a cunning machine had been built, with a silver rod, at the top of which the figure of a silver dolphin played. Taut ropes ran from the machine within the altar to the starting gates for the race.

The moment the last chariot team was locked in its stall, the Chief Judge stood up—the horse teams must not be kept waiting any longer than necessary, lest they injure themselves in the confined space—then the Chief Judge held high a white cloth for all to see, and dropped it.

At once the assistant starter, who stood at the altar, turned the silver rod. The silver dolphin at the top end fell. At the other end a silver eagle with wings spread wide rose into the air. The turn of the rod caused a wheel within the altar to turn, which pulled the ropes that ran to the horse-starter. The ropes operated the first two of the releases, one at each wing of the V. As the releases dropped, the two outer teams surged off with whips flying. They were at opposite ends of the V, but they were racing each other. Those two were the only ones running until they reached the next stalls along the V. At that moment the restraining ropes dropped for the next two teams, the waiting drivers flicked their whips, and now there were four in the race. They continued like this—teams released as front runners reached them—until everyone was out of the stalls. The system ensured every team had an equal start, and an equal chance of gaining the inner line of most advantage.

"That's a brilliant device," Markos marveled.

"Of course, it's brilliant; it was invented by an Athenian," I said.

The racers reached the apex of the V, the rope restraining the last two teams fell away, and now forty chariot teams jostled for position, all down the centerline of the course in a perfect start.

The crowd screamed and cheered.

"Ten drachmae says Sparta beats Athens," Markos shouted to me over the noise. The racers were clumped so tight, it was impossible to see who was in the lead, but I could clearly see Iphicles in his chariot toward the back of the pack—he had drawn one of the center stalls and got off to a slow start. The chariot bearing the owl of Athens was on the outside but moving up well and shortly behind the rich red of Sparta. I knew nothing about chariot racing, but one thing I was sure of: I wouldn't let this Spartan go one up on me at anything.

"Done," I said. "And five drachmae says Athens wins." It was a foolish bet. In this race there was no certainty Athens would even finish, but my blood was up.

"Only if you give me the same for a Spartan victory."

"Done."

"And done."

The cluster of chariots drove into the glare of the morning sun, approaching the turning post at the east end of the course. At this end, too, was the ancient stone altar called Taraxippus—the "horse-terror"—whose power caused even experienced beasts to panic.

No driver was willing to let another have first turn at the

post. They all drove straight for it, wielding the whips and cursing. Forty teams of four frantic horses each tried to fit into a space for one. Metal-rimmed wheels ground against each other producing sparks and a mass squeal that set every man's teeth on edge. Drivers close to one another struck out with their whips, hoping to distract their opponents. Maddened, frothing horses ran shoulder to shoulder; even with the bits in their mouths they tried to bite the drivers in the chariots ahead. Every driver whipped his team.

One driver in the middle of the pack was too aggressive, or misjudged the turn, or perhaps his team was spooked by the curse of Taraxippus. His left wheel caught the turning post and tore off. The wheel bounced high into the air and flew into the crowd at the far end, where it struck down several spectators. The chariot overturned to the right, spilling the driver, whose right arm was caught in the reins. The chariot twisted and broke its coupling and tumbled into the altar, where it smashed to pieces. The driver somersaulted in the air and hit the ground headfirst. His unconscious body was tossed to the side like a broken doll while his team continued to race inside the pack. Directly behind came Iphicles. He had no time to swerve. His horses trampled the fallen driver, and then his wheels drove over the body. If the driver hadn't been dead when he hit the ground, he certainly was now. Iphicles's chariot swerved from side to side over the uneven bump, and for a moment I thought he would tumble, too, but Iphicles pulled with one arm and then the other, using his main strength against the tension in the reins and the pressure of his feet on the platform to stabilize his vehicle. Everyone shot by as he swerved to the outside to regain control. Men cheered his skill.

"Good driving," Markos said, and I had to agree. He'd lost time, but Iphicles had done well to stay in the race. The moment the last driver had passed, a recovery team ran onto the course to drag away the corpse and manhandle the driverless horses to the side. Another group picked up as many pieces of shattered chariot as they could before the racers returned from the other end.

The first turn forced the pack to string out. Corinth was in the lead; neck and neck behind them were Argos and Cyrene.

As they approached the turn, the Corinth driver hauled hard on his left rein and threw his body to the inside. His chariot actually rose on its inner wheel, and for a moment the crowd gasped as we all thought he'd fall. But his outer beasts were pulled, and the chariot almost spun on the spot. When it righted with a bounce, the chariot had turned on a drachma and the driver whipped the team into a sprint down the straight.

Men in the crowd beat one another in excitement and screamed.

Cyrene was to the outside of Argos. As things stood he was certain to come out of the turn third, but the Cyrene took aim for the corner and whipped. He cut across the path of Argos, and the Argos driver had a choice: ram his opponent or brake. His nerve failed for an instant, and he hauled reins. It was a tight squeeze; the Cyrene got around first, but his momentum took him out wide and the slower Argosian made the tighter turn. When they straightened, Cyrene was ahead by a neck. Both drivers whipped their horses as if they didn't care whether they lived or died—in the lust for victory, they likely didn't.

Athens had forced his way through the center of the pack. Cyrene pulled ahead to a clear second.

Athens led the main pack and made the second turn without incident, but the chariot immediately behind flipped. The driver screamed as his flimsy vehicle slammed into the team coming up on the outside and sent them both into the outer wall, a tangled wreck of thrashing horses.

Recovery teams ran out to retrieve what they could. I saw one driver still move as they carried him off. The other dangled limp between two men. Three men with swords appeared and finished the horses with broken legs. They sliced the harness so the survivors could be stood to walk off. The owners must have cried. A fortune in pedigree beasts had been reduced to dog meat. Indeed several dogs had already smelled the blood and hovered at the edge of the ring. An attendant chased them away.

The other teams had to rein in or join the wreckage. They lost time edging about the inside.

The dust rising from the hippodrome had enveloped the racers. Now the slight breeze carried it over the crowd, and men sneezed as they screamed. Tears ran down our cheeks. Markos beside me gasped and banged on his chest. I looked at him in alarm, but he shook his head.

"Don't mind me. This always happens when the air is thick. I'll be better when it clears."

Corinth-Cyrene-Argos-Athens. Then a confused mêlée of teams, and Iphicles of Thebes bringing up the rear.

But Iphicles had an advantage over every other team: there was no one to interfere with his drive; he accelerated into the race as if it were an exercise.

Iphicles caught up with the main pack over the next six laps—there are twelve in all, plus the half lap to start. As he did so, Iphicles passed the rapidly growing tail of failed teams: teams with horses lamed in the scrimmage; chariots with damaged wheels, so easy to happen in the grind of the pack; teams that couldn't maintain the punishing pace set by the leaders; and teams whose drivers had failed at this ultimate test, unable or afraid to compete against the best of the best. None of the failures would give up, but soon they would be lapped.

Iphicles passed all these and by the next turn was at the back of the pack. Markos wheezed but watched in intense concentration.

At the next turn Iphicles came out wide and whipped his team like a madman. He surged past all the main pack but the team from Chios, leading the group, which saw Iphicles pass and charged with him. Thebes and Chios were half a lap behind the leaders. The Athenian must have heard the renewed cheers of the crowd, because he looked behind him—something even I knew you should never do—to see the challenge coming fast upon him.

Iphicles's chariot seemed to stagger for a moment. Then suddenly his outer wheel came loose and ran alongside before it veered to the right and sped out of the hippodrome and into the crowd. A few spectators were bowled over.

I gasped. So did everyone else.

The disaster happened so slowly it was like watching a shipwreck rather than a chariot crash. Iphicles had automatically flung himself to the left, so his weight was over the remaining left wheel. I supposed he'd endured such an accident in training, because his response was immediate. He kept his balance long enough that some fools in the crowd thought he could stay that way and cheered him on. Inevitably the remaining wheel wobbled over a piece of wreckage that lay in the dirt, and Iphicles was flung off.

He didn't let go of the reins. Iphicles looked back and saw his danger. The Chian team was right behind him and behind the Chian, a small pack of chariots that couldn't see him in the dust and wouldn't stop even if they could. If Iphicles let go, they would run him over and serve out the same fate he himself had delivered to the first man to fall.

The frightened horses dragged Iphicles along the ground, tearing away his skin, but he was still conscious and held on to avoid being trampled. The pain must have been excruciating.

The turning post at Taraxippus was coming up fast. If he didn't do something, his horses would slow at the end, and Iphicles would be crushed, if the drag didn't kill him first. All the Hellenes watched, almost silent despite the race, as Iphicles the charioteer fought for his life.

My witness was about to die.

"Come on!" I said to Markos. I jumped over the low wooden fence that served as barrier.

"What are you doing?" Markos shouted at me.

"That's our witness out there. You want to lose him?" I ran for Iphicles.

"Nicolaos, you idiot, wait!" Markos cursed, jumped the barrier and ran after me.

Iphicles had fallen near the hippodrome's entrance, but we were closer to the Taraxippus end. If I ran at an angle, I could catch them despite their speed. I picked a spot by eye and ran for it. The Chian had seen Iphicles's disaster ahead of him, but that wasn't going to stop him from driving straight for the turn. It was a question whether I could reach Iphicles before the Chian horses trampled him.

Iphicles had finally lost it. The reins slipped from his hands, and his unconscious body lay there for the chariots behind to crush him.

The four stampeding beasts of the Spartan team rushed past me. I ignored them.

I reached the body. With one movement I scooped up Iphicles and tossed him onto the center line between the turning posts. He was safer there than on the track.

His limp weight had made me lean into the throw, and as he left my arms, I fell face forward into the dust.

Somewhere outside myself men screamed. Were they screaming at me? I shut it out. I knew that, somewhere to my left, the Chian chariot was fast approaching. I recalled the body of the driver that Iphicles had run over, how his body had flopped in the dirt like a rag doll. I pulled in my legs and hoped.

I felt the rush of air as the Chian chariot passed me by.

I laughed in triumph and at the relief of still being alive. Then I scrambled up.

Right into the path of the back markers, the final three racers. They were three abreast, twelve horses in a row, headed straight for me.

I can't explain how I felt. Something rooted me to the spot, and I could only watch the drivers whip their horses as my end approached. They were too wide to avoid.

I was about to die. I hoped Diotima would forgive me.

Something hard and heavy hit me and threw me to the side. At that instant the final three chariots passed by. I could hear their drivers cursing. The screech of their wheels was in my ears and their dust in my mouth.

I suddenly realized I was shaking.

"What in Hades were you thinking, you idiot?" Markos screamed from on top of me; our faces were so close I could have kissed him. He had dived into me to save my life, and if he'd made a mistake, he would have gone to Hades with me.

"I'm sorry, Markos, I was—"

"No time for that now."

He was right. The front-runners were making their turn at the end. They'd soon be on top of us.

We scrambled up, and I spat the gritty circuit dust from my mouth. We each took one of Iphicles's arms and dragged him to the edge of the ring, where a recovery team hovered and cursed and abused us for interfering. We handed over our vital witness. They carried him away to the iatrion—the aid station—still swearing at Markos and me.

A fat man who sweated profusely waddled over from the judges' box, a mighty scowl upon his face. He snarled that the judges would see us when the race ended and ordered us to the room behind the official stand. We nodded our understanding.

Markos and I helped each other along the way. We were both bruised and bleeding, but I hoped it had been worth it. I didn't know if Iphicles would live or die, but for the moment at least our vital witness still breathed.

"All we can do is pray to the Gods that he survives," I said.

"He doesn't have to survive," Markos replied. "All he has to do is live long enough for us to question him."

Which I thought was a trifle callous, if accurate.

Behind the stand where the judges stood to watch the race was a low wooden building. We sat on the floor and nursed our cuts and bruises while the rest of the race was run. All we could do was listen to the roar of the crowd over the squeal of the chariot wheels and the cries of the horses.

Trumpets announced the end of the race, after which everything quieted down for the presentation of the crown. I wondered which team wore the olive wreath of victory. Presently, Exelon the Chief Judge entered the room, followed by the other judges. None of them smiled.

"What in Hades did you think you were doing?!" the Chief Judge shouted at us. Markos and I stood at attention before him. I was used to being shouted at by Pericles, but it made a nice change having Markos for company. The Chief Judge was louder than Pericles but not nearly so cutting.

"Saving the life of a witness, sir," I said. I quickly explained why we needed Iphicles alive.

"You had no business to be on the hippodrome in the middle of a contest. Spectators are not permitted on the field, even to save a life."

Markos said, "If I may point out, sir, you did induct Nicolaos and me as Olympic contestants."

"Not in the chariot race, you idiot."

The Judge had a point.

"Sir," said Markos, "it was your express order that we must do everything possible to solve this crime. If we had stood by and watched while an important witness died—a witness Pindar the poet had told us had information—what would you have said to us then?"

"The word of Pindar is like the word of the Gods," said one of the other judges, rubbing his chin, a tall scrawny man. "It's true, Exelon, such young men as these could hardly be expected to use sound judgment in such a situation."

"That's why they were chosen," Exelon said. "Because, contrary to current evidence, they're supposed to be smart."

"The contest ground for the chariots is the hippodrome, is it not?" said Markos.

"Certainly."

"And the contest ground for the athletics is the stadion."

"Of course. What's your point?" said Exelon.

"That the contest ground for Nicolaos and me is all of Olympia, sir," said Markos. "There is no boundary."

The Chief Judge growled. "Let me make this clear. You took the oath, so you are beholden to us judges, and not to your own cities. That doesn't give you the right to meddle in the Sacred Games. Understand?"

"Yes, sir!" we said in unison.

"Any questions?"

"Yes, sir," I said. "Who won the race?"

The Chief Judge glared at me. "The team from Cyrene. Athens was second. Sparta third."

I held out my hand.

Without a word, Markos put a hand beneath his exomis and withdrew a money bag. He untied the leather thong and made a great show of counting out ten coins. Then he spat on the coins and slapped them into my palm.

I grinned. "A pleasure doing business with you."

"I'll win it back next time." He grinned back.

The judges stared at us as we both broke into hysterical laughter. It was the shock and relief of being alive.

"Get out. Both of you get out."

"Yes, sir."

As we walked from the building, I said to Markos, "If you ever want a job in the law courts at Athens, let me know and I'll introduce you around."

He laughed. "I'm happy in Sparta, thanks."

Men covered the hippodrome in the aftermath of the race. They congratulated one another or stood silent and glum, according to whether their teams had finished or lay among the

carnage. My own father, Sophroniscus, was across the other side
of the field. He stood among a cluster of men who waited to congratulate the owner of one of the teams.

Pieces of chariot and dead horses littered the arena. The
cleanup crews had begun to pick up the mess. As soon as the
wreckage was cleared, the next event could begin: the bareback
horse races.

"At least Iphicles is still alive. Speaking of which, we should go
to him straightaway. He might tell us something."

"He won't be conscious for hours, I should think," said
Markos. "Not if he's lucky. I felt a few broken bones when we
moved him."

"We have to check," I insisted.

Markos sighed. "Very well."

I had no idea where to find the iatrion. We asked. Someone
eventually pointed us to a large tent erected between the stadion
and the hippodrome. We could hear the screams as we approached.
Markos and I shared a look. This was going to be unpleasant.

"I hope that's not Iphicles."

We pushed through the flap. The tent material smelled new.
Inside was a row of camp beds, and on six of them lay chariot
drivers. The man who screamed was closest to the entrance. His
right arm pointed straight into the air, or, rather, what was left of
it did. I could actually see the bone sticking out past the elbow.
The flesh from that point was simply gone, to leave a ragged end.

I swallowed to hold back the bile.

Two men pressed him back onto the bed. Another man stood
over a brazier that burned hot.

"What happened to him?" I asked.

"Lost his grip and came off his chariot backward. The one
behind ran over his arm."

I'd seen it happen. I'd had no idea the injury was as bad as
this. Markos peered at the wounded arm curiously but showed no
reaction. Perhaps these Spartans were as tough as everyone said.

"Since you're here, you can help," said the man at the brazier.

"We actually came for Iphicles," Markos said.

"I need you now. This man will die if we don't act at once. Then you can see your precious Iphicles."

Markos nodded assent.

"Are you a doctor?" I asked.

"Heraclides of Kos, yes. How do you do?" he said mildly, as if we'd just met at a symposium and not over the mutilated body of a screaming man. "What we need to do," he said as he pushed the bar about inside the fire, "is close the wound so the poison can't get in. If we do it right, he might even live." He looked over to the man who held a wineskin to the lips of the driver. "How's he doing?"

The other man shook his head. "Too busy screaming to drink."

"Oh, well. We're hot enough here. You two"—he pointed at Markos and me—"you hold him down. I need the other two to keep his arm steady. Unlike you, they know what they're doing." He gave us a searching look. "Can you do it?"

Markos said, "Of course."

I swallowed and nodded. I told myself we were saving this man's life.

"Right. Keep his body still. Don't worry about the legs; I'll avoid them. Ignore the noise; this one's a screamer."

Markos and I made ready on either side of the driver. We pressed down.

"Harder. He'll jerk like a dying fish."

I pressed harder. The other two assistants held the arm with two strong hands each and grim expressions. The man at the brazier wrapped wet rags about the end of the bar to make a handle, pulled it out, and in a single smooth motion pushed it against the wound. It sizzled. I smelled the flesh burn and gagged.

"Hold him down!"

The man had been right; the driver jerked like a dying fish. I pushed with all my might and turned my head to avoid seeing what happened so close to my eyes.

When it was finished, the driver curled up in a ball and whimpered. The end of his arm was a blackened stump.

"That was awful," I said to the man as he put the iron bar, now cool, back in the brazier. "But at least he'll live."

The man shrugged. "Maybe. Maybe not. Sometimes they sicken anyway and die in a fever. Who knows? You said you wanted Iphicles. He's in the bed at the end."

Iphicles lay there and gasped. Niallos the team manager crouched beside and trickled cool water on his driver's head. Niallos looked up as we approached.

"Is he all right?" I asked.

"Of course he's not all right," Niallos snapped. "Look at the man. He can barely breathe."

Iphicles coughed, tried to scream but couldn't, and coughed again. Flecks of blood spattered the face of Niallos.

"I'll kill those bastards on the crew! Did you see the way the wheel came apart? Without being hit, even."

"The chariot drove over some wreckage, and a body, on the first lap," Markos pointed out. "Perhaps it was damaged then."

Niallos spat his disdain. "Maybe. But the wheels are built to handle that, or they bloody well should be. It's a chariot race, curse it, you expect to hit wreckage."

Heraclides joined us.

I asked, "What are his chances, doctor?"

He shrugged. "Sometimes a man gets hit in the chest and the ribs cave in and then this happens. I was at the race. Iphicles took a big blow, and he didn't let go. Those horses dragged him cruelly."

"Iphicles did the right thing," said Niallos. "If he'd let go, he'd have joined that fellow over there with the crushed arm, only he'd have lost his legs. Maybe worse."

"Can he talk?" Markos asked.

"Doubt it."

Iphicles moaned. The eyes rolled in his head.

I quickly knelt by his side and said, "Iphicles, is there something you wish to say?"

He nodded, slowly, and opened his mouth.

I said, "Markos, he's going to speak!"

Markos said, "Zeus and Apollo favor us," and leaned over, the
better to hear.

Iphicles rolled toward me and coughed up a little blood.

He whispered, "My . . . my lucky whip . . ."

"He wants his whip."

Niallos placed the whip in the right hand of Iphicles and gently closed his fingers about the handle.

Iphicles smiled for a moment and then gasped. I thought he
must have cleared his airways. Then a great surge of blood came
from his mouth and hit me right in the chest.

Iphicles died before our eyes.

I WALKED OUT, unable to stand it any longer. As soon as
I emerged into clean air, I tried to wipe the sticky blood off my
exomis, but it was no good. I undid the pins that held the material
together, let it fall to the ground, and kicked it out of the way. I
stalked off naked, with only the pins in my hand and anger at the
Gods in my heart.

"Wait up there, Nicolaos." Markos ran to catch up. He took
my arm. "I don't know about you, but I could use some wine
about now. Let me buy you a drink."

He led me toward the wine stalls of the agora, temporary,
grossly overpriced stands there to rip off the tourists. Even so, it
was hard not to enjoy the place. A normal agora is a fresh food
market with household wares on the side; the agora at Olympia
was an all-day carnival of entertainers and hot food sizzling in
braziers.

A troupe of young women juggled balls. Markos and I stopped
to watch in appreciation as various parts of the girls wobbled in
time to the juggling. We tossed coins at their feet. A fat man sang

and a thin man rode by while standing on the back of his horse. He flipped over to stand on his hands as the beast rode on. Strong men dressed as Heracles lifted heavy stones over their shoulders. A small man slipped through the crowd, and we came almost face-to-face. He took one look at me, said "Eek!," and ran off. It was my own Heracles, the scrawny fellow who had attacked Diotima and me the day before. Crowds gathered wherever there was something to see, which was pretty much everywhere.

I shook my head. "I wonder how many thieves there are in this crowd."

Markos laughed. "I've already caught two hands searching for my purse."

He bought the first round, and we downed our cups in one go. I said, "This was a great idea, Markos. I've seen some ghastly things, but that tent was one of the worst sights ever."

He said, "We need to talk."

"So we do."

I bought a small amphora for the second round. He carried the cups and I carried the wine, and together we walked up Mount Kronos. It was a long way to go, but we both felt the need to escape the crowds. We found dry rocks to sit upon and a view of Olympia worth the effort of the climb. He poured, and together we drank, watching the activity below as if it were some play put on for our benefit.

I felt better. Being slightly drunk helped.

Markos said, "Nicolaos, back in the forest last night, you said you didn't know what an ephor was. I told you it matters a great deal, but I don't think you believed me."

"I didn't," I admitted.

"You're an Athenian; I guess you know about political factions and hidden agendas."

"Conspiracy is in our blood," I had to concede.

"Yet you really don't know how it works with us Spartans, do you?"

Markos explained. His explanation took so long I poured him another cup to keep his throat smooth.

"Sparta has two kings, not one like in any normal kingdom."

"Why two?"

Markos shrugged. "That's the way it's always been. They're descended from two different ancient lineages. Then there's the Gerousia, a council of old men who advise the kings, twenty-eight of them. You have to be sixty to be invited into the Gerousia, and then you're a member for life, if you can call it life when you're that old."

I nodded. "I know what you mean. Why do they always leave important decisions to the old men? Everyone knows your mind turns to water when you get old."

"Tell me about it." He sighed. "But to continue, then there are five ephors, and they're the scary ones. They're elected annually from among all the Spartans. Their job is to be . . . auditors. The ephors see to it that the kings rule according to the law. Whenever a king leaves Sparta, two ephors must accompany him. Any two ephors together can overrule one king. All five ephors can overrule both kings."

"So the ephors are the real rulers of Sparta."

"No, because the ephors have no power to command, they can only veto."

"Then the two kings rule."

"Only so long as the ephors agree with them."

"Then what of the Gerousia?"

"They advise the kings in the background and act as a final court. Did I mention the ephors consult the Gerousia on questions of the constitution?

"And I thought Athenian politics was complicated."

"No, it's really quite simple. The kings tend to be our progressive thinkers, because they have to rule for the long term. The Gerousia are conservatives to a man. The ephors are a throw of the dice; much depends on who's elected in a given year, whether they support the kings, and we get progress, or block the kings, and we get conservatism. On any one issue the kings might have differing positions, in which case the ephors can veto one and support the other."

I thought this over. "King Pleistarchus is here at Olympia. Where's the other king?"

"King Archidamus is in Sparta. The Spartans like to keep one king at home at all times, in case of an emergency."

"So useful to have a backup. Like having a spare knife."

"Exactly. Your metaphor is more perfect than you know. That's what our kings are: very dangerous knives. They're capable of anything, for the good of Sparta."

For the good of Sparta . . . the phrase resonated with a favorite saying of Pericles. He liked to justify his actions as being *for the good of Athens.*

I said, "There must be two ephors here with Pleistarchus."

"Xenares and a fellow named Phalakrion. I wouldn't call Phalakrion weak-willed, no one could ever say that of a Spartan, but he will go along with a strong opinion."

"Xenares decides for them both."

Markos nodded. "You see what I mean, Nicolaos? You do need to know about Spartan politics."

"Thanks for taking the trouble, and call me Nico, will you? All my friends do."

He smiled and said, "Nico."

"I guess you've been looking into Arakos from the Spartan end?"

"Of course."

"Tell me about him. If we're lucky, this might turn out to be a run-of-the-mill domestic killing."

"Then you're out of luck already." Markos grimaced. "Did you notice at the opening ceremony that Arakos had no father or brothers with him?"

"Yes?"

"Arakos was an orphan. His father was one of the Three Hundred who held the pass at Thermopylae, one of the heroes who died to the last man rather than surrender to the Persians. At the time, of course, Arakos was a babe in arms. There was a grown brother by a previous marriage, but the brother died in the fighting later. Our victim was raised by the state."

"Tough childhood."

"Yes and no. The orphans of the Three Hundred received special attention. But it makes things tricky for you and me. To assault a child of the Three Hundred is an insult to all Sparta. That makes this murder political."

It was my turn to shrug. "It was political already."

"True enough. But there are Spartans who are going to take this personally."

"Did you know Arakos before this?" I asked.

"Not the way you know the accused. No."

I paused. "Tell me, do you think Timodemus killed Arakos?"

"Not enough evidence," Markos said promptly, earning my immediate approval. "But on what we've got, the answer is probably yes."

"We don't have anything."

"Nico, we might have to agree to disagree on our politics, and the Gods and all men know your city and mine are mortal rivals, but fortunately we don't have to agree on such things to run an investigation. Surely we two can agree on facts, even if our interpretations are at odds?"

"I was about to suggest the same thing," I said. The shared danger on the hippodrome had brought us together, and Markos struck me as a man very like myself. "But Markos, what if we find Timodemus is not the killer?"

Markos shrugged a third time. "Then that's what I report, and it's up to my leaders to make of it what they will. More important, Nico, what if we prove your friend killed Arakos?"

I gulped wine, and it went down the wrong way. "In that

case," I choked, "it's what I report, and Timo is a dead man. But I repeat, there's nothing connecting Timo with the scene."

Markos nodded. "I was sure you'd say that. You seem to be a man much like myself." He hesitated. "I . . . er . . . I'm not sure you're going to like this, but I know if it were me I'd want all the evidence . . ."

"Yes?" I prompted.

"I'm afraid that connection you mentioned exists. The first thing I did after I left the scene was search the tent of Arakos. I found this." He handed me an *ostrakon*, a pottery shard into which a note had been scratched with the point of a knife. People used ostraka all the time to write short notes. This one was larger than normal.

Timodemus says this to Arakos: I offer to meet you in the woods across the river tonight.

As I read, wild cheering erupted from the stadion behind us. Someone had just won an Olympic crown.

"MARKOS HAS A perfect set of evidence." I groaned. "I'm sure he only showed me that ostrakon to rub it in."

"It doesn't look good, does it?" said Diotima. "Maybe he's hoping you'll give up?"

I'd gone to consult with her at once, to reveal my fears and hear her news. We'd met at the agora to compare plans and to eat honeycomb. Diotima had discovered a stall that sold the sweetest food you could find in Hellas. On our previous job, we'd both been spoiled by the decadent Persian desserts, but Diotima in particular couldn't get enough of sweet foods now. It was a good thing she was an heiress, because I could never have afforded the stuff. We sat on rocks with honeycomb in our hands and on our lips and sticking our teeth together. It made kisses an interesting challenge.

"We're doing this the wrong way," Diotima said. "We have

to find realistic evidence against someone. Someone other than Timodemus, that is."

"Good idea," I said. "How do you suggest we do it?"

"I only think of the plans. It's up to you to make them work."

I said, "If Timodemus wanted to destroy Arakos in a fair fight, why wouldn't he wait a mere four days for the pankration? Then he could kill Arakos in full view of thousands of men and not only get away with it but even be praised for his technique."

"That's easy," said Diotima. "Because Timodemus didn't think he could win." She saw my expression and said at once, "Sorry, Nico, but that's what Markos will say: Timodemus decided on an early murder because he didn't think he could win in the ring."

"Timo had already beaten Arakos, at the Nemean Games."

"Maybe the contest at Nemea was lucky. Maybe your friend didn't think he could do it again."

I knew she was wrong, but I couldn't prove it.

Diotima had been checking the evidence at the women's camp while I dealt with the men. After all, Timodemus had been arrested there. I said, "Did you discover if anything suspicious happened at the women's camp?"

"Among hundreds of drunk men looking for sex? What do you think? Everything that happened that night was suspicious."

"Isn't that reverse logic?"

"I asked among the pornoi," Diotima said. "Not easy, by the way. The girls are all exhausted." She finished licking her own fingers clean and began on mine, taking each and sucking on it gently. The effect was . . . distracting.

"Late nights?" I asked, trying to keep my mind on the subject and failing miserably. We were out of sight of anyone else; I put my free arm around her and cupped her breast.

"Doing a roaring trade. The more popular ones had men queuing outside the tents. Timo's story that he blundered into

Klymene's tent rings true. It happened to me, you'll recall; it could have happened to Klymene, too."

I played with her nipple beneath the material of her chiton. Diotima breathed a little more heavily.

"Did anyone spot Timo?" I asked.

"One man among many? No. But one of the girls did see someone interesting."

"Oh?"

"Arakos."

"What!"

I unhanded her. Diotima grabbed my hand and put it firmly back.

"One of the pornoi saw Arakos in the women's camp."

"We'd better see her at once."

"No, Nico, we have to go to my tent at once."

"Why?"

Diotima gasped. "Because my other nipple is feeling jealous. The rest of me needs attention, too. Come on. Quickly!"

"WHAT I REALLY want to be," said Petale the pornê, "is a hetaera. Those girls have it made: their own house, regular clients, big money." She twisted a stray brunette tress around her little finger and looked thoughtful. "I'm working my way up, gonna have my own place someday."

Would Petale make it? I glanced at Diotima for her reaction, because Diotima was the daughter of a hetaera, and a highly successful one at that. Diotima might cringe at her mother's history, but she knew the business as few respectable women did. When Diotima nodded, ever so slightly, I knew she rated Petale a chance to reach the top of her profession. I wondered why; it certainly couldn't be based on her possessions.

We sat in Petale's tent, patched and barely large enough for its purpose. A man could stand if he hunched. A couple could lie on the rug, a trifle worn but thick enough and scattered with cushions to cover the stains and the spots where moths had eaten holes. Petale had produced cheap pottery cups and served us wine, which somehow she had managed to chill despite the heat of the day. She had served us with grace, and perhaps this was what Diotima saw. Petale was poor—everything she owned could be rolled up within the canvas of her tent—but she did the best with what she had.

I glanced at Diotima. She glanced at me.

"Did I say something funny? How come you're both smiling?" Petale asked.

"We're naturally happy people," I said. "Where are you from, Petale?"

"Corinth."

"Long way to haul your tent," Diotima commented.

"There're men with big carts and donkeys. We girls rent space for our stuff and walk alongside. The bastards charge a small fortune, but what can you do?"

"Pay in kind?"

She laughed. "Not them. They want the money."

"Listen, Petale, it's important we know about the man you told Diotima about."

"The huge guy, built like a small fort?"

"That's him. What time did you see him?"

"You think I watch the time?" She gave me a pitying look. "I was in this tent from the moment the Games ended for the day until the middle of the night. The guys couldn't wait to get across the river and at the girls."

"So how did you see Arakos? Was he a customer?"

"I had to piss. A girl can only take so much before the pressure starts to tell. So I crawled out of my tent and there he was."

"Waiting outside?"

"Freaked me out, I can tell you. For a moment I thought he was a client, and I had this vision of being crushed to death. Thanks be to Aphrodite, he wasn't waiting."

"He didn't stop?"

"Walked straight by. I don't think he even saw me, seemed preoccupied, or maybe he was looking for something. I dunno."

"Are you sure it was Arakos?"

"My client recognized him, too. We crawled out of the tent together and he said, 'What's he doing here?' He was from Sparta, too."

"You could tell from his accent?"

"He wanted to pay me with those weird iron bars the Spartans use for money. I wouldn't take it."

I glanced across at Diotima. She looked as frustrated as I felt. Here we had someone who could help us trace the victim, but she couldn't tell the time.

"Was Arakos with anyone?"

"On his own."

"I don't suppose there was anyone following him, was there?" I silently offered Zeus a sacrifice at every Olympics for the rest of my life, if only we could solve this crime with one simple witness. Besides, such an oath would be a good excuse to come and see every Games.

Petale shrugged. "There was no one else."

I canceled the sacrifices.

"This client, what was his name?"

Petale gave me a withering look. "Heracles. They're all named Heracles. Or Achilles. The ugly ones call themselves Apollo."

"Right, scrap that. Can you describe him?"

"He looked just like all the other men I saw that night."

I threw my arms up in despair. "You must have some idea of the time."

"Why? I was flat on my back the whole night." Petale looked reflective. "Um, no, actually I was on my knees most of the time or standing or bending over. Mostly bending over, come to think of it; we get a lot of cheap asses here."

"You're kidding."

"Wish I were. We charge by the position, you know."

"You do?" said Diotima, whose knowledge of these things was limited to the high end of the business. "I had no idea. Did you, Nico?"

"No idea," I agreed innocently.

Petale said, "They walk in demanding the best—that's them on top or me riding—then when I quote my fee they whine and end up going for a cheapie."

"Which is?" Diotima asked.

"Me bending over and them behind. Costs less because it's so impersonal, you know? But it's quick; I can get through more guys in a night and I don't have to smell their breath, and let me tell you that's a bonus. Hard on the calves, though. I get lots of practice touching my toes. I'm very flexible. Want to see?"

"Sure, I'd love to—" I caught Diotima's hard eye. "—er, that is, no thanks."

Diotima said, "So most of your clients were cheap. I guess you remember how many were on your back?"

"Only one."

"Kneeling?"

"Three."

"Standing or bending?"

"That's what I don't remember. More than twenty, for sure."

"Busy!"

"I told you we girls were full up, so to speak."

"This is all very interesting if you like prurient statistics," I said, "but it doesn't help. We have to know what time Petale saw Arakos."

"I can see the details of this wouldn't interest a man," said Diotima. She looked thoughtful. "Time's running away on us. It's almost midday already, and there are so many other lines we need to pursue. Why don't you look into them, Nico, while I continue with Petale?"

It seemed to me Petale was a dead end, so I was happy to agree. But I reminded Diotima, "Don't forget our fathers meet this evening, to discuss you know what." I wasn't inclined to let Petale in on our personal business.

"How could I forget?" said Diotima. "Don't worry, I'll be there." She gave Petale a calculating look. "Leave this with me, Nico. You have other things to do."

TIMODEMUS WAS HELD in an ancient stone cottage, one among a row of such ruins at the foot of Mount Kronos. The cottages were normally used by itinerant artisans who came to work on the grounds of Olympia. Now one cottage held an accused murderer, and another housed the murdered man. The smell as I passed the cottage that held Arakos was a trifle rank. An honor guard of two Spartans, unarmed, of course, stood at the door. They glared at me as I passed.

The cottage that held Timo had guards too, but they weren't for honor, and they were armed soldiers of Elis, the host city. They let me in without a word.

Timo sat on a pile of straw on the floor. This was supposed to be his bed. There was no chair, and it felt wrong to stand over him, so we sat side by side with our backs to the wall. The room was claustrophobic, as the rooms in ancient buildings often are. We sat so close our knees touched. The smell of Timodemus was everywhere, but I didn't smell any fear.

I handed Timo the ostrakon that Markos had discovered, in which he demanded a meeting with Arakos in the woods at night.

Timodemus turned the ostrakon round and round.

"I never wrote this." He stared at it. "Never."

Timodemus handed the ostrakon back to me. I inspected it once more in search of any clue. To scratch a message into an ostrakon is an inconsistent business. The knife slips, much depends on how hard the clay is, and what part of the broken pot is used. I could ask Timo for a sample of his own writing, but I could never match a sample with the evidence. The best I could do was take him at his word, or not.

"All right, Timo, tell me what you know and, for both our sakes, tell me the truth."

"Do you think I killed him?" he asked.

"I don't know what to think, other than that if we don't come up with some useful facts soon, you'll take a short flight."

"Thrown off Mount Typaeum," he mused. "Exelon picked the most shameful death he could."

"Let's start with the priestess. You were found naked in her tent. I look forward to hearing how that happened."

Timo was silent for a moment. He looked down at the ground. Then he said, "That was a mistake."

"Oh, really?"

"All right, Nico, you can be as sarcastic as you like. The truth is I happened to be passing, and I, uh, stumbled in by accident."

"Timo, there are so many things wrong with that statement, I don't know where to begin."

He didn't reply, merely sat there, eyes on the ground.

"Well?" I tapped my foot.

"This is embarrassing," he muttered.

"Embarrassing as in I wish my best friend didn't know what I'm about to reveal, or embarrassing as in I'd rather die than anyone know this?"

"All right, you made your point." He paused. "I was looking for a woman."

"Any particular woman?"

"No, as long as she was presentable." He hung his head. "This is all the fault of Dromeus."

"Your trainer?"

Timo nodded. "He prescribed sex as part of my training regimen. He says regular sex relaxes the body and makes it more supple."

"How regular?"

"Every night for the last ten months."

"You lucky bastard." I slavered in envy.

"You think so? It was easy enough back at home, plenty of slave girls there."

I nodded. A slave girl couldn't say no, not to the son of her owner, at any rate. Most Athenian men had their first taste of sex at home with their mother's slave girls.

But there was one well-known problem with that system.

"Didn't they get pregnant?"

Timo shrugged. "A couple of them, but Father didn't care. Anything that helps me win an Olympic crown is fine by him."

"What will you do with the babies?"

"The girls hadn't birthed when we left. Father left instructions to expose them, unless they're healthy boys, in which case to keep them as slaves. I didn't like it, but, well, those were Father's orders. What could I do?"

The child of a slave is a slave, even if the father is a citizen. Whoever owns the mother can do with the baby what he will, even expose the baby to die. It is ugly stuff, people don't like to talk about it, but everyone knows it happens, and One-Eye wasn't exactly sentimental.

Timodemus continued, "When we moved to Elis, in preparation for the Games, it became a problem. No handy slave girls, and I could hardly use respectable women. Which left the pornoi."

"I'm not seeing the problem. Sex every night at your father's expense? It's every man's dream."

"You might find this hard to believe, but it became sort of like, well, work."

He was right. I found it hard to believe. "So when you walked into Klymene's tent you were on your nightly excursion . . ."

"I thought the tent belonged to a pornê, a wealthy one. I wasn't the only one doing this, by the way. Other trainers tell their charges to go have sex. Mostly they hit the brothels."

"Why didn't Festianos stop you?"

"Festianos?"

"When you sneaked out of the tent, after I left?"

"Festianos wasn't there."

"He wasn't?" I blinked, and moved on quickly. "I guess you must be anxious to get out of here," I said.

"Lying in damp straw isn't the best training regimen."

"Worried?"

"No, I'm not, oddly enough. Want to know why? Because while I'm stuck in here, no one has any expectations for me. No one's wishing me good luck. I don't have Father constantly on my back, encouraging me to train a little bit harder."

I could see his point.

"You know what, Nico? Lying here with nothing to do, I've been thinking. I could get used to being a normal person."

That worried me. "Timo, I have to ask this. You didn't deliberately attack Arakos in front of everyone to get out of having to compete, did you?" Because in a bizarre way, I could see how being *too* aggressive might be an honorable way to avoid the Olympics without having to admit he didn't want to go on.

Timodemus laughed. "You know me, Nico. I'm not that clever. That sounds like something only you'd think of. No one else thinks the way you do."

I'd known Timo since we were boys, and this was the first time he'd ever accused me of originality. Did he really think of me like that? I was just another young man, trying to get by; I didn't think of myself as all that unusual. On the other hand, speaking of unusual acts . . .

"That reminds me, do me a favor, will you, Timo? If you meet Diotima, don't tell her about your fun with the slave girls. Diotima was almost exposed herself as a baby, and she has strong feelings about it."

I'd brought a flask of watered wine and some garlic lentils and bread. I knew Timo would be hungry. We took turns dipping our hands into the wooden bowl to eat. As I licked my fingers, I said, "What was Arakos like? Did you get on?"

"Arakos didn't have friends; he had targets. Not that I cared.

I was only there to win. It's easier if you dislike the man you're hurting. Arakos was abusive."

"Why did Arakos abuse you on the walk from Elis?"

Timo wriggled again. He plainly wasn't comfortable. "Playing mind games, I suppose, before the contest. I was his main rival. If he could have disposed of me, he'd probably have won."

A flash of inspiration struck. "With you and Arakos both out of it, who's likely to win the pankration?"

Timodemus thought. "Korillos," he said. "Maybe Aggelion. But my money would be on Korillos. He's good. What are you thinking, Nico?"

"That a man who wanted to win the pankration would improve his chances by killing one of you and framing the other."

"Nah. They're honorable men; they fight fair." Timo paused, then said, quite abashed, "Nico, I'm sorry to spoil your Games like this. You came to Olympia for fun, and here you are at work. I really am sorry, Nico."

They fight fair, Timo had said. It was the highest praise he could give a man. It was the reason I didn't want to believe he had murdered Arakos; because if Timo was the killer, it meant he'd abandoned a code of honor that he'd maintained ever since we were children.

Once upon a time a boy was lying in the street, bruised and bleeding. He was surrounded by a small gang. The boy tried to stand, but his persecutors pushed him down again. He called for help, but the men in the street walked on. After all, they were only boys playing. The boys taunted, called him coward and girl. They trod on him, and he ate the dust of the street.

He didn't see what happened next; he only knew the boys had taken their feet off his back, and there was shouting. When he lifted his head, he saw another boy who hadn't been there before. The new boy shouted and punched and kicked, and the gang was scared of this little terror. He fought like a whirlwind; he was incredibly fast, never where his enemy struck, always hitting hard and bouncing out of the way. They were many, and he was one, and even lying in the dirt the first boy could see that, if only the gang coordinated, the boys could have surrounded their tormentor, but they fought like individuals and lost like little boys. The gang yelled insults and ran down the street.

"Are you all right?" the new boy asked, bending down to help up the one in the dirt.

"Yes." He sat up. "Thank you. They were going to beat me."

"I know. Cowards. They should have fought you one at a time, not all in a gang like that."

"What would you have done, if they had?"

"Let them, and watched what happened. If they fight you one at a time, then it's honorable. That's what my dad says."

"Is that why you helped me?"

He shrugged. "It wasn't a fair fight, them beating you up all together," said the small boy who had taken on a dozen and won. "Besides, I saw you try to hit them, even when you knew they were going to beat you. You didn't give up like a coward."

Timodemus became my firm friend from that day on, two lonely boys together. By rights every boy in the city should have admired him, but they didn't. They feared him. Timodemus was mild until someone pushed him a step too far, and then he had a terrible temper, which always ended in someone else getting hurt. I think I was the only boy he never hit in anger. Because of that, we often sparred together when he needed to practice—no one else his own size would face him—and though I never had Timo's natural talent I came to know something of the art of pankration.

I know why I liked and admired Timodemus. I had never before met anyone so completely unaware of his own virtues. I don't know what he saw in me, a boy who didn't get on with other boys.

I said, "Don't worry about it, Timo. Investigation is what I do. You know I'm happy to help."

Timo was depressed. "I didn't kill Arakos, but there's no way I can prove it. They're going to execute me, aren't they?"

I thought of the boy lying in the street, and I said, "No, they're not, Timo. I'm going to save you."

I'D AGREED TO meet Markos at the Athenian camp so we could interview One-Eye and Timo's uncle Festianos together. I got there first. A slave took great delight in telling me I'd wasted my time; Festianos wasn't there, and One-Eye had walked out of the camp, heading south. I left a message for Markos with the slave and threaded my way south, crouching so my head didn't show over the height of the tents to avoid my father.

My head was so low I ran into a man as he walked north to the Games.

"There you are," Father said. "Have you lost something?"

"I, uh . . ."

"I almost died when I saw you run onto the chariot track. What in Hades were you thinking? Never do such a thing again."

"Sorry, Father."

He put a hand on my shoulder. "It was well done. All the men around me remarked on your bravery. I was proud to tell them you were my son." He paused and looked me over. "Are you all right?"

I was shaking, not from the recollection of near death under the wheels of a chariot, but because they were the first words of praise I'd heard from my father in a long time.

I swallowed and said, "Yes, Father. I'm fine. Scratched and bruised, but fine."

Father took me by the arm and led me to our own tents. "That fellow who pulled you out of the path of the chariots. Who is he?"

"Markos, of Sparta."

"A Spartan, eh? Well, he saved the life of my elder son. Tell him he's welcome in my home—or my tent—anytime."

"Thank you."

Sophroniscus was dressed in his best formal chiton, an old but respectable ankle-length garment that covered his body, arms, and legs. It had once been brightly patterned in red, green and yellow, but the dyes had faded, the borders were a trifle frayed, and the material stretched across his paunch. He looked about as comfortable in formal wear as a sheep wearing sandals. Father usually wore a short exomis to leave his arms and legs free to move, essential for his work, since he was a sculptor. It was strange to see him not covered in gritty marble dust. When I looked at Father, I imagined I could see the future Socrates, which wasn't hard, because Socrates at that moment sat outside our tents, turning something over in his hands and ignoring our conversation.

"I'm sorry about Timodemus, son. I know he's your friend. Are they to execute him?"

"Not if I can help it."

"Don't go getting yourself killed along with him. Your mother would never forgive me."

"I'll do my best, Father."

Then he frowned. "Pythax came to see me today about this supposed marriage. He's not a happy man. Why did you have to act so rashly? Now we have this mess to sort out."

"You could approve the marriage?" I said in hope. "Pythax is happy for it to go ahead."

"Of course he is!" Sophroniscus thundered. "How many former slaves can marry their metic daughters to a citizen?"

A metic was a resident alien with permission to live in Athens. The prejudice against marriage with metics was strong and getting stronger all the time. Pericles even talked of a law to make the children of such marriages non-citizens. If that happened, Diotima and I would have a problem.

"Please don't blame Diotima's family."

"I don't. I blame you. If you wanted to be married, son, all you had to do was ask me. Didn't I just tell you every man at Olympia remarked on your courage this morning? By the end of that race, any man in the hippodrome would have been pleased to match his daughter with you. In fact I had two offers as I left. It's not too late; I can still find you a good girl."

"I did find a good girl, Father."

"You found a non-citizen. How do you know she won't turn to her mother's trade?"

I laughed. "One thing I can guarantee you, Father: Diotima will never be involved in prostitution."

Sophroniscus sighed. A long, deep sigh like I'd never heard from him before. "We'll have to see what sort of a dowry this Pythax can offer to accompany his daughter."

Had I really heard that? I felt an unexpected flutter of hope. "You mean, sir, you might consider taking Diotima after all?"

My father's shoulders tensed, and he shuffled his feet like a guilty man. "I hate to admit it, son, but business has been slow. Too slow. The truth is, we're close to the point where I'll not be able to feed the family."

"Oh. I didn't realize."

"I know you didn't. You've been too busy gallivanting about. But if your Diotima comes to us with enough dowry to keep our heads above water . . . well, I'd have to consider that very carefully."

"Is there anything I can do, Father?" I asked. I was genuinely, deeply, and suddenly concerned. He lived for sculpting. If he were unable to continue, it would break him.

"I need work, son. Perhaps one of these athletes will commission me for his victory statue."

Dawn lit up for me. "So that's why you've flocked to congratulate the winners! I thought you'd become a sports fan."

"If it will help win work, I'll join the mob." He sighed. "There are too many good sculptors. Onatas of Aegina is here. So is Myron of Eleutherae." Sophroniscus named the most fashionable, most popular, and most expensive sculptors in Hellas.

"If I see a chance to help—"

"Oh, so you have time to work with your father now?"

"No—I mean, yes! But Father, if I find someone who needs a statue—"

"You'll mention it. Yes, I know you will, son. By the way, there was a message left for you."

"A messenger? What did he say?"

"No messenger, a written message, and we don't know how it got here. It's all a bit of a mystery. Socrates has it."

Socrates sat outside our tents. He'd ignored our conversation. Instead he stared at something in his hands. He'd obviously fallen into one of his trances, during which he was oblivious to the world. Father and I had both become accustomed to his strange behavior.

"Socrates!" Sophroniscus yelled into my brother's ear. "Wake up, will you?"

Socrates looked up as if he'd suddenly noticed the world existed. "What?"

"Show Nico the message," our father said.

Socrates held out the thing in his hand. It was an ostrakon, a piece of broken pottery, red on the outside and black on the inside. On this one, words had been scratched in stark white into the inner black:

He said the secrets would kill me to if I told you but I had to do sumthing the Athenian dinnt do it the secrets killed the Spartan

"Where did you find this?" I demanded.

"In the middle of our tent," Socrates said. "When I returned from the chariot race. It lay in the middle, where you couldn't miss it."

The tent flap had been up. Anyone could have tossed it in as he walked by.

"What secrets could kill a man?" I asked myself aloud.

"Many," Sophroniscus said. "You're old enough to know that."

I inspected the ostrakon closely to deduce what I could from it.

I hoped for a clue as to who might have thrown it into our tent. Then I sighed.

"It's difficult, isn't it, Nico?" Socrates sympathized.

"It certainly is."

"Yes. Other than that the writer was a nervous, left-handed man with a blunt knife and tawny-colored hair, there's almost nothing we can get from it. But you know that, of course."

I almost dropped the ostrakon. "You can't possibly know all those things," I said, but I was afraid he could.

"Sure you can, Nico," he said. He was too absorbed in the problem to notice the insult. "See here where the knife has slipped? It slipped from left to right. So he held the ostrakon in his right hand and the knife in his left."

Now that he pointed it out, it was obvious. "All right," I granted. "But the blunt knife?"

"The same slip happens here and here and here," Socrates pointed to the slight scratches. "The knife point wouldn't hold."

I had to concede he was right. "And the nervousness?"

"He can spell secrets, but not didn't. He couldn't think straight."

I knew what to look for now. I rotated the shard until I found the short hair trapped in a crack at the bottom edge, where the break was particularly ragged. I didn't know how a hair could have caught there, but there was no doubt it was tawny colored.

I put the ostrakon in a cloth pouch and tied it to my belt. I had no idea what it meant, but I'd find out. This was the first evidence that Timo might be innocent.

"Good work, Socrates."

"Thanks, Nico!" Socrates beamed.

I FOUND ONE-EYE in a dusty patch he'd taken for an exercise ring, surrounded by dry, spindly grass. Not an official athlete, One-Eye wasn't permitted use of the Olympic facilities. He danced about in the dust in a sequence of oddly elegant movements, each ending in a blow, a kick or a punch against the empty air. One-Eye practiced the standard routine of a pankratist. He danced naked and glistened with sweat. The red, empty eye socket gave him the forbidding look of an angry Cyclops. He snarled and grunted, dodged, swerved, and struck so smoothly that I knew I observed a daily routine. One-Eye might have been an old man, but I for one wouldn't have wanted to face him. I doubted anyone but a current contestant could have taken him on.

One-Eye saw me, but he didn't stop his practice. If anything, his momentum increased ever so slightly. Had he picked up the pace to impress me?

I said nothing but waited for the routine to slow to a halt, which finally it did.

"Nicolaos," he acknowledged me. He began to alternate jogging in place and straining his arms against a large piece of granite.

"Very impressive, sir. Are you finished?"

"The heavy, useful part of the routine is over, yes. I must cool down slowly now, or the muscles will knot."

"Does Festianos exercise like this, too, sir? Where is he?"

One-Eye laughed, but without humor. "My brother has let himself go these last years. But perhaps I shouldn't criticize too much," he allowed. "My brother has been afflicted with poor health. No, Festianos has gone to the stadion to watch the pentathlon."

"Oh, of course." I'd forgotten for a moment there were Games on. "I don't suppose you know where I could find him on the hill?"

"He left late. I imagine he'll be toward the back, close to the entrance." One-Eye continued his warm-down exercise without pause while we talked.

"Don't you want to watch, too, sir?" I asked.

"There's only one sport I care about, young man, and it's not the pentathlon."

"I see."

"You're the one assigned to free my son. Why aren't you out doing it?"

"It's why I'm here, sir. There are some questions I have to ask."

"I know nothing about the killing," One-Eye said at once. "Except that it was thoroughly deserved."

"Arakos didn't *deserve* to die," a voice said. Markos came to a halt beside me. He was surprisingly calm considering One-Eye had just consigned a Spartan to Hades.

One-Eye looked him over. "You're the Spartan they assigned to make sure my son dies."

Markos said mildly, "I'm the Spartan assigned to investigate a murder."

"Then perhaps your time would be better expended elsewhere. Chasing the killer, for example?"

The tension oozed between One-Eye and Markos, between One-Eye and me. I said, "One-Eye, I understand your love for your son makes you anxious—"

"My love? When I learned my wife was pregnant, I sacrificed to Zeus for a son. I sacrificed every day of her term. Do you understand why?"

"Er . . . because you wanted a son?"

One-Eye snorted. "If that's your idea of incisive deduction, then my son is doomed. Yes, you idiot, I wanted a son so that I could pass onto him the family tradition of the pankration."

"Why did you say just now that the death was deserved?" Markos asked, then added, his voice dripping with irony, "Please don't mind my feelings in your answer."

One-Eye turned to me. "I know you've talked to my son. He must have told you what transpired on the march here."

I knew, because Pindar had told me. Timo hadn't thought to mention it. It occurred to me that my friend Timo hadn't told me everything. I said, "I heard. Arakos harassed Timo."

"Arakos had it coming. Like most Spartans, he was an arrogant bastard." One-Eye glared at Markos, daring him to interject. Markos kept his face a carefully controlled mask. He was a superb interrogator. One-Eye went on, "Whoever got him, I'll wager it was someone understandably angered beyond control."

I wondered if he realized that description might apply to him or to his son. For the first time I noticed how Timo's propensity to wild anger had been inherited from his father.

I asked, "Did Dromeus really prescribe sex as part of the training regimen?"

One-Eye frowned. "Dromeus says it keeps the athlete's muscles relaxed, and I have to admit the results seem to prove him right. It's one of those newfangled theories, like the meat-only diet everyone swears by these days." One-Eye shook his head. "It's unbelievably expensive. Do you know what red meat costs?"

"So you disagreed with Dromeus on Timo's training regimen."

"Oh no, I'm not getting into that argument! Haven't you wondered why I, an expert in the pankration, hired an expensive personal trainer for my son?"

"I did wonder." In fact, it had never occurred to me, but I didn't want to appear stupid.

"It's because a father is not always the most objective when it comes to his own son. A more dispassionate eye can see and correct faults an indulgent father might pass over."

One-Eye thought he was indulgent?

"You were my son's friend—"

"I still am."

"And for that I forgive you these impertinent questions. But there will be no more from either of you. Free my son, Nicolaos. Preferably by tomorrow. Being cooped up in that room is terrible preparation for the contest."

Markos said, "Sir, the Judges of the Games set Timo's trial for the last day of the Games." Markos didn't add the obvious: that they'd done so in order to execute him at once if the judgment went against him.

"Then bring forward the trial."

"What?" I couldn't believe him.

"You heard me. The pankration is the last event on the fourth day. Timodemus must be free by then, or he won't be able to compete."

I said, "Sir, it's for the judges to decide."

"But if you told the judges you could prove his innocence they would hear you early, would they not?"

"I suppose so," I said, with the greatest reluctance. "But One-Eye—"

"Good, then tell them."

"Wouldn't it help if we solved the crime first?"

"Young man, you don't need to find this killer. You merely need to prove it could not be my son. Surely you can do that."

Markos and I looked at each other in disbelief. For the first time, Markos was at a loss for words.

"Right now, One-Eye, I can do no such thing. In fact, on the face of it, Timodemus did kill the Spartan."

"You don't believe that." He tossed weights into the air and caught them.

"No, sir, but it's what any impartial judge will decide. Let me do my job in the time allotted, sir, and if Zeus grants me the victory, then your son will return home with you, alive and free."

"I hoped for more than that."

"More? I don't understand, One-Eye."

"Timo won at Nemea last year, no matter what they say. You should ignore the ugly rumors."

I blinked. "What rumors?"

"I just told you to ignore them. If Timo wins here at the Sacred Games, then it remains only for him to win at Corinth and Delphi—both easier competitions—and he will have won every major title on the competition circuit. Those who achieve such a feat are entitled to name themselves *paradoxos*."

Paradoxos—"the marvel"—Timodemus the Marvel, because to achieve four straight victories is almost impossible.

Dear Gods, his son was held in a prison awaiting execution, and One-Eye could only think of how they would win the next contest.

"The advantages that accrue to a *paradoxos* are great indeed," One-Eye went on.

Had the man no grip on reality? He'd be lucky if Timo still breathed come the next contest, let alone won it.

Markos said, "Then it would help, sir, if you could give us any clue as to who might have killed Arakos. You've been around the pankration all your life. You know everyone in the sport. What do you think?"

"It wouldn't surprise me in the least if Dromeus killed the Spartan."

I blinked. Had One-Eye just shopped his own head coach for the crime? He'd said it as easily as if he discussed the weather.

"Are you serious?" I had to ask.

"Certainly I am."

"Why would Dromeus want to kill Arakos?" Markos asked.

"Dromeus saw some hard times after his Olympic crown. He was widely considered the weakest Olympic victor ever. He turned to coaching to bolster his reputation, and he achieved some success, which is why I hired him, but Timodemus is the first of his charges to have a real chance at the crown. Dromeus is desperate for this win."

And you aren't? I thought to myself, but didn't dare say it. Instead I said, "Merely wanting to win a sporting contest hardly seems a motive for a serious attack."

"Doesn't it? Look at me, Nicolaos."

He grabbed me by the shoulders and pulled me so close that my entire vision was filled with his face. His hot, angry breath blew on my face.

"Here now!" Markos moved to save me, but I waved him back.

"What do you see?" One-Eye rasped.

I could see the broken nose from his many fights, the pock-marked skin dark and splotchy from years of practice under the sun, and, above all else, the ugly red hole where his right eye had been. It was scarred and puckered. A layer of grime lay within the empty socket, where the sandy dust of the practice ring had settled.

"A man who has spent his life in the pankration," I whispered. I wondered if Timo would one day look like this.

"Do you know how I lost this eye?"

"Timo told me once, long ago."

"Did he tell you the details?"

I shook my head.

"It was at the Nemean Games, when I was the age my son is today. I was a pankratist, one of the very best. Not the best—there was no clear best—but I was among the top four or five, let us say; any one of us had a hope of Olympic glory.

"I'd reached the semifinals of Nemea. I was confident. Very confident. I'd won easily in every round. I knew I was fighting better than every man present, and these were the men who'd be going on to the Sacred Games the next year. I allowed myself to hope that if I kept up my training, and worked hard, then perhaps the crown of the Sacred Games was within my grasp."

One-Eye's one remaining good eye glistened. If it had been anyone else, I might have suspected a tear was forming.

"My opponent in the semifinals was weak. He wouldn't have made it so far, except the Gods had seen fit to grant him a bye in the earlier round. I faced him, and by his stance, I knew I could take him. I could see in his eyes that he knew it, too.

"The umpires called time, and we entered the ring. We faced each other and I let him approach. Then sand flew into my eyes. He'd thrown it. He'd kept his hands clenched to hide the grit he held.

"I was blinded and fell back. He jumped on top of me. The

next thing I felt were the fingers hooked behind my ears and the thumbs in my eyeballs. I could hear the umpires screaming and the whips striking his back, but he didn't stop. I tried to turn my head to save my sight. But I felt my right eyeball slide out."

That was definitely a tear on his cheek. I thought that One-Eye was about to weep, but he held it back.

"I still have nightmares. For one hideous moment I saw my own face. Then it was gone, and I was left screaming on the ground. They carried me away, my trainer and my father, to the doctor to save what they could. He applied the branding iron to cauterize the wound."

One-Eye shuddered.

"It was a Spartan who gouged out my eye. He claimed it was an accident, which made him a liar as well as a cheat. All he got was a beating, while I . . . I could have been an Olympic victor."

One-Eye let go of me, and I staggered back.

"So guess what. I don't give a shit about any dead Spartan. But hear me on this, friend of my son." In his rage, the spittle flew from his mouth. I felt it spatter my face. "Timodemus gets his chance to go where I failed. And that means you've got to get him out in time for the pankration."

"What if I can't?"

"Then it doesn't matter whether he lives or dies, because his whole life will have been wasted."

"NICE FRIENDS YOU have," Markos said as we walked away.

I was shaking. All these years I'd known Timodemus—been at his house, played there as a boy—yet never had I talked to One-Eye long enough to realize what a driven, brutal man he could be.

"The father of Timodemus isn't my friend."

I recalled the horrible sight of Arakos as he lay faceup in the dirt. There'd been ugly red holes where his eyes had been torn out, holes that matched the terrible scar in One-Eye's own face, and One-Eye had admitted a Spartan disfigured him. I hoped Markos didn't make the same connection.

Markos and I had to push our way through the entrance to the stadion. The way was narrow, the crowd immense. It squeezed the shambling men to two abreast, down a roofed passage not more than fifteen paces long.

A voice beside us said, "The Hellenes pass through the birth canal of the entrance into the clean, open world of the stadion."

We both turned, startled, to see Pindar at my elbow. Even in this crowd he carried the manner of a priest. Men about us gave him room, and he slid in to join us, with Markos to his left and me to his right.

"I noticed the two of you push your way into the queue," he said. "I was intrigued, of course, so I slipped in behind. Are you young gentlemen hot on the heels of the malefactor?"

"If Zeus favors us," I said, and then, hearing my own words, said, "Curse it, Pindar, I'm beginning to sound like you."

"That would be a distinct improvement."

"Did I hear you say 'birth canal'?" Markos said.

"Consider the layout, my friends," Pindar said, as the crowd of which we were a part shuffled into the tunnel. "The goddess Hera—she who is wife to Zeus and matron to the Gods—her temple opens directly onto this path down which we tread. Men are squeezed into the short tunnel before us, whence we emerge into the open stadion. So Hera gives birth to us all."

I was aghast.

"You're not serious, are you, Pindar?" Markos said.

"It's a metaphor, lads. Poets are very keen on metaphors. They sell like honey cakes. I thought of the birth canal idea many Olympiads ago, when I was a young man. I've always wanted to get it into a victory song, but I never found the opportunity."

"I can't imagine why," Markos said. "Unless they introduce Olympic childbirthing as an event."

"No sillier than Olympic detecting," Pindar pointed out.

"And I must beg to disagree with you on the chance of Olympic childbirth. What would our illustrious ancestors say if they knew these days we have an Olympic mule race? Never underestimate the power of human stupidity, my boy. After the acts of the Gods, the mistakes of mortals are the single greatest decider of our fates."

"Did you really write a victory song for the mule race?"

"I did. But I used one of my generics."

"Generics?"

"I prepare them in advance and then fill in the victor's name later."

We found Festianos where One-Eye had guessed he'd be, standing at the back of the crowd on the low hill that ran the length of the stadion. Which was a good thing because we could never have pushed through the densely packed men to find him anywhere else. The hill had been covered in grass when I first saw it two days ago. Now I felt nothing but bare dirt between my toes. Ten thousand men walking across it for two days had had the expected effect.

"Festianos," I said. He looked up at me in surprise, then to my right where Markos stood. His eyes narrowed.

Festianos had the family height, which is to say, not much, but unlike One-Eye and Timo, Festianos had let himself run to fat. He was pudgy and entirely bald. His eyes had dark rings around them. I guessed that was due to excessive partying.

"We need to talk to you," I said to him.

Suddenly my feet felt wet. I looked down. I'd trodden into a puddle where someone had pissed where he stood rather than miss the Games. I glanced behind me. A man with a deep black beard grinned back.

"Does it have to be now?" Festianos said. "They're in the middle of the pentathlon."

There were no athletes on the field, which meant they were between events. The pentathletes are permitted a short break in between each of the five events—discus, javelin, long jump, wrestling, and running.

Droplets of sweat had appeared on Markos's brow. I, too, was sweating freely. The men were packed in like sheep, and the heat that rose from the bodies was incredible. It was the middle of the day, but anyone who wore a hat had it torn off by the men standing behind.

"Where are they up to?" Markos asked. He seemed to be easily distracted by the sport.

"They've finished the discus and the javelin. The long jump will start at any moment."

Even as Festianos said it, the athletes emerged from the tunnel carrying their weights, accompanied by an aulos player with his V-shaped flute. They walked single file across the stadion to the long side immediately before us, where the *skamma* lay, a long strip of soft earth in which the long jumpers would land.

While the athletes stretched and warmed up, I said, "That night outside Timo's tent. You said you'd keep an eye on him after I went to bed. What happened?"

Festianos groaned. "I knew you'd ask that eventually."

The pentathletes were naked, of course, but for the only item of wear allowed: the *kynodesme*—the "dog leash"—a leather cord that tied around the tip of the penis and then wrapped around the scrotum, to stop bits from jiggling while the athletes competed. They carried in each hand heavy weights to assist with their jumps.

The first man to jump stepped up to the line.

The aulos player put his V-shaped flute to his lips and played a hymn to Apollo. The hymn was catchy and the rhythm so regular that I found myself tapping my foot.

The first jumper swung his weighted arms back and forth in time to the music, stared intently at the skamma, and bent his knees in preparation. The swings became progressively more violent till I thought he must surely be lifted off his feet. At the next swing forward he leaped, arms and legs outstretched.

The moment his feet landed in the softened ground, he swung his weighted arms back, bent his knees, and barely managed to hold his place. If he'd fallen or taken a step forward, he would have been disqualified.

Immediately one of the judges rushed to the landing spot with a measuring rod. The athlete walked back to the group with head hung low. Men about me shook their heads and muttered. One of them was Markos.

"Not the best," he said.

"No," Festianos agreed. "But he needn't worry yet. He still has four more attempts." He paused. "The tent, yes, I know. I'm not avoiding the question. The truth is I went for a walk to clear my head. To be honest, I knew Timodemus wanted to sneak off."

"*And you let him?*" I couldn't believe it. After all the effort I'd gone to.

Festianos snorted. "I'm a middle-aged man. Middle-aged men don't stop young men when they want to party with the women."

"You knew he was looking for women?"

The next pentathlete had stepped up to the line, and the aulos player picked up the tune. The athlete made a huge leap—well beyond the first—but try as he might he couldn't stop himself from taking the tiniest step. The crowd jeered, and he walked away without a measurement. Like the first man, he still had four tries.

Festianos resumed the conversation. "Timo has been creeping from our rooms in Elis for the best part of a month. Where else do young men go in the dead of night?"

"But the Spartans might have been out to get him."

"I was a trifle worse the wear for drink. You probably noticed. I suppose it affected my judgment."

I felt like throttling Festianos. If he'd done what he'd said he'd do, Timodemus wouldn't be in trouble now.

"So you let him go to the tents of the pornoi."

"The pornoi? Timo has better taste than that. No, the lad's picked up a girlfriend."

That wasn't what he'd said to me! I was careful not to let my surprise show. In the most neutral voice I could manage, I said, "What's this girlfriend's name?"

"I've no idea. He got her in Elis. Apparently she followed him here."

I thought of how Festianos had promised me he'd watch Timodemus, then let him out on his own the moment my back was turned. Festianos was capable of lying.

"You sure you don't know this girl's name?"

"I swear by Zeus," Festianos said. "Why don't you ask Dromeus? I bet he knows. That bastard never takes his eye off Timo. I don't know who's more driven for my nephew to win: my brother or Dromeus."

DROMEUS SAT IN a corner of the gym with four other trainers. It seemed the ban against Team Timo didn't extend to a former Olympic champion. Dromeus and his friends had laid wet cloths across their heads, no doubt to keep them cool in the heat. Even with the open courtyard to let in the breeze, the gym was like an oven.

Dromeus had won the pankration twenty years ago; among these men he was a celebrity. I wondered how much it had cost One-Eye to hire his services. The Timonidae were a wealthy family, but to hire a man like Dromeus must have stretched even their fortunes.

The trainers spoke among themselves. They sat upon the benches that lined the walls. There were bowls of food scattered between them and wineskins in their hands. Markos and I were about to interrupt their lunch. The thought made me realize that I'd probably be missing my own; there was too much to do.

As we approached, I heard Dromeus speak the words, "If you ask me, I reckon it was one of those two what did it—" He broke off his conversation when he saw us. "What do you want?"

They all five looked at Markos and me, standing side by side.

I said, "Dromeus, we need to ask you what happened in the procession."

"You were there?"

"Yes."

"Then you know." He turned his back on us.

I stood my ground. "Dromeus, what did Arakos say?"

Dromeus turned. "Listen, kid—"

"My name's Nicolaos."

"Listen, kid, I've got a reputation to think of. You understand?"

I nodded. "You don't want to be associated with a killer."

The trainers burst into laughter. Dromeus said, "This young idiot thinks I don't want to be seen with killers. Hey Theo, when did you last kill a man with your bare hands?"

Theo scratched his head. "Eight, nine months ago? At that contest in Thebes. I got this guy in a real neat choke hold, and he just wouldn't give up. Bastard grabbed my balls and twisted, so I jerked his—"

"Thanks, Theo," Dromeus broke in. "Eosilos, how many men you killed?"

"You know I can't count high, Dromeus! I'm an athlete, not a philosopher." They all grinned while Eosilos counted on his fingers, slowly. "Reckon I've done for eight men as I recall." He paused. "Not counting Persians, of course."

"Barely worth the effort of killing," Dromeus agreed with a straight face. He turned back to me. "You see, kid? Every man here has killed with his own hands, except for you and your friend."

He was wrong, in my case at least. I'd killed two men, but neither was something I could talk about. Markos kept his

expression carefully neutral and hadn't said a word, but I felt
rather than saw his muscles tense, and I guessed he too had seen
his share of mayhem.

Dromeus had made his point.

"Murdering don't mean a thing, kid. You know what they do
before the pankration? They give us a blanket pardon for murder.
Because all those kids you saw take the oath? Chances are one of
them's going to kill another before these Games are over."

"One of them already has," Theo said.

"But the next one will be fair and square."

"Where were you when Arakos died?" I asked.

"You're not suggesting I—an Olympic champion—had something to do with this, are you?"

"As it happens—"

Theo and Eosilos raised their fists.

"Er . . . no, of course not, Dromeus."

"Good."

Markos cut in smoothly, "But consider, sirs, if we know where
everyone was, then it helps us to eliminate the innocent from
suspicion, you see? Also, anyone you saw must be innocent."

Markos, the calm voice of reason; once again he was doing
better than I in an interview. This was becoming a habit I didn't
want to continue.

Dromeus considered Markos's words. "All right," he said.
"After the ceremony, where my moron of a student made a complete ass of himself in front of everyone, I dragged the young
idiot here to the gym. Well, you know that, Nicolaos, you turned
up later."

I nodded. I could still feel the bruises.

"No one hung around after you left. Timodemus had his rub-
down. Then his uncle led him away."

"Not One-Eye?" I interrupted.

"He wasn't there. You know that."

So I did. One-Eye had gone to see Pericles and then the judges.

"What about that night? Did you see Timodemus then?"

"Didn't see him the entire evening."

"What about One-Eye?"

"Didn't see him neither."

"Is that reasonable? You train his son, who was scheduled to fight in only a few days."

"No, he isn't. Timodemus is a prisoner. Remember?"

"You didn't know that then."

Dromeus shrugged. "All I can say is I didn't see One-Eye nor his son nor his brother the whole night, and I stayed up late, let me tell you."

"Oh?"

"I stayed at the gym to greet my friends. It was dark when we left here."

"It took that long?" Markos asked.

"I have a lot of friends. Then we went out to dinner together."

"All of you?"

"Most."

"Anyone can vouch for you?" I asked.

"Yeah." Dromeus nodded at Theo and Eosilos. They grinned back at me, or, rather, they bared their teeth.

"I saw Arakos," Theo said. Every head turned, and Theo looked surprised at the attention his statement got him.

"What?" Dromeus said.

"When? Where?" I added.

"It was when I left you guys. After dinner. Remember, I said I was off to get a woman?"

Heads nodded. Everyone agreed Theo had been off to get a woman.

"Well, I was walking to the women's camp, and Arakos passed me by."

"Wait, when was this?" I demanded.

Theo scratched his head. "I dunno. To tell you the truth, I'm not too good at telling the time . . ."

"He means he was plastered," added Eosilos helpfully.

Theo looked hurt. "That ain't true, Eos," he said. "I walked in a straight line all the way from here to the women, didn't I?"

"You was walking in a straight line when you left," Eos allowed. "All right, so you was mellow."

"Mellow. Exactly." Theo nodded. "Mellow's fine. Means you can still get it up. Not like plastered, 'cause in that case with a woman you got to—"

"Could we get back to Arakos please?" I asked. "Can any of you remember when Theo left your company?"

They all looked blank.

"Was the moon still rising, or was it falling?" I asked in desperation.

"Rising," said Dromeus. "I remember. Not long before it peaked."

Close enough to midnight, then.

"Excellent. Now, Theo, think hard—"

He gaped at me with an open mouth.

"Where did you see Arakos?"

"We crossed the ford together."

"Did he see you?"

"Sure. We spoke."

"What!"

"I said I was going to get a woman, and he said he was, too, and then he was going to meet Timodemus to beat the little bastard senseless."

"In the name of Zeus, why?"

"In revenge for what happened at Nemea."

"What happened at Nemea?" Markos asked, looking confused. "What's Nemea last year got to do with this?"

"Arakos lost. Timodemus won," Theo said simply.

"I've heard there was some unpleasantness at Nemea," I said.

Silence, but a few eyes turned toward Dromeus.

"Theo, why didn't you tell me this before?" Dromeus said.

"You didn't ask, Dromeus."

"I would have stopped a fight."

I asked the trainers, "Would it be cheating if two pankratists decided to batter each other in private, *before* the contest?"

They had to scratch their heads about that one. "I dunno," said Eosilos. "I never heard of it happening, but there's nothing in the rules against it, is there, Dromeus?"

Dromeus shook his head. "Nothing in the rules says no, but if my student agreed to meet Arakos in the woods, I'd kill the idiot before the judges did."

"Dromeus, when I walked in, I heard you say, 'I reckon it was one of those two what did it.' Who were you talking about?"

"Never you mind."

There was nothing I could do to force him to answer.

"What would you say if I told you someone—I won't say who—has accused you of the murder?"

Dromeus laughed bitterly. "I'd say One-Eye was full of donkey crap."

I gaped. "What makes you think it was One-Eye?"

"The look on your face, for one. But I know 'cause I can read people, and let me tell you that bastard would do anything to get Timodemus off. Do you know the most important skill of a pankratist?"

"Hitting people?"

Dromeus snorted. "If that's all there was to it, any big man could be a champion. Look at Timodemus, he's a small guy, but he can mix it up just fine. No, kid, the secret is in reading your opponent. Where he's looking can tell you a lot. So can his body, which muscles are tense, which relaxed."

"So you're saying Timodemus can read people?" Markos said.

"Like a scroll. It's why he's the best. He's never where the other guy's about to strike. It's almost impossible to hit the little bastard."

It occurred to me, if Timo could read other people so well, then he knew Arakos was about to needle him before Arakos opened his mouth. Then how could he claim he was so enraged by Arakos that he acted without thought?

Markos said, "I take it you don't like One-Eye."

Dromeus shrugged. "I gotta train his son. I don't have to like the father."

"What about Timo himself?" I asked.

"Timodemus is all right," Dromeus said. "Listen, kid, I like you. You took on Timodemus when you didn't have a hope in Hades. You knew he was going to beat you to a pulp, didn't you?"

"I told you we fought as kids. You said Timo needed to get the anger out of his system."

He nodded. "I like that. A man ready to take a few lumps for a friend."

"You said fighting me would get the anger out of Timo's system. Did it work, Dromeus?"

"I think it did."

"Then how can you think Timo killed Arakos?"

"You got it wrong, kid. You asked me before who the two were, the two I reckon did it."

"Yes?"

"One-Eye and Festianos."

The others in the room showed no surprise. It must have been common gossip. I said, "Why?"

"Isn't it obvious? They want their boy to win."

"Festianos says you're desperate yourself."

Dromeus snorted. "I'm a professional. Sure I want my student up there. Doesn't mean I'm gonna cheat for it. I told you I didn't see One-Eye and Festianos that night, but I tried. I went around to their tent. Neither of them was there. I reckon they were off, seeing to Arakos."

THE MOMENT WE left the gym, Markos took my arm and led me to a quiet spot in the shade of the building. Quiet meant there were only ten other men sitting there, fanning themselves and talking sport. Olympia really was crowded.

Markos said softly, so the others wouldn't hear, "Nico, this evidence of Dromeus agrees with the ostrakon I found, the one that demanded a meeting."

"I know, Markos, but Timodemus denied writing it."

"He's your friend. I understand," he said sympathetically. It was the tone of a man who spoke to the bereaved, or the soon to be bereaved.

"I don't know, Markos. Give me some time. I need to think."

Had Timo lied? I didn't want to think about it, so instead, I wondered what Diotima was doing, whether she'd made any progress, and suddenly I was gripped by the empty feeling of not having her with me. So I said, "Come on, Markos. I want you to meet my wife."

WE FOUND HER at Petale's tent. A queue of men waited outside. Diotima sat at a table beside the entrance with a stack of coins and a water clock dripping away the time.

A man emerged smiling from behind the tent flap. He blinked, adjusted his tunic, and sauntered off.

"Next!" Diotima called, without taking her eyes off the clock. It had only a few drops left to run. At the last drop, Diotima turned it over and made a mark on a wax tablet. She consulted her notes and said to the man at the head of the queue, "Let's see, you're doggy." She handed him four obols from the stack of coins.

The man said, "But what if I want something else?"

"If you want free sex, then you do it my way," she told him. "You're wasting time. Get in there and stop screwing about—er." Diotima realized what she was saying. "That is, *do* screw about."

The man grinned and went inside. A moment later, we heard a brief squeal from Petale.

"Diotima!" I said, shocked.

Diotima looked up, pushed back a wisp of dark hair from her eyes, and said, "Oh, hello, Nico."

"What in Hades do you think you're doing?"

"We need to know how long Petale spent with clients. Didn't I say to leave it me?"

"Petale doesn't remember how many clients she saw."

"I found a way to work out her payments. Most of them, anyway."

"No one can look at a jar of coins and deduce in what handfuls they'd been put in. I know you're smart, Diotima, but I can't believe even you could do it."

Diotima blushed. "I . . . er . . . had some help."

"Who could possibly do such a thing?"

"Hi, Nico!" came a boy's voice from under the table.

I bent to look. There was my little brother, Socrates.

"Socrates worked it out," my wife admitted sheepishly.

"You asked a child?"

"Well, he is my brother-in-law, you know."

"It was fun, Nico," Socrates said eagerly as he crawled out from under the table. "A really unusual puzzle. But I solved it!"

"How?" I said, unbelieving.

"Say there are fourteen obols in the jar. Then it must be for a man on top and a doggy. Because man on top is ten obols, and doggy is four." Socrates paused. "Er . . . I thought at first doggy had something to do with—you know—dogs. I wondered where they all were. It was a bit of a relief when Diotima explained about the different ways. Hey Nico, which positions do you and Diotima—"

"Can we get back to Petale?" I interrupted. "Why couldn't it be for something else?"

"Oh, sure. Well, woman on top is nine obols, and standing is three, and there just isn't any other way to make fourteen. That's only an example, of course. You see?"

I saw. "That's really quite clever. But I saw Petale's money jar. There must more than a hundred coins."

"Yes, Nico, but the customers come from different cities. Lots of different cities. There weren't more than a couple of customers from each place."

"Go on," I said, intrigued despite myself.

"Well, every city has its own coins, and everyone paid *in their own currency*."

It struck me like a hammer. "Dear Gods, Socrates, that's brilliant!"

Socrates smiled like the rising sun. "Thanks, Nico! Do you know, I think that's the first time you ever said I did something smart? All the other times you—"

"Don't get carried away," I told him. "Go on with your calculation."

"Oh, well, in the jar there are only a handful of coins from most cities. So it's easy to work out all the different ways they could have been paid. Lots of the solutions are obviously ridiculous; we can eliminate those."

"And where there's ambiguity," Diotima added—I heard the *I-told-you-so* in her voice—"it usually doesn't change how many men paid." She shrugged. "Sometimes we took the high answer, sometimes the low. It'll even out close enough that we know how many men she saw."

"But the coins from different cities have different values."

"Sure."

"To do this you'd have to know the fees in the coins of every city in the country for every way of having sex."

"Oh, that's all right," Socrates said. "I memorized them all. Petale told me all the going rates."

Terrific. My wife was running a brothel, and my little brother had memorized the cost of every sexual position with a prostitute for every currency in Hellas.

Diotima said, "I'm timing the same number of men, duplicating the positions as close as we can get them. Pretty soon now I'll be able to tell you what time Petale saw Arakos the Spartan."

The answer would be a gift of the Gods, but I still had trouble believing the answer could have been divined.

"Socrates, tell me the truth, did you really work out how many men she serviced? You're not making this up, are you?"

"No, Nico," he said, and he sounded hurt. "I can prove it. Honest. I'll show you every step."

"No," I said at once. "I believe you, Socrates. I'm sorry I asked. So how many men in all?"

His eyes and mouth became large as plates. "*A lot.*"

"You've done well. Good thinking, Socrates."

"Thanks, Nico!" He beamed.

"Uh—don't mention this to our father." I pulled Diotima to the side. "You've been teaching Socrates about sex," I hissed.

"He was surprisingly ignorant for a twelve-year-old," she said calmly. "Fortunately he didn't need to know much to solve the mathematical problem."

"*That's not the point.* I told Father you'd never be involved in prostitution. What if he finds out?"

"It's more important to get the answer." Diotima looked at Markos, who'd listened to all this with a bemused expression. "Who's your friend?" she asked in a loud voice, quite blatantly changing the subject.

"Markos, meet my fiancée, Diotima. Diotima, this is Markos of Sparta."

They looked each other up and down.

At that moment the man emerged from the tent.

"Oh!" Diotima rushed back to the table and ran her finger down the list. She grabbed a handful of coins and thrust them at the man first in line.

"She's on top. Go!"

The man nodded his head and stepped in quickly. Diotima might not have approved of the seamier side of life, but she certainly knew how to run a brothel.

She became preoccupied with her chart, checking her figures.

Markos and I looked at each other, both desperately trying not to laugh. Markos grinned and said, "Your remarkable lady would have made a fine madam."

"I wouldn't say that to her if you wish to live."

"I don't suppose Diotima has a sister, does she?"

"Sorry, Markos, you'll have to find your own clever priestess."

As I said it, I thought what a pity that was. I would have enjoyed having Markos for a brother-in-law.

Diotima turned her attention back to us. "What have you two learned?"

Markos and I took turns telling her what we'd been up to while Diotima listened closely. From time to time as we spoke, she had to break off the conversation to usher in another client for Petale.

When Markos and I finished, Diotima said, "Dromeus accuses Festianos and One-Eye. One-Eye accuses Dromeus. Festianos implies either Dromeus or One-Eye would have been happy to do the deed. The only person everyone agrees would not have killed Arakos is Timodemus, and he's the one who's arrested."

"How do you like Uncle Festianos or One-Eye as murderers?" I asked her.

"They'd be a start."

It occurred to me my friend Timodemus might be a trifle miffed if I saved his life but got his father or uncle executed. I said, "Why do you think Dromeus named them?"

"For the traditional reason," Diotima said. "He hates them. But they're all members of Timo's team."

"No one else has a motive," Markos pointed out.

"Is there no one among the Spartans?" she asked. "Had this prickly pankratist no enemies at home?"

Markos considered. "It's a reasonable question," he conceded. "But why, if you were a Spartan, would you pick Olympia to murder a fellow citizen? Surely there'd be better opportunities. In fact, I know there are."

Diotima opened her mouth to argue, but Markos raised a

hand. "Wait! I agree it needs to be checked. I'll see if anyone in the Spartan camp had a particular reason to kill Arakos."

I wasn't entirely happy, but we had to trust Markos in this. If Arakos did have an enemy in the Spartan camp, Diotima and I could never hope to discover him. The Spartans would refuse to talk to us.

It was hard to concentrate with the sounds of passion emanating from the tent behind us. Markos seemed distracted, too, but Diotima didn't seem to notice.

The line of men had shortened to the final two when the slave with the runny nose appeared from around the corner and walked up to us.

"Not you again." I backed away.

He sniffed loudly. "Got another message from Pericles. The great man wants to see you." He jerked his thumb in the direction of the main camp.

"Tell him we'll be there shortly," Diotima said.

"You're coming, too?" I asked.

"I'm almost finished here," she said.

Markos said, "This is an Athenian-only meeting, I'm sure. I'll see what I can find at the Spartan camp while you consult your leader."

"Pericles isn't leader of Athens," I said. "He's influential, but he's a citizen just like any other."

"Then why do all you Athenians jump at his beck and call?" Markos asked.

It was a good question.

DIOTIMA AND I pushed our way into Pericles's tent without bothering to knock. Pericles was equally abrupt. Without greeting, he asked, "What progress?" And then, seeing who was with me, demanded, "What's *she* doing here?"

Pericles and Diotima didn't exactly get along. It may have had something to do with the fact that Diotima had once blackmailed him.

"Diotima's my partner, Pericles," I said. "If you want this job done in three days, I need all the help I can get."

"Hmmph." He knew I was right. He also knew I would walk away if Diotima was excluded.

Rather than argue about it, I caught him up on everything we'd learned.

When I finished, Pericles said, "I want you both to understand how important it is to Athens that Timodemus not be guilty of this killing."

I nodded. "Yes, it would be shameful if an Athenian cheated in such a way."

"I don't think you've quite understood me. I said it's important *Timodemus be found not guilty*. I didn't say anything about him actually being innocent."

"You're not suggesting we deliberately ignore evidence, are you?" Diotima said.

"Not at all. Unless it's inconvenient, in which case yes."

"Pericles," I said, offended, "I swore an Olympic Oath to find the killer of Arakos. Timodemus is my closest friend, but if the facts lead to him, I have no choice."

"Yes, you do. How many men are dead of this debacle?"

"One."

"If we're not careful, the victims of this crime will expand to thousands." Pericles picked up the bronze stylus he'd been playing with the last time we'd met in his tent and began to twirl it in his fingers.

"Did you know there was a battle between Athens and Corinth while you two were away in Ionia?"

"In the war for control of Megara? Yes."

"Corinth sent an army to settle the issue," Pericles said. "We were committed to so many wars, in different parts of the world, that all we had left to send were old men and boys. Old men and boys against an army of veterans."

"And?"

"The old men and the boys won. The army from Corinth was driven off. Our lads erected a victory tripod."

"Good for them."

"The Corinthians can't have been pleased," Diotima said.

"They weren't. The people of Corinth sent their army straight back, with orders to do a better job. The Corinthian army erected a victory tripod, too, claimed they'd won, refused to fight, and took off for home a second time."

We all laughed.

Pericles said, "It may seem very well, but I've heard news this day. As I warned you might happen, Corinth is using this killing to egg on the Spartans to join the squabble. We must do nothing that would give the hawks in Sparta an excuse to declare war. Stretched as we are, we'd certainly lose it."

"I see."

"This time I think you do. If Sparta and Athens ever go to war, it will be like two giant lions mauling each other."

"Could it come to that?" I asked, concerned. I was as ready to fight for Athens as any man, but I hated the discipline of army life.

"I begin to think a fight might be inevitable," Pericles said. "There've been incidents. Small parties of Spartans have waylaid Athenians on their own, to rough them up. Our men defended themselves. There's yet to be open fighting, but it's only a matter of time. We're not at war at the moment. I don't wish to be when these Games end."

"Can't you stop this, Pericles?"

"No, but you can."

"Me!"

"You. The Spartans won't like it, but if Timodemus is officially innocent then there is no cause for dispute. Tension will fall. There are many things that could come of this debacle, Nicolaos, but there is one that must not: *Athens and Sparta must not go to war*. Ouch." Pericles looked down to see blood flowing from his palm. In his excitement he'd stabbed himself with the stylus.

Diotima said, "But Pericles, Nico's sworn an oath. What if we discover Timodemus did kill Arakos?"

Pericles said coldly, "Then Nicolaos must decide. Is he an investigator first, or an Athenian?"

DIOTIMA AND I walked out of Pericles's tent, out of the Athenian camp, and out of Olympia. Our path took us past the camp of the Spartans, as it had the night Arakos died. A handful of Spartans who lounged about the entrance saw me. One of them knocked another in the shoulder and pointed as we passed. I ignored them. I knew I'd become notorious; everyone had seen me take the Olympic Oath.

We went to the woods, which were quite pleasant to stroll in if you didn't think of them as a murder scene.

"What do you think?" I asked her.

"Pericles has a point," Diotima conceded. "Is it worth delivering justice for one victim if it kills thousands more?"

"I'm tempted to give in and do as he asks."

"Yet the entire thing is unethical."

The pressure to exonerate Timodemus was enough to make me shake. His father, his uncle, Pericles, and the Athenians had made clear the result they expected. What would my life be like back in Athens if he were found guilty? I'd be known for the rest of my life as the man who destroyed one of our own.

A hand pushed me in the small of my back. I stumbled against a large oak tree.

"Athenian." A voice spat the word. I turned to see five men, one of whom stood before the others. He was tall, and the muscles in his arms bulged. The other four looked tough too. None of them smiled. They had the look of men who spent their days in the sun, and to a man they looked deeply uncomfortable in civilian dress.

Spartans. These were the men we'd passed. I'd been so absorbed I hadn't even noticed them follow me. Too late I recalled Pericles's warning that the Spartans were targeting Athenians on their own. Not that I was alone, but these men would have discounted Diotima.

The five stepped smoothly, almost dance-like, to form a semicircle around us.

Diotima moved instinctively to cover my back. I was proud but worried. The last thing I wanted was her hurt.

"You're a troublemaker, Athenian. A *biased* troublemaker."

"What are you talking about?"

The leader spat on the ground, narrowly missing my foot. "Word is, you're a friend of the man who killed Arakos."

"The supposed killer," I corrected.

"The killer. You'll do whatever it takes to get him off, won't you? 'Cause he's an Athenian, and the man he killed's a Spartan, and that's what you Athenians do, isn't it? Tell lies. And cheat." All five Spartans glared at me.

"I swear to you, if I find the killer of Arakos, I'll denounce him before every man."

"Sure you will. What are you waiting for?"

"Some evidence."

"Plenty of that. Problem is, it doesn't suit you."

I was uncomfortably aware that this was close to the truth. There *was* enough to convict Timo in any Hellene court. "It's not good enough. It's not *certain*. I need to prove it could only have been Timodemus."

"We reckon you'll hold out until you can cook up something that'll get him off."

I forgot myself and stepped forward in anger. "That's a lie."

Instantly the Spartans surrounded me. One of them grabbed Diotima by the arm and flung her aside. She skidded across the rough ground. When she came to a halt, she picked herself up and ran. She ran out of the vegetation, out of the woods, and back down the path to Olympia.

Good. At least she was safe.

They pushed me, and I stumbled into the man at my right. He

pushed me back and I fell against the men on the other side. This went on so long I became dizzy. It was like a boys' ball game, but played by men and with me as the ball. If they'd done this on the grounds of Olympia, passersby would have interceded at once to stop them. But no one could see us here.

"You don't mess with the Spartans," the leader said. "And you don't cheat them either. But you're an Athenian, you always cheat, don't you?"

"He needs a lesson, Skarithos," another Spartan said.

"That he does," Skarithos agreed.

Me against five Spartans. There was only one way this could end. I might as well go down fighting. I drew in a deep breath and prepared to strike first. I hoped it wouldn't hurt too much.

"I don't think so." Markos shouldered his way past my tormentors to stand beside me.

I don't know who was more surprised, the Spartans or me. They stopped pushing.

Markos and I stood side by side, and suddenly I felt much more confident. One against five was a certain loss. Two against five was survivable, especially when the two were Markos and me.

Skarithos said, "I wouldn't have picked you for an Athenian lover, Markos."

"No, Skarithos, I love Sparta," Markos said. "And unlike you undisciplined idiots, I can follow orders. King Pleistarchus commands the investigation run its course."

"So you protect the Athenian." Skarithos spat in the dust.

"He can look out for himself. I protect Sparta."

"Step aside, Markos. Or suffer with this bastard."

Markos smiled and shook his head. "As I said, I follow orders."

"Then you'll get your lesson, too, Athenian lover."

They didn't say a word, merely circled and feinted. Sometimes one jumped to startle us, waiting for Markos or me to trip or make a mistake.

"What are you doing here?" I said to Markos out of the side of my mouth, as our enemy circled us like sharks.

"You mean you didn't send her?" he said, puzzled.

"Her?"

"Diotima. She ran straight into the Spartan camp, knocked over the guard who tried to stop her, and screamed my name. I came at once."

Markos and I turned so that we stood back-to-back. We both crouched, waiting.

"I hope you can do this," Markos said to me quietly.

"Don't worry about me," I said. "I'll still be standing when you're down."

"No, you won't, Athenian."

"Ten drachmae say I will."

"Twenty."

"Done."

None of us had weapons, or Markos and I would have been dead within heartbeats, if that was their plan.

Skarithos attacked first. He punched at my head. I dodged and kicked to the side, guessing there would be another man there. There was. My foot connected with a knee, and a man shrieked. Behind me I heard grunts of pain, and I hoped it wasn't Markos. There was a snap, and one of the Spartans screamed, "Bastard broke my wrist!"

I smiled.

That was when they all attacked at once. The two facing me grabbed an arm each.

A third man appeared, the one whom Markos had hurt. He nursed his left wrist in his right hand. He kicked, swift and hard and strong, into my balls. I screamed and my knees buckled, but I told myself I mustn't fall.

"Why don't you give up, Athenian?" Skarithos breathed in my ear, his hands tight on my forearm. "Go down, and it'll all be over."

I gasped, "And pay twenty drachmae to Markos? Never!"

I kicked both my heels against the damaged wrist of the man in front—suddenly my pinioned arms were an advantage—and my heels connected with a satisfying crunch. I could feel his bones move between my feet as I rubbed them together. He screamed and fell back. Skarithos let go to punch me hard, one-two, in the diaphragm. The other man got an arm across my throat to choke me. I was about to buckle. Desperate, I reached behind, searching for something to grab. I knew it wouldn't stop Skarithos from killing me.

A knife came out of nowhere to strike Skarithos in the side of the head.

It was Diotima. She'd returned, and she'd thrown her priestess knife with perfect accuracy. All that practice in her tent had saved me. A priestess knife is for sacrifices. It has a razor-sharp edge but no point to speak of. If it had, Skarithos might have died. As it was, the blade bounced off his skull, and he fell back.

I found what I was grappling for and twisted without mercy. The man behind screamed, and the arm across my throat disappeared. Enraged, I turned and rabbit-punched the man who'd denied me air. He dropped like a stone.

I looked around. Both the men who'd attacked Markos were down and unconscious. "What did you do to them?" I rasped through my burning throat.

Markos shrugged. "They weren't very good." He grabbed Skarithos by the shoulder. "One to go."

We both took ahold of Skarithos, whose wits had been addled by the blow from the knife. That wouldn't stop either of us from beating the stuffing out of him.

"After you," I said courteously to Markos.

"No, no, my friend. After you."

"You're too kind. Perhaps if we hit him together?"

"An excellent suggestion. On the count of three, then."

We both drew back a fist.

Markos counted, "One, two—"

"Hold!"

Markos and I looked around to see King Pleistarchus staring at us. We let go of Skarithos. He staggered back, his eyes rolled up, and he flopped to the ground.

Pleistarchus looked at the carnage. "Am I interrupting anything?" he asked.

Markos stood to attention and said, "No, Pleistarchus. Only some light exercise."

Pleistarchus stepped over the body of the unconscious Skarithos. "Always good to get in some exercise," he said with a straight face. "Keeps men fit for combat." He counted bodies. "Speaking of which," he continued, "why are you still alive?"

"Training standards aren't what they used to be, sir," Markos replied, matching the deadpan tone of his king.

"They certainly aren't if you two could stand against five of our best. These men are supposed to be officers. I'll have harsh words for them." He toed a groaning body. "When they're conscious."

"You didn't send them, King Pleistarchus?" I asked.

He looked at me in surprise. "Me? Of course not. What makes you think that?"

The demons were whispering in my ear, telling me what to say. "Because Arakos was killed by the secrets. I wondered if those secrets were yours." I didn't know what it meant. I hoped he did.

Pleistarchus turned gray. Markos stared as if I were some *psyche* he'd crossed in the night.

The Spartan king stood silent for a moment before he said, "I see. Come with me." He turned and strode off without looking back, assuming we'd follow his abrupt order. Which, of course, we did. Diotima stepped in between Markos and me. She was breathing hard, her chiton was dirty where she'd skidded across the dirt, and her hair straggled down her face, but she looked excited. I didn't think I'd ever loved her more.

"Thanks," I said to her. She gave me a smile.

Pleistarchus led us to the camp of the Spartans. He didn't stride so much as march. Men instinctively stepped out of his way, and Pleistarchus barely noticed. He went straight past the guards at the entrance—one of whom glared at Diotima—and stopped at the opened flap of his tent to motion us inside.

"No one disturbs or hears us," he ordered the guard within. The man nodded and went out. The tent was furnished with one camp bed and one travel chest. That was it. The king of Sparta traveled with less than Diotima. In one corner, a small folding table and a camp stool. Only one stool. We stood in the middle space to talk.

"Gentlemen—and lady—we have a problem," Pleistarchus said. "I find there are things I must tell you, if you are to succeed. In fact, the security of Sparta may depend upon it. You—Nicolaos?—yes, before I continue, you must swear by Zeus and Athena that you will not reveal what you hear to any man, and particularly not to any Spartan. Do you agree?"

"Yes, Pleistarchus." It meant I couldn't use what I learned as evidence before the Judges of the Games, but it might lead me to the killer. I would worry about evidence later. "May Zeus destroy me if I reveal what you tell. May Athena persecute me."

Diotima nodded. "Artemis, hear my oath," she said.

"What do you say, Markos? Can these Athenians be trusted to keep an oath?"

Markos looked at me as if I were livestock for sale. After a moment he said, "Yes, Pleistarchus, Nicolaos is an honest man. Surprisingly honest, considering the work he's in."

Pleistarchus grunted. "Whoever heard of an honest Athenian?"

"Be it so, Pleistarchus, you can trust him."

Pleistarchus shook his head and said to me, "The fact is, if you and Markos continue to blunder about as you have, if you make a mistake, it could start a war and thousands will die."

It was so similar to what Pericles had said that Diotima gasped. Pleistarchus noticed her reaction.

"The Spartans fear Athens, young lady. That's not something I'll admit in public, but the Spartans fear your democracy. If it spreads, what will happen to the Spartan way of life? Some demand war at once, before Athens becomes stronger. The ephors are among those for war. Others hold that it is none of our business, as long as Athens does nothing to upset the balance in the Peloponnese, which is ours by right of strength."

"I understand, Pleistarchus," I said, and Diotima nodded.

Pleistarchus said, "Do you Athenians know what the *hippeis* are?"

"It means 'cavalry' . . . 'knights,'" I said.

"So it does, a title of great honor. The hippeis are elite soldiers. The best of the best. In war they're our scouts, trained to act independently; in peace the hippeis are the royal bodyguard."

"Many cities have a similar system," I said, wondering why Pleistarchus told me this.

"This much all men know," he went on. "That they are scouts and bodyguards. But the knights of Sparta have a third job. One of great importance."

"*A third job?* Don't these people have lives?"

"No. Combine the first two tasks and what do you get?"

"I have no idea."

"In war the knights gather information about the enemy. In peace they guard the state."

Diotima said, in surprise, "Men who gather information to protect the state!"

Pleistarchus nodded. "The knights are Sparta's security service." He paused. "Markos is one of their best."

Which made Markos the best of the best of the best. Suddenly I felt less confident of victory.

Markos smiled at me. "Surely this is no surprise, Nico. My job is much the same as yours. I wager we have the same skills and the same expertise."

Except I was a sole individual, with little or no support and no official position, forced to live by my wits and reliant on the largesse of Pericles. I noticed King Pleistarchus showed not the slightest surprise at Markos's revelation about my own profession. Obviously Markos had reported on me to King Pleistarchus.

Pleistarchus continued, "Now as to what I'm about to tell you . . . you have sworn never to reveal. Not under any circumstances."

"Then why tell us?"

"Because if I don't, you will probably die."

It sounded like a good reason to me.

"Within Sparta there is a tradition—closely kept—which we call the *krypteia*."

"The 'secrets'?"

"Just so. The *krypteia* is a rite of passage for Sparta's most promising young men from across the entire army, the ones likely to become officers. They're sent alone into the countryside with only a dagger, no food or water, and orders to survive without being caught."

"What if they're caught?"

"The failures are beaten to within an inch of their lives. There's no place in our officer class for losers."

That made my own army training look like a picnic.

Pleistarchus said, "Each young man is required to kill a few of our slaves, the people we call helots. It's our way of getting the young men used to killing before they have to do it much more dangerously on a battlefield."

I looked to Markos in astonishment. "You did this? You murdered a helot *for practice*?"

Markos shrugged. "It's what we do."

"But—"

"It's not murder," Pleistarchus said. "Every year, at their inauguration, the ephors declare war on our own helots, so that it's legal to kill them at any time."

"Oh, well! That's all right then!"

"It's been this way for centuries, Nico," Markos consoled me. "If it makes you feel better, we only target the troublemakers who would have gotten themselves killed sooner or later anyway."

Pleistarchus went on, "A few of the young men, the ones who demonstrate unusual aptitude at the helot-killing part of the test, and who are judged to possess the personality to match, are recruited by the ephors to join a secret organization of the same name: the krypteia, the Secrets. When something unsavory has to be done for the good of the state, the ephors turn to the krypteia. Like the hippeis, the krypteia serves the state, but where the hippeis exists to secure the state in the light of day, the krypteia works in the dark to . . . er . . ."

"Eliminate problems?" I suggested.

"Just so. I don't understand what's happening, Nicolaos son of Sophroniscus, but when you tell me 'the secrets' killed Arakos, you are probably thinking of hidden information. But it might mean something quite different."

I asked, "Does Arakos have anything to do with this?"

Markos said smoothly, "Arakos was neither a knight nor, as far as we know, a member of the krypteia. He was just a big oaf who was good at hitting people."

"Markos is offensive but correct," Pleistarchus said. "Arakos was an outstanding if slightly dimwitted warrior—a fine man in the ranks, but not officer material. Now he's become an excuse for war for those who want it. If there's any danger of you exonerating the Athenian, it will be cause for war."

So if I saved Timo, who was only one man, then many thousands of men might die in battle. Terrific.

Diotima said to King Pleistarchus, "Why don't you simply ask this krypteia organization if they're involved? And if they've acted without orders, why can't you simply order the krypteia to stop whatever they're doing?"

"The krypteia wouldn't obey me, even if I knew who they were."

"You don't know?"

"As I command the hippeis, so the ephors command the krypteia. They're entirely different units within Sparta. Only the ephors know the members of the krypteia. I won't risk open conflict with the ephors, neither here at Olympia nor back in Sparta. When you three walk out of this tent, you're on your own."

"Are Skarithos and his friends krypteia?"

Markos said, "I should hope the ephors have better taste than that. But who knows?"

"Surely, Pleistarchus," I said, "the ephors would not dare challenge the authority of the kings?"

Pleistarchus snorted. "This wouldn't be the first time the ephors have acted against the kings. Why, my own grandsire . . ." He trailed off.

Diotima said, "King Pleistarchus, would a Spartan assassin really kill another Spartan, and if so, why? This is hard to believe."

"Then I must take you to someone who will convince you, someone who, frankly, I'd rather avoid."

"Who's that, sir?"

Pleistarchus shuddered. "My mother."

PLEISTARCHUS DEPARTED TO arrange the interview.

I said, "Quick, Markos, what do you know about Queen Gorgo?"

"Daughter of one king, wife to another, mother to a third," he replied. "Gorgo's been the power behind the kings of Sparta for three generations. They say she's the smartest woman in Hellas."

"A likely story," sniffed Diotima, who had her own pretensions in that area. "They always make these claims about royalty."

"Well, you're about to have your chance to find out," Markos told her.

A guard came, and we were escorted, Diotima, Markos, and I, to the tent of Queen Gorgo, in the very center of the camp.

I would never have guessed the tent contained royalty, for it looked like any other. The dowager queen of Sparta sat within upon a hard wooden chair, the only concession to comfort an upright back. A guard stood at attention behind her, and it wasn't merely for show; the man looked ready to kill the slightest threat.

Gorgo was so thin I could count her bones. Her hair was tied back and gray, which exposed the outline of her skull. The image was accentuated by perfect teeth that seemed too large for the rest of her. Her hands were like the claws of a bird. Her dark eyes had the look of an alert and merciless eagle.

Gorgo noticed me, and I felt like some bug crawling underfoot.

She said, "So you're the ones they say are causing so much trouble."

I waited for Markos to defend us, but when he stood silent I replied, "I think the one causing the trouble, Queen Gorgo, is the man who murdered Arakos."

"No need to get uppity with me, young man. I said that's what people in Olympia are saying. I didn't say I agreed. My son tells me you need to know about the krypteia."

"We asked the question," I said. "An anonymous note claims secrets killed Arakos. Pleistarchus thinks it might refer to the Spartan krypteia, but there are other interpretations. Would the krypteia really murder one of their own citizens? And if so, why? Especially since, except for his ability to fight, there was nothing special about Arakos."

"Nothing special," Gorgo repeated, then said, "There's one thing about Arakos, but I cannot conceive of it as a motive for murder. Did you know that the father of Arakos was one of the Three Hundred?"

"Markos told me."

"His father fought and died at the gates of Thermopylae, alongside my husband Leonidas. After the war, I personally made sure that the children of the Three Hundred were cared for. If anyone harms a child of the Three Hundred, it's as if they harmed my own. You understand?"

"Yes, Queen Gorgo."

"Tell me what you know."

I did. It was the first chance I'd had to explain to Markos the anonymous note on the ostrakon and its strange message. He exclaimed when he heard it.

I finished by saying, "And so we want to learn whatever we can of this krypteia."

"I see." Gorgo was silent for a long moment. Then she said, "There's a family history . . ."

"Yes?"

"My father, Cleomenes, was king of Sparta. My father—how shall I put this delicately?—my father went stark raving mad."

"That's delicate?" I asked the Queen of Sparta.

"I'm known for speaking my mind."

"Insanity is sent by the Gods," Diotima pointed out. "Usually to punish."

The Dowager Queen examined Diotima head to foot, like an officer examines a soldier. "You are?"

"I am Diotima of Mantinea." Diotima lifted her chin proudly.

"Your accent says you're Athenian."

"Yes, Gorgo. I go by the name of my mother's city." I could tell Diotima was favorably impressed by the way she stood a little straighter, as she would before a high priestess.

Gorgo said, "You're right, Diotima of Mantinea. Insanity is the curse of the Gods. In my father's case, in the war against the Argives, he dragged prisoners from a temple sanctuary and cut them to pieces."

I winced. "That would do it." To abuse temple sanctuary is almost the greatest crime there is.

"So the Gods cursed my father, and his condition worsened until the family had no choice but to put him in chains. Can you imagine the shame? A king of Sparta in chains? Then, one day soon thereafter, they found him dead." Gorgo sat up even straighter, if that were possible.

"The official story is that, while still chained in his cell, my father obtained a knife from the helot who was set to guard him. My father used the knife to skin himself alive, beginning at the shins, and laid his own flesh in strips beside him, all the way to his thighs. When he was finished there was only the meat and muscles and veins. The feet he left. I don't know why. It made the sight all the more horrific, to see those normal feet at the end of legs with the meat hanging off." Gorgo shuddered, her first sign of humanity.

"Then he started on his groin. I won't tell you what he did to himself there. He died as he sliced the last of the skin from his stomach."

"This is terrible," said Diotima, truly shocked.

"The moronic guard claimed my father had threatened him if he didn't hand over the knife. I didn't believe his story. I insisted the fool be executed."

"You said that was the *official* story," I prompted.

"Your stress on the word is correct. My father was mad, I don't deny it, but he wasn't insane enough to strip the flesh of his body with his own hands. My father's condition was an embarrass-ment to the Spartans." Gorgo waved an arm, almost dismissively. "Something had to be done. I suspect something was done. I have no proof, but I believe he was killed and the death purported to be his own act. The krypteia are the natural suspects. You asked if the krypteia could kill a Spartan. They could. They'd even dare to murder a king."

I said, "None of this explains why the ephors or the krypteia would target Arakos. The motive escapes me."

Gorgo laughed, without the slightest trace of humor. "You're the ones who asked the question. It may be, as you suggest, that these secrets are not Spartan ones. Arakos spent an unusually long time on his own, out of Sparta, on account of his athletic prowess." She thought for a moment, then said, "I don't know if it's relevant, but I talked to him last year, after the Games at Nemea."

"Yes?"

"He was very unhappy with the result. Well, who wouldn't be? He came in second."

"Second's better than last," I said.

"In a war, second *is* last, and Spartans don't raise losers. Arakos seemed to think there'd been cheating. I put it down to anger at losing."

"Thank you for telling us this," I said.

"There's no requirement to thank me. I do this purely out of self-interest." Her expression didn't change as she added, "I'm an ill woman; soon I will depart for Hades, and there's no telling what those idiot men will do without me to guide them. I need to engineer a period of peace while I still can, but this investigation threatens to destabilize all of Hellas. I need you to find a solution that gives me a chance to keep people calm."

That seemed to be what everyone wanted. The problem was, everyone disagreed on what constituted the right solution.

"And if we find Timodemus did kill Arakos?" Diotima asked. "What will you do then, Queen Gorgo?"

"Cheer on my men as they lay waste to Attica."

I nodded automatically. This was the wife of Leonidas, who had led the Three Hundred. She had watched and waved to her own husband as he marched off on a suicide mission. The Queen of Sparta would do whatever had to be done.

"Are there any of these krypteia at Olympia?" Diotima asked.

"If there are, I'll discover it and let you know."

"How?" Markos asked. He probably thought that if he couldn't find the answer, then no woman could, not even a queen.

"I have my sources, young man, and they're not for you to question."

Markos bowed his head.

"The head man at Athens, who is it these days?" Gorgo asked.

"Athens is a democracy," I said at once. "We're *all* the head man. No one's vote counts for more than anyone else's, no one can tell us what to do, and we share the decisions."

"Don't give me that rubbish," said Gorgo. "I was doing power politics when you sucked on your mother's teats." Diotima stifled a laugh. "Now, tell me who leads Athens."

"Pericles," I said, reluctant to admit it to an outsider.

"I'd heard the same," Gorgo said. "The son of Xanthippus, isn't he?"

"Yes."

"I know Xanthippus. Not as great a man as my late husband, of course, but a good man. He would have made a reasonable Spartan. Tell me, is the son like the father?"

"Pericles?" I was nonplussed for a moment. How would one describe Pericles? "When Pericles talks, people listen."

Gorgo grimaced. "I know the type. I wager he's untrust-worthy."

"Er . . ."

"That's the problem with these elected rulers," Gorgo said. "They always make short-term decisions to make themselves look good. The ephors are the same. Now if Athens had a king to run things, no one would be under pressure to get re-elected, and the people could be ruled well for the long term."

"What if the king's not too bright?" I objected.

"Then they listen to me. I've advised the Spartans since I was eight years old."

"*Eight*? The Spartans listened to *a child*?" I couldn't believe it. "What could an eight-year-old possibly have to say?"

She smiled grimly, but answered in a matter-of-fact tone, "I advised my father, the king, not to invade Persia, which he was considering. It was my first move into foreign policy. One of my better decisions, too, if I may say."

"I'm impressed, Queen Gorgo," Diotima said. "For all your

life, the Spartans have followed your advice, while I, who live in a democracy, have no chance of being listened to. How is that you Spartan women are the only ones who can rule men?"

Gorgo turned her eagle eyes on my wife. "It's because we're the only ones who give birth to real men."

Diotima looked Gorgo in the eye. "We'll see about that," she said.

There was nothing more to say. We turned to depart.

"Athenian!"

I stopped. "Yes, Queen Gorgo?"

"I like your woman. Bring her back sometime."

MARKOS SAID HE had things to attend to at the Spartan camp. Diotima went to look for Socrates, whom she'd volunteered to keep an eye on and then neglected. A child was safe enough at Olympia, but she thought she'd better at least confirm he was still alive. I went straight to Pindar. Whatever had happened at Nemea, it was clear we needed to know about it.

Pindar was easy to find, because the afternoon of the second day is reserved for religious rites. I found him in the Sanctuary of Zeus, where he stood upon an unoccupied stone pedestal and declaimed poetry. He might have been a statue himself, the way he stood with his back straight and clutched the front of his formal chiton in a dignified manner.

A small group of men and women had clustered about.

He saw me but ignored my hand waves to come down.

". . . Not every truth is the better for showing its face undisguised . . ."

I waved so frantically that a respectable woman beside me thought I was a madman and stepped away. It had no effect on Pindar.

". . . and often silence is the wisest thing for a man to—whoa!"

I dragged him off his pedestal.

"My apologies, everyone," I told the crowd. "The great Pindar has been summoned." A few muttered, but there were plenty of other attractions, and the people moved on.

"Summoned by whom?" Pindar demanded. "If it's anyone less than a head of state, the Furies will be as nothing compared to my wrath—"

"We need to talk," I said. "I need information."

"You? You dragged me away for *you*?" I led him by the arm. "Where are you taking me?"

"Do you like to drink?" I asked.

"I'm a poet."

"I'll take that as a yes."

We stopped at the nearest wine cart. Olympia was dotted with the things. They wheeled in at first light, sold wine by the cup at amphora prices, then disappeared when it was too dark to count the coins.

"What's your best wine?" I asked the man behind the cart. He was dark and covered in warts. From the way he wobbled and his eyes glazed over, I guessed he'd been at his own wares.

"Got some from Lampsacus lying around," he slurred. "Lampsacus is in Ionia," he added helpfully.

"Yes, I know." I bought the wine and didn't worry about the cost. If Pericles and Pleistarchus were both so desperate to avoid a war, one or the other of them could fund me for a few cups of wine. Pindar followed me while I carried a cup in each hand to the shade beside the Heraion, the Temple of Hera. We sat on a bench that was, miraculously, unoccupied.

I said, "Pindar, I have a question for you. Gorgo says that, straight after the competition at Nemea last year, Arakos complained to her. He said there were irregularities. One-Eye told me to ignore rumors before I'd even heard them. This has come up too many times now. What really happened?"

Pindar fixated on only one point. "Gorgo?" he said. "Queen Gorgo's at Olympia? I had no idea. You want to avoid Gorgo, Nicolaos. She knows people who kill people. Lots of them."

"You're too late," I told him. "We've already spoken to her.

She seems quite nice, once you get past her innate feelings of total superiority."

He rubbed his chin. "Her feelings are well founded. I do have great regard for both her and her glorious husband. I viewed the battlefield, you know, before the bodies were buried. I never saw such carnage before or since, but one thing I can tell you: every Spartan who died sent a hundred Persians to Hades before him."

There was something I'd always wondered about that most famous of last stands. "Tell me, Pindar, is it true you wrote the epitaph for the Three Hundred? 'Passerby, go tell the Spartans that here, according to their law, we lie.'"

They were the best-known lines of poetry in the world, but no one who'd been present when the memorial stone was raised had ever claimed the credit.

"I'm not going to talk about that," Pindar said without hesitation. "The late, great Simonides and I were both on the mission to praise the fallen. We agreed the deeds of the heroes were greater than the words of any poet and swore never to reveal the author. It might not even have been either of us; other poets were there too."

The way he said it, I knew this was a rehearsed line that he'd repeated many times. I wasn't surprised. *Everyone* wanted to know who wrote those lines. It told me something else about Pindar: for all his massive ego, the man was a patriot.

"Gorgo's contribution to the war was as great as her husband's," Pindar said. "When the Persians gathered their army to invade, a Spartan then exiled in Persia sent us a warning. The Persians would have stopped him, so he had to write in secret. He scratched his invasion alert on the backing board of a wax tablet, which he covered over with fresh wax, and then sent it home. When an apparently blank tablet arrived in Sparta, none of Sparta's so-called wise leaders understood the meaning. They took it to Gorgo. She deduced at once that there must be a secret message, ordered the wax removed, and so read the warning to prepare for war. We'd all be Persian slaves today if it weren't for her clever deduction."

"Let's get back to the unpleasantness at the Nemean Games," I said.

"Why ask me?" he evaded.

"Because you're the one who first mentioned it. Just before the chariot race," I said.

"You'll have to ask the ones involved."

"Nothing escapes the eyes of the famous Pindar," I wheedled. A little flattery wouldn't hurt to deal with a man with an ego the size of Pindar's. "I need to see through your eyes, brilliant Pindar, because you see what other men miss. Surely the greatest poet since Homer would notice the subtle relationships between men: who hated whom, who was jealous, who was plotting. Come on, Pindar, greatest of bards, tell me what *really* happened."

"Good Gods, man, are you trying to butter me up?" His tone was angry.

"Er . . . yes."

"Listen, flattery will get you nowhere with me. I lay it on thick with honeyed words better than any man alive. I could teach you tricks of sycophancy that would make your eyes water. What do you think it means to be a *praise singer*?" Pindar stood and drew himself up to his full height to announce, "I, Nicolaos, am a *professional* flatterer." He sat down again. "So don't try to cozen me with your amateur efforts. It would be like attacking a well-armed Spartan with a blunt knife." He looked me up and down before adding, "A *very* blunt knife."

Pindar drained the cup. Again. It was my plan to loosen his tongue with wine, but I was starting to wonder how many amphorae it would take. I took the cup from his hands without a word so I could be ripped off by the wine seller for a third time. "I hope you're sober enough to answer questions," I said when I returned.

"You asked about Nemea." He burped. "Your friend Timodemus had an easy run to the final." He paused, no doubt for dramatic effect. "A *remarkably* easy run. Every single man Timodemus faced, he disposed of in short order."

"Timo's good."

"No one's that good. Pretty soon everyone noticed that all the other bouts were fiercely fought, but against Timodemus, it was as if his opponents lay down for him like weak women. I wasn't the only one to notice. Accusations were made, of cheating."

Cheating happened. Men didn't like to talk about it, but sometimes two pankratists would arrange a result in advance. Then money would change hands.

Pindar continued, "The judges of those Games looked into it. The only problem was, if he'd bribed his opponents to take a fall, then *every single man* must have been involved."

"Were they?"

"Every one of them stood before the altar of Zeus at Nemea and swore there'd been no arrangement. In truth it's hard to see how Timodemus could have suborned *everyone*. The judges decided there'd been no bribery. They swore every man present to secrecy that the question had ever arisen."

"Then how come you know about it?"

"I was present at the swearing, as a witness. The judges wanted someone who could report later that all had been done according to the law."

Pindar had begun the conversation with the claim he hadn't been involved. I decided not to point out his obvious lie. Perhaps it was an attempt to be discreet, as his position required.

Pindar said, "The judges concluded that collusion was impossible, but no, that wasn't the end of the matter. There was another explanation."

"What was it?"

"Witchcraft."

"NICO, DO YOU think it could be true?" Diotima asked.

I found Socrates and Diotima at her tent, where we'd agreed

to rendezvous. She'd searched for my errant brother and bought sweet cakes along the way. He'd been willing to go with her because, as he put it, "The chariots were fantastic, but not enough people get killed in the athletics."

Now we nibbled on the cakes and discussed the revelation that Timodemus really might have cheated. To curse an enemy is so simple and easy, anyone could do it.

"I don't know," I said, glum. "A few days ago I would have laughed. Now, I'm not so sure."

"I'm sorry." She put a hand on my arm. This was why a man wanted a wife, for comfort. "There were too many good reasons for Timodemus to kill Arakos," she said. "To silence his taunts, to silence his accusation that Timo cheated, or maybe even . . . to cheat."

I winced.

"I know he's your friend, Nico, but I have to tell you—"

"Yes, I know. Three days from now I'll stand before the judges to condemn my own friend. Did I tell you, by the way, One-Eye demanded I bring the trial *forward*?"

"The man must be mad."

"Merely willing to sacrifice his own son to reflect in Olympic glory. Diotima, you're a priestess—this tale of witchcraft . . . is it possible?"

"Oh, Nico, priests and priestesses don't do magic!"

"Magic is different?"

"Completely. Utterly. If a hundred people want to honor the Gods together, then someone has to perform the sacrifice, *someone* has to say the prayers, *someone* has to pour the libations and clothe the statue. They can't all do it, so the priestess does it for them. That's all being a priestess means, when you get down to it. But curse magic, that's asking the Gods to hurt someone to your advantage."

"How?"

"The curse is always written on a tablet."

"Pindar didn't say anything about curse tablets. Where would you look for one?"

"Down a well. Most curses invoke Hades, Lord of the Underworld, to do something nasty to the victim. The closer you can get the curse, to Hades, the more likely the God is to read it. Most people scratch it on a strip of lead."

"That must be bad for the well."

"It's only lead; it can't hurt you. Also, if you hire a professional to write your curse it has more chance of working."

Did Timo know any magicians? "You said anyone could write a curse tablet."

"True, but a professional magician knows what to write and how. Magic is all about persuasion. No one can coerce the Gods, no matter what some charlatans claim. Mortals can only ask and hope the Gods feel charitable that day. Does Timodemus know any magicians?"

"I have no idea. I doubt it. If he *has* been writing curses, what would they say?"

Diotima picked up her wax tablet and scratched some words, which she handed to me.

I call upon Hades, he who rules in the land of the dead, to whom all men must go, to bind my opponent Arakos in the pankration. May his arms grow weak. May his strength wane. May his hands fail to grasp. May his legs grow heavy and his knees fail. Do this for me, mighty Hades, Lord of the Dead, so that Arakos loses miserably and I am victor in the contest.

I put it down in shock. "This really is cheating."

"Timodemus would write one of these before each fight," Diotima said. "He'd name his opponent and say what he wants to have happen."

"Why not write one generic curse? *May all my opponents lose.* Something like that."

"Because it's very unlikely to work. The Gods need a name to work with. If you wrote something like *please make me rich*, would you expect wealth to arrive at your door?"

"No."

"Right. It's too general. You're asking the Gods to do your thinking for you. The Gods aren't nannies looking out for us. But if you said, *please Poseidon, make sure my merchant ship makes it to Chios this trip*, then you're in with a chance. He may or may not do it, but at least Poseidon knows *exactly* what you want."

"I see. If the priests and priestesses don't do magic, how do you come to know all this?"

"People beg priests and priestesses for an effective curse all the time. You're not the only one to make the confusion. After a while I became interested and looked into it. You know how it is."

With Diotima I certainly did. She absorbed knowledge like a sponge.

She went on, "But this can't be the answer, Nico. Arakos didn't lose in a contest; he died in a forest."

In fact, if Timo had cursed Arakos, then he wouldn't have needed to kill him. I said, "Strange as it may sound, if we can prove Timo cheated, then it might just save his life. Let's say Timodemus cursed Arakos. Where would he put the tablet here in Olympia?"

"There's no well. Everyone gets their water from the river."

"In the river, then?"

"Too shallow and too easy to see."

"Dig a hole?"

"Wouldn't that be obvious?"

"Dig a hole in the woods?"

"If he did, we'll never find it."

I nodded glumly. "If we can't find the tablet, it means nothing; merely that we couldn't find it."

"Of course, you don't have to find the tablet," said Socrates. He'd been uncharacteristically quiet.

"What do you mean?" I demanded. "Of course we do."

"But Nico, if Timodemus planned to curse his opponents, doesn't he need a lead strip for each one?" Socrates said.

"Diotima said so. All you have to do is search his tent for the other lead strips."

Diotima and I looked at each other in despair.

"I hate it when he's right," she said.

WE BURGLED THE tent of my best friend at once while the Games were in full swing and there were few around to see us. If Timodemus had belonged to any other city, it would have been a problem—strangers walk into an empty tent, questions are asked—but Timo was Athenian, and the men of the neighboring tents had seen me before. We didn't even have to sneak in Diotima. It was forbidden for women to view the contests, but the tent camp was fair game.

We left Socrates on guard outside—I ignored his bitter protests—and went in.

There was a camp table in the middle, the kind an officer might take with him on campaign. A camp bed lay along the far side. I tested it. Quality stuff, well strapped, and made of solid wood. This thing was heavy. How did they transport it? Ah yes, that explained the long line of donkeys tethered outside.

The tent seemed extraordinarily well appointed. Because he traveled to so many contests, he lived under canvas more often than any man but a military officer. He needed the comforts to keep his body in condition. Though I'd known him all my life, I'd never thought of this before, and Timodemus didn't like to talk about himself.

Diotima had unrolled a bundle of papyrus sheets on the small table, using her palms to prevent the sheets from curling. She frowned as she read.

"What do you have there?" I asked.

"Love poetry," Diotima said.

"Timo reads *love poetry*?" I said, aghast.

"I don't know about reading, but he certainly writes it." She looked up at me. "And it's very, very bad."

"Give it to me," I said, intensely curious to see what my best friend had written. I grabbed the pages.

"No!" Diotima snatched them back before I could see a word. "I can't let you do that, Nico. It's personal."

"Then how come you're reading it?"

"That's different; I'm a woman."

There were no curse tablets, nor strips of lead, nor an engraving tool to inscribe into the lead we didn't find. There wasn't even anything to write with.

"This is awful," Diotima said. "I was so sure we were on the right track."

"I'm relieved," I admitted. If Timodemus had been practicing witchcraft, what would I have done?

Diotima understood. She hugged me. "Timodemus might have hidden his curse equipment somewhere else," she said.

"In this crowded place?"

"Buried it in the woods, maybe? What do we do now?"

I said, "I want to look into the tent next door." Where One-Eye and Festianos slept.

"Why?" Diotima was puzzled.

"There's a demon on my shoulder, whispering in my ear."

The tent of Timo's father and uncle was barely furnished. Two camp stools. Two camp beds. Two traveling chests, pushed together in the center of the space to make a table.

"Where are the books?" Diotima asked at once, perplexed. The tent was far too utilitarian for her taste.

"I don't think they're the reading sort."

Diotima looked at me as if such a thing was beyond her comprehension. Which it was. For her, the marks that men made were a gift of the Gods, and only the sacrilegious ignored them. Diotima was one of the few women who could read; she read so often she could even do it without having to say the words out loud or move her lips, a level of expertise few men ever achieved.

I opened one of the chests, Diotima the other. Within mine

were jars of ointments, leather gloves like the ones used in boxing and for practice, spare clothing, expensive and well used.

"I'll bet this belongs to One-Eye," I said.

Diotima rummaged through hers. "Nico, I've found a wooden case." She pulled out a box, wide, deep, and flat. The sort of thing in which you might carry paper-writing tools. It was the right size. She hefted it. "It's too heavy to hold papyrus," she said, following the same thoughts. "In fact," she said, and gave me a meaningful look, "it's heavy enough to contain lead." She jiggled the box. Something inside rattled.

"Open it!"

Diotima pressed on the lid, but it wouldn't open. "There's a catch."

I tried to take it from her, but she pulled it close to her chest. "Oh no, you don't. Finders keepers." She ran her fingers around the edge, probing. "Ah." She pushed a tiny lever. I heard a click within. Diotima slowly lifted the lid while I crowded close to see over her shoulder.

Lying within, in neat rows, were vials. They were ceramic, in a nondescript red with no decoration, and each stoppered tightly.

"What are they?" I asked.

Diotima picked one up and—keeping her thumb over the stopper—she shook it.

Something sloshed. She removed the stopper.

"Careful," I warned her.

Diotima took a gentle sniff, then a longer one. She screwed up her face in distaste.

"What is it?" I asked.

"I'm not sure," she said, "but I think this is hemlock."

WE HURRIED BACK to the closest private place—my own tent—with the evidence in hand and pulled the flap closed behind us so we could inspect the booty. Diotima had developed a new theory: that Arakos had been fed hemlock.

"All right," I said. "Tell me how Uncle Festianos persuaded Arakos to drink it. You think Festianos went up to Arakos the Spartan and said, 'Here, old chap, there's hemlock in this cup. Quaff it off like a good chap, would you now?' I don't think so. We don't even know for sure this is truly hemlock."

"I'm sure it is, Nico," said Diotima. "Everyone knows hemlock tastes like a dead mouse."

"Do they? How could anyone know such a thing?" I demanded.

"Well, it doesn't kill at once," Diotima said. "Anyone who's been executed with it could tell you before he expired."

"Have you ever spoken to a man dying of hemlock?" I asked.

"No."

"I could try it and see," offered Socrates. He picked up the poison.

"Don't be stupid, Socrates," I said. I snatched the vial from his hand. "You're not to go anywhere near hemlock, you hear me?"

"Yes, Nico."

Diotima said, "There are doctors who use hemlock to treat patients with aching joints."

"Don't the patients die?"

"I didn't say they were *good* doctors."

"So these vials might be—"

"Medicine."

"Then the whole thing could be totally innocent. How do we know if the dose in the vials is fatal or therapeutic?" I asked.

"A doctor could tell us if this is medicine," Diotima said. "But where will we find a doctor?"

I smiled. "Leave that to me," I said. "I know just the man."

"YES, I REMEMBER you," said Heraclides of Kos. "You were in the tent when I operated on the chariot driver."

"What happened to him?"

"He's still alive."

"I'm pleased."

"So am I. There's more chance I can squeeze my fee out of his father. What can I do to help you?"

Diotima, Socrates, and I sat before him on three folding stools in his expansive tent. Heraclides himself sat on a chair.

He was a man in his prime years, strong and healthy looking. I supposed that was important for a doctor. Who'd trust a physician who couldn't keep himself healthy? The most unusual aspect about Heraclides the doctor was the writhing, squirming thing on his lap that he struggled to contain.

"Is that a baby?" I asked.

"Clever of you to notice. I see you have the makings of a doctor. This is my son." Heraclides smiled proudly. "My wife left me to amuse him while she went to the agora." He jiggled the creature up and down and cooed. It was obvious Heraclides was more than happy to entertain his son.

"We need to consult you," I said to him, in an attempt to keep his attention.

"Is one of you ill?" Heraclides held the baby's tiny hands, wiggled them back and forth, and went, "Coo—coo—coo—"

"We aren't ill, Heraclides," I said, wondering if there might be another doctor in the camp city.

"Your wife is pregnant, then."

"The Gods forefend!" Diotima interjected.

Heraclides turned to her. "I'm afraid the Gods are usually uncooperative on that score," he said.

"I'm not pregnant," Diotima said with finality.

"In fact we only have some questions for you," I said.

"Questions count for the usual consultation fee," he said at once.

I said, "Oh, of course, being a doctor, your only concern is—"

"The health and welfare of your patients," Diotima broke in. "How much for your wise and knowledgeable advice, worthy Heraclides?" she asked smoothly.

"Twenty drachmae for the consultation."

"Agreed," I choked, and hoped One-Eye would pay. After all, we were doing this to save the life of his son, whose brains might soon be dashed out on the rocks of Mount Typaeum. If that didn't count for a medical emergency, I didn't know what would.

"We have this vial, Heraclides," I said. We had brought it along inside a canvas bag to conceal the evidence. I pulled it out to show him. "Is this hemlock? And if so, is it strong enough to kill someone?"

Heraclides threw the baby into the air and caught him with practiced confidence. The baby giggled and smiled. Heraclides threw the baby again, so high he almost bounced off the canvas roof.

"Is that good for him?" I asked.

"Perfectly," Heraclides said. "Babies enjoy the sensation of flying. It's because the throw takes the baby closer to Apollo, who is a god of healing and health. The theory's perfectly sound, I assure you. Why do you ask?"

"My mother says babies shouldn't be tossed in the air."

"An old wives' tale."

"My mother's a midwife," I told him.

"Is she now? In that case, here, hold the baby for a moment, would you?" Heraclides passed the child over as if it was the most natural thing in the world to hold a baby. I put my hands out by reflex, without a chance to object. I'd never held a baby before in my life.

The baby immediately tried to crawl off my lap.

I was afraid he'd fall and hit his head on the ground and die. I held on tighter. The baby cried at once. I was suddenly afraid I'd hurt the thing and relaxed my grip. The baby fell off my lap.

"Whoa!" I grabbed him as he fell.

Diotima laughed at me.

"Here, Diotima, play with this baby, would you?" I dumped the baby in her lap before she could object.

Diotima, being a woman, knew exactly what to do with it.

"Here, Socrates," she said, passing over the child. "Play with this baby, would you?"

"How come I'm the one left holding the baby?" he whined.

"Because I'm bigger than you are," Diotima said coolly.

"Then how come Nico dumped it on you?"

"Because he's bigger than me," Diotima said, delivering an important lesson in power politics.

"He vomited on me!" Socrates said.

"Babies do that," Heraclides said absently as he searched through a leather case full of scrolls. "He'll be all right. Cute, isn't he?" Heraclides pulled out a scroll and began to read. "Ah, yes."

"What are you doing?" I asked.

"I'm just reminding myself about hemlock. I myself don't usually prescribe it. Those who do use it to treat severe pain in the joints and uncontrollable tremors."

He took the vial from my hands and held it close to his eyes.

"What makes you think this contains hemlock?" he asked.

"The smell," Diotima said.

"This vial is of a type used by doctors to contain medicine. It might be a prescribed dose." Heraclides opened the stopper and took the lightest sniff. He made a face and put back the stopper. "It's hemlock, all right." He rummaged once more through the scroll jar beside him. He pulled one out and unrolled it. "Ah yes. The normal dose for medicinal use is one leaf, two at most."

"What would be a fatal dose?" Diotima asked.

"Six leaves, according to the authorities. I can't say of my own knowledge. A man taking hemlock to kill himself will typically make sure of it by taking much more, ten or twelve leaves. The roots and berries are more toxic than the leaves."

"How long would it take to kill a man?" I asked.

Heraclides shrugged. "It's highly variable. A man who drank a cup of the potion and then exercised vigorously might die quite quickly. But a large man who lay still could take as much as half a day."

"But a man wouldn't drop dead on the spot?"

"No."

"Can you tell the dose in these vials?"

"Do you have a spare dog you don't want?"

"No."

"Then you're out of luck. The only way is to try it."

"Let's say this is medicine, a leaf per dose," I said. "Does that mean if I drink six vials in a row that I've taken a fatal dose?"

"Yes. Don't do it."

Diotima asked, "What should a man do, if he accidentally takes a fatal dose?"

"Say farewell to his friends."

"There's no cure?"

"There are things you can try. I once had to."

"To save a man from hemlock?"

"It was back at my home on Kos, where I have some small renown for my skills. I had only sat down to supper, when the door of my house crashed open and a wild-eyed fellow ran in, a young man, he could not have been more than thirty. He barged into my courtyard before the house slave could even announce him, fell upon his knees, and begged me to save his sire. It seemed his aged father had decided to end it all with an infusion of hemlock. The practice is well established on the islands—traditional even—the man who has chosen to die eats a final meal in pleasant surroundings, says farewell to his friends and family, makes any last bequests, and then downs the cup of hemlock. All perfectly reasonable."

"Of course." The practice is illegal in Athens, where to commit suicide is considered a crime against the state, but I knew some of the islands preserved the ancient custom.

Heraclides said, "Do you know what the bloody fool did then? He changed his mind. There he was, surrounded by his family, his son at his side. He'd drunk the infusion to send him peacefully to Hades, and *then* he gets scared. He started to cry and grabbed his son by the hands and begged his son to save him. He behaves in this cowardly fashion before his friends."

"Oh dear."

"Indeed. It must have been a pitiful spectacle, and it put the poor son in a dreadful position. If he refused to help his father, he'd risk the curse of the Gods, but if he tried in good faith and failed, men might have wondered if the son had helped along the father for his inheritance. I should add this fool was a wealthy one."

"Tricky. So the son ran to you," said Diotima.

"Sensible of him. If *I* killed the old man, no guilt attached."

"What did you do?"

"Tripled my fee at once. Then I induced vomiting, to remove as much of the poison as I could. It's the nature of hemlock that it's a relatively slow death. Unfortunately considerable time had passed before I was called. The patient had already lost feeling in his feet, which meant much of the poison had already entered his body."

"Is that normal?"

"That's how death proceeds. The patient loses all feeling in his feet, then his legs. The lack of sensation progresses upward until it reaches the heart, which stops."

"I see."

"That's why I never prescribe hemlock. It is much, much too easy to make a mistake." He held up the scroll. "But I must say it's unlikely anyone would accidentally take too much. The taste is distinctive."

"What if it were mixed in wine?" Diotima asked.

Heraclides thought about that for a moment. "Possible," he conceded. "Especially if the wine has been made with fenugreek. The fenugreek would mask the taste."

Most Hellene wine has fenugreek added.

"But I doubt a fatal dose could be hidden that way," Heraclides finished.

"What about a succession of nonfatal doses?" Diotima asked.

"That's possible. But there'd be no lasting effect."

"What are you getting at, Diotima?" I asked.

"The vials are small," she said to me.

"All right, but this can't be how Arakos died," I said. "We've gone down the wrong path."

Diotima asked, "Is there some way to tell if a man has died of hemlock poisoning?"

"None, once he's dead. It's indistinguishable from death by natural causes."

"There'd be no sign at all?"

"Well, the aroma of the hemlock might remain in the mouth. But that's not a medical sign."

Diotima said, "Heraclides, would you come with us to the body of Arakos? I'd like your opinion on how he died."

Heraclides looked at Diotima as if she'd asked him to descend into Hades. "You expect me to go near a corpse? Are you mad?"

"Don't you do it all the time?"

"I'm a doctor. The idea is to *not* be with a corpse."

Heraclides took back his son from Socrates. The two had been staring at each other and making faces.

"He's cute when you get used to him," Socrates admitted.

"When he's grown, we'll practice medicine together," he said proudly. "They'll call us Heraclides and Son."

"What's his name?"

"Hippocrates," said the proud father. The baby looked up with big, round, loving eyes.

AS WE WALKED, I said, "Diotima, what was all that about Arakos taking hemlock? We know that's not how he died."

"But think, Nico. The guilt of Timodemus hangs on the fact that only he could have beaten Arakos to death."

"Yes?"

"What if someone poisoned Arakos with hemlock? Not enough to kill him, but enough to slow him down."

"Dear Gods, you're right. Even a weak woman could beat to death a man who can't move."

"It needn't be even so much hemlock. Merely enough that a normal man could do him in."

"Which means—"

"The killer is not limited to Timodemus. Anyone could have beaten Arakos to death, as long as they had access to his food. Of course, this is only a theory—"

"Come on." I took her by the hand and dragged her along the muddy path.

"Where are we going?"

"I want to smell the mouth of a dead body."

"THERE MIGHT BE a slight smell of something, but . . ." I knelt back, disappointed. "I don't know, Diotima. I can't smell a thing over the . . . er . . . over the other smell." I tried not to breathe as I spoke.

"He's been dead a while now," Diotima admitted. Indeed, it was a hot summer, the taint of corruption was strong about the body of Arakos, and a cloud of flies had settled in for the long term.

"There's no evidence here," I said.

"Sorry, Nico."

"Don't be. Your idea was brilliant."

"There's only one thing we can do: confront Festianos with the evidence, and see what he says. Nico, I think perhaps I should learn something about medicine," Diotima mused, almost to herself.

"Why?" I exclaimed.

"You heard Heraclides. Doctors wouldn't be seen dead around a corpse. Don't you think it would be useful if we could study a corpse?"

"No, I don't."

"Yes, you do. You just don't want your wife to do it."

"Are you arguing with me?"

"Yes."

"Oh."

I didn't know what to say to that. Wives are supposed to obey their husbands. It hadn't occurred to me that someday my wife might refuse to obey me.

I asked, "Is Festianos a doctor?"

"How should I know?" Diotima said.

"Nico, I've been thinking," said Socrates. "I'm pretty sure the uncle isn't a doctor."

"Oh come now, Socrates, how can you possibly know?" Diotima said.

"Did you see all the instruments and things in the tent of Heraclides? He had jars of scrolls and bronze instruments."

"So?"

"I sneaked a look inside while you searched the uncle's tent. Festianos had none of those things."

Diotima looked at Socrates in wonder. "Try not to think so much, Socrates. It'll only get you into trouble."

"Yes, Diotima."

APOLLO'S LIGHT WAS well to the west. This being the middle of summer, the Sun God would remain with us longer.

Soon it would be dinnertime. This was the evening assigned for the negotiation between our fathers for the marriage between myself and the woman who, as far as I was concerned, was already my wife.

I sent Socrates to our tents with orders to make sure everything was ready and to collect wine. I escorted Diotima to her tent to dress for the dowry negotiation. Typically the prospective bride and groom would go nowhere near such talks, but in the special circumstances our attendance was required.

Diotima entered her tent while I waited outside.

I waited a long time.

"Are you all right in there?" I called. "What's keeping you?"

"Everything!"

I went in.

I found Diotima naked, which was nice but not quite according to plan. How long does it take to change a chiton?

"I can't decide what to wear," she wailed. "Should I dress as a modest young woman or a forthright woman of the world?"

Diotima, indecisive?

"Go with the modest maiden," I advised, thinking that would most likely please my father.

"A bit too late for that, but I'll try for modest," she said nervously.

I was nervous too, more than I'd been in a long while. Whether or not our fathers could agree would affect the rest of our lives; whatever decision they reached would bind us, and I had no idea what was about to happen.

Diotima, on the other hand, had a clear view.

"This meeting is all about the state of my genitals," she said as she wrapped about herself an unrevealing chiton of dull browns and reds.

"That's true," I admitted.

"So why can't I speak for myself?"

"Because your genitals are the concave sort," I said. "Listen, Diotima, I'm very happy about the state of your genitals."

"You better be. They're your doing."

"You don't regret it, do you?" I asked, alarmed at the bitter tone of her voice.

She smiled. "No, Nico, I don't. Not at all. I'm sorry if I sound tense, but I'm worried about this meeting between your father and Pythax."

"So am I."

Poor girl, she was embarrassed about the whole thing. This problem existed because she'd chosen to get into bed with me—with, it must be said, substantial encouragement on my part—and now two old men were about to discuss her sex life.

I lifted the tent flap for her to exit. Outside, she said, "Your father doesn't like me."

I nodded. There was no point denying it. "It's not you personally, Diotima; it's so important to him that his grandchildren be citizens, and your family is . . . er . . ."

"Unconventional?" she supplied helpfully. "I guess I'm the lucky one."

"No," I said, "that's me." And I took her in her arms and kissed her, just as a woman with two girl children walked past. The woman turned her head and sniffed. The young girls watched closely.

"We're in public!" Diotima, the girl with the unconventional family, had the most conventional morals in Athens. To kiss one's wife in public is scandalous behavior.

So I dragged her back into her tent.

"Nico!" Diotima said, startled. "What are you doing?"

"Making sure your genitals are still concave."

Diotima squealed.

"Sorry. Cold hands."

I ESCORTED DIOTIMA to my father's tent, eventually.

"You're late," he complained.

"Sorry, Father, something came up."

Not being a camping or fighting man by inclination, Sophroniscus hadn't his own canvas. He'd hired one from the local scam merchants. It was tattered and smelled of decay, but it kept the sun off our heads and was warm enough at night. By rights we should have met at the house of the bride's father, or in this case his tent, but Pythax had refused, I suspect because he was embarrassed.

Pythax had come to respectability late in life. Perhaps that was why he held onto it so tightly. He dressed in a formal chiton, dyed in bright reds and greens, that hung all the way to his ankles and covered a body that would have done credit to a man half his

age. He wore sandals on his wide, flat feet, feet that had never
before known any protection. A himation of the finest Milesian
wool draped about his shoulders and trailed down his left arm. It
was the dress of a wealthy gentleman, and it must have cost him
a small fortune. On a man like Pythax, who had spent his life in
leather armor, the effect was faintly ridiculous. Or perhaps that
was because I'd known him when he was still a slave. On his head,
a circlet of flowers sat askew. Beneath it, his craggy features and
scarred, sunburned skin gave lie to the entire pose.

Pythax and Father sized each other up, and it was almost
comic to see: the large, well-muscled man who looked so totally
out of place, and the short, stocky sculptor.

"I never thought I'd negotiate a marriage opposite a northern
barbarian," my father said.

I winced.

"And I never thought I'd be negotiating with an artist weakling," Pythax growled.

I forced a smile. "Can I bring you refreshments, sirs?"

They ignored me.

They sat down on either side of a low traveling chest to face
each other. The camp stool onto which Pythax lowered his bottom creaked under the strain, but didn't quite splinter.

I set out cups and poured wine for them both. The more the
better, I reasoned, and poured only an equal measure of water.
For a business meeting the ration would normally be three water
to one wine.

Sophroniscus said, "We are here to negotiate the marriage of
my son Nicolaos with your stepdaughter Diotima."

"They're already married," Pythax said.

"They are not," said Sophroniscus.

"They are," said Pythax. "They say they did the ceremony."

"Then perhaps we should review what happened."
Sophroniscus turned to me. "Nicolaos, did you perform the rite
of marriage with Diotima?"

"Yes, sir." It wasn't the answer my father wanted, but it was the truth, and I didn't regret it.

"There, you see?" said Pythax.

Sophroniscus persisted. "In this ceremony you say you performed, did the girl hand her girdle to her mother?"

"No, Father, how could she? Diotima's mother wasn't there."

"So the girl wasn't prepared by her mother. Did either of you bathe in the morning?"

"No."

"Did you walk from our home to hers, to collect her from her father?"

"No."

"Did you place her in a chariot drawn by a horse, to lead her to her new home?"

"Father, everything you ask was impossible."

"Precisely," said Sophroniscus. "It is impossible that the marriage ceremony could have taken place as it is practiced by the Athenians. Therefore no marriage has occurred."

Pythax turned a dangerous red. "You're saying my daughter's been used and now you won't do anything about it."

"It would help if we weren't doing everything backward." My father said to me, "It's traditional to negotiate the dowry *before* you bed the girl."

Diotima had sat silently behind Pythax up to this point. Now she sat up straight and angry and said, "That was *my* choice, thank you very much!"

Pythax said angrily, "Sophroniscus, if you try to deny this marriage, I'll sue you."

"On what grounds?" Father demanded.

"Damage to my property."

"*Property?*" Diotima fairly screeched. "I'm pretty sure those bits are *my* property."

But Pythax was right. No father in his right mind would contract a non-virgin for his son. After what had happened, if we returned Diotima, she'd only be good as a second wife for older men whose first had died.

To calm the situation, I said, "We didn't mean to get married, sirs. It sort of just . . . happened. Sorry."

"Don't add lying to your father to your crimes. You're not sorry at all," Father said. He sighed. "Pythax, I'll be honest with you. I'm not against my son marrying your daughter, not necessarily anyway, but I insist we negotiate on the basis that nothing has yet happened. There is no fait accompli here, no certainty, and certainly no presumption that the girl has been accepted without a dowry."

"All right," Pythax said gruffly. "Can't say I agree, but it sounds fair. What do you call a reasonable dowry?"

"The normal arrangement would be the girl's inheritance from her late father. I've looked into this, and I know she's in line for his house and his farm."

I had to stifle a gasp. Diotima's late father had been comfortably well off, not dirty rich like the aristocrats, but worth far more than my own father. Such a dowry would more than double our family's wealth. It seemed an outrageous demand, and yet Father was correct. Tradition clearly required the woman to bring her inheritance with her. Anything less amounted to theft by the stepfather.

For the first time I realized this negotiation might not be as simple as I thought.

Pythax said, "I can agree to the house in the city, but the farm has to stay with me. The city house will give the young couple a place to live."

Away from my Diotima's new in-laws, Pythax didn't say but clearly implied. It's the custom that the bride will join the family of her husband in his family home, where she must live in the women's quarters with her mother-in-law. It wasn't the most comfortable arrangement for the bride, who would frequently be bossed and lectured by her mother-in-law, but she would learn the ways of her new family very quickly. The son of a very wealthy man might move out of the family home with his bride—Pericles had done so—but only with the permission of his father.

Father shook his head. "That won't work," he said. "A city house is a sink for wealth, not a source of it. How could my son maintain such a household?"

"You could help him," Pythax said.

"I'm not made of money." Father carefully avoided revealing his financial straits. "The farm must come with the house, or Nico will have no way to maintain his household. I must insist."

"Take the city house," Pythax urged. "I'll throw in the house slaves."

As he sat thinking, my father glanced over the shoulder of Pythax and caught my eye. I nodded vigorously.

Father said, "I'm sorry, Pythax, but I can't agree to this."

"It's the best offer you'll get," Pythax said.

Sophroniscus said, "Then we have an impasse."

And no marriage. I gripped Diotima's hand, out of sight.

Diotima could contain herself no longer. She burst out, "Dear Gods, I don't care about the farm! Why don't we all just share the bloody thing?"

Pythax said, "It's not that big, Diotima. There's enough to feed one family, but not two."

Sophroniscus nodded. It was the only time the two men had agreed on anything. "Such arrangements never work," he said. "It always leads to fighting and court cases at harvest time."

Pythax said, "I got nothing against your boy, Sophroniscus, but I got to say you're overrating him. What would you ask for if you didn't know my girl was an heiress? Nothing like what you're demanding from me, I'll bet. The house on its own is more than you'd get from any other father."

Pythax had a point. An average dowry between two artisan families might run to a year's wages, say, four hundred or five hundred drachmae. I had no idea what it cost to buy a house, but it must surely be many times that.

"We must acknowledge the obvious fact that the girl's family is not an asset," Father said.

I suppressed a groan. I'd expected Father would raise this, but hoped he wouldn't. In Athens, a marriage is as much a union of families as a union of two young people. The wife's family is expected to bring to the party prestige and advantage.

"You can't say that," Pythax protested. "The girl's dad was a great statesman."

"Forgive me, Pythax, I would not raise the subject except that it's an essential point, but I must point out the girl's mother was a hetaera."

Pythax controlled his temper most admirably. "Not anymore."

"Granted, but it's the family history that people remember. The girl was born illegitimate—"

"Not any longer; they made her legitimate so she could inherit."

"Granted again."

"And you're in no position to complain, Sophroniscus. If your boy marries my girl, he'll become the heir."

"That's why all the property must come to him."

There was no point in going on. The meeting broke on inability to agree about the farm. I knew Father's need for money. I knew he couldn't accept less. All Pythax had to do was say yes, and Diotima and I would be married. I was so frustrated I wanted to scream. Why wouldn't Pythax release what was Diotima's?

Sophroniscus and Pythax agreed to consider their positions and talk again—back in Athens after the Olympics.

I left the tent in a daze. Diotima followed, and I think she suppressed a sob. I held her tight, and didn't give a curse what any passing man thought. She said in my ear, "We came so close, Nico. So close."

Over Diotima's shoulder I watched Pythax's back retreat, an angry and insulted man. He stamped down the muddy path that was lined with burning torches, lit so that the Olympic party could continue all night.

"Pythax!" I called.

He stopped and turned. I said to Diotima, "Wait for me here," then ran to Pythax.

We stood together in the mud. I said, "Pythax, I'm sorry about what happened in there."

"So am I, little boy," he said sadly. "I'm gonna do the best for my girl, and Diotima wants you. Gods know why. There's not much meat on you."

"Thanks a lot, Pythax."

"Well, look at yourself, lad. You look like you ain't got a muscle in your body." He grabbed my upper arm and pinched it. I winced. "You're way too skinny to be my son-in-law. You better put on some meat, or I'll be embarrassed to be seen with you at the gymnasium."

Pythax gloried in the gymnasium as few men did. When he was a slave it had been forbidden to him. Now, he expressed his citizenship by frequenting the place as often as he could.

"But I gotta be honest, little boy. If your father don't change his mind, it ain't gonna happen."

"My father is unreasonable," I said bitterly.

Pythax sighed. "No, little boy, he ain't. Your dad's doing exactly what he ought to, and he's got right on his side. Diotima inherited the house and the farm from her dad; she's got every right to take it with her when she marries. I know that."

"Then . . . er . . ."

"Why won't I release it?" Pythax was shamefaced. "It's like this, lad. When I was a slave, I didn't need to worry about where I would sleep or what I would eat, or how I would pay for it. Right?"

"Sure."

"Then I became a free man, and a citizen. Free men don't get nothing for free. And I got a house now, and a wife."

"Oh." Suddenly I realized what the problem for Pythax must be.

"I don't know how to make money," Pythax said. "Never had to. That farm Diotima inherited from her dad, it's the only income I got."

Diotima's mother had very expensive tastes. She was used to the best, and Pythax was too besotted to deny her.

"Don't tell anyone, all right? It'd destroy me if men knew I couldn't support my own family. They'd say it was because I used to be a slave. They'd say I wasn't a real citizen."

I knew what a big admission this was for Pythax. For a man of his pride, for what he'd achieved and how he'd risen, it must have been painful beyond words.

"I understand, Pythax. Keep the farm. I don't need it."

"Yes, you do. Your dad's right about that, too. But I ain't got no choice. I tell you, nobody better get in my way today, or—"

"Yaah!"

"Yaah!"

Two Heracles imitators in lion skins jumped in front of us and swung their clubs.

Pythax grabbed their necks, smashed their heads together, and tossed their unconscious bodies to the side of the path.

"Or I might get angry," he finished and strode off to the Olympics, a desperately unhappy citizen.

THE ABORTED MARRIAGE negotiation left me very depressed. It would require godlike powers of persuasion to reconcile everyone's differences. Maybe Pericles could have talked his way through, as he had so many times with the people of Athens, as he had with the judges to get Timo back in the Games, but Pericles would never involve himself in our domestic dispute.

If only I possessed the honeyed tongue of Pericles. But

Pericles had told me when we first met that I had a poor voice. Even the great Pindar only yesterday had derided my speech, and he should know, because he was a professional.

Pindar!

My rhetoric might be poor, but my investigation skills were top-notch. I tracked Pindar down at an extended late night dinner party beside the sacred altar, which was already decked out in flowers for the festivities to come the next morning. I knew I could rely on Pindar being wherever the biggest audience was to be found.

I said, "Pindar, when last we spoke, you said you could teach me tricks of flattery. Did you mean it?"

"Perhaps." He sounded evasive in the face of my enthusiasm. I hopped from one foot to the other.

"*Would* you teach me? You see, I have a problem." I explained the situation with Diotima and my father and Pythax. I didn't explain it well; I came to a confused halt.

Pindar buried his chin in his chest and thought. "I see. Affairs of the heart, a family in dispute, yes, this is the stuff of poetry. It lacks only a ten-year-long war to reach Homeric proportions, or perhaps a murder in the family. I don't suppose you have a close relative that you're willing to sacrifice?"

Socrates was a temptation, but . . . "Sorry, I'll have to disappoint you there."

"A pity. Nevertheless, that only affects the aesthetics, not the solution, which is simplicity itself."

"It is?" I blinked. Could the answer to my problems be so easy? "Tell me what to do!"

"Not you. Me. I will write a praise song in your honor."

I laughed. "That's impossible, Pindar. I've done nothing that qualifies for a song." Praise songs are always in honor of war heroes and sports victors.

"Not so. You're a contestant in these Olympics, are you not? I distinctly heard the Chief Judge take the oath from you. When you catch this killer, then you, Nicolaos, son of Sophroniscus, will be an Olympic victor."

It hit me like a fist. Pindar was right; I could win at the Olympics!

"Dear Gods, Pindar, you're a genius!"

"Yes, I know. When your father and prospective father-in-law hear your name sung in praise before the assembled Hellenes, all your difficulties will vanish in their pride of being the father of an Olympic victor, whose song is sung by the greatest poet since Homer," he said modestly.

"Didn't you say this morning that you were immune to flattery?"

"I'm immune to yours. I'm totally vulnerable to my own."

I thought about it, then asked, "Can you get in a mention of Diotima?"

"It's immoral to praise a woman, but I'll try to squeeze in a brief allusion. Maybe something about Hera, helpmeet to mighty Zeus?" he mused. "Leave it with me; I'll think of something."

"Thanks, Pindar!" I said in gratitude.

"You know, don't you, that a praise song doesn't come cheap?"

"I knew there'd be a catch. How much?"

Pindar named a sum.

I staggered back in shock. "Dear Gods! People pay that?"

"It's the going rate. Normally my clients are in such euphoria from their victory that they don't stop to think. You're unusual in that you're currently rational."

The taste of reconciling my family was too sweet to refuse. I didn't have the money, I had no idea how to get it, but I'd think of something.

"Start writing my song, Pindar."

"There's one final point."

I sighed. "Yes?"

"You have to catch the killer, Nicolaos."

"Well, of course."

"I don't think you've quite caught my meaning. *You* have to catch the killer, not the Spartan. If the Spartan Markos beats you to it, then he has the victory, and you have no victory song nor, it would seem, any hope of a marriage."

DAY 3 OF THE 80ᵀᴴ OLYMPIAD OF THE SACRED GAMES

HOMER'S ROSY FINGERS clutched the dawn. Timodemus had two days to live. Three, if you counted the day on which he'd be tried and executed.

At least today I wouldn't have to drag reluctant men away from the sport to question them, because most of Day Three is dedicated to the worship of Zeus.

One happy effect of this was that the men could sleep in. Whereas the sports began at the crack of dawn, the service could not begin until the main attraction had been driven in from wherever it was kept waiting.

I woke in my tent and pulled on my chiton, the only decent clothing I had, and wandered out to blink at the sun and wonder if there was anything to eat.

Socrates was already outside, protesting loudly. "I won't wear a chiton," he said.

"Yes, you will," our father said. "This is a sacred festival and I won't have you wandering about looking like a small child. You can wash in the river, too."

"I'm clean enough," Socrates grumbled.

Father looked to me, and I knew what to do. I picked up the bucket of water that lay between our tents and threw it on Socrates.

"Now you're clean," I said cheerfully.

Socrates sputtered and gave me a look that said he would have as cheerfully thrown a bucket of snakes at me. Nevertheless he was clean—an unusual state for him. I held Socrates down while

Father pulled the chiton over him. This was an old, cast-off garment of our father's, which had been cut down to size by our mother for Socrates to wear. Or, rather, almost to size. Mother had allowed room for my little brother to grow. The sleeves ended somewhere slightly past his fingers, and the bottom edge trailed along the ground. Socrates almost tripped over it when he took a step. Father hitched up the chiton, tied a rope belt around Socrates's waist to hold up the extra material, and cheerily declared we were ready to go.

We joined the crowd streaming to the Sanctuary of Zeus, where we met up with Diotima, as we'd arranged. Women might not be allowed in the stadion when the Games were on, but these were religious rites, and the sanctuary was open to everyone.

I saw Markos with the other Spartans, though he stood somewhat apart. I guessed he was unpopular with his fellows since the fight with Skarithos. I beckoned and he came to join us.

A vast cloud of dust hung in the air above the road from Elis. If I hadn't known better, I might have called it smoke from a forest fire, or perhaps the coming of the Gods. But I knew what to expect, and so I stood, Diotima and Socrates beside me, and we stared.

From the base of the cloud emerged a large, plodding ox, and alongside it walked a man. Both were difficult to make out; the ox's coat was white against the gray of the road dust hanging in the air.

Another ox and man emerged behind the first, and another, and another, until one hundred oxen were visible on the road. The procession was so long that by the time the last appeared out of the dust raised by their hooves, the first ox had entered Olympia.

Each ox was garlanded in bright ribbons and crowned with an olive wreath. But there was something more spectacular than the colorful adornments.

Socrates gaped. "Is that real?" he asked.

"It is," said Diotima. "Each ox to be sacrificed today has a coat of pure white."

"I thought it was road dust," Socrates said.

"No, they breed them like this."

"How?"

Diotima shrugged. "Don't ask me."

"They allow only the bulls with white coats to mate," said a man beside us in the press. "If a calf is born with an absolutely perfect coat of white, then it's made an ox and reserved for sacrifice."

"It's incredible," Socrates said, and for once I had to agree with him. This was one of the most amazing sights in all of Hellas: one hundred pure-white oxen, garlanded in flowers and with bright ribbons about their horns.

Each ox was led through the entrance into the Sanctuary, where the grand altar of Zeus was ready and waiting. The Hellenes were about to make their greatest sacrifice to Zeus, for these hundred white oxen, especially bred for their fate, were on their way to the god.

The first of the oxen was led by his keeper to the altar, where waited the Butcher of the Games with the tools of his trade.

The crowd walked along with the first of the sacrifices. Men called out good luck to the ox and wished it well and thanked the beast for consenting to be sacrificed. Those who could reached out to pat it gently.

The priest of Zeus spoke to the beast. I couldn't hear what he said, but he seemed happy with the result because he stood back, and the Butcher stepped forward. He was a huge man with bulging triceps that would have compared favorably with Pythax's or even Arakos's.

The Butcher swung a large mallet and struck the ox direct on the forehead. The stunned animal stood stock-still, but lowered its head as if to nod in agreement.

The crowd sighed in happiness.

The Butcher dropped the mallet and picked up a large, very sharp knife. This he thrust into the beast's neck and sliced to cut its throat. The blood spurted at a tremendous rate. Priests who stood waiting with large bowls hurried to catch the sacrifice's lifeblood. As each bowl filled, another took its place, until slowly, but with tremendous grace, the animal's legs gave way and it sank to the ground.

"It was a fine sacrifice," Sophroniscus said.

Diotima pulled me aside. "Nico, did you see that? A mallet to the head would be just the thing to stun Arakos."

"Before they beat him to death, you mean?"

"Yes. I've seen lots of sacrifices, I've performed plenty of them myself, but it's never quite . . . er . . . struck me the same way."

"What about your idea that he was disabled by hemlock?"

"This is the same, but with solids."

The priests and attendants stood back, and what seemed like a hundred slaves stepped forward. The ox had been led up onto a wooden platform, the underside of which dripped with grease of pig fat to make it slippery. An aulos player put his V-shaped recorder to his lips and began to play sacred music. The slaves took up ropes and began to heave in time to the music. The remains of the sacrifice slowly but surely glided along the path— thanks to the slippery fat—to the waiting barbecue pits.

The Butcher of the Games and his attendants would spend the rest of the day dismembering the sacrifices to prepare them for the feast tonight. The Feast of the Oxen is one of the most popular for one simple reason: at no other time in the next four years would we have a chance to eat so much meat of such high quality. There were poor men present who might not even see such meat again until the next Olympics.

The Butcher was already spattered with blood, which made for an interesting effect on his formal chiton. Large drops of grease had fallen from the passing sled and formed small pools of slip- periness in the muddy ground. I wondered if anyone would step in it. That put me in mind of Socrates and his clean tunic. I said, "Socrates, look out for the slippery patches, and for Father's sake, try to keep your chiton clean, all right?"

No answer. I'd expected a sarcastic comment.

"Socrates?"

I looked about me. He wasn't there.

I said, "Diotima, weren't you keeping an eye on Socrates?"

"No," she said shortly. "He's my brother-in-law, not my child."

I said, "Has anyone seen Socrates?"

No one had. Socrates had disappeared.

He was probably safe. Any normal boy would spend the day running between the grown-ups, playing in the crowd, stealing extra meat from the barbecue, and then make his way back to camp that night for his scolding. The only problem was, that was what any *normal* boy would do. Socrates, on the other hand, was fully capable of climbing into the barbecue pits to see how they worked.

Father remained admirably calm. He said only two words: "Find him."

We spread out. I reasoned that he couldn't have gotten far, not because Socrates couldn't move fast but because the press of people made it impossible. The same press made it difficult for me to move, too. I became overly acquainted with the sweaty armpits and backs of the men and women I brushed past.

It was Markos who found my errant brother.

"He's over here!" Jumping up onto the plinth of a statue, I saw Markos standing near the fire pits, which reignited my fear that Socrates had fallen into one. Markos waved and shouted. Somehow over the chaos I managed to hear him. Diotima heard, too, and she was closer. She pushed her way through to Markos before me.

Slaves were already at work on the pits; they'd kindled a hundred fires. Wood chips had been added and the smoke smelled sweet. When the fires burned strong, the slaves would add stones to glow red hot and be the base on which the oxen would roast. Other slaves prepared the wooden frames to hold the carcasses. Tonight the Hellenes would enjoy the largest barbecue in the world.

Then I saw what had attracted the attention of my over-inquisitive little brother. Socrates sat on a stone, in earnest conversation with a man who wore a large flowing robe of the deepest purple, tall and thin, with a nose long enough to double as a spear. Upon the man's feet were sandals that were quite obviously made of bronze. How he walked in them I don't know, but they glared in the sun so that you couldn't miss the odd footwear.

Beside the strangely dressed man was a fire pit, much smaller than the hundred official pits. The small pit looked quite forlorn. A shovel and heaped dirt lay discarded beside it. The stranger leaned over a pile, almost as tall as me, of gray, squishy bread dough. He kneaded the dough, handful by handful, as he conversed with Socrates. In fact I saw he'd handed some dough to Socrates, who was also kneading. Already the two of them had attracted a small crowd.

Socrates looked up and said without apology for wandering off, "Oh, hello, Nico. This man is making an ox!"

"You mean he's cooking an ox," I corrected.

"No, he's making one. Out of bread."

I said to the man, "Can I ask a question?"

He nodded as he kneaded the dough on his lap. "That's why I'm here. I was once a fish, you know."

It wasn't entirely the answer I'd expected. "You don't say?"

"And a bird."

Light dawned. Yes, this was exactly the sort of person Socrates would take up with.

I said, "You're not a philosopher, by any chance, are you?"

"My name is Empedocles, son of Meton, and I am indeed a lover of knowledge. How did you guess?"

"Just a feeling I had. Why are you making an ox out of bread?"

He clapped his hands in happiness, and bits of dough splat-
tered over us. "That's the question I hope many will ask. The
answer is because it's immoral and unethical to consume meat.
My plan is simple yet brilliant," he elucidated. "Tonight I will
hand out pieces of my bread ox. Then everyone will see we can
all eat bread instead of meat, and there's no need to kill our fellow creatures."

Socrates asked, "But why did you say you'd been a fish and a
bird? Did the Gods transform you, sir?"

"What happens when you die?" Empedocles asked Socrates
in return.

Socrates looked confused. Everyone knew the answer to that.
"Er . . . my psyche goes down to Hades?"

"Not so!" Empedocles said. "The psyches of the dead are
reborn in other living creatures. We've all lived past lives."

If we had, this was the first I'd heard of it. I could tell from the
expressions of Diotima, Markos, and Socrates that they, too, had
never heard of such a thing.

Empedocles continued, "In my own past lives, for example,
I've been both a fish and a bird. When we hold a beast in our
hands, it could be our own son, our mother, our daughter from a
previous life. When we consume the flesh of the sacrifice, young
boy, it's nothing less than cannibalism."

"Yech!" Socrates said.

Empedocles said this not only to us but to the rapidly growing
crowd that had come to watch. Empedocles worked as he talked,
trying to mold the bread dough and failing miserably.

After a while of watching him struggle with the dough, Socrates
remarked, rather rudely, "It doesn't look much like an ox."

"Anyone can be a critic," Empedocles said to him. "Can you
do better?"

"Sure I can," Socrates said. "Nico and I are the sons of a
sculptor."

Empedocles blinked. "You are? Good, then you can both help

me," and before I could object he handed us trowels and a set of sculpting tools so new they shone in the sun.

I couldn't see any harm in it. Socrates was interested in talking to Empedocles, and I was simply relieved that we hadn't found my brother grilled with the oxen. Together we wrestled the dough into something that approximated a bovine body. Everything sagged.

Diotima and Markos laughed at our efforts. That made me determined to do the job right. After a time I stood, tossed the tools on the ground, and announced, "There!"

Empedocles looked thoughtfully at my creation, rubbed his chin, and said, "It looks more like a cow, doesn't it?"

"It's definitely an ox." I turned to Diotima and Markos. "It looks like an ox, doesn't it?" I said. They both nodded gravely.

"Definitely an ox," Markos said. "I see it clearly."

As we worked, Socrates questioned Empedocles closely on the doctrine of reincarnation, as he called it. Empedocles was puzzled that a mere child should show an interest, so I explained proudly that Socrates had once met the philosopher Anaxagoras, who told us everything was made of infinitesimal particles, and—

Empedocles almost exploded. "That mountebank!" he shouted. "I know this fellow you talk of, and let me assure you, he's no more a philosopher than this boy here." He gestured at Socrates. "Tell me, have you ever seen these supposed particles?"

"Well, no," I admitted.

"Have you touched one?"

"No."

"Heard one?"

"No."

"And nor will you, because they don't exist." Empedocles snorted. "The whole idea is simply bad philosophy. I've solved the riddle of matter, and it has nothing to do with these ridiculous particles."

"Then what is it, sir?" Socrates asked eagerly, because he was always desperate to learn from philosophers.

"All matter is composed from earth, air, fire, and water. They combine in different portions to form everything around us."

Socrates thought about it, his head cocked on one side, then he asked, "But sir, what moves the earth, fire, air, and water to combine in different portions?"

"That's simple. Love and strife. Love and strife, young boy, are what move everything in the universe."

Love and strife move everything. Empedocles might be crazy, but he'd given me an idea.

"Nicolaos!" It was an old woman's voice. I turned to see Gorgo with two men at her back, both twice her height. She, too, had come to see the spectacle of the oxen.

"Where's your woman?" Gorgo asked.

I pointed to where Diotima and Markos stood together. Gorgo motioned, and we all stepped away from Empedocles, who had begun to harangue the amused crowd.

"Why were you making a bread cow?" Gorgo asked, obviously intrigued.

"It's an ox."

"Looks more like a cow to me, but that's not important now. I have information for you." She looked about, realized we were in the middle of a crowd that had come to watch Empedocles's strange protest against meat, and signaled for us to follow. Gorgo's two Spartan guards cleared a path for their queen. Gorgo led us, at her slow walk, to a place behind some statues of former Olympic victors. Here there were only a handful of men, quietly taking turns to drink from a wineskin. The guards made these drunks feel unwelcome, and they departed with rude gestures and empty threats.

When they were gone, Gorgo said, "I've done some checking of my own, as I told you I would. You're still interested in the krypteia?"

"Yes."

"Then you'll wish to know there are definitely krypteia at Olympia."

"Who?" I asked, excited.

"I have no names. I begged a favor of a member of the Gerousia—that's our council of elders—from a fine man who once served with my husband. He's of a conservative disposition himself and in with the current ephors. He tells me that Xenares said to him, when they were both well in wine, that he—Xenares, that is—wants to promote a war against Athens while he's here at Olympia, and that a member of the krypteia is assisting him. I'm told Xenares appeared quite confident of success."

That didn't bode well for Athens.

"The difficulty is, I don't know what this plan is, or in what capacity the krypteia might play a part. Olympia, as the location suggests, involves other city-states. The agent may simply be a go-between among allies."

"Thank you, Gorgo," Diotima said.

"I've also looked closely into the life of Arakos. I searched for any motive someone who knew him might have had to kill him. I find that Arakos was an exemplary Spartan."

I said, "Tell me, how many krypteia are there in total, Gorgo?"

"The exact number is unknown, of course, but it's possible to deduce. There are eight thousand serving Spartans—"

"So few!" I'd always thought of the Spartans as being a large army, but this was less than half what Athens could put into the field.

"You forget that any one Spartan is worth ten men from any other city. The test of the krypteia is reserved for those who might one day become leaders in combat. Perhaps one young man in ten is selected for the test. Of those, perhaps only one in a hundred shows such resourcefulness and expertise at silent killing that he's selected by the ephors. From this we may guess the entire membership of the krypteia is probably not more than ten."

"Do you mean to say we're worried about only ten men?"

"We're probably only concerned with *one* of those ten, and we're right to be worried. It would require a man of extraordinary talent to face down one of these hidden killers and survive. My Leonidas could have done it; I know of no other man who would stand a chance." Her eyes glistened as she spoke of her husband, and I realized with a shock that Gorgo was close to crying.

"Is there nothing that betrays them?" Diotima asked quickly. She wanted to spare the queen of Sparta the indignity of tears before strangers.

"They live ordinary lives," Gorgo said. "They're only called upon to provide their special service when the need arises. The only thing that marks them is they must all be of the officer class. I speculate that the krypteia deliberately restrain their abilities in day-to-day life, so as not to be too obvious."

"Terrific," I said glumly. "We'll never spot him. If he even exists, that is. There are at least two other ways to interpret the word 'secrets' in that anonymous note."

Gorgo said, "Your next step is clear. You must speak with Xenares. Only he can tell you more."

"Will he agree to see us?"

"He will, because I'll order it, personally. For all his faults, Xenares is a good Spartan, and there's one thing you can rely on from any good Spartan. Markos, what's the first lesson of our people?"

Markos smiled. "To follow orders, Queen Gorgo."

Gorgo returned his smile. "It makes life so much simpler."

FOLLOWING ORDERS MIGHT make a man's life simpler, but it certainly didn't make him happier.

"There are no krypteia at Olympia," Xenares said, or, rather, snarled. "And even if there were, I certainly wouldn't discuss it with an *Athenian*."

As Gorgo had predicted, Xenares the ephor of Sparta had

agreed to meet, but that didn't mean he had to like it. We stood in
a room at the Bouleterion, Xenares, Markos and I. Though there
were couches along the walls, he remained standing in the center.
Xenares clearly intended this to be a short discussion.

"I've heard otherwise," I said.

"I can't control what other people say. More important, how
does an Athenian come to know of the krypteia and where its
members might be?" Xenares looked pointedly at Markos, and
there was no doubting whom he thought had talked.

Markos met his gaze with a bland expression.

"Markos told me nothing," I said. "My source is higher up
than any of us."

Xenares frowned. "Higher than me?" He had no trouble
guessing whom I meant. "Then this will be a subject for discussion at the next meeting of the ephors."

I'd probably just caused trouble for Pleistarchus and Gorgo, but
that was better than exposing Markos to the wrath of the ephors.

I said, "Tell me the names of the krypteia at Olympia."

"What part of 'no krypteia at Olympia' did you not understand?"

"Do you want this killer punished?" I asked.

"This goes without saying."

"Then why won't you help us catch—"

"Because he's already been caught. Let me ask you, if our
roles were reversed, if Arakos had been an Athenian and this
Timodemus were a Spartan, would you be looking so hard for
evidence to exonerate him?"

I had no answer to that, because Xenares was right.

Markos said, "Xenares, may I remind you, Nicolaos has been
ordered to do his best for the accused, as I have been ordered to
do my best to convict him. We can hardly blame a man for following his orders, can we?"

That gave Xenares pause. "I see. Yes, Markos, you're right.
Very well then, it does not matter how many krypteia are here at

Olympia, nor who they are. They will never act without orders.
Do you know what the krypteia are?"

"Assassins," I said.

"Patriots," Xenares corrected me. "Highly talented patriots,
who have dedicated their lives to the good of Sparta."

The way he said it reminded me of the saying of Pericles, *for
the good of Athens.*

"So you're saying the krypteia only act on the orders of the
ephors," I said.

"The Spartan system is one of balance," Xenares said. "The
ephors are elected to represent the people, the Gerousia represent the wisdom of age, and the kings act for us all."

One thing struck me. "The ephors are elected by *the people*?
You mean by all the Spartans?"

"Certainly."

"I thought Athens was the only city with democracy."

"Democracy?" Xenares shuddered. "Are you insane?
Democracy is for weaklings. We ephors are elected by the people
to act as a balance against the kings, so they cannot get above
themselves. The system works. The kings make the best decisions they can because they know if they don't, we ephors will
veto them."

"Does *veto* include tearing the skin off a man who's out of his
mind?"

Xenares looked like he'd swallowed something distasteful. "I
see you've heard the rumors about Cleomenes, who was grandfather to our current king Pleistarchus. How should I know what
happened back then? It was before my time. Whatever happened,
I'm sure it was for the best for Sparta."

"But the ephors could order such a killing?"

"We never discuss the government of Sparta with outsiders,
and particularly not with an Athenian."

"Why do you hate Athens so?" I asked, genuinely curious,
because I'd never understood it.

"Is that a serious question?" Xenares said. "Athens disturbs the balance. Athens uses her wealth to bend other cities to her will. Every merchant from every city must deal with you, because you're so rich. You set unfair rules that serve only to increase your wealth and power, and then the richer you get, the more you extend your unhealthy influence. Athens is like a cancer among the city-states." Xenares was shouting now and waving his arms. He stopped abruptly when he realized what he was doing.

"Where were you, Xenares, when Arakos died?"

I thought for a moment he was going to strike me. "I didn't even know the man," he said at last.

"Purely for the record, Xenares, so we can eliminate you."

"Eliminate me, eh? If you must know, I was with a delegation from Corinth. We talked through most of the night. They'll vouch for me."

Considering Corinth was a close ally of Sparta and a mortal enemy to Athens, that didn't mean much. To test him, I asked, "Oh? What did you talk about?"

Xenares glared at me. "A subject dear to all our hearts: how best to destroy Athens."

"HE'S PROBABLY TELLING the truth," I said to Markos. "If he wanted to lie, he surely would have made up a story that put him in a better light."

"I hate to have to tell you this, my friend," Markos said, "but to many people in Hellas, wanting to destroy Athens *does* put him in a good light." He thought for a moment, then said, "We must consider the possibility that the information Gorgo gave us, that there's a krypteia agent assisting Xenares at Olympia, is tangled up in these negotiations with Corinth."

I nodded. "If so, then he has nothing to do with Arakos, and we've gone down another dead end."

"I'm sorry you had to hear all that from Xenares, Nico," Markos said. "It can't have been pleasant for you."

"Do men truly praise Xenares because he hates us?"

"That's how most Spartans see it."

"Is that how you see it?" I asked him.

Markos hesitated for so long I thought he might refuse to answer, but he said, "How I feel doesn't matter, Nico. I follow orders. You and I don't get a say. Maybe one day, when we're as old as Xenares, you and I will be able to sit down together and resolve all the differences between our cities."

"I know what you mean," I said, thinking of my orders from Pericles to get Timo off the charge at all costs. That in turn reminded me of my new idea. Empedocles had said that love and strife moved everything in the universe. To me, it sounded like two good motives for murder.

I left Markos behind and crossed the river, where I waited outside the tent of Klymene, under a nearby tree for the shade, until the tent flap lifted and the priestess's personal slave—the girl with red hair, whom Klymene had called Xenia—emerged carrying a large jar with two handles. The girl settled the jar on her head, where it remained, perfectly balanced, and walked easily toward the river.

"Going for water?" I asked as I joined her on the path and matched her steps.

She glanced at me in contempt. "What a stupid question."

"Then let me try a better one. Where do you sleep at night, Xenia?"

"Are you hitting on me?" She didn't break stride for a moment.

"I'm a married man."

"Well, at least you're honest!"

"I only want to ask a few questions."

Xenia scoffed. "That's a different approach."

We reached the riverbank. Xenia waded in. She stopped in the middle of the stream, took down the jar, and slowly submerged it in the river.

As the air bubbled up she said, "You're the one who came to

the mistress's tent with the pretty dark-haired girl, aren't you? Why do you care where I sleep?"

"I think you're like most slaves in a camp; you sleep outside your owner's tent."

She nodded. "All right, that's true enough."

"But in the women's camp at Olympia, it's not safe for a lovely girl like you to be asleep outside a tent, not with all those drunk men staggering about looking for a pornê."

"So?"

With a grunt she heaved the jar back up on her head and waded out. I pulled her the last few steps up the bank.

"Thanks."

We walked back toward the camp.

I said, "So I think you sleep in her tent, at the entrance, so that any man who blunders in will trip over you first and not bother the Priestess of the Games."

Xenia walked on, saying nothing.

"Here's the thing, Xenia. When Klymene screamed in the night and the guards came to take Timodemus, why weren't you there first? In fact, why didn't Timo trip over you?"

The jar fell from Xenia's head. I almost caught it as it fell, but it was wet and slipped through my hands and hit the ground at my feet. I was sloshed head to foot.

"Gods curse it! Now I'll have to fill it again." Xenia bent to pick up the jar, which must have been beloved of the Gods because it hadn't broken.

This was what I realized when Empedocles spoke of love and strife: that neither Klymene in her testimony nor Timodemus nor the guards had mentioned Xenia.

"What's the answer, Xenia?" I said.

"You can't make me talk."

"I don't have to. The judges will see to it if I call you as a witness. I suppose you know they torture slaves when they give evidence in court."

Xenia went pale.

"A thumbscrew's what they usually use."

She said, "You mustn't tell the mistress I told. Promise me."

Aha! "I swear it by Zeus. May I lose the contest if I reveal."

Xenia whispered, "Klymene sent me away."

"Why?"

"Why do you think? Because a man was due. It wouldn't be the first time."

"Timodemus?"

Xenia nodded.

"Had he been to her before?"

"Not here at the Games."

Which meant in Elis.

"Do you like your mistress?"

Xenia stopped to think about that. "Yes," she said finally. "On the whole, I do. She's had a tough life."

This from a slave. I wondered what had been so tough for Klymene, but that didn't matter now.

Xenia looked worried. "Remember you promised not to tell the mistress."

"I promise."

So now I had the alibi for Timo that I'd wished for right from the start. But Timodemus had lied to me about how he came to be in Klymene's tent. What else had he lied about?

"IT'S ALL LIES." Klymene said. "There was nothing between Timodemus and me. I'm the Priestess of the Games, you know!"

"I know," said Diotima. "If I were Priestess of the Games, and I'd been fooling around, I'd deny it, too."

I'd brought Diotima the news, and together we'd waylaid Klymene at the Sanctuary of Zeus, where everyone had congregated to party and drink while they waited for the oxen to cook. Already the aroma of sizzling, well-cooked meat was drifting across Olympia.

Diotima and I dragged Klymene into the Bouleterion for a private discussion. The inside of the council house was divided into one large meeting hall and a number of small rooms. We chased a couple of slaves out of the smallest, quietest room, where they'd been hiding to shirk their duties, and then we accused Klymene, not of murder, but of lust.

She'd denied everything, over and over.

Diotima and I shared a look. We knew we were running out of time; even with my official status, we couldn't keep a priestess locked away forever, especially not if they needed her when the Games resumed.

Diotima sighed. She said, "Very well, then. How do you explain the love poetry?"

"What?" Klymene was nonplussed. So was I, for a moment. Then I remembered.

"We searched his tent," Diotima said. "Timodemus writes poetry about you. Did you know that?"

"Does he really?" Klymene said. Her expression was one of wonder. "You mean . . . he really likes me?"

"Shall I go fetch it?" Diotima said. "You can see for yourself."

Klymene turned away to stare at the blank wall, ignoring us entirely.

I dragged Diotima to the other corner. "Why didn't you tell me before about the poetry?" I hissed.

"I did," Diotima said. "You saw me reading it."

"You didn't tell me he was writing about Klymene! You could have saved me having to question Xenia."

"Er . . . there's a slight problem there," Diotima admitted, somewhat abashed. "The poetry doesn't *actually* mention Klymene by name."

I was appalled. "Then how can you possibly know it was meant for her?"

"I used some intuition. Also a bit of logic. Everything Timo has here at Olympia, he brought with him from Elis, right?"

"Yes."

"Then he must have written the poetry beginning in Elis. Who did he meet there? Who else could it be for? Do you see any other nubile women around here, to use his words, *with breasts like melons?*"

"Timo wrote that?" I asked.

"I told you it was bad poetry. Listen, Nico, we can prove Timo wrote the words. Considering he was captured in her tent, that should be enough."

Klymene turned around. "All right, I'll admit it." She twisted a tress around her fingers. "Timodemus and I were having an affair. How did you know to look for poetry? I suppose that little vixen Xenia told you all about us first. She's hated me ever since we were children."

"You knew Xenia as a *child*?" Diotima asked.

"Oh yes. Xenia is my father's, he got her on a barbarian slave he once owned. That's why she's called Xenia. He kept her because he thought she might be a useful companion for me. I'm older by a year."

"It wasn't Xenia who told me. I guessed the truth," I said, to cover for the slave-woman. "The scream that brought the guards running to your tent. That wasn't you being scared; that was you having an . . . er . . ."

"Orgasm," she finished for me. "If you ever want one, Timo's your man."

"Thanks anyway."

"I shouldn't have screamed, but you know how it is when the moment's upon you. When those moron guards came running, we had to make up a story, fast. Timo jumped off the bed and pretended to have stumbled in by accident."

She didn't bother to say she willingly let him sacrifice himself to protect her reputation. I didn't know whether to deplore her ruthlessly self-centered attitude or applaud the way she carried it off. Timo must have been an idiot to bed this woman.

"When did Timo come to you?"

"After I'd dined."

"Diotima, when did Petale look outside her tent to see Arakos?"

"After the moon had reached its peak."

Diotima took hold of my hand and squeezed gently. Timodemus had been less than innocently engaged at the same moment Arakos was discovered breathing his last. Klymene's testimony would prove Timodemus was innocent.

"You were seeing Timodemus back in Elis, weren't you?" Diotima said. She added, "There's no point trying to hide anything, Klymene. We know enough to be able to force your personal slaves to testify before the Judges. They'll certainly tell us everything you've done."

They certainly would. It was the law that slaves could only testify in court under torture. The young women who served Klymene would fold in an instant.

Klymene knew it, too. She sighed. "Yes, I admit it. Both Timodemus and Arakos," she said.

And Arakos. It took a moment to sink in. Diotima and I stared at each other in open shock.

"What, at the same time?" The thought of small Timo and the huge Spartan—

"Of course not, silly! They hated each other. You couldn't imagine two more different men. Like salt and honey, the two of them."

"Which was salt?"

"Oh, Arakos. He's strong, not subtle at all. He really makes a woman feel like a woman. Or he did, rather. Timodemus is *smooth.*" She smiled. "And sweet."

"So all this hatred between the two of them was rivalry over you," I said.

"Oh, I have a feeling it went deeper than me. Not that I'm not deep, you understand."

"I can imagine."

"I met Arakos first, in Elis, at the time the athletes arrived for the compulsory training period before they move on to Olympia. Part of my job is to welcome the new arrivals. Arakos took a shine to me at once."

"And then you . . . er . . . welcomed him."

"He welcomed me first! Grabbed me when we were out of sight behind the temple walls and kissed me properly. I felt like a powerless rag doll in his hands." She smiled happily.

"What happened when Timo arrived?"

"That was many days later. This time it was me doing the welcoming. What a good-looking man!"

"And Timo took a shine to you."

"Oh, yes," she said, matter-of-factly.

"Arakos must have been furious when you dumped him," I observed.

"Dump Arakos?" Klymene looked at me strangely. "Why would I do that?"

Diotima's jaw dropped. "You mean you—"

"Had affairs with them both. I told you."

There was a refreshing directness to Klymene that I was beginning to appreciate. Klymene probably didn't have many friends among the women of her own class, but back in her home city the young men must have queued up to meet her.

"What about your father?" Diotima asked.

"You have a disgusting mind for a priestess!" Klymene said.

"Er . . ." I said, taken aback. "What Diotima means is, didn't your father object?"

"Oh. He never found out. But even if he had, what could he do? I'm his only child. He can't rid himself of me; he needs to marry me off to get an heir. Besides, if I did something to hurt him . . . well, that's all to the good, I say. He deserves it. My father killed my mother."

I gasped. "*Your father* murdered *your mother*?"

"It wasn't anything as merciful as a knife. No, what he used to kill my mother was his penis."

I boggled at the mechanics of such a killing. "Is that what they call a blunt instrument? How did he hit her—"

"She means her father got her mother pregnant, Nico." Diotima rolled her eyes.

"Well, how was I to know?"

Klymene nodded. "When she was too old to carry, he got her pregnant because he was so desperate for a son."

"You're the only child," Diotima guessed.

"Yes, but it wasn't for want of him trying. I remember when I was a child, he was always happy to go to his parties or use the slaves and leave Mother and me to our lives in the women's quarters. We had enough food, weaving to be done, chores to do . . . we were happy together, Mother and I. I loved her so much.

"All except for every tenth night. Then Father came to our quarters, and I was sent away. I'd stand outside the door and listen to the moans and groans and screams. When he was finished, the door would open and he'd step out. He always saw me there. He'd look at me but not say anything, just walked past without a word, like I didn't matter, which when I was older I realized was true. A girl child's no better than a slave, is she? We wouldn't see him for another ten nights. That's how I learned to count to ten, by marking off the nights before he'd come back. The tenth night chore, my mother called it. But nothing ever happened. Then, when everyone thought nothing could, that she was past her days, Mother fell pregnant."

Klymene had tears in her eyes. They rolled down her cheeks, and she had to wipe. Diotima offered a small cloth, but Klymene waved it away. She said, "Suddenly nothing was too good for my mother, no food too expensive. Father had every doctor in Elis come to give advice. Not that any of them looked at her. The doctors cast their divinations, or they sacrificed a ewe and inspected its liver. Either way they pronounced everything would be fine, took their coins, and departed. Father forbade Mother to work, for fear she might fall and harm the baby. He bought more slaves to work for her." Klymene paused. "The lying-in was awful."

"You were there," I said, a statement, not a question.

"They said I was old enough. All through the labor she swore and writhed and cried in awful pain. And while that baby slowly killed her, she said it was all my father's fault because he had to have his son. When the pain was worst, she asked to hold my hand. She held so tight I thought my bones would break. She looked in my eyes and said she loved me. She said it over and over. And she said it was all my father's fault," she said again. "Those were the last words I ever heard her speak. The midwife couldn't stop the bleeding."

"What happened to the child?"

"It was a boy. A dead one. The cord wrapped around the neck. I was glad."

I wondered for the briefest moment if perhaps the baby had been strangled with its own cord after birth by a frightened and upset little girl whose mother lay dying. But I put the thought away at once. The midwife would certainly have attended to a son first before seeing to the mother.

"I'm sorry, Klymene," Diotima said.

"So am I. So am I."

I was struck all at once with a dreadful fear. The danger of childbirth. It was something my Diotima would face one day.

Diotima was saying, "What were you going to do if you fell pregnant?"

"Oh, there are herbs to fix that," she said. "I know a witch-woman. I've already had to use them once."

I wanted to put my hands over my ears to blot out the horror. Klymene saw my reaction and turned on me. "What would you know about this? You're a man."

"My mother's a midwife. I don't know everything that happens in the birthing bed, but I hear enough. You know no father will accept you for his son if word gets out." Even as I spoke, in a blinding flash like a revelation from the Gods, suddenly I understood my father's attitude to Diotima. I might not like it, but I understood.

Klymene snorted. "I'm the daughter of a wealthy man. I'll only be married to another wealthy man, one twice my age. He'll probably stink. He'll certainly use me for breeding and take whatever hetaera he frequents for his pleasure while I go old and gray looking after his brats. It's for certain he'll be no good in bed; old men can't keep it up any longer than it takes to spit. And that's it for the rest of my life. Sometimes I wonder if a quick death would be the better fate."

I thought Diotima would be disgusted. She surprised me by nodding in sympathy. "I know what you mean. I was very lucky to escape exactly that fate. What do you want from life, Klymene?" she asked.

"A proper man," Klymene said promptly. "One who'll treat me like a woman. A young man who can keep up with me."

"It'll never happen," I said at once. Because Klymene's estimate was right. Even Timo would have agreed. He'd talked of having his father find him a young virgin when he was thirty. "You've made a mistake."

"Who are you to complain about sex before marriage?" Klymene looked pointedly at Diotima and me.

"This is my fiancée," Diotima said through gritted teeth.

"Got caught out, did you?"

"As it happens, yes, but in a good way. I was caught by my heart. How many other women get to marry for love?"

"Well, I won't be one, that's for sure. But the way I heard it, you two aren't properly betrothed."

"We will be," I said confidently. At least, I hoped I sounded confident. "Our fathers are arranging the details even as we speak."

Klymene laughed. "Point proven, then. You two have been at each other before it's official, so don't whine at *me*."

Klymene was so right that it was embarrassing. To change the subject, I said, "What happened after your mother died?"

"Father married again. It was part of a commercial deal, alliance of families, you know how it works. She hated me, I hated her. Then she died."

"Of anything in particular?" I asked, wondering if there'd been a murder.

"A wasting disease. I made sure I didn't catch it by going nowhere near her."

"You can't catch wasting diseases," Diotima pointed out.

"Oh? I wasn't aware. Anyway, that was the last time Father tried marriage. I begged to join the priestesses; at least it gets me out of the house."

I said, "This is all irrelevant to the important point. We'll take you at once to see the judges, Klymene. Your testimony will clear Timodemus of the murder." I smiled to myself. This was mission accomplished. Between us, Diotima and I had proven Timodemus innocent. Pericles was going to be impressed how quickly we'd solved this one.

Klymene looked at me as if I were mad. She said, "No."

"What?"

"I said no. No chance. Have you thought this through? I can't give Timodemus his alibi without admitting what we were doing. Do you know the penalty for polluting the Priestess of the Games?"

Death. I didn't know what the law said, but it was obvious. Timo's alibi would result in his execution in *any case*.

Klymene said, "I'm sorry. Really I am. I like Timo. I like him a lot. But he gets executed either way, and if I can't save him, I see no reason to join him in disgrace."

For the first time in the conversation Klymene sounded genuine and sincere. She had a point. We would have to do this without her.

"If your father finds out about your fun, he's going to kill Timodemus," I mused.

"He already is," Klymene said.

"What did you say?"

"Are you hard of hearing? My father's already ordered the death of Timodemus."

"B . . . b . . . but . . ." I stammered. "The judges . . ."

"Oh, didn't I mention that? My father is Exelon, the Chief Judge of the Games."

WHAT A MOTIVE to kill Arakos. And Timodemus, too, for that matter. Fathers regularly killed young men who despoiled their daughters; every year there were one or two cases in Athens. Usually the fathers got off, because jurors have daughters too.

With that thought, I realized how lucky I was that Pythax had not murdered *me*. I'd despoiled his stepdaughter. When you got down to it, Pythax had shown remarkable restraint. He must really like me. And I liked him. The thought made me more determined than ever to make everything right between us.

Diotima and I talked it over. Exelon, the Chief Judge of the Games, had just gone straight to the top of our suspects list. He could have murdered Arakos to make it look like Timodemus had done it. Then as Chief Judge he could simply find him guilty and execute him, not only with perfect legality but with an apparent fairness that men would admire, and in so doing he would eliminate both men who'd been with his daughter. The thought amazed me. It was almost the perfect crime.

There was only one problem: I tried to imagine Exelon murdering anyone, but the image eluded me. The man was so rigid in his uprightness they could have used him for a temple column.

"There's another possibility, Nico," Diotima said. "Something else we can try. If Exelon learns that we've found a motive for him to have killed Arakos, if he knows that to convict Timodemus means exposing his own reputation and that of his household, he might drop the charges."

She said it as if it were the most reasonable thing in the world, but there was one problem with Diotima's suggestion.

"You want me to blackmail the Chief Judge?"

"No, not at all!" she said calmly. "Merely point out an unpleasant consequence of his intended actions. You're an officer of the judges, Nico, after you swore the Olympic Oath; you should bring this detail to his attention."

"It sounds like blackmail to me!"

"Pericles would tell you to do it, wouldn't he?" she wheedled. "All Pericles wants is for you to get Timodemus off. He doesn't care how you do it."

It was an odd thing that Pericles and Diotima, who couldn't stand each other, were so alike when it came to ruthlessly achieving their objectives.

I sighed. "You're right. I'll talk to Exelon." I told myself I'd be more diplomatic about it than Diotima.

We'd missed most of the lunch, but we could smell it, and we headed that way. As we walked across the Sanctuary of Zeus, discussing the case, we came across a man lying in the dirt. I recognized him at once.

"Niallos, are you all right?" It was the manager of the Theban chariot team, who had tried to protect Iphicles from our questions and who had sat with the charioteer while he died.

"No, I'm not bloody all right," he said, his face in the dirt. "I killed my friend."

His hair was shredded almost to nothing. He'd cut it with a knife, and either the knife had been blunt, or he'd been mighty careless as he hewed, because there were ugly wounds in his scalp that had barely scabbed over. To cut one's hair is the traditional sign of mourning, but usually it's a polite shear. Niallos had really meant it.

I helped him up and wrinkled my nose. Niallos hadn't washed

or eaten or, if the way he clutched a wineskin was any indication, done anything but drink since Iphicles had died the day before. The dust caked on his face had tracks where the tears had fallen.

He said, "If only it had been a decent death, I could accept it, you know? Racing's a deadly game, always has been. If another chariot had gone into him, or his team went down, or he didn't make the turn, then it'd be the will of the gods. I could accept that. If only it weren't my chariot that killed him."

He stifled a sob.

"It wasn't your fault," I said.

"Of course it's my bloody fault! I'm the team manager. Iphicles died because I gave him a faulty vehicle. Did you see the way that wheel came off?"

"Accidents happen," Diotima said. I heard the pity in her voice.

"Yeah, well, that's what I tell myself, but it's not much consolation." He swayed from side to side, and his face was gray. For a moment I wondered if Niallos was about to pass out.

Instead, he said, "I've known Iphicles ever since he was a lad. He used to hang around the chariot teams and bother the drivers, when he was, oh, I don't know, eight or nine years old? That boy was born to race."

"You'd been together that long?"

"All he ever wanted was to be a driver. Back then, I was a crew member, a chariot specialist. All I wanted was to be manager. I was working my way up."

He upended the wineskin. I thought about taking it from him, but it would have been cruel. He needed to forget.

Niallos went on, "The drivers are the stars, you know. They thought Iphicles was just another fan boy, but I knew the lad loved the race as much as I did. He and I used to talk chariots long into the night. Now see what it's brought us."

The way he said it, I could tell they'd done more than just talk. Niallos had lost his love.

"Can we help?" Diotima asked gently.

"You can't bring back the dead, can you?"

Diotima was silent.

Niallos began to sob once more. All we could do was sit him in the shade with his wine and leave him alone.

"These Games are cruel," Diotima said.

EXELON WAS A hard man to catch, which was not surprising for someone running the largest athletic event in the world. I eventually managed by waylaying him at lunch, where he sat with the other judges before bowls of steaming ox meat.

I pushed my way into their group with mumbled excuses. "Exelon, I must ask you some questions."

"Now?" he said. He looked meaningfully down at his bowl of hot food.

"Have you any idea how hard it is to get hold of you?"

He said angrily, "I've been working since before dawn yesterday morning. It's the middle of the day; I will be up half the night and at work again before Apollo rises tomorrow. So yes, young man, I have some vague awareness of how busy I am. What do you want?"

I studied the man who was hated so very much by his daughter Klymene, and I wondered which of them was in the right. For my purposes, though, the answer didn't matter.

"Exelon, new evidence has come to light that, when you've heard it, will probably cause you to drop all charges against Timodemus." I began praying that Diotima's idea would work.

Exelon looked amazed. "That's an extraordinary statement, young man!"

"It's extraordinary evidence, sir." I took a deep breath. Then I whispered, so quietly that no one else could hear, "Exelon, I must report to you, in your official role as Judge of the Games, that the Priestess of the Games may be a tad . . . er . . . impure."

Exelon looked left and right to make sure no one had heard

me. "Shhhh! Don't say that out in the open, you idiot." He set aside his bowl of food. "Come with me at once."

He dragged me across the grounds of Olympia to where the judges had their tents, in the best, most central location. He ushered me into his own tent and went straight to an ornately carved traveling cabinet I knew must hold wine, since it was decorated with the figure of the god Dionysos surrounded by grapes. He opened the door to pull out a cooler in the shape of a flying heron.

Exelon poured himself a slug of wine into a cup fashioned and painted to look like an egg. He took a hefty swallow, then collected himself and held the cooler up to me. "Do you want some?"

"Yes." I felt I was about to be as depressed as he looked.

Exelon pulled out another egg-shaped cup from a chest and handed it to me. I was surprised at the weight and then saw that it was solid silver.

"They're family heirlooms," he said when he noticed my interest. "My family is one of the oldest, wealthiest, and most respected in all of Elis. I come from a long line of judges stretching back generations, but I believe I am the first of my genos to be Chief Judge of the Games. For the Chief Judge, young man, the Games he runs define the success or failure of his entire life. I'm not the suicidal type, but I wonder if by the end of this disaster I might not feel like it."

"Has it been that bad?"

"What do you think? How many Games have seen contestants murdered? No matter what trouble this might mean for Athens and Sparta, for me it's a personal disaster, and now Olympia is becoming an armed camp. Will this be the first Olympics in history to be abandoned due to war? And to top it off, there was that impious *idiot* with the cow made of dough."

"It was an ox."

"My Olympics will be a laughing stock because of him.

A hundred years from now men will still be calling this the Olympics of the bread cow, and they'll laugh."

"I'm pretty sure it was an ox."

"An ox, you say? You must have looked more closely than I." Exelon emptied his cup and filled himself another. He fell back on a comfortable stool. "Now you may say what you have to say."

"I've said it. Your daughter, the Priestess of Demeter, was having it off with two of the contestants. Arakos and Timodemus. Quite a coincidence, wouldn't you say?"

Exelon snorted. "What you bring me is no news at all, and it's no coincidence. The pankratists are the stars of the Olympics. It seems my daughter likes them strong and flashy."

"What?"

"I'm not blind, young man. I know what you're thinking: why didn't I stop it? Well, by the time I found out, the damage was done. If I made a fuss, it would have hurt her more than them."

It wasn't what I was thinking at all. "How did you find out?"

"My daughter is a featherhead—I may be her father, but I'm not deluded—she left enough hints that anyone would have known. I see that I must tell you the whole story, but you must never reveal what I'm about to say."

"I'm sorry, Exelon, I can't promise you that. Not if it proves Timodemus is innocent."

"You have no choice," he said. "I remind you, young man, that you swore an Olympic Oath."

"I could hardly forget it. I must discover this killer no matter what the consequences."

"You're wrong," said the Chief Judge of the Games. "Nothing in your oath *requires* you to catch the killer. But you are required to obey the orders of the Judges of the Games."

It took a moment for it to sink in. Then I almost shouted, "You deliberately wrote the oath so that I must obey you!"

"No," he said. "You spoke the standard oath. But it so happens in your case the words take a different meaning from any other event. I therefore order you, Nicolaos of Athens, not to reveal my daughter's activities."

I was honor bound by oath to Zeus to obey.

Angry, I said, "You realize, don't you, Exelon, that this makes you a suspect."

"It does not."

"A man whose daughter was despoiled by the victim *and* the accused? You must hate them both."

"On the contrary. I called Arakos and Timodemus to my house in Elis on the day before the procession."

I imagined the scene, the two bitter rivals, standing side by side, facing the man who would soon decide their fate in the Games, the event for which they'd trained since they were boys, the event they'd been born to contest, and both knowing they'd been screwing this man's daughter.

"I suppose you tore strips off them?" I said

"I was the voice of reason, after I finished shouting at them. I told them that I knew what had been going on. They both turned a distinct green color."

"I can imagine. They both probably expected to be disqualified. It would have ruined their lives."

"And the life of my daughter, too. She could never survive the scandal and find a husband. But equally I did not dare let them go unpunished. One or the other of these two over-endowed idiots was certain to win the pankration, and when he did, he would be untouchable. The winner could boast that he'd despoiled the daughter of the Chief Judge and be immune from my revenge. Happily, I had the perfect punishment."

"I can't imagine what it was."

"I congratulated them and said that one of them was about to become my son-in-law. I told Arakos and Timodemus that whichever of them won the Olympic crown would also win my daughter in marriage."

He paused.

"So you see, one of them would lose the Olympics, and the other would be stuck with my daughter. I'm not sure which is the worse fate, but either way, why should I wish to kill my future son-in-law? Especially when he's about to become an Olympic champion."

"WHEN DROMEUS ADVISED you to have regular sex, he probably didn't mean with the Priestess of the Games."

Timo shrugged. "Can I help it if I'm irresistible to women?"

I'd marched to the makeshift prison via the fire pits, where I'd snaffled a rib of succulent meat that dripped with fat, maybe the best I'd ever tasted. Timo and I sat on the dirty floor and ate it. I needed to confirm Exelon's statement with the only man left alive who would know. Also, I had a few bones to pick with my supposed friend, the one who'd sworn he'd told me the truth.

"Besides," Timo went on, "Klymene is good in bed." He paused. "She's really good."

"Oh?" I said, deeply interested. "What does she do?" Then it occurred to me Diotima might not approve that line of questioning, so before he could answer, I said, "You're going to be really dead if anyone finds out the Games are being blessed by a ritually impure priestess. Timo, why did you lie to me?"

"I didn't want to get Klymene into trouble."

"So instead you thought it might be a good idea to die?"

"When you put it like that . . . perhaps I wasn't thinking straight."

Or perhaps my friend was more in love than he knew.

"What's this story about Exelon pulling you and Arakos up in front of him?"

Timo sighed. "It's true. There was Arakos and me, side by side, in Exelon's private office. I've never been scared of anything, but I was shaking in that room! I thought to myself, this is the Chief Judge. If he wanted, he could find some way to destroy my chances in the Sacred Games. Then, when Exelon announced the winner of the pankration would wed his daughter, I was almost relieved. It meant my chances in the Games were still good."

"What about Arakos?"

"I hated him then, knowing he'd been with Klymene."

"And he hated you."

"He was insanely jealous."

"I've heard about the accusations of witchcraft at Nemea, Timo."

"Oh." He was crestfallen. "It's not true, Nico. I swear it isn't."

"Did you cheat at the Nemean Games?"

"No."

"Did you kill Arakos?"

"No."

"After the way you've lied to me, is there any reason why I should believe you now?"

Timodemus paused, then hung his head and said, "No."

I REPORTED BACK to Diotima what Exelon had told me. She was in her tent, reading.

She focused on the issue closest to her own heart. "You mean he *allowed* his daughter to have affairs?"

I nodded.

"Why couldn't I get fathers like that?"

"It's rather the reverse of our problem, isn't it?" I paused. "Diotima, is being really good in bed a basis for a marriage?"

"Hmm? How would I know?"

"Thanks a lot!"

"Oh Nico, I didn't mean it like that." Diotima put down her scroll. "What I mean is, we have so much more in common than merely sex."

"*Merely* sex?"

"We have our common work. We get on—mostly. We respect each other. You're good to me, Nico. You listen to what I say."

"That's because you're right more often than I am," I admitted.

"You see? How many men would admit that? Why are you asking these questions?"

"You heard Klymene say Timo was the man to see for an orgasm. Later, Timo told me that Klymene is *really good* in bed."

"Oho!"

"Yes. Of course, their fathers would have to agree."

"Which as we know all too well isn't certain."

"Right. But I wouldn't want Timo to make a mistake. I don't know what sort of wife Klymene would make."

Diotima considered. "She doesn't seem marriage material at first glance, does she?"

"No, and to top it off, she's not a . . . er . . ."

"Not a citizen of Athens?" my non-citizen metic wife finished in a frigid tone. "And is that a problem, *husband*?" She picked up one of the throwing knives beside her and balanced it on a finger.

"Not for me, and well you know it, *wife*. But for most men, yes, it is."

"Well," said Diotima, "it won't do either of them the slightest good if Timodemus is executed."

"But we've proven he didn't do it. He was in bed with Klymene."

"An alibi we can't use."

I nodded unhappily. "The only way to save Timo is to find the real killer."

"Then let's review the possibilities."

"All right," I said. "One-Eye and Festianos. They killed Arakos to give Timo an easy run in the Games. The hemlock is suspicious."

"Maybe," Diotima said. "But it leaves us with the problem of how they could poison Arakos with hemlock before they beat him."

I nodded glumly.

"Dromeus has the same motive," Diotima said. "I don't trust Dromeus. He makes a living teaching young men how to beat up other young men."

"Would Dromeus take such a risk for what, after all, is only a job? Dromeus is a hired hand."

"Who can say? We need to know more about Dromeus," Diotima said. "There might be more to him. What about Exelon? Do you believe his story?"

"Timo confirms the facts, but . . . I don't know, Diotima. He has a fantastic motive."

"I agree."

"What about these mysterious secrets?" I asked. "Any idea?"

Diotima threw up her arms in confusion. "Your guess is as good as mine."

"Have we missed any suspects?"

"The other contestants," Diotima said at once. "What better way to improve their chances than to kill one front-runner and frame the other?"

I'd had the same thought but never followed it up. "You're right, and I haven't done a thing about them. We better get on to that."

WE COLLECTED MARKOS on the way, since the rules of this game required us to see the same evidence and hear the same witnesses. I'd played very loose with those rules, and I was sure he had, too. I debated with myself whether to tell Markos about the hemlock. I liked him, and I was sure that together we could make faster progress. I decided in the end that this was a competition, and he was my opponent, and that mattered more than friendship, particularly when my other friend's life was the stake of the game.

Timodemus had told me the top three men in pankration, after himself and Arakos, were Korillos from Corinth, Aggelion from Keos, and Megathenes from Megara. We found all of them at the gym, as expected. The pankration was on the next day, a dismal reminder that Timo's time was running out. The pankratists were in final preparation—not working to the limit, but enough to keep themselves loose.

Diotima had to wait outside. Markos and I found the three we wanted, the three with the most to gain from the elimination of Arakos and Timo. Their trainers tried to stop us, but we invoked the rule of the Chief Judge: Markos and I had access to anywhere and anyone.

"Can we go somewhere we can't be seen?" one of the men—Korillos—asked. They were as young as Marko and me.

Together we crossed the Sanctuary—Diotima rejoined us on the way—to the Avenue of the Victors, part of the road into Olympia, lined with the statues of past winners. The statuary varied wildly in style, from the recent winners, so realistic you'd swear they could step down from the plinths to win again, to statues of winners from so long ago they looked like something out of Egypt.

All three of our suspects seemed worried. Aggelion, from Keos, was small and fast, like Timo. Megathenes of Megara had more the look of a runner than a fighter. Korillos of Corinth was a big man, exuding strength.

"Why are we hiding?" I asked. "Is what you have to say so sensitive, or is it embarrassing to be seen with the investigators?"

Aggelion said, "It's nothing to do with you."

"The thing is, we're regulars on the circuit," said Megathenes. "We don't want the other regulars to think we might be talking about them."

"The circuit?" Markos repeated.

Korillos said, "The Isthmian Games, the Pythian Games, the Nemean Games, the Olympic Games. The big four, plus all the little contests in between that no one ever mentions. We go from one to the next, competing at each. It's a punishing pace, but while we're fit and young is the time to do it. We hardly ever see our homes."

"We're closer to each other than we are to the people in our own cities," said Megathenes. He smiled at Korillos, and Korillos returned a grin, in a way that instantly caused me to think they might be very close indeed.

"You were to compete against Arakos then," Markos said.

"Right," said Korillos.

"Are you from a sporting family?" Aggelion asked me.

I smiled. "Hardly. My father's a sculptor."

"How can someone who doesn't understand sport solve a sporting crime?" Aggelion asked.

"I don't need to understand the game to solve who killed a man."

"Sure," said Aggelion, obviously unconvinced.

"How well do you know Timodemus?" I asked the pankratists.

"Like us, he's been on the circuit," said Korillos.

"All three of you were at Nemea?" Diotima asked.

"Yes," he said shortly. He was clearly unhappy to talk to a woman.

Diotima saw it, too. She said, "Do you understand we're empowered to ask any question?"

"No, you're not," said Aggelion. "That's the two men. We don't have to answer to you."

"When Diotima speaks, it's as if I speak," I said at once. "Please answer her questions."

Diotima had held her temper remarkably well. She said, "The rumor is Timodemus cheated at Nemea."

Korillos looked to his friends and competitors. They nodded. "It's no rumor. Timodemus definitely cheated at Nemea."

Markos cast a look of triumph my way, which I studiously ignored.

Megathenes spoke for the first time. "All three of us fought against Timodemus. We all felt the same thing."

"Felt what?"

"Heavy legs."

Korillos nodded. "Lethargic, like I didn't want to move. I was fine before the match, I was fine the next day, but when I faced Timodemus, all I wanted to do was lie down."

"Everyone knows he cursed us with witchcraft," Megathenes said.

I kept my face passive. I already knew this from Pindar, but I didn't want Markos to discover I'd hidden the information from him.

"I've got a question," I said. "It's nothing to do with the investigation, so please excuse me if this is rude and don't answer if you don't feel like it . . ."

They looked at me in surprise.

"You, Megathenes, you're from Megara."

"Yes."

"And Korillos, you're from Corinth."

"Right."

"Your cities are at war, and Athens is involved, too. Your little war could drag every other city in Hellas into an all-out conflagration."

"I get the impression you're not pleased about that," said Megathenes.

"I'm not. I have better things to do than march in a phalanx. Has it occurred to you gentlemen that if Hellas goes to war, we five might have to kill each other in battle? But here's the question you don't have to answer. How can you, Megathenes, and you, Korillos, maintain your . . . ah . . . friendship when your cities are at each other's throats?"

"It isn't easy," Korillos said at once, and he reached out to hold Megathenes's hand. Megathenes squeezed back.

"We've talked about it. A lot," said Megathenes. "But what can we do? We have to hope it all settles down."

"Any hope of that, do you think?" I asked.

"Megara would make peace in an instant," said Megathenes. "My people only want to be left alone."

"But Corinth won't tolerate it," said Korillos. "Megara began as a colony of Corinth, and that's how my people insist it stays. It wouldn't be such a big deal, except Megara ran to Athens for help."

"My people could hardly do otherwise when they have no chance against Corinth on their own."

Korillos and Megathenes seemed to have forgotten us. They faced each other in their own little argument.

"But bringing in Athens turned it into a matter of prestige," said Korillos. "Now my people can't back away without looking weak."

Megathenes said, with some heat, "That's not fair."

"Don't fight, you two," said Aggelion. Which I thought was rather silly for one pankratist to say to two others.

"You see how it affects us all," said Aggelion, and Korillos and Megathenes looked rather shamefaced. "Now kiss and make up," Aggelion ordered, and the two friends did.

"You see the real reason we didn't want to be seen," Aggelion said. "There'd be an uproar if a man of Corinth and a man of Megara fraternized."

I wondered if Aggelion sometimes joined in the frolics with his friends. "So you three have a real interest in keeping the peace," I said.

"Rather funny for a bunch of professional fighters, isn't it?" Aggelion observed, and he smiled.

"Where were you on the night Arakos died?" Diotima asked.

"In bed," said Aggelion.

"That's not much of an alibi."

"In bed together. All three of us."

"Oh."

"Please don't tell our trainers."

"THE CASE SEEMS clear," Markos said, after the three friendly pankratists had made their way off. "Timodemus of Athens cheated at Nemea. Not only cheated, but used witchcraft to curse his opponents, a terrible crime. He continued his ways here at Olympia, only now he's graduated to murder."

"Why wouldn't he continue to use curses?" Diotima asked. She and I knew the truth, that Timo could not have been in the clearing with Arakos, but we couldn't tell Markos that.

"Perhaps Arakos had proof Timodemus had cheated before. That would be more than enough motive for murder."

Indeed it would, if it were true.

"I'm not sure I believe Timo cursed anyone, Markos," I said.

"You'll have to believe it if everyone who fought against your friend tells the same tale. You realize, I'm sure, the evidence of those pankratists make it certain your friend practiced witchcraft. Heavy legs, indeed! It sounds like a typical binding spell."

"I don't even know if curses work," I said.

"Oh, come on, Nico. I know you have to do your best for your friend, raise every reasonable doubt, but *everyone* knows curses work."

"Have you ever tried one?" I challenged him.

"No, of course not," he said. "That would be immoral."

"Then you don't really know."

"Everyone's heard of a case."

"Right. You hear the stories, but you never see one."

"Well, now you *are* seeing one, and you refuse to believe it," Markos said, reasonably enough.

I shook my head. There was something wrong with that logic, but I couldn't work out what it was. Perhaps Socrates could tell me.

"I just feel we need to look for a more rational explanation," I insisted.

"You've been hanging around too many of those philosophers you have in Athens," said Markos.

"Ain't that the truth," I told him, and I nudged Diotima, who considered herself to be a philosopher.

"He'll be hanging around one for a lot longer," she said, and took my arm.

Markos laughed. "It's a pleasure to work with the both of you. I'm sorry that I must prosecute your friend. I hope you understand, my liking for you won't prevent me from doing my utmost to see him punished."

"You keep calling him my friend," I said.

"It's true, isn't it?"

And of course, Markos was right. No wonder people didn't trust me. It made me wonder if perhaps Markos was right, if my friendship for Timo had blinded me to the evidence, because he was right about that, too. On the face of it, those pankratists had been cursed.

WE NEEDED TO know more about Dromeus of Mantinea, the trainer of Timodemus. Dromeus had been at Nemea. He was here at Olympia. He had every reason to want to see Timodemus win. And another thing: everyone assumed only Timodemus could have beaten Arakos, but what about a previous victor? Surely a man who'd won the crown and kept himself in good condition could take on a current contender, especially in a surprise attack in the dark.

But who was Dromeus, really, and what sort of man was he? I knew just the people to ask. Heralds not only have the loudest voices, but every one of them is a sports fanatic.

Diotima and I bid farewell to Markos and wished him a happy feast in the evening. Then we went to find the Heralds of the Games.

The heralds sat in a cluster at one corner of the stadion. It was one of the perks of the job that they had access to the field. When I approached, I saw they were eating a picnic on the most hallowed sporting ground in the world. Most of them carried paunches over which their chitons had to detour on the way down. It seemed odd that men who loved sport should themselves be in such poor condition.

"I'd like to ask you a few—"

"Shhh!" They waved at me to be quiet. "Can't you see we're playing *kottabos*? He's about to throw."

"Oh." I shut up.

Now that they mentioned it, I saw they lounged in a ring around a central point, where they'd placed the upright stand necessary for the party game called kottabos. The stand was half the height of a man, a polished wooden pole set into a wide, bronze base. A small hook had been placed in the top of the pole, from which hung an ornate bronze disk. Carved into the disk was the image of Dionysos, the God of Wine.

One of the heralds drained his wine cup down to the dregs. Then, using only the forefinger of his right hand to hold the cup handle, he took careful aim and flung the dregs at the kottabos stand. The dregs sailed through the air as one alcoholic glob to hit the small bronze. The disk wobbled back and forth, once, twice, three times, then came loose of the hook and fell into the bronze base, where it landed with a loud metallic clatter.

"Yes! Yes! Yes!"

He pumped his hands in the air. If he'd won the Olympics he couldn't have been any happier. I struck while there was joy all around.

"You heralds are the world's greatest experts on sport," I said.

"Of course we are," said the kottabos winner. "That's 'cause we watch it most."

"Right. What can you tell me about Dromeus?"

"Which one?"

"Dromeus the Olympic victor."

"Yeah, which one?"

It took me a moment to realize what he meant. "You mean there are two Olympic victors named Dromeus?" I asked.

"Of course, there are. Don't you know nothing? There's Dromeus of Stymphalos who won the *diaulos*—"

I looked at him blankly.

"The *diaulos*, where they race two lengths of the stadion. Diaulos—two lengths—get it?"

"Sure."

"Well, he's the Dromeus what said athletes should eat nothing but meat, and he won, so ever since athletes have been on meat-only diets. That philosopher who preached this morning, the one with the bread cow—"

"It was an ox."

"He'll be lucky to leave these Games alive if he keeps talking against meat. That bread cow was a laugh, though."

"What about the second Dromeus?"

"That's Dromeus of Mantinea. He won the pankration in the seventy-sixth Olympiad."

"I'm after Dromeus of Mantinea."

"You're wrong," another herald spoke up. "Dromeus won in the seventy-fifth."

"It was the seventy-sixth," said the first.

"You're both wrong. It was the seventy-fourth," said a third man.

"Don't tell me what's what. I can name every Olympic victor in every event going back to the days of my father."

The second man spat in the dust. "That's nothing. I can name every running victor since the days of my grandfather. My grand-daddy memorized the winners in his own day, and he passed it on to me dad, and me dad passed it on to me. And when my son is grown he'll know the victors for four generations."

Diotima spoke up. "Gentlemen, could we get back to the issue at hand?"

"What's *she* doing in the stadion?" one of the heralds demanded. He stared at her like she was some creature from the underworld.

"Are the Games on?" I asked.

"No."

"Then she can be here." I was right, and he knew it. Women were only barred during competition. "So as my wife says, what was Dromeus like, as a competitor? Aggressive? Smart? Tough?"

"You mean, how he fought? Ha!" They shared a good chuckle before one of them deigned to explain. "You know how Dromeus won his crown, don't you?"

"I imagine by beating his opponents."

Now all the heralds guffawed.

"That's where you're wrong," said the kottabos winner. "Dromeus won without raising a fist."

"That's impossible."

"No, it ain't. That year there was only one other contestant for the pankration." He shrugged. "It happens, some years. Anyways, the other man was Theagenes of Thasos, and he'd also entered for the boxing. Theagenes won the boxing, then claimed he was too exhausted to fight the pankration."

"I'm not surprised."

He spat. "Surprise or no, the man was a coward. It's an insult to Zeus to enter the Games and then refuse to fight. The judges fined Theagenes two talents."

"Urrk." That was more money than I ever expected to see in my life. Two talents were twelve *thousand* drachmae, enough to feed a family for thirty years.

The herald said, "Yeah, but here's the thing. Dromeus of Mantinea stood to fight, and no one stood against him. So they had to award him the crown for nothing. And ever since then, men have said he's the weakest Olympic victor ever. That's gotta burn him to the core, don't you reckon?"

"THAT'S THE BEST motive I've heard for killing someone in, oh, at least half a day," Diotima said as we wandered away.

"It certainly makes it more likely he'd kill for a win," I agreed.

"The more I hear about this Dromeus, the less I like him," she said.

We stopped dead, because there, in front of us, stood Diotima's stepfather, Pythax. He looked gray and old, two words I would never have associated with the Pythax I knew. Had he been taken ill?

He said to me, "I've just been talking to your dad. He's officially turned down my dowry offer unless I throw in the farm."

"Throw in the farm," Diotima said at once.

"Do you want your mother to starve?" he said quietly.

Diotima paused for a long moment. "No."

Pythax turned back to me. "So it's like this, Nicolaos."

I blinked. It was the first time Pythax had ever called me anything other than little boy.

Pythax said, "I gotta find another husband for my daughter.
I would have liked you, but it ain't gonna happen. Diotima
might not be my natural daughter, but she's mine all the same,
and I'm going to do right by her. I'll find her someone decent,
I promise you that, 'cause I ain't giving her to no one but a
decent man."

I nodded. "I understand, Pythax."

"I thought you would. We both want the best for her, right?"

I almost choked. "Of course."

"Yeah, and the best place to find someone is right here at
Olympia."

Pythax might not be the smartest man in Hellas, but he wasn't
stupid. Many men brought their daughters to Olympia to find
them matches, and many men came here to find a wife. Diotima
was a beauty. Pythax could find a husband who'd want Diotima for
herself, whose father didn't need another farm.

"Don't I get a say in this?" Diotima demanded.

"No," Pythax and I said simultaneously.

"I'll talk to my father," I said.

"He ain't gonna budge."

"I know." And I knew why. If Father accepted Diotima on
the offered terms, we'd be bankrupt within a month. He was too
proud to tell Pythax that, and Pythax was too proud to admit he
couldn't make it as a citizen without Diotima's wealth. They were
both trapped by poverty.

"Go back to the women's camp, Diotima," Pythax said. "If
you're seen alone with Nicolaos, everyone will know you two've
been . . . er . . . friendly. Fortunately we're at Olympia. There're
a lot of eligible bachelors here, from other cities. Men who don't
know . . . er . . . aren't aware of . . ."

"My unfortunate family history?" Diotima supplied. Her tone
could have frozen an ocean.

"Well, yeah." Pythax shuffled his feet. He could command hundreds of guards with ease, but one stubborn woman was beyond him.

"If you think I'll agree to this, *Pythax*," Diotima said, "then you're quite insane."

There were fathers who would have struck their daughters for such rudeness. Pythax wasn't one of them. He was silent for a long moment. He seemed sad. Finally, he spoke.

"Then there's only one thing left I can do," Pythax said. "I'll give Sophroniscus the farm. You can marry Nicolaos, and I'll hire out as a mercenary."

Mercenary?

Diotima exclaimed, "No! Father! You can't do that."

I agreed with her. For all his tough talk and tougher ways, Pythax was a man who ended fights, not started them.

"If I ain't got the farm, I got to do something to earn money to support your mother. Mercenary is honorable work, even for a citizen," he said, then added, "And it's something I can do."

"I won't have this," Diotima said.

"Then go back to the women's camp," said Pythax.

"You'll have to go, Diotima," I said.

Diotima knew it, too. She offered me one look of despair, and walked away.

We watched her go.

"Nicolaos, I want you to know I'm ashamed about this."

"I understand, Pythax," I said. "I don't like it, but I understand. I would have liked you as a father-in-law." I forced a grin. "I never thought I'd say that, after we first met."

"Yeah, well, we still don't take piss-poor little mama's boys in the Scythian Guard."

He paused.

"Of course, you ain't one of those anymore."

I said, "Pythax, I was just about to go into the gymnasium. There's someone there I need to talk to. Want to come along?"

His sad eyes brightened. "See the Olympic gymnasium? 'Course I do."

"Come on."

Dromeus was exactly where I'd left him, with his cronies, Eosilos and Theo and the rest of them, old warriors recalling old times. There was no reason Dromeus should have moved; he didn't have a student to train.

"Dromeus," I said at once. He and his friends looked up from their talk. "You said your friends were with you the night Arakos died. Is that right?"

"That's right."

"I've seen how close you pankratists are to each other. You might have tried to kill each other when you were young men, but I reckon you'd die for each other now."

"I reckon you're right," Dromeus said, and his friends about him nodded.

"Which makes me wonder if your alibi is any good. Did you kill Arakos?"

He snorted derision and said nothing.

"I wonder how much you needed Timo to win. I wonder if you needed this victory as much as One-Eye?"

"You're crazy. I'm an Olympic victor. Nothing could compare to that, not even if my man wins."

"How did you win your victory, Dromeus?"

He glared at me. "You know. Everyone knows what happened. I stood to take on anyone who cared, and no one came forward. I can't *make* them fight me, can I?"

I said, "It's true, isn't it, Dromeus, men consider your victory lesser because it was unopposed?"

"Listen here, weakling, it's Zeus who grants the victory. At my Games, that's the way he chose to do it." Dromeus was almost shouting.

"What do men whisper behind your back? 'There goes the man who won his crown for nothing.'"

Dromeus picked me up with one hand and slammed me against the wall. He was so fast, I didn't know until it had happened. My legs dangled off the ground. I could feel his hot breath on my face.

"Is that what you say?" he asked.

"Er . . ." Something had gone horribly wrong. I'd wanted to provoke Dromeus into an angry admission, not a beating rage.

Dromeus drew back his fist to punch me in the face.

From seemingly nowhere Dromeus was thrown to the side. I dropped to the ground.

Standing behind Dromeus was Pythax.

Dromeus rolled like the expert he was and sprang to his feet ready to fight. Pythax stood there, solid as a rock, with bulging muscles. The two huge men faced each other: the expert pankratist and the hard-muscled barbarian.

Pythax said, "Leave him alone. I know he ain't much, but he's a friend."

Dromeus sized up Pythax and spat at his feet. "Stay out of this, barbarian. You shouldn't even be here. The Sacred Games are for Hellenes."

"I'm a citizen of Athens," Pythax said in his barbarian accent, and even I winced at the sound of it.

Dromeus laughed. "They make men out of dogs now, do they?"

I thought Pythax would strike—he turned angry red—but instead he said, "I reckon Nicolaos got it right. A man who wins a crown for nothing ain't worth much."

Dromeus flushed. "I earned my victory!"

"A real man would've refused the crown, 'less he had to fight for it."

"Anytime, barbarian."

They squared up to each other like two angry Titans.

"The agora. Before the light closes. I like to see a man when I kill him."

"I'll see you there, barbarian."

Pythax and I backed out of the gym; it was that sort of tension. When we were out the door, I said to him, "You realize you just agreed to take on a professional fighter?"

"I had to, little boy. That bastard questioned my right to be here. Me, a citizen of Athens."

And who was I to question that? Pythax had defended the greatest privilege any man could have.

"Pythax, when you meet Dromeus, let me back you up."

He clapped me on the back, and I almost fell over. "I knew you'd say that."

"At least I discovered something important."

"What?"

"That Dromeus was capable of killing Arakos. I didn't even know he was about to attack me until my head hit the wall."

Pythax shook his head. "You picked a dangerous trade, little boy."

This, from a man who was about to face a trained bare-handed killer.

The feeling between us at that moment was intense. If we'd both been Hellenes, we would have hugged. But I refrained. Pythax was a barbarian, and I didn't want to embarrass him. Then I remembered Pythax was trying so hard to be Hellene.

But the moment had passed. I watched Pythax's back as he strode to the agora.

"You look rather depressed," a voice said from behind.

I turned around to see Markos.

"I am."

"The man you were speaking to, when I saw you just now, that's the father of your fiancée, isn't it?"

"That's Pythax, and that's why I'm depressed. The wedding with Diotima is officially off."

"What's this?" Markos asked, surprised.

"They can't agree on the dowry," I said shortly, unwilling to tell him the details.

"I see." He rubbed his chin. "Well, it happens, even among the Spartans, but I'm sorry for you. They say fathers know best about these things. What happens to Diotima now?"

"Pythax hopes to find her a suitable husband here at Olympia."

"A girl like her, she's bound to get offers before the Games are over."

"Is that supposed to make me feel better?" I asked.

He put a hand on my shoulder.

"Nico! Nico!" Socrates ran up, stopped in front of us, panting. "Another message! It was dropped in our tent, just like the last one."

Socrates handed it to me. Into this ostrakon, scratched in shaky, barely legible letters, were these words:

Why haven't you arrested them? I'm scared but I have to do something. Meet me at the Temple of Zeus at dusk and I'll tell you but only you or I'll run away.

"Did anyone see him?" I asked.

Socrates shook his head.

I said, "Who is this man?" But there was no answer. I would have to find out when I met him.

It was unfortunate Socrates had found me in the presence of Markos. Though we were supposed to share everything, this meeting was an advantage I could have held. I turned the new ostrakon over and over, in hopes of gleaning something more.

"The shard was taken from the side of a broken amphora," I said, and Socrates nodded.

"How can you tell?" Markos asked.

I held it up for him to see, vertical and sideways. "See the curve of the clay? If it came from a small pot, then the curve would be tighter. This comes from an amphora, or some other pot of similar size."

"I see. Then it might also be from a krater for mixing wine?"

"No. Kraters are always decorated on the outside." I turned the shard to show the outer face. "It's not glazed. Only the dull red of the original clay."

"Very good, Nicolaos! I understand exactly."

"Thanks, Markos." I was oddly pleased by his approval. "The only problem is, it doesn't help us at all. There must be hundreds of broken amphorae all over Olympia. A distinctive glazed decoration and a maker's mark would have been so much more useful."

"Your correspondent has been careful to remain anonymous. Yet he arranges a meeting. Why didn't he simply come to you?" Markos asked, puzzled. "It would be as easy as to leave the message."

"I don't know. I wonder why he sent this to me, and not you?"

"Because I'm a Spartan," Markos said ruefully. "He's afraid I'll suppress any evidence that exonerates an Athenian."

"Markos, do you want to be there?"

Markos hesitated. "Do you swear to tell me everything he tells you?"

"I swear it, by Zeus and Athena."

"Then I won't go. I might scare him off." Markos looked up at the sun and squinted. "You have a while before you need to be there."

"That's good, because I have a fight to referee."

PYTHAX AND DROMEUS met at the field of the agora. There was nothing unusual in that. The agora was the site for all manner of sideshows. For two men to test themselves against each other was nothing special, except these men were Pythax and Dromeus.

By the time Dromeus arrived, word had already spread and a ring had formed, defined by the men who had come to watch the weakest pankratist ever take on a mere barbarian with pretensions to Hellenism.

Pythax had stripped and stood waiting. Dromeus did the same as he arrived, flanked by the pankratists from the gymnasium. They backed their man for the honor of the pankration.

Pythax spat in the dust. I stood at his side.

"Gentlemen," I called. "The contest is between Dromeus of Mantinea and Pythax of Athens. The rules are those of the pankration—"

"No rules," Dromeus said.

Pythax nodded. "No rules," he agreed.

I stepped back. So did the friends of Dromeus. I hoped this didn't turn into a free-for-all, because there was only me to back Pythax.

In the crowd I saw my father, Sophroniscus. His eyes were impossible to read from the distance. I hoped Father would stay out of this. He was an old man, in no condition for these games.

Pythax's eyes were dark and angry. For some reason I noticed how thick and bushy was his beard.

"Begin," I said.

Pythax took a swing at Dromeus and knocked his head around. Dromeus returned the blow with a swift punch to the neck. Pythax dodged, but the blow hit him over the heart, and he grunted.

Pythax knew every dirty trick there was. I knew, because he'd taught me most of them, but he used none of them now. He was determined this was to be a test of pure strength. Dromeus likewise eschewed every technique of the pankration and concentrated on battering Pythax into submission. Blow after blow they traded, until I was sure one or the other must fall.

The two men staggered back and forth, barely on their feet. Blood streamed from their noses, their mouths, their ears, and gashes on their faces. Their chests had taken a pummeling that would have killed lesser men.

"Dear Gods, what's happening!" A voice behind me. Diotima. "What are you doing here?"

"I realized I don't care what happens to me; I refuse to hide like a weak woman in my tent. I heard about this in the women's camp. All of Olympia is talking about the fight. *You* got Pythax into this, didn't you?"

I told her what happened as the pummeling continued. Dromeus had his head down and smashed Pythax in the dia-phragm over and over while Pythax hammered the head of Dromeus.

"Nico, if you love me, you have to stop this," Diotima said. He voice sounded strained.

"Why?" I asked.

"I was cursing Pythax because he won't give in to your father's demands and let me marry you. Then I thought about Klymene and her vitriolic relationship with her father, and I realized that I might not like it, but Pythax has looked out for my interests like I was his own birth-daughter, and I love having him as my father, and Nico, you have to stop that fight."

"I can't," I said.

"Nico—"

"Diotima, this is an act of catharsis for both these men. It would be the worst cruelty to stop this before they've proven themselves before their fellows."

"You mean to say Pythax and Dromeus can fix their lives by battering each other until neither can stand, while other men watch them do it."

"Precisely."

"Aaarrggh. Why are men so stupid?" Diotima grimaced.

As she spoke, they both went for each other's throats. Their arms locked in a sheer test of strength. Their grins turned to ric-tus smiles of ultimate effort. The muscles in their arms strained so hard I could count every tendon. The sweat poured from their brows. At any moment the tendons would tear through the flesh that barely contained them. It was a dead heat for sheer animal strength. I seriously considered the possibility that Dromeus and Pythax might be about to kill each other.

"Aaarrgh!"

Someone with a panel of wood torn from one of the stalls whacked Dromeus in the face. He fell back, not expecting the blow.

It was Diotima.

"Aaarrgh!"

She hit Pythax in the face. He was too surprised to block. He, too, fell to the ground, panting and exhausted.

Diotima stood in the center; she owned the field of victory.

She shouted, "Stop this, both of you!"

I shouted too. "Diotima, get out of there!"

"Diotima?" Dromeus said from where he lay in the dirt. "Young woman, who are you?"

I realized Dromeus had never before seen Diotima in my company. He had no idea who she was. Dromeus stared at her as if she were some psyche ascended from Hades, which, given her fury, was a reasonable assumption.

I said, "I'm sorry, Dromeus. She's a bit hard to control."

Dromeus waved away my apology. "Who are you, woman?"

Diotima lifted her chin and said with pride, "I am named Diotima of Mantinea." Pythax, lying in the dirt and panting, winced. His action caught Diotima's eye, and she added in a softer voice, "And, too, I am daughter to Pythax, Chief of the Scythian Guard of Athens."

"I care nothing for your father," Dromeus said. "Your mother," he said. "Tell me the name of your mother."

"Why should I tell you?" Diotima never admitted her mother if she could help it.

"Just tell me, woman."

"No."

"Then tell me yea or nay, does she go by the name Euterpe the Hetaera?"

Diotima gasped.

Then it struck me like a blow to the head: Diotima was known as Diotima of Mantinea, after her mother's hometown, because her father had never married her mother, and here was Dromeus. Dromeus of Mantinea.

I glanced at my father. Sophroniscus looked from Dromeus to Diotima and back again, and stroked his beard, and I thought I saw the beginning of a smile.

Dromeus scrabbled to his knees, took Diotima by the hand, and between broken teeth said, "Greetings, cousin. I haven't seen you since you were a baby."

DROMEUS HAD POLITELY asked permission of Pythax to speak to Diotima. Of course Pythax granted the privilege; it's perfectly acceptable for a close male relative of a respectable woman to speak with her.

I invited Dromeus to our tent, and Pythax, Diotima, my father, and I gathered around to hear his story. I dragged in a table and kicked about some loose sacking to give us something comfortable to lounge on. The terrible injuries Dromeus and Pythax had inflicted on each other were forgotten—no, that wasn't quite right; they had become marks of respect for each other. Two tough men united by a woman: Euterpe, the mother of Diotima.

"Your mother was a wild one," Dromeus said to Diotima as he sipped our wine. "No man could tell her what to do."

"Not like her daughter at all, then," I said.

Diotima jabbed me in the ribs.

"She ran away from home twice, and twice her father—my uncle, your grandfather—dragged her home. When she ran the third time, he let her go. He said she was more trouble than she was worth."

Pythax growled. This was his wife that Dromeus spoke of.

Dromeus said, "I understand your feelings, friend. I report what happened, not my own thoughts."

Pythax nodded. "She's a good woman," he said.

"I know it. Speaking of which, where is she now?" Dromeus asked.

"Back in Athens," Pythax said. "The Olympics are no place for a respectable lady."

As soon as he said it, every male head turned to look at Diotima. We were all thinking the same thing.

She stuck her tongue out at us.

Dromeus laughed. "That's what I've always remembered about your mother: her independence."

I wasn't sure that Diotima really wanted to know how much she resembled her mother.

"When we heard she'd become a prostitute, that was the end of her as far as the family was concerned."

"Did you ever see her again?" I asked Dromeus.

"I did. When I came of age, I thought to look her up. We knew she'd moved to Athens. It was easy for me; a man on the tournament circuit moves around."

Like Korillos and his fellow pankratists. Yes, that made sense.

"She'd become a fine woman with a big house. I was impressed. When I knocked on the door, she thought I was a client. It was disconcerting."

I nodded in sympathy. I'd had the same experience, and barely survived.

"Well, I explained who I was, and she remembered me, and there were tears, and she swore me to secrecy, and then she revealed that she was a mother. So proud and happy, she was." He said to Diotima, "I held you in my arms when you were barely a newborn."

Diotima wiped away a tear. "What was I like, as a baby?"

"You peed on me. Euterpe whisked you away, and that was the last I ever saw of you. Your mother had a comfortable life, and I'd fulfilled my duty as a male relative, so I wished her well and left. I'd always wondered what happened to her."

As we went our separate ways—Diotima hugged Dromeus; Dromeus hugged me; Pythax, after an awkward moment of hesitation, stepped forward to hug Dromeus—my father pulled me aside and said quietly, "This puts your marriage to the woman Diotima in a different light."

"It does?" My spirits lifted.

"The daughter of a prostitute is one thing," said my father. "The cousin of an Olympic champion is quite another. The prestige of an Olympian in the family may overcome the defect of the mother. Of course it would have been nice if the Olympian had been anyone but Dromeus."

My spirits fell. "Dromeus couldn't help it if no one else came to fight him," I said, oddly echoing his own defense.

"Hmmph." Sophroniscus half-grunted. "There are still two problems, are there not?"

I stared at him blankly.

"There's still the issue of the farm, and did you not tell me Dromeus is a suspect for this murder? We could hardly have a murderer in the family."

It was a good point. Dromeus, so convenient a suspect for both Pericles and the Spartans, would now destroy my last chance of marrying of Diotima if he proved a murderer.

Diotima had no such fears. "I can barely believe it, Nico. I have a male relative, a *respectable* male relative."

"Not merely respectable. He's an Olympic victor."

"I don't care about that." She brushed aside the highest accolade any man can win. "The important thing is I can mention him in public and not have to blush. Not a single taint. Not a slave, not a prostitute. Nothing but respectable."

"That's good?"

"Good? It's *wonderful*. Don't you see? All my life I've been saddled with this awful reputation that wasn't my fault. Now suddenly I've got some respectability to balance it."

"I thought you didn't like Dromeus."

"I've changed my mind."

I hoped it stayed that way when our investigation finished. But it would soon be dusk, so I left Diotima to contemplate her

newfound relative while I departed for the secret meeting with
the secret informant. I'd have to hurry, or I might be late, and
this was a meeting I definitely didn't want to miss.

THE NEW TEMPLE was a massive building, visible from
anywhere within Olympia, and it only became more impressive
as I approached. I stopped in the Sanctuary of Zeus to admire it.
There, standing with his back to me, was Pericles. He too looked
up at the massive temple.

I stopped beside him. Pericles turned his head, startled, saw it
was me, and relaxed.

"Oh, it's you," he said. "Have you come to report progress?"

"No, but with any luck, I'll have some good news for you
before the night is out."

"That would be nice, because we're running out of time, in
case you hadn't noticed. The pankration is in less than a day.
Timodemus will die the day after."

Pericles and I stood side by side and gazed. The Temple of
Zeus was painted in red and blue. A line of gold ran all around
the outside of the roof.

"What do you think?" he asked.

"How can they make so much stone stand upright?" I marveled.

"Don't ask me," Pericles said. "I'm no architect. It's impressive, isn't it?"

I had recently come from Ephesus, where I'd seen its
Temple of Artemis, said to be the most beautiful building in
the world. The Artemision had beautiful lines and was covered in the finest sculpture, but for majestic awe this Temple
of Zeus at Olympia with its stark, simple lines beat it hands
down.

"It's incredible," I said.

Pericles nodded. "Athens needs something like this. Something
that shows the world Athens is a force to be reckoned with, not

only in strength of arms, but that we lead the world in the arts
and philosophy and culture."

"Do we?"

"Not yet, but we will, if I have anything to do about it."

I said, "Remember when we first met, Pericles? I was walking
up to the Acropolis, to think about a new temple, and you were
coming down—"

"Having considered exactly the same thing. And in between us
was a dead body."

"Can we do it again, do you think?" I asked him.

"You mean find a dead body?"

"No, think about building a new temple to Athena atop the
Acropolis."

Pericles looked at me curiously. "Why do you care so much,
Nicolaos?"

It was a good question. There'd been a time when I wondered
if Athens deserved my support. I'd even considered abandoning
my city, not that I would admit that to Pericles. "Athens is my
home," I told him. "It's my future. If I'm to have a position of any
importance in the world, it's in Athens, Pericles, and I'd rather
my city were one of power. Who wants to be a powerful man in a
weak city? Best to be powerful in a place of power."

"You're ambitious."

"Yes." I'd committed myself to Athens. Now I wanted Athens
to commit to me.

We were not the only ones in awe of the new building. A
constant trickle of men wandered in from the direction of the
stadion and stopped in the Sanctuary where we stood. Every man
did the same as us: stared up at the tall columns of stone and the
massive roof.

The roof was tiled in marble. It must have cost a small fortune
every time a tile slipped, but it was worth it. The play of light
across the thin, polished marble gave the roof the sheen of a still,
deep pond.

"I like the roof tiles," I said. "Can we have tiles like that?"

"I'll see what I can arrange," Pericles said.

"You know we're wasting our time even talking about it, don't you?" I said. "Athens can't afford anything like this."

"We'll have to see. Certainly the state coffers are low. But Nicolaos, a decent-quality Temple to Athena should not be beyond the Athenians."

"Who paid for this one?" I asked.

"The Eleans, using booty they pillaged long ago during their war against the Pisans."

"Then all we need to do is pillage someone," I said lightly.

"Yes, I'd come to the same conclusion," Pericles said in all seriousness. "I must think about that."

Dear Gods, *I* would have to think about that. Was Pericles serious?

"I must leave you," I said. "I have an appointment."

The entrance to the Temple of Zeus faced east, as most temples do, so that Apollo's first rays of the day can shine within. I avoided the ramp and instead climbed the three large steps.

A man stood inside. I didn't notice him at first because it was much darker within and it took my eyes time to adjust. When they did, I saw he was a shifty-looking fellow with a black beard who wore the exomis of a tradesman. I wondered if he was the one I'd come to meet. I stood in the center to give him a chance to approach me, but he didn't move, merely watched me from the side.

Looking around the inside, I could see spots where the builders hadn't finished, areas not yet painted, decorations not carved, in the corners and out-of-the-way places. Torches hung in wall brackets, and braziers stood in the corners and along the sides, but none of them were lit.

"What do you think?" the man with the black beard asked.

"It's amazing." I rubbed my hand along the walls. "It looks like marble."

"It's not. It only looks that way. You touch stucco which has been craftily applied to have the look of marble. Beneath, it's limestone."

"You seem to know something about it," I observed.

"So I should, young man. My name is Libon. I'm the architect."

I realized I had just made a fool of myself.

"If it isn't a rude question, Libon, what are you doing lurking in the shadows?"

"You stand in my life's work, young man. I will do nothing greater. The reaction of the Hellenes to my temple over the next three days will decide whether my life has been worthwhile. If you faced that sort of judgment, what would you do?"

"I would lurk in the shadows and watch everyone's reaction," I said.

"Exactly."

To talk to Libon would be the perfect cover while I waited for my meeting. I had no idea what the man looked like, but he obviously knew me. With Libon I could stand in the middle of the temple in perfect innocence, yet make it easy for the informer to spot me.

Libon was as eager as I was. "Let me show you my temple." He dragged me across to the entrance through which I'd come.

"Main entrance," he said, when we were outside on the steps. "Look up." He pointed to the pediment, the triangular area that closed off the end of the roof. In a temple these are always filled with a sculpture in relief.

Though it was dusk, and the entrance faced east, there was still sufficient light by which to see, because it was the middle of summer and the moon was already rising bright. The relief sculpture showed two men and their attendants, each man before his chariot. Zeus stood in the center of the scene, from which position he took oaths from the two men, who were obviously about to race.

"Is this an Olympic chariot race?" I asked.

"Older than the Olympics," Libon said. "Or perhaps the first Olympic race, depending on how you look at it. Do you know the story? Do you know who the drivers are?"

"No."

Libon pointed to a very ancient ruined building to the north, halfway between the Temple of Zeus, where we stood, and the Temple of Hera.

"Do you see the ruined house over there, with only the shattered walls still standing? That is, or was, the *megaron*—the great house—of King Oinomaos. He ruled this land long ago, before even the time of Homer." Then Libon pointed to the relief, at the figure beside the second chariot. "That is King Oinomaos there."

"I see."

Libon turned me slightly to the left. "Now see that mound beside the megaron?"

It was a large burial mound, of the kind used by the ancients, enclosed within a wall of five sides.

"That is the burial mound of the hero Pelops. The hero-king for whom this land is named, the Peloponnesian Peninsula."

"Let me guess. The other driver in the relief is Pelops."

"Correct. According to legend, King Oinomaos had a daughter, a girl of great beauty, by the name of Hippodamia. Whoever should marry Hippodamia would inherit the rule of the land.

"Needless to say, a great many unsuitable men asked for the hand of the beautiful Hippodamia, so many that it became an irritant. Oinomaos developed a way of discouraging suitors. He challenged them to a chariot race. If Oinomaos won, then he killed the foolish suitor with his bright spear. But if the suitor won, then the suitor would marry the girl and become heir to the kingdom. Many men died in the pursuit of beauty and wealth.

"Then the hero Pelops came along. He asked for the hand of Hippodamia. Oinomaos set the usual condition.

"Luckily for Pelops, Hippodamia fell in love with him. She bribed her father's charioteer, a man by the name of Myrtilus, to remove the linchpins from the wheels of her father's racing chariot. His reward if he did so would be half the kingdom and the first night in the bed of Hippodamia.

"And so the race was arranged. The hero and the king swore their oaths before mighty Zeus—it is the scene you see in the pediment—then the race began. Pelops surged to the lead. It seemed Pelops must win. But the chariot of Oinomaos made ground.

"Oinomaos raised his spear to slay Pelops as they raced, when at that moment the wheels of his chariot flew off. Oinomaos, caught up in the reins, was dragged to his death.

"Pelops married Hippodamia, became king at once, and they all lived happily ever after. Except for Hippodamia's father, who was somewhat dead."

"What about the charioteer Myrtilus?"

"He reaped the usual harvest for treachery: Pelops murdered the fellow when he was brazen enough to claim his reward. Myrtilus was buried under the Taraxippus at the east end of the hippodrome. It's the reason there are so many accidents at that turn. The psyche of Myrtilus remains to terrify the horses."

I had looked about us as Libon spoke. He noticed my inattention and broke off.

"Am I boring you?" he asked.

"I'm sorry, Libon. The fact is, I arranged to meet someone here and I'm looking for him. But the problem is, I don't know what he looks like."

"Won't that make it harder to find him?"

"You've spotted the nub of my problem. I rather hoped *he* would find *me*."

"Ah, I understand. You humor an old bore like me so that you can be visible in the middle of the temple without at the same time being conspicuous."

"No, it's not like that at all . . ." I trailed off at the look of disbelief on his face and sighed. "All right, it *is* like that. But I was interested in everything you said. Truly." Now I felt guilt that I'd used him. He seemed a nice man.

"Then let us see if we can find your anonymous friend," said Libon, with more grace than I would have shown. "Is there anything you can tell me about this person?"

"Well, he's probably a bit nervous," I said nervously.

"We will begin at this end and work our way through," said Libon. We reentered the building past the three large doors, all of them open.

The first room was the *pronaos*.

"I used a standard design for the temple, as you can see, Nicolaos," Libon said, ending with my name in a loud voice. He had obviously decided to make my presence very obvious in the hope of attracting my informant. Every man in the room had jumped at the sudden loud voice. Everyone knew Nicolaos was present.

The room was full of men but empty of decoration, except for a burning brazier of bronze. This was the room where men, wishing to dedicate something precious, could offer it to Zeus by hanging it on the wall. There was only one such offering so far: at nose height beside me was a kynodesme, the cord an athlete used to hold down his penis while he competed. No doubt the kynodesme had belonged to one of the winners, and he wished to dedicate it to the God who had granted him the victory.

"Look at the floor," Libon instructed.

The floor had been paved in tiny colored pebbles. The pebbles had been artfully arranged to make a scene: silver fish in a blue sea, white seabirds and, in the middle, a Triton.

"Now let us move on."

We walked from the pronaos to the *naos*. The naos was the main room of the temple. Two rows of seven pillars each supported the ceiling, which was high-quality wood, oiled and polished till it gleamed. The naos was divided into four sections.

"The statue of Zeus will go in the third of the four quarters," Libon said. "They haven't begun it yet."

I peered into the darkness of the large room, and I wondered if this was why the mysterious informant had specified dusk. In this light, he could speak to me, and it would be difficult to recognize him later.

"The statue is planned to reach halfway up," said Libon.

I looked up; it was a long, long way to that wooden ceiling.

"Zeus will be sculpted sitting on his throne. If the God stood up, his head would hit the ceiling."

"Let's hope he doesn't, then," I said. "A God with a bad headache is to be avoided."

Libon and I had made as much noise as possible and called attention to ourselves.

"Are there any more parts to this temple?" I asked.

"There's the *opithodomos*, of course," he replied. "It's a room about the size of the pronaos, but on the west side. It has no connection to the inside; it's more like a covered porch with a bench running along the back wall."

"What's it good for?"

"Meeting your friends in bad weather."

Libon led me out the entrance and around the building to the west side. Many men were there to talk and admire the sunset. Libon and I again made a fuss of ourselves, but no one approached, except to ask us to speak more quietly.

"Are you sure this person is coming?" Libon asked. "I'm afraid, Nicolaos, son of Sophroniscus, that you have been stood up."

"I am afraid, Libon, master architect, that you are right. Could we make one final sweep in the naos? It makes sense that is where he would go."

"Why so?"

"Because it is darkest there, and so easiest to hide." As I said it, Apollo dipped below the forest on the other side of the Kladeos to begin his journey around the underside of Gaia.

"Not anymore," Libon said.

"What do you mean?"

"When Apollo descends, the slaves light the torches within the temple. The naos will soon be as bright as day."

We hurried back to the other side for the entrance. I grabbed a torch from a passing girl slave. She wanted to protest, but when she saw Libon she subsided.

Men began to leave for whatever parties they had planned for the evening. It made my job easier. I walked all around the edge of the room. There was no one who looked like he might be skulking.

I said, "Libon, I notice some flagstones are pulled up where the statue is destined to go."

"The flooring is receiving extra reinforcement to support the weight to come. Those are limestone blocks you see raised."

"Mind if we have a look?"

"Be my guest."

Together we looked down into the space created where the floor stones had been raised. There, lying in a pool of blood, was the weedy man in the Heracles costume.

I heard Libon gag. But that didn't stop him from leaning over for a closer look in the semi-dark.

"There's something odd about him," Libon said, puzzled.

"So there is," I agreed. "He has four eyes."

HIS EYES WERE wide open. Many people died like that. But the killer had carefully placed an extra eyeball facing upward on each cheek. Combined with the ragged lion skin, he had the look of some strange creature out of myth.

He stared at me accusingly (with all four eyes), as if his death was my fault. For all I knew, he might be right.

The slave from whom I'd snatched the torch took one look and screamed. She had to be led away, sobbing.

"What is this?" Libon exclaimed, and then, "Who is he? Is this your friend?"

"I think he must be. As to his name, I have no idea, though we met once. I don't suppose you know him?"

"Not I."

I gave a slave directions to the tent of Diotima and ordered him to bring her. It was rude of me—the slave wasn't mine to command—but Libon gave no protest. Perhaps it was because of the torchlight, but his skin had noticeably grayed.

"I'm sorry if the presence of the corpse disturbs you, Libon," I said. "I wouldn't have had it happen after your kindness."

Libon's voice was harsh when he said, "I manage a building site, young man. I've seen dead men aplenty in accidents."

"This was no accident."

"No, and that's what disturbs me."

A disturbance at the entrance. Heads turned. Diotima ran in, followed by a panting Pindar.

"I saw this young lady of yours race across the sanctuary, and I knew something of importance must have occurred," he explained between gasps. "I'm getting too old for this sort of thing. What's happening?"

I told them both of the note and the meeting.

"I suppose you've let the informant get killed." Diotima got straight to the point.

"Thanks very much for your confidence."

"Is it the informant?"

"Well, yes." I had to concede. "But I didn't *let* him die. He got himself killed without my permission. Remember the weedy-looking fellow who accosted us at the agora? It's him, Diotima."

She looked down at the corpse. She turned pale.

"The eyes," she said.

"Yes."

We looked at each other, no need to say a word. The eyes of Arakos had been removed. Here they were.

"Notice anything else strange?" Diotima asked.

I looked carefully but saw nothing beyond. "He's dead?" I suggested.

Diotima glared. "Thank you, Asclepius. Where's his club?"

"Club?"

"He swung a club at us."

"Maybe he didn't bring it."

"A pity. He could have defended himself."

The blood had poured from a gash in his throat.

"We'll never know what he had to say," Diotima said. "And the Temple of Zeus is polluted, *right in the middle of the Sacred Games.* Have you any idea the damage it does when someone dies in a temple? They'll be up all night ritually cleansing the place. What a mess. Well done, Nico," she accused me.

"Me? I didn't do anything."

"Why must you always get there *after* the witness has been killed?"

Pindar had listened to our argument with something like a half smile. Now he asked, "Has this sort of thing happened before?"

"All too often," Diotima grated.

Pindar said, "Perhaps if in the future Nico could arrive at secret meetings early?"

Markos ran in. He was hot and sweaty. "I just heard." He looked down at the corpse. "Unfortunate. Who is he?"

Diotima said, "You knew about this meeting?"

"Yes."

"Then each of you is as bad as the other. Why weren't you here, Markos?"

"My presence probably would have scared him off."

I added, "The note specifically said only me."

"I don't suppose it occurred to either of you that Markos could have covered the outside of the building? You might even—" She glared at me. "—have considered telling me. I could have visited the Temple of Hera, which is right next door to the Temple of Zeus. Between Markos and me we could have observed everyone who went in and out, and we could have been in place long before the meeting time. We could have spotted any man going in who looked nervous. We could have noted anyone who followed another man. As it is, anyone could have walked in and out of the building without Nico seeing him."

A long silence followed. Markos broke it with the words, "I think we've been told off, my friend."

"Diotima's right," I said.

"She is indeed. I'll never conduct an investigation without her approval again. You're lucky to have her."

It was the worst thing he could have said, because Diotima wasn't mine. We both froze.

Markos looked from one to the other of us, then he remembered. "Oops," he said. "Nico told me, but I forgot. I apologize."

"You told Markos about the dowry problems?" Diotima said. I could hear her anger.

"Er . . . yes."

"How could you?"

"Let's concentrate on who could have killed the fake Heracles." I said hastily, to change the subject. "Who knew he'd be here?"

"You and Markos, but not *me*," Diotima said pointedly. "Does anyone know who he is? Other than a fake Heracles, I mean."

Silence.

"Perhaps we should wait to see who reports a missing man," Diotima said.

Markos and I both stared at her in surprise.

"In Olympia?" I said. "That's like waiting for one particular drunk in a dockside inn."

"Men wander between the camps all the time," Markos added. "You could go missing and no one would notice until the Games were over."

"I'll wager that happens," I said.

Markos nodded. "It does. At the end of every Games there are always a few tents still standing when all the others have been pulled down. That's when men look at each other and say, 'Where's Ariston?' Or 'Where's Lysanias?' Or whatever the fool's name is. So they search for Ariston or Lysanias, and they find him dead drunk in a ditch. Or they find he fell into the river when he was dead drunk, and now he's just dead."

"You sound like you speak from experience," Diotima said gently.

"I do. I was assigned to the security detail in the Spartan camp at the last Games. One of the missing men was my own father. We found him floating under the weeds by the bank."

"I'm sorry, Markos," Diotima said.

Markos shrugged. "There's nothing anyone can do about it now."

I said, "No, and there's nothing we can do about this murder either. Probably our best witness just died."

DAY 4 OF THE 80TH OLYMPIAD OF THE SACRED GAMES

NEWS OF THE second murder spread like plague. The temple slaves took great delight in telling anyone who'd listen that the corpse had been discovered with four eyes. The gory detail was enough to make men shudder.

Men began to say that the Games were cursed. The body had been found in the brand-new Temple of Zeus; surely there could be no stronger confirmation that Zeus had deserted us.

I had to admit, when you put it all together, it didn't look good. First the murder of Arakos—a cursed event if ever there was one—the Games are first and foremost sacred to the Gods. Then the affair of the ox of dough. At any other Olympics it would have been laughed off. Now, it was another item on the list of sacrilegious disasters. Empedocles had to quietly leave Olympia that night, for his own safety. I thanked the Gods no one had recognized me; the crowd had been too busy watching the more interesting philosopher.

As to why Zeus had abandoned us, men didn't look far for a reason. Too many at Olympia had also been at Nemea: the pankratists, Pindar, probably the heralds, no doubt others. People began to talk. By the time the moon had reached its peak, every man at Olympia had heard the ugly rumor, as One-Eye had called it, that Timodemus, the man accused of murdering Arakos, had somehow cheated at the Nemean Games.

Clearly, Timodemus had cursed the Sacred Games.

The guards, who had been set to keep Timodemus in, now found themselves keeping a lynch mob out.

Spartans, Skarithos vocal among them, claimed that Athens was to blame. The Athenians were as vocal in claiming a conspiracy against them. The men of other cities supported one side or the other, as their alliances or inclinations led them. What had been a predominantly Sparta-Athens dispute now consumed every man present.

Overnight, Olympia deteriorated into islands of armed camps. Men moved carts, packing boxes and supplies—anything they could find—to create low walls around the tents of each city. With so many blacksmiths and weapon-makers present, it was a simple matter to turn tent poles into serviceable spears. Despite the Sacred Truce, a few forbidden swords appeared as if from nowhere. Where a man might the day before have walked between camps unhindered, now guards protected each entrance. They stopped and questioned every visitor and passed through only the men of allied cities.

A strange thing had happened.

"Olympia has turned into a microcosm of Hellas," Pericles said to me within the privacy of his own tent, next morning, the dawn of Day Four. He was bleary eyed. Pericles had spent the night consulting with the leaders of the other cities and doing what he could to keep men calm. Despite which, he was oddly exhilarated. Sport might have bored Pericles senseless, but he lived for politics.

"Is that bad?"

"It's fascinating. I'm beginning to think there might be a point to the Olympics after all. Do you realize, Nico, what we're seeing here is how each city would react if it came to general war between the Hellenes? What happens here will inform our foreign policy for years to come."

"And what *is* happening?"

"The cities of the Aegean Islands are supporting us, for the most part. It's in their best interests. They're closest to Persia; they need a strong Athens to protect them. The cities of the

Peloponnese are supporting Sparta. No surprise there. If they didn't, they could expect a Spartan army at their gates. All except Argos."

"The men of Argos don't fear Sparta?"

"The men of Argos have hated Sparta since time immemorial."

"Oh. What of the cities to the north?"

"The opportunists from Thebes are negotiating with both sides. Delphi is staying out of it."

"Is anyone playing any sport through all this?"

"Apparently, but I'm not paying any attention. We must consider the alignment of forces if a fight breaks out."

"At Olympia? With the Sacred Truce?"

"I know. But Nico, the way things are going, it could come to blows between Athens and Sparta. If it does, every other city will be drawn into it. We should be thankful the Sacred Truce forbids bringing arms into the district. If it *does* turn into a fight—and I wouldn't put it past the Corinthians to egg everyone on—then the lack of weapons will limit the deaths."

I had a sudden thought. "Do the Spartans have any better idea than us on how to control this?"

"No. Worse, if anything. Spartans make excellent bullies, but terrible diplomats."

"Then no one knows what will happen if it comes to blows."

"I sincerely hope no one wants to find out. But we must prepare, Nicolaos. We must prepare for the worst."

"What should we do?"

"There's only one thing you should do." He glared at me. "Find the answer to who killed Arakos. And it had better be the right answer. Without that, I can guarantee a war inside Olympia."

DESPITE ALL OUR theories, we were no closer to proving a killer. There was only one thing left that I could try. Libon's

guided tour of the temple had inspired me. I wasn't sure it was
a good idea, but I'd discussed it with Diotima anyway, late last
night, after everyone else had left the temple and before she'd
returned to her tent in the women's camp. I always talked
things through with her. I wondered how I'd cope when she
was some other man's wife. Diotima and I had both agreed my
idea was unlikely, but with so little time, any hope was better
than none.

I took Socrates with me to the Sanctuary of Zeus, where
Niallos continued his mission to drink himself to oblivion.
Luckily for me, it was early morning. Niallos had had most of
the night to sleep off the previous day's effort. Even so, the smell
was horrendous.

I slapped him around until he came to. Niallos peered at me
with eyes that were red from excessive drink and copious tears,
and he mumbled, "You again? Go away. Every time you turn up,
it's bad luck for someone else."

That was so true I didn't bother arguing. Instead I said,
"Maybe not this time. Listen, Niallos, do you want to do something for Iphicles?"

"There isn't anything anyone can do for Iphicles."

"Yes, there is, but only you can do it."

"What? Why me?"

"Because you know better than anyone all the parts that make
up a chariot. You'd recognize even the tiniest piece, wouldn't
you?"

"Sure."

"I want you to go with this boy—his name's Socrates. He talks
a lot, but try to ignore that—and I want you to search the hippodrome for pieces from Iphicles's chariot."

Niallos looked at me as if I were mad.

I told him what to search for, and why. It was the first Socrates
had heard of my idea. When I finished, Socrates looked at me in
admiration and said, "Nico, that's brilliant."

Niallos rubbed his chin and sat up straighter. "I see. If this were true—"

"I don't know, Niallos, but do this for me, will you? Socrates will help."

Niallos dusted off his clothing. He looked human again already. "If you're right, we can do this quickly."

I WAS TORN over what to do about Diotima. With the fighting that was about to break out, would she be safer in the women's camp or in the middle of the Athenians? I went to see her.

Pythax was with her in her tent. He was black and blue from the beating Dromeus had delivered. There was a lump over one eye, and his hair was still matted with traces of blood. But I was relieved to see him. If it came to a battle, Pythax would see Diotima safe.

"You're not needed," Pythax growled.

Technically, he was right. Diotima was no longer my responsibility, but that wouldn't stop me protecting her.

"What's your plan, Pythax?"

"Diotima's safe enough," said Pythax. "She's got a Spartan admirer."

"What's this?" I noticed Diotima's eyes were red. Had she been crying?

"I told you I got to do my best for my girl."

"Yes."

"I got an offer."

"Already?"

"Surprised me, too. I hadn't even asked around yet, not with all the troubles. But he said he knew Diotima had become free. It's a good offer. He's a Spartan, good family, got a high position. And he don't want much in dowry."

"What position?"

"Says he's a knight. That's high up."

"Dear Gods." My heart raced.

"His name is Markos."

He'd asked me if Diotima had a sister, and I'd told him he'd have to find his own beautiful and clever priestess. It seemed he had. Markos had betrayed me.

"This Markos, what's he like?" Pythax asked.

I wanted to say he was evil. I wanted to say he was poor, and a coward, and he beat women. But Pythax had to do his best for Diotima, and I had to help him, because I wanted the best for her too. I thought about my answer for a long time, before I came to a reluctant conclusion.

"I admire him," I said. "But Pythax—"

The tent flap flew open at that moment and Socrates ran in, followed by Niallos, who was both excited and sober.

"Nico! Nico! Look what we've got!" Socrates skidded to a halt in front of me and held up a tiny piece of metal, as if he'd discovered the world's greatest treasure.

"What is it?" I stared at the bent bronze. It was a thick piece of wire.

"It's the linchpin from a chariot," said Niallos. "From our chariot. You were right, Nicolaos; it's just like the story of Pelops and Oinomaos."

"Where did you find it?"

"On the floor of the team box," said Socrates. "Niallos showed me where to search."

Diotima and I stared at each other. "Then that solves it," she said. "But . . . I can barely believe it. Who would have thought?"

"Not me," I said. "It's almost impossible to prove." I thought about it. "We'll have to trick everyone."

"And I know how to do it. Listen to this." Diotima spoke for a long time. I wasn't happy with her idea, but I knew she was right.

Pythax growled. "I'll see to my end of it."

I nodded, reluctantly.

Diotima put an arm around me. "I'm sorry, Nico. This'll be so painful for your friend."

IT WAS THE afternoon of Day Four. At any moment, the wrestling would begin. Then it would be the boxing, and finally, the pankration.

I went to see Timodemus in his prison. The walls were scarred where an angry mob had attacked because they believed Timodemus was the cause of all their troubles. At one place there was actually a hole smashed all the way through, where someone with a pickaxe had repeatedly struck the weakened ancient stones. It occurred to me that Timodemus was lucky to be alive. I thanked the guards as I passed, though. One of them spat. "Don't thank me. If it weren't for the Priestess of the Games, I would've handed over the little bastard."

I blinked. "Klymene was here?"

"She stood where you are now, folded her arms, and dared the mob to pass her. She said they'd only get to Timodemus over her dead body."

Well, wasn't that interesting.

Timodemus paced in his room. It was obvious he'd been at it some time.

"I'm not used to the lack of exercise," he explained. "I need to keep moving."

"Not much room," I said.

Timo shrugged. "I've been doing jumps and push-ups. It's enough. The forced rest may even have done me some good." He smiled wryly. "Do you think it's important for a man who's about to be executed to be healthy?"

Timo did indeed look better than he had in a long time. He'd always worn training scrapes and cuts and bruises; three days with no practice had given them time to heal.

"Why do you fight, Timo?" I asked.

He smiled. "It would hurt if I just stood there and let them hit me."

"No, this is a serious question. Why do you walk into the ring, time after time?"

Timo stood for a long while, contemplating. Then he scratched his balls.

"I dunno," he said.

"That's the sum total of your deep personal introspection?" I asked.

"Listen, Nico, have you ever known a time when I *didn't* fight?"

"No."

"There you are, then. Fighting is what I do. If I stopped, I wouldn't be Timo anymore."

"You fight because your father told you to fight," I said.

"Well, yes," he admitted reluctantly. "But that was when I was a child, so long ago it doesn't matter anymore."

"Do you *want* to go on?"

"Why are you asking me this?"

"Your father demands I move your trial forward, to before the pankration."

"So I can compete."

"If you survive the trial, yes. And listen, I think I know what happened. But trials are tricky things, my friend; the result might not turn out the way you'd want."

"Then it's like the pankration. No matter how good you are, you can never be sure how it'll end."

"There's something else of which I must warn you, Timo. After this trial is over, even if the judges acquit you, you might not feel like competing."

"I see." He sat there and said nothing. I wondered if he truly did see.

"Timo, what do you want me to do? If you want to fight, the trial has to be right now."

Timo thought for a moment. "The choice is mine?"

"Entirely yours. If you say you want to wait to tomorrow, then that's what we do. I'll tell your father it was my decision. One-Eye will never know it's what you wanted."

Now Timo really did think, staring at the floor. I sat as quiet as I could to not disturb him while he considered his fate.

Timo looked up and said, "Let's go for it."

"PINDAR, I'VE GOT a job for you."

"What, another commission?"

"You'll want to do this one for free."

I explained what I needed and why.

Pindar laughed. "You're right, my young friend. I'd do this purely to see the looks on their faces."

"That's good, because I couldn't afford you twice. Speaking of which, how's my praise song coming along?"

"At the moment I actively seek inspiration and explore the exciting possibilities, all within the efficient confines of my febrile imagination."

"What does that mean?"

"It means I haven't done a thing. But don't worry, I always do my best work in a rush, right before the deadline."

"So do I. I hope."

AS I WALKED through the Athenian camp I came across Festianos outside his tent.

"Have you heard the news?" I said to him.

"No, what?"

"The judges have agreed to try Timodemus this afternoon."

"A day early?"

"I told Exelon I have enough evidence to clear Timo's name. Markos says he's ready to prosecute. They agreed to bring it forward. If he's found innocent—and with my evidence I'm feeling confident—they'll allow him to compete. I don't know why you look so surprised, Festianos. This is exactly what your brother One-Eye demanded."

"Yes, it is. But I never thought the judges would agree. I'm not . . . that is, we're not ready. Timo hasn't trained at all these last days."

I shrugged. "There's nothing I can do about that, I'm afraid. Will I see you at the trial?"

"Yes, of course."

I continued on my way down the path and out the camp entrance. As I rounded the corner, I passed Pindar and Socrates.

"Don't lose him," I said out of the corner of my mouth.

Everything was set in motion, and there was no way to recall it. Timodemus would live or die according to whether our plan worked.

THE TRIAL OF Timodemus was held in the central room of the Bouleterion. To arrange the matter at such short notice, with the presence of the judges required at every event, the trial had to be held between the boxing and the pankration.

I waited inside for the judges and the witnesses to arrive. Markos waited with me.

I barely knew what to say to the man who'd offered to marry Diotima. I settled for, "You asshole! I thought you were my friend." I resisted the urge to punch him down.

"But . . . it's over between the two of you," Markos said. "You told me so yourself. That's why I thought I was free to say something."

"That doesn't mean I like it. Couldn't you at least have had the decency to wait until the Games were over?"

"I didn't want to risk another man offering first. Would *you* risk losing a prize like her?"

"No," I said bitterly.

Markos put his hand on my shoulder. "I'm sorry, Nico, that was insensitive of me. If I'd thought you were still in with a chance I wouldn't have said a thing. I'll go to her father after the trial to withdraw my offer."

"Don't bother." I shook my head. "I can't blame you for doing what I want to do myself. Forget it, Markos. We both have the trial to think about."

"The trial, yes." Markos, hesitated for a moment, then said, "Nico, I've come to love you as a friend, but I'm sorry, once we go to trial, it will be a fight between you and me. I warn you I'll hold nothing back."

"It's like the pankration," I said, echoing Timodemus.

"Exactly," Markos agreed.

"It's all right, Markos." I grinned. "I won't think the less of you when you lose."

"What makes you think I'll lose, Athenian?" He grinned back, the moment of anger between us gone. "It'll be me who takes the first-ever winner's crown for investigation."

"Twenty drachmae says it'll be me."

"Fifty."

"Done."

The Ten Judges filed in. They'd come straight from the stadion. They were covered in sticky sweat to which a layer of dust had adhered. Their hair was plastered down. Behind them came Pericles; King Pleistarchus and his mother, Queen Gorgo, who stepped slowly; Xenares One-Eye, and Festianos followed by Pindar; and, in the middle surrounded by guards, Timodemus.

The judges sat behind a long bench table. At once slaves placed cups of watered wine in their hands. As one they downed the drink and held out their cups for more. If the red skin on their faces and necks was any indication, being under the sun for four days had given them all severe sunburn.

Exelon opened the proceedings. "I have a pounding headache. Can we make this quick?"

Quick, to consider a man's life?

"The situation is unusual," Exelon continued with the under-statement of the Games. "But we will proceed along normal lines." Exelon nodded at Markos. "We begin with the prosecution case against Timodemus."

Markos stepped forward and said suavely. "I'll be brief." Ten judges nodded in appreciation. Under my breath, I cursed his self-assurance. Why couldn't I be like that?

"Gentlemen, we can twist and turn all we like," began Markos. "We can consider one hypothesis or another. We can list suspects. We can check their alibis. We can consider motive until the Gods themselves go gray of advanced age. We can do all these things, but we can't escape one fact: who could beat to death the second-best unarmed fighter in Hellas, other than the very best? That, gentlemen, is the heart of the issue. I need hardly mention that everyone saw Timodemus attack Arakos on the morning of the murder."

Markos spoke with such authority, his words measured and reasoned, that I found myself unconsciously nodding in agreement. When I realized what I was doing, I stopped. But I knew what effect his words must be having on the others.

"And the motive for this killing?" Xenares the ephor asked.

"Timodemus cheated at the Nemean Games. Arakos knew it and intended to expose him."

Exclamations from the judges, though I knew at least half of them must have heard the rumors.

"And the method of cheating?" Xenares prompted. The two must have prearranged this dialogue.

"Witchcraft," Markos said.

Gasps, and murmurs of shock.

"Is this true?" one judge demanded.

"I believe so, sir," said Markos. "Arakos, who had been at Nemea and lost to Timodemus in the last round, stood ready to expose what had happened there. Of course such news would disqualify the accused for the Olympics."

"These are lies!" Timo shouted.

"The rumors about Nemea are rife," Markos said calmly. "You can check them for yourselves."

Several men nodded. It seemed they already had.

"The final evidence is this." Markos tossed onto the bench the ostrakon he'd found in the tent of Arakos. It clattered across the wooden top, loud in the sudden silence of the room. A judge picked up the broken pottery to read the message I'd seen two days ago: *Timodemus says this to Arakos: I offer to meet you in the woods across the river tonight.*

"The implication is clear," said Markos. "Timodemus lured Arakos to the woods with this message. Timodemus struck Arakos on the forehead without warning—you've all seen the body—then beat him to death."

Markos stepped back.

"A brilliant summary, Markos. Short, succinct, conclusive," said Xenares.

"What says Athens?" Exelon demanded.

"I can explain this, sirs," I said. "But . . . uh . . . it might take a little while."

Ten judges frowned. I licked my lips, and tasted salty sweat. I hadn't realized until that moment how hot and close was the room.

I plowed on. "Timodemus stands accused of cheating through witchcraft, a charge for which there's no defense; it's all but impossible to prove innocence in such cases."

I paused.

"I call upon Festianos, the uncle of Timodemus, to give evidence."

"What's this?" Festianos stepped to the center. He looked worried.

"Only that you were at Nemea, Festianos."

"As were hundreds of men. Most of them are at Olympia."

I ignored Festianos and said to Exelon, "Sir, I'll need some other evidence. I call for Diotima, a lady of Athens."

"You're bringing in a *woman*?" Exelon said.

"Uh, two women actually, sir. The other one's a pornê. I also have a doctor. Oh, and my little brother."

Before Exelon could object, I opened the door, where stood waiting Diotima and Petale and behind them Socrates and Heraclides.

Diotima walked in and placed on the table before the judges a large canvas bag. It rattled and clattered. She untied it and pulled out the case of vials.

"Festianos, can you tell me what this is?" I said. Diotima opened the case for all to see the vials inside.

Festianos was bug-eyed. "Where did you get this?" he said.

"From your tent."

One-Eye exclaimed, "You searched our tent?"

"For a good reason, One-Eye," I said. "Bear with me."

"This is medicine," said Festianos. "For my arthritis and the shakes with which I am sometimes afflicted. A doctor prescribed it."

"Is your doctor here at Olympia?"

"In Athens."

"Then there's no way to corroborate your story."

"Why should there be? It's medicine."

"This is poison hemlock."

"I don't deny it," said Festianos. "The doctor warned me not to take too much at a time."

"Or else?"

"Or else it could kill me. I am to swallow a vial when the pain in my joints is particularly bad or if my body begins to shake, and at no time am I to take more than one vial every two days."

Heraclides, who stood at the back of the room, nodded in approval. He said, "The statement of Festianos agrees with what many doctors would prescribe."

I said, "Sirs, allow me to introduce Heraclides, a doctor from Kos. He told me that a potion made from a single leaf is medicinal, but that as few as six leaves are certain to be fatal."

Festianos shrugged. "I wouldn't know. I'm not a doctor."

"How much hemlock is in each of these vials, Festianos?" I asked.

"I believe two leaves."

"You don't know?"

"All right, yes, it's two." Festianos wiped his brow.

"Heraclides?" I asked.

The doctor said, "Two leaves in a healthy man would not be a fatal dose."

"But it would make a man sick?" I asked.

"He would feel lethargic, numb. He would be leaden-footed. Any movement would be a struggle."

"Like an athlete having a bad day," I said.

"The symptoms might resemble an athlete off his game," Heraclides agreed.

"Sirs," I turned to the judges, "I have spoken with the pankratists who competed at Nemea. They say that when they fought against Timodemus, they felt as if they had heavy legs."

"Nicolaos, what are you thinking?" Pericles said, beside himself. He wrung his hands. "Have you forgotten your orders . . . ?"

Pericles trailed off. He dared not admit his orders to me before the assembled personages.

I said, "My Olympic Oath requires me to prove or disprove Timo's guilt in the matter of the death of Arakos. I can only do so by discovering what really happened at Nemea last year."

Pleistarchus said, "We all know what he's thinking, Pericles, and I must say the idea's an interesting one. Do you intend to protect this man?"

"You know I can't," Pericles said testily.

"Nicolaos suggests this man Festianos gave mild poison to everyone except his own nephew," said King Pleistarchus, plainly intrigued. He had followed the conversation closely. I was sure he knew where this was going. "It appears we may have been a little hasty in condemning Timodemus." Pleistarchus was obviously enjoying every moment of this. "What do you think, Exelon?"

The Chief Judge looked at the King of Sparta with some irritation. "I think we need to hear the answer from Festianos."

"This is ridiculous," One-Eye protested. "First my son is accused of murder, then my brother of poison. This is nothing less than a conspiracy against my family and I demand—"

"You haven't proven a thing," Festianos interrupted. "How did I get the poison into the athletes?"

"In their water bottles," I said promptly. "The relative of a competitor is almost invisible, and no one watches the water bottles. Why should they?" I faced the judges again and began to pace back and forth, a habit I'd picked up from Pericles. "Sirs, at midday today, I told Festianos that Timodemus had been given permission to contest the Games, if he's found innocent."

"Which is true," said Exelon.

"Yes, sir. Festianos immediately poisoned the water of the other contestants."

Festianos said, "You're making this up."

I smiled to myself. "I thought you might say that." I stopped pacing. "Pindar?"

Pindar stepped forward to stand beside me. The Ten Judges stirred in their seats. The greatest living poet of the Hellenes was about to speak.

Pindar cleared his throat.

"Honored Judges of these Games most sacred to mighty Zeus," he began in his beautiful voice, "as Apollo with well-strung lyre sung before the Gods of high Olympus, so I stand before you with these few simple words of—"

I stamped on Pindar's toes. "Save the panegyrics for the paying crowd!" I hissed. "We have a man to redeem."

"Er . . . to cut a long poem short . . ." Pindar glared at me and rubbed his foot. "I affirm that I, Pindar the Praise Singer, watched this man Festianos leave his tent, carrying the box you see. I observed him walk into the gym, where were assembled the athletes for the pankration. I saw him walk back to his tent soon after."

"Lies," said Festianos.

"The word of Pindar is beyond doubt," said a minor judge.

Timodemus had watched his uncle's testimony with something like horror in his expression. Now he walked in front of Festianos, turned his back on the judges, and thrust his face so close to Festianos that I thought they might kiss. Or bite.

"My win at Nemea wasn't a fair fight?" Timodemus whispered.

"I didn't poison the bottles, nephew," Festianos rasped.

"It's all been a lie. I'm not the best at all." Timo turned away and hid his face in his hands.

Diotima reached into the evidence bag and withdrew a leather bottle. She placed it on the table. Festianos stared at it in surprise.

I said, "I took one of the contestant bottles after you left the gymnasium. Here it is." I paused for dramatic effect. "Would you care to drink the water, Festianos?"

Festianos glared around at the assembly. He was a trifle wild-eyed. He reached for the leather bottle, opened the stopper, upended and drank it down in rapid gulps.

"There, you see?" he coughed a little. "River water mixed with wine. That's all it is, and not very good wine at that."

The faces about us showed disappointment. All except One-Eye, who registered confusion, and Pericles, who looked relieved.

Diotima reached into the evidence bag. Slowly, deliberately, she pulled out another bottle and placed it before Festianos.

"Now try this one," she said. "Nicolaos took more than one bottle."

Festianos stared at the bottle, at me, at the bag.

The room was totally silent.

Diotima reached into the bag for a third time. Without a word, she placed a third bottle before Festianos.

I said to him, "If you told the truth, your bladder will fill, and you'll be a little drunk. Nothing more."

We waited, but Festianos only stared at his doom.

"The bottle you drank can't harm you, but three bottles is six leaves, enough to kill a man. Of course, if as you say, there's only water and wine in there, then there's nothing that can hurt you, right?"

Festianos made no move.

"Drink the water, Festianos," Exelon ordered.

Festianos reached forward. He took the next bottle and brought it to his lips. His hand shook. In one sudden motion he upended it onto the floor. The liquid splashed out. Droplets fell on our feet. Then he leaned forward onto the table, head in his arms, and cried.

"So it was Festianos who murdered Arakos," murmured the Chief Judge.

"Oh no, sir," I said. "That's quite impossible. A man with arthritis like Festianos could never have raised his arms against Arakos."

They all looked at me in shock. A judge shouted, "Are you playing with us, young man?"

The answer was yes. I deserved some revenge after what these men had put me through. But what I said was, "No, sir! It was necessary to demolish the motive that Sparta alleges against Timodemus."

"How do you know Timodemus wasn't in it with Festianos?" Xenares said.

"You need only look at him," I said.

Everyone did. Timodemus had buried himself in the corner of the room, his head against the whitewashed wood of the wall, oblivious to everything.

I said, "No, sirs, Timodemus had an extremely good reason to murder Arakos, but this wasn't it."

"*Had a good reason?*" Pericles seemed close to apoplexy. Good. This would teach him to order me to fake an investigation.

I said, "Rivals in love, Pericles. But I'll let someone else explain that."

Diotima opened the door. Klymene stepped in, shaking. Her skin was the color of dough.

"Klymene, daughter of Exelon, has important evidence for us," I told the assembled men.

Klymene said, "Timodemus could not have killed Arakos." She drew a deep breath. "Timodemus could not have killed Arakos because he was with me." She paused. "In my tent," she added, to make the point clear. Then, in case anyone in the room was terminally stupid, she finished, "We were having sex. Lots of it."

At least five judges dropped their cups of wine.

One said in a horrified squeak, "But this means the entire Games have been observed by a priestess in a state of pollution."

"Yes."

"The last four days are *invalid*?" If he hadn't been sunburned, the judge would have turned dead white. "If the people find out, we'll be slaughtered."

The judge beside Exelon turned to him and said, "I'm sorry, Exelon my friend, but the penalty is prescribed. She must be thrown off Mount Typaeum."

Exelon said merely, "No," in the faintest of voices.

Klymene smiled bravely. "It's all right, I've had my fun. Timo and I can go together."

"Why do you tell us this?" another judge demanded. "Are you in love with this Timodemus?"

"If love is liking someone, in bed and out, then I suppose I am."

To get us all back to the important point, I said, "Timodemus didn't do it. This leaves us with the problem of who did kill Arakos."

"I suppose you know who that is," Exelon said sarcastically.

"I call upon Petale the pornê to give evidence. She will be assisted by—I'm very sorry about this—my brother."

Petale explained that she had seen Arakos leave the women's camp, and no one else.

I said, "My brother Socrates will now explain how he used the coins in Petale's jar to calculate what time Arakos was seen walking into the woods."

Exelon stared in distaste at Petale and Socrates, a prostitute and a boy, holding hands. He muttered, "I think we'll take your word for it, for the moment at least."

I breathed a sigh of relief. The idea of Socrates trying to explain anything to anyone was terrifying.

"The evidence of Petale fixes the time of the murder," I said. "Something the killer certainly didn't want. He needed to ensure there was some moment during the night when Arakos might have died, and Timodemus had no alibi. You'll notice the ostrakon that demands the meeting is deliberately vague about the time. How is this possible? How could they have met? The only possible answer is, the killer lured Arakos with a verbal message, one that gave a fixed time, and then planted the ostrakon later." I paused to let that sink in. "Which means the killer went to all this trouble to frame Timodemus."

"It means nothing," Xenares the ephor said. "All we have is the word of a whore, and—" He stared at Klymene. "—and the word of a girl who should be."

Pleistarchus said, "More to the point, it doesn't necessarily imply the killer had anything against Timodemus, other than that the young man had made himself the perfect target for a false accusation."

"I acknowledge the truth of what you say, Pleistarchus," I said gratefully. "Let's move on to the death of Iphicles the chariot driver."

"An unfortunate accident," said Markos.

"Very unfortunate, because Iphicles saw the murderer."

"No, he saw Arakos."

"Then why didn't Petale see Iphicles?" I shot back. "Petale says she saw Arakos and no one else leave the women's camp."

I paused for them to consider.

"Iphicles, while blind drunk, followed a man through the women's camp and into the forest. It must have been either before or after Petale left her tent to relieve herself. The man directed Iphicles back onto the path to the river ford. That man must have been the murderer."

"We'll never know now," said Markos.

"No, we won't. There's been an unfortunate tendency for witnesses to die. Let's consider the fake Heracles, who was murdered in the Temple of Zeus."

Markos turned to the judges. "I remind you, sirs, the question in hand is the murder of Arakos. Any other deaths, however regrettable, are incidental."

Exelon nodded. "Markos makes a fair point. This trial is for the murder of Arakos." Thus was the death of the pathetic little Heracles consigned to the same insignificance as his life.

I tossed my two ostraka on the table to rest with the one Markos had presented.

"The first message declares Timodemus innocent. The second asks for a meeting in the Temple of Zeus. Clearly the fake Heracles knew something about the murder."

"The killer's name?" suggested Pleistarchus.

"No, the murder weapon," I said.

"There are no weapons at Olympia," said Exelon at once.

"Yes, there are," I replied. "The clubs carried by the Heracles imitators! Perfect to beat a man to death, even a top pankratist, if he doesn't expect the blow, and especially if it comes from someone he has no reason to distrust. Arakos was stunned by the first blow to his forehead, just like the oxen in the sacrifice. After that it was a simple matter to finish him."

Silence while everyone absorbed that. I could almost feel the ideas rearrange themselves in the minds of my audience.

I said, "Someone took the club from the fake Heracles and used it to kill Arakos."

"You still have no proof," said Exelon.

"You're right, Chief Judge. It's not certain proof, but it was enough to make me look for certain proof."

I held up the twisted bit of metal for everyone to see. "This is the linchpin from Iphicles's chariot."

Then I turned to the murderer.

"You made one mistake, Markos. As soon as you knew Iphicles had seen you, the chariot driver had to die. You remembered the story of Pelops and King Oinomaos, and how the groom Myrtilus pulled the linchpin. So you pulled the linchpin straight after the crew had checked the equipment. I even watched you crouch to do it. The entire pit crew can swear you were the only man who could have pulled this pin."

Silence. Everyone waited for Markos to speak. His expression gave nothing away.

Without a word, Markos pulled out a handful of coins. He placed them in a single pile on the table, where everyone could count them. Fifty drachmae.

Markos was no fool; he knew the door would be heavily guarded.

So he ran for the window.

Gorgo stood between him and his escape. Markos raised his arm to strike her out of the way, and I gasped. Even a slight blow could kill the weak queen, but there was no time to reach him.

Diotima threw her priestess knife. The blade slid across his arm and sliced the skin. Markos yelped and skipped around Gorgo and dived through the open window.

"After him!" A dozen voices shouted.

I ambled over to watch.

Markos ran down the narrow lane. Standing at the end, blocking the path, was Pythax. Pythax snarled. Markos had no club with which to beat a larger man now. He skidded to a halt, turned, and sprinted in the other direction.

Straight into Dromeus, who advanced from the other end. Dromeus hammered him hard. Markos staggered back.

Pythax and Dromeus converged on Markos. They beat him with their fists. As far as they were concerned, Markos was a dead man. Markos, to his credit, took it in silence and hit back when he could. I'd always admired him.

"Gentlemen! If we could have him alive, please?" I shouted.

"HERE'S WHAT I think happened," I said, after a dazed, bruised, and bleeding Markos had been hauled back between Pythax and Dromeus.

"Even before the Games began, Xenares gave Markos orders to stir up trouble between Athens and Sparta, because the ephors want a rallying cry to take down Athens."

"But Markos is a member of the hippeis!" Pleistarchus objected. "Not the krypteia."

"Actually, Pleistarchus, he works for both. A double agent. When we interviewed Xenares about the krypteia, Xenares assumed automatically that Markos had told me there were krypteia at Olympia. He hadn't; it was your mother, Queen Gorgo, who discovered it through her own sources. Markos belongs to the hippeis, and the krypteia are famously secretive. Why would Xenares assume Markos could say where they are? On its own it might not have meant much, but combined with the proof that Markos had performed the killings, and that Gorgo confirmed there was no particular motive for any Spartan to murder Arakos, and that Markos barely knew his victim, the only remaining reason was to cause trouble between Athens and Sparta, which it certainly did. The man at Olympia who hates Athens the most is Xenares, and the krypteia take their orders from Xenares."

Every eye turned to Xenares. He stood, unrepentant. "I remind you, Pleistarchus, that a serving member of the ephors cannot be indicted for any crime."

"Your term has only six months left to run," said Pleistarchus coldly. "Then you are vulnerable."

"That's as may be. Much can change in six months."

Pleistarchus and Xenares stared at each other, both men full of hatred. It was going to be a frosty trip back to Sparta.

I said, "Arakos wasn't killed for rivalry in either sport or love. He was killed to start a war between Sparta and Athens. The philosopher Empedocles told me strife and love move everything. Arakos wasn't killed for love; he was killed for strife. It almost worked, too. How close are we to open fighting?"

"Close. Very close," Pericles said, and Pleistarchus nodded.

"So Markos arrived at Olympia already with an eye out for opportunities to cause trouble. What's the first thing he sees? Timodemus attacks Arakos during the opening ceremony, in front of thousands of witnesses. It was a genuine case of rivalry between two great athletes, in a squabble over a woman. Then and there, Markos has his plan. He will murder Arakos in such a way that everyone believes only Timodemus could have done it.

"My guess is, Markos was inspired when he ran into the fake Heracles. Weapons are banned under the Sacred Truce, but no one considers those clubs a weapon. Markos snatched the club from the fake Heracles, just as I did when he swung it at Diotima and me earlier that same afternoon. I imagine Markos threatened the fake Heracles. He said the krypteia would slit his throat if the Heracles said anything, and the fake Heracles, being from the Peloponnese, would be aware of the charming Spartan custom known as the krypteia, of cutting the throats of irritating locals.

"Markos lured Arakos into the woods with the false message, then beat him to death with the club. Astonishingly simple, really. But Olympia is a very crowded place. There was always the risk someone would see something.

"Iphicles, dead drunk, followed a man into the forest. As soon as Iphicles told us this, before the race, Markos crouched, ostensibly to inspect the chariot, but in fact to hide his face before Iphicles recognized him. While he crouched, Markos had to think quickly. He pulled the linchpin, with the reasonable hope Iphicles would have a terrible accident on the track, and so it proved.

"That would have been the end of any hope of solving the

crime, except the fake Heracles overcame his fear long enough to write me the two messages."

"Why didn't the fellow approach you directly?" Pleistarchus asked.

"He tried, twice," I admitted ruefully. "After he watched me take the Olympic Oath and once when I walked through the agora. But both times he ran away. Now I know why: he ran both times because I was with the murderer. After that, he resorted to anonymous messages. It was sheer bad luck that Markos was with me when I received the second message."

"What about the eyes?" asked Pericles.

"Markos tore out the eyes of Arakos because it made the killing look more like the work of an angry pankratist. Putting the extra eyes on the body in the temple was his little joke. His sense of humor runs that way."

I turned to him. "I'm sad, Markos. I thought we were friends. A couple of days ago I thought to myself, I'd like to have you for a brother-in-law."

Markos smiled through his bleeding lips and broken teeth. The flesh about his eyes was already puffing up.

He said, "For my part, I thought you were an idiot. Congratulations, the way you hid your intelligence fooled me completely."

I decided not to tell him it was mostly Diotima who had out-thought him.

"I suppose you're not as inept as you appear," he went on. "But I must say, keeping you alive was hard work. I had to save you twice. First at the hippodrome, then with Skarithos."

"Why did you?" I asked, genuinely puzzled.

"Because the whole point was to make Athens look guilty. With you alive, either you'd agree that Timodemus the Athenian was guilty, or you'd blatantly whitewash your man in a way no one believed; either way, Athens would look terrible, and Sparta would have her rallying cry, as my orders demanded. But if you'd died, then Athens would have looked less guilty, and other cities might have had some sympathy for Sparta's enemy."

Gorgo was visibly shaken. She said, "You, a Spartan, chose to murder a child of the Three Hundred?"

Hung between Pythax and Dromeus, Markos turned his head to speak to her. "It's not murder when you're acting under orders," he said. "Is it not the case, Queen Gorgo, that sometimes an officer will sacrifice a man, perhaps many men, perhaps even himself, if it's the only means to win the war?"

"Do not seek to lecture *me* on the nature of sacrifice, young man," Gorgo said.

"Then you'll understand, Queen Gorgo, that the death of Arakos served Sparta more than his life could ever have done. What would have happened if he'd lived? He would have come in *second* in the pankration. You said it yourself, my Queen: coming in second means coming in last. But by his death, Arakos gave Sparta the chance to come in first in a much more important contest: the competition for Hellas. That's what my orders demanded, to begin that contest between Athens and Sparta."

Every eye turned to Xenares. The ephor remained impassive under our united glare. Xenares the ephor wasn't on trial here. He couldn't be, because he had killed no one. But I guessed from the expression of extreme anger on the face of Pleistarchus that the ephors of Sparta would be in some difficulty the moment the Spartans were all back home.

Markos had spoken with no trace of remorse. There was no reason why he should. A good soldier doesn't feel guilty for what happens on the field of battle, and Markos was the best of the best. The Spartan ritual of the krypteia was a test of silent killing, and Markos had excelled at it. That test had marked Markos for a duty far removed from the common lot of a soldier in the ranks. Markos had been given the most demanding duty any elite trooper can be asked to perform: targeted assassination for political ends.

The difficulty was that Markos seemed to enjoy his work. But then, what man doesn't take pride and pleasure from doing what he does best?

Pericles cleared his throat for attention. The chatter ceased. He said, in a pleasant voice, "I think we can all agree Arakos was not killed by an Athenian?"

Every eye turned to King Pleistarchus.

Pleistarchus said, "Sparta acknowledges that the murderer was a Spartan. There's no need to continue this trial. This is now an internal matter for Sparta. We'll deal with it."

"No need to continue?" exclaimed Exelon, angry. "After all we've been through? After this man almost started a war on sacred Olympic soil? I don't think so!" Behind him the other judges nodded. "The crime was committed at Olympia. It's an Olympic matter."

"It's Spartan," said Pleistarchus. "The victim is Spartan. The murderer is Spartan."

"Olympic, I say," Exelon repeated. "We can enforce this."

"You and whose army?" Pleistarchus said quietly.

And there it was, out in the open. The threat of armed force against the religious authority of the Sacred Games.

I noticed Pericles couldn't keep the self-satisfied smile from his face. I should have been pleased at his happiness, but I wasn't. I held my breath.

Exelon said, "You wouldn't dare. All of Hellas would fight such sacrilege."

"Wait." It was the voice of an old woman. Gorgo stepped forward, slowly. Her steps hesitated for a moment, and Diotima took her arm to support the dowager queen of Sparta.

Gorgo's hawklike eyes took in the entire party as if we were prey. She said, "Before you men start slaughtering each other, let me make a point. If Sparta committed sacrilege, then you are right, Exelon; even our closest allies would turn against us. But think of this: have these Games truly been Sacred? Forgive me for mentioning it; I know the young woman is your daughter, but the Priestess of these Games is about as ritually clean as a sewer."

Ooh, that was a low blow. When it came to political pankration, Gorgo was Olympic strength.

Klymene laughed. Timodemus scowled and stepped toward Gorgo, but One-Eye hauled him back.

Exelon stood as if stunned.

Gorgo said, "Is it not possible the Gods cursed these Games because of the state of the Priestess? If they heard the story, the other cities might think so. Better, don't you think, for us to sort out these problems quietly?"

Exelon looked ready to kill, but he whispered, "Perhaps, under the circumstances, this matter is best left to Sparta."

Gorgo smiled. "Very wise. Now, Exelon, I notice this beautiful new Temple of Zeus puts the rest of Olympia to shame. The place needs brightening up. My son was about to mention that."

"I was?" said Pleistarchus.

"You were, my son," said Gorgo firmly. "I'm sure Sparta would like to send a gift to Olympia. Something substantial."

"Oh! Yes, I see. Good idea, Mother. Exelon, Sparta would be pleased to donate. I'm not quite sure what yet. If you have any ideas—"

"Perhaps some new statuary?" I put in quickly.

Everyone looked at me in surprise.

"I can recommend a good sculptor," I explained.

"You can?" Pleistarchus laughed. "I feel we all owe you, Nicolaos. Very well then, Sparta would love to commission new statuary for the grounds in the spirit of our eternal friendship. What do you say, Exelon?"

"That would be agreeable," Exelon grated. "And now, before my happiness at this outcome can grow too great to bear, I must insist we depart for the stadion. The next event is the pankration, and it's long overdue."

THE JUDGES LED us in, followed by Timodemus, then King Pleistarchus and Pericles, and the rest of us followed in a confused gaggle. Timodemus now wore that same bored expression that he always did before a fight. He was about to do what he was born for: compete at the Olympics.

Klymene took her box.

The stadion was packed to overflowing with men. The trial of Timodemus had taken longer than everyone but Diotima and I had expected, and now from the loud buzz I deduced there was a certain amount of irritation with the judges for their delay. The murmurs rose higher when men in the crowd noticed Timodemus among us.

The other pankratists and their trainers stood in a group; among them I saw Korillos, Aggelion, and Megathenes. They were shocked to see Timodemus enter.

"You allow him to compete?" Megathenes asked.

"We have determined two things," Exelon the Chief Judge said to the pankratists and the trainers. "First, that Timodemus did not kill Arakos. Second, that this will be a fair contest."

Timo didn't break step. He walked over to his fellow pankratists. He spoke in his normal conversational voice so that they and those of us near him could hear, "Men, I've only this day discovered that I won unfairly at Nemea. I never knew; may Zeus slay me where I stand if I lie." Timodemus drew in a deep breath. "I revoke my Nemean crown, which means the victor of Nemea becomes Arakos of Sparta."

The men murmured among themselves.

"And I promise you I will compete today with the same disadvantage that you suffered at Nemea. That's only fair." Timo turned around to face me. "Nico!"

"Yes, Timo?"

"If I know your cleverness, you have more than three of the poisoned bottles in that bag, don't you?"

"Yes, I have them all." Diotima and I had swapped every

poisoned bottle, fearing that Festianos might manage to slip some to the athletes.

"Good, because I'm thirsty."

I blinked. "What? But Timo, you mustn't—"

"I said I'm thirsty, Nico. Give me something to drink." I had never heard such command in his voice. I could see the strain he was under, the tension in his neck muscles. I hesitated. Timo repeated, "Nico." He held out his hand.

Against my will, but unable to deny him, I handed over a bottle of hemlock.

Timodemus held the poison to his lips and drank it down, swallowing over and over until he'd drained it to the last drop. Timo threw the bottle to the side and said, "Now let's fight."

A voice behind me said, "I forbid it." One-Eye pushed past me to stand before his son. "Timo, stop this now."

"Isn't this what you want, Father? Isn't this what I was born for? Didn't you train me every moment of my childhood for this one moment when you could see me at the Olympics?"

"Not like this," said One-Eye. "I expected you to . . . to . . ."

"Survive?" Timo smiled, a grim, grim smile. "Did you know about Festianos?"

"No, son, I didn't."

"But you suspected, didn't you?"

One-Eye looked away.

Timo said, "This time there'll be no cheating. This time, Zeus really does grant the victory."

One-Eye hesitated for the longest moment, then he nodded and did something I am sure he had never done in his life: he took Timo in his arms and held him tight. They hugged for the longest time, while all the Hellenes watched them.

Timo broke away and walked over to me. "Thank you, Nico," he said.

"You don't have to do this, Timo," I said, quiet but urgent.

He smiled sadly and said, "You of all people know I can't abide a fight that isn't fair."

"What happened at Nemea wasn't your fault."

"It wasn't a fair fight."

They were the same words he'd used when he'd saved me as a boy, all those years ago.

"Listen, Nico, I want you to do something for me."

"Sure."

"Look after Klymene, will you?"

"Er . . . look after her how?"

"She might be in trouble with her father, when all this is over. I don't want her hurt, and with Arakos dead and with me . . . well, the pankration's dangerous, you know that."

"I thought she was just for fun. Good in bed, you said."

"Maybe I like her a little bit. You're my only friend. Swear you'll do your best to protect Klymene. That's all I ask."

"I swear it." I felt like I pronounced a death sentence.

I stepped back to join Heraclides alongside the box where the trainers stood. It meant I was among the officials, where I could see and hear everything, but at this point no one seemed to care.

Timo walked over to the other pankratists. The lots were drawn for the bouts.

The Chief Judge called, "Begin."

There were four matches, to be held at the same time, in four circles set out in a line along the stadion.

At the call to begin, all eight pankratists advanced. Timo downed his opponent quickly with some swift kicks and a hard punch to the neck. The man went down unconscious, and Timo was declared the winner. He waited by the side while the other fights, more evenly matched, came to their completion. Two bodies were carried away, neither dead, both merely unconscious.

I said, "How is it, Heraclides, that Timo hasn't collapsed?"

"You forget that he's taken but a medicinal dose, the equivalent of two leaves. As the poison seeps through it will slow his reactions but not kill him. But I fear . . . oh yes, he's doing it now."

Timodemus had picked up another of the bottles and downed it. For the next bout.

"Four leaves is survivable," Heraclides said. "Unless the person is old or weak, and your friend is certainly neither of those."

Timodemus was noticeably slower in the next fight. He faced Megathenes. Megathenes hit out and landed some hard blows, though everyone could see Timodemus try to react.

Dromeus leaned over the box where he stood with the other trainers and said to us, "You see what's happening? Timodemus sees the blows coming but he's not fast enough to dodge."

Heraclides said, "It's the drug." He shook his head.

The skill of Timodemus showed despite his slowed reflexes. He allowed Megathenes to come at him, grabbed him about the waist, and rolled backward. Megathenes rolled over him. Timodemus finished on top. He struck Megathenes in the head, one, two, three, four times. When Timodemus climbed unsteadily to his feet, Megathenes remained down and unconscious.

Exelon called the final round.

Timodemus picked up the final bottle.

"No!" Klymene stood in her box. "No!" she shouted again, and the whole stadion of men looked at her in stunned surprise.

The Priestess of the Games had spoken. She stepped out of her box and went to the judges, who were clustered next to where I and Heraclides and the trainers stood.

"I refuse to see these Games," Klymene declared.

"What?" The Chief Judge could not have appeared more surprised if his daughter had declared herself to be a Gorgon. "You can't mean that."

"I do. Don't you see Timodemus plans to kill himself with the poison?" Klymene demanded.

"As long as the Games proceed, that's the important thing. Daughter, he might well have died in the contest in any case."

"But he was to be your son-in-law!"

"We may be revising that plan."

"Timodemus is a good man. He's a better person than I am." Klymene looked abashed.

Timo had walked over when Klymene abandoned her box. He seemed preternaturally calm. Now he said, "That's not true, Klymene, you're a better person than you know. You saved my honor in the court."

"Timo, don't do this," Klymene begged. "Our lives are brief enough as it is, don't go making them any shorter."

Timo winced. He said, "This is a matter of honor, Klymene."

"What honor? Your uncle cheated, Timo. You want to make up for his crimes? Then go ahead and lose these stupid Games. But your uncle didn't kill anyone. You don't have to die for what he did."

"Don't you understand, Klymene?" Timo said, perplexed at her words. "*It wasn't a fair fight.*"

Klymene threw her arms up in despair. "You men are idiots. If you're bent on suicide, I'll not help you."

Klymene stalked off without another word, leaving her father to stand there alone while the assembled Hellenes watched a man unable to control his own daughter. Klymene couldn't be stopped: the Chief Judge didn't dare beat the Priestess of the Games; to do so would have brought down the worst luck imaginable.

Exelon slowly turned to face the crowd, his face gray. He drew in a great breath and shouted, in a voice that carried across the stadion, "Hellenes, we have no priestess to observe the Sacred Games. Therefore I must declare—"

"Yes, you do," Diotima called out. She stood at the stadion's entrance. Everyone turned to stare at her.

The Chief Judge said, "Women are not permitted—"

"I'm a priestess," she said loudly, so that the whole stadion could hear her words.

Diotima waited at the entrance for an invitation to enter. Every man present watched in silence as the Chief Judge walked the hundred paces across the field, to speak to her in private. I hurried across, too, anxious to find out what Diotima thought she was doing.

"Are you a priestess of Demeter?" the Chief Judge asked her quietly.

"Artemis," she said. "Do you have time to be choosy?"

"The priestess of the Games must serve Demeter. When the crowd finds out they'll—"

"I won't tell them if you don't. Why don't we pretend you never asked me that question."

Exelon looked at her for a moment, then at the crowd, and I could see the rapid calculation racing through his mind. If he stopped the Games now there would be a riot. Already we could see a few ripples in the crowd, where scuffles had broken out.

Exelon said, "Take the stand." He walked to the stadion center to tell the crowd that the Goddess Demeter in her wisdom had seen fit to send a replacement.

To the background of loud cheers I said, "Diotima, you know what you're doing, don't you? Timo wants to poison himself."

"How would you feel if your life's greatest moment turned out to be a lie?" she asked. "Timo needs this extirpation."

"Even if it kills him?"

"That's his choice," said my Priestess of the Hunt. "What do you think Timo's life will be like if he lives? What will men say of him? Besides, I seem to recall two men who battered each other almost to death in public, and *you* refused to stop it."

I could only hang my head. Diotima stepped past to take her place in the box Klymene had vacated. She spurned the chair and stood, her hands gripped the railing like a judge about to pass sentence. She was every bit the haughty priestess.

I went back to the cluster of people from the trial.

Timodemus drank down the final bottle.

"Six leaves," Heraclides said to me. "A fatal dose."

The Chief Judge of the Sacred Games looked to Diotima for permission.

Diotima nodded.

"Begin," Exelon called.

The referees took their positions, and Timodemus began the contest that would kill him.

Heraclides scratched a note into an ostrakon. "Socrates, I want you to take this note to my wife. Tell her I want these medicines and instruments laid out before I arrive."

Socrates took the note and ran.

"Will Timo make it to the end, do you think?" I asked.

Heraclides said, "I don't know which is stronger, the poison or his remarkable reserves of willpower."

Korillos punched Timo, hitting him in the same spot in the diaphragm, over and over, obviously hoping to deprive him of any chance to breathe.

Timodemus doubled over and spewed.

"Good," said Heraclides. "We can hope that's taken out some of the poison with it."

"You mean he might live?" I said.

"Who knows? His extreme exertions spread the poison much more quickly, and he's a small man. But he's also in outstanding condition, and there's no telling how much of the poison that vomit might have brought up."

Korillos landed a massive kick against Timo's leg. Everyone saw it coming, but Timo couldn't move. The whole stadium heard Timo's leg snap. They could see the bone poking through his skin. Every man gasped and waited for the inevitable moment when Timo raised his arm in defeat.

But Timo didn't. He kept on fighting.

"Dear Gods, he's fighting with his bones sticking out!" I heard someone exclaim. I looked beside me for the voice and saw it was Pericles. He looked distinctly ill at the ugly sight. In the crowd behind me, someone retched.

"He doesn't feel a thing," Heraclides said in astonishment, and then, "Oh, but of course! The poison's deadened all feeling in his legs! While he's in this state, there's nothing Korillos can do to hurt him."

Timodemus stood there on his broken leg and ignored the blows raining down upon him. He grabbed the throat of Korillos and squeezed. There was no art in what Timodemus did, but he had no time for art.

Korillos fell to his knees. Timo didn't relent for an instant. He grinned the rictus smile of supreme effort.

Any moment now, Korillos would expire for lack of air. His face turned blue. It was surrender or die.

Korillos raised his arm in defeat.

Timodemus let go, staggered sideways, forward, backward, forward. He dribbled uncontrollably, then doubled over and vomited again. He gasped for breath. His eyes rolled up, and he collapsed.

The crowd gasped. Men wept and beat each other.

"Timodemus of Athens is the victor," the Chief Judge called. He stood over the inert form as if this had been nothing but a normal bout.

Heraclides said to me, "There might still be time. As soon as the ceremony is over, bring him to the iatrion as quick as you can. I'll wait there for you."

I nodded, not trusting myself to speak.

Heraclides picked up the skirts of his ground-length chiton and ran out of the stadion and down the path like a woman.

One-Eye walked to the center of the ring. I thought he too might collapse, but he picked up his son, who was entirely limp, and carried him to the altar where the Olympic crown waited.

One-Eye laid his son on the altar as if he were a sacrifice. There was nowhere else to put him.

On Pericles's face I saw immense satisfaction.

A small group gathered about the body. I hovered behind. I had no standing to be there, but I had to be close.

For a moment, no one moved. Unable to keep the urgency out of my voice, I said, "Crown him, and be quick about it!"

Diotima took up the olive wreath. She blessed it and passed it to Exelon.

The Chief Judge declared to every man present, to all the Hellenes, "Timodemus, son of Timonous One-Eye, an Athenian, wins the pankration. Zeus has granted the victory!"

All around the stadion, men cheered and sobbed in equal measure. It was a famous victory by a man who had expunged family dishonor by the manner in which he chose his fate.

Exelon placed the olive crown on the head of the still form. My friend had won the Olympic Games.

Everything that had to be done was done.

I pushed my way through, picked up the body of Timodemus, slung him over my shoulder, and ran.

DAY 5 OF THE 80TH OLYMPIAD OF THE SACRED GAMES

IT WAS A fine afternoon at Olympia. The closing ceremony had finished, and men packed their tents for the journey home. The Sacred Truce would last long enough for everyone to travel back to their cities, after which we could all go back to fighting one another.

Not that I was likely to notice any difference.

The closing ceremony had been particularly fine and, for me, the only time in the last five days that I'd been able to relax. I thought what a pity it was Timo hadn't been there to see it. But Timo was ensconced in the iatrion with Heraclides, unable to move.

It had been a tense and stressful night. Heraclides had worked right through, first to keep Timo breathing, and then, when it was certain Timo's breath wouldn't stop and while the effects of the hemlock were still upon him, to reset the shattered bone in Timo's left leg. Timo didn't feel a thing, which was good because the pain would have been excruciating. Timo would walk with a limp for the rest of his life. He could never fight again, but I had a feeling he wouldn't mind.

Klymene tended Timodemus throughout. Diotima had to tear her away at dawn, because the Priestess had to oversee the closing ceremony. The moment it was over, Klymene had returned to Timo's side. One-Eye and Exelon had begun negotiation for the marriage.

"Do you think the fathers will agree?" Diotima asked me.

"I'm sure they will. The sooner they can both put their

children's pasts behind them and look to the future, the better for everyone."

Diotima smiled. "Good. Marriage is a fine thing."

The night before, Diotima had been present when Pythax and Sophroniscus signed our marriage agreement. King Pleistarchus had already commissioned my father for statuary at Olympia. With the money that Sophroniscus would earn, we were provided for, and Pythax could keep the farm. Pythax and Sophroniscus had imposed one new condition: that we replay the marriage ceremony in our mothers' presence. I protested, but Pythax, one of the toughest and most dangerous men in Athens, had explained the situation with great clarity.

"If you don't, your mothers will kill us," he'd said.

My father had nodded agreement with his new relative. "Don't take on any new commissions until then, do you hear me, son?"

"There's no fear of that, Father."

The body of Festianos had been discovered that morning, slumped over the altar at which the oxen are sacrificed to Zeus. His throat had been slashed from ear to ear, just like the sacrifices. The altar to Zeus stands at the busiest point in Olympia, yet not a single witness had stepped forward. This was one death I would not be investigating.

Not that there was time, even if I wanted. Diotima and I had been summoned to Queen Gorgo.

"YOU HAVE SAVED the Spartans and the Athenians from war, young lady," Gorgo said. "A war that would have weakened not only both our cities, but all of Hellas. You've done well."

"Thank you, Queen Gorgo," Diotima said.

I waited for Gorgo to praise me, too, but apparently I hadn't saved anyone.

"I have something for you," Gorgo said.

Diotima knelt before Gorgo, and Gorgo placed into Diotima's hands a stained backing board and four pieces of thin wood.

"What is it?" Diotima asked, confused.

Gorgo said, "This is what's left of the wax tablet that held the secret message, the warning that the Persians were about to attack. Do you see the message itself scratched into the wood? I saved the city-states when I deduced the existence of that message—not only my own city, but all of them. Do you take my meaning, girl?"

"I understand you," Diotima said. Her voice quavered.

Gorgo looked into Diotima's eyes. "I've waited twenty years for a Spartan woman of the next generation, one to whom I could pass these bits of wood. Now I find they must go to an Athenian."

Gorgo looked to Pleistarchus and me. "Leave us," she said, in a voice that commanded kings. "This young lady and I have a few things to discuss."

IT'S NOT EVERY day you get to shoot the breeze with a king of Sparta.

Pleistarchus and I walked through the camp while we waited for his mother and my betrothed to end their conversation.

Pleistarchus said, "I could almost wish the Persians would come at us again."

"You can't be serious," I said, surprised. His father had died fighting Persians.

"You're right, I'm not serious. But we Hellenes had something back then that we've lost: unity of purpose. When it looked like we might all die together, we fought as one. The moment the pressure was off, we went back to our old internecine bickering ways. I hate it."

"You're a king, Pleistarchus. Why don't you do something about it?"

He laughed a bitter laugh. "You went through the last four days, and you don't know the answer to that?"

"You could change the rules, rule without the ephors."

"The last man to try that was my mother's father. He ended up minus a certain amount of his skin."

All about us, as we ambled, Spartans packed their belongings with military precision. They paused to salute Pleistarchus wherever he passed.

"Traditions should change when they no longer work," I said, sure of my point. Wasn't that what had happened when we Athenians created the democracy?

"I see you have no future as a Spartan," Pleistarchus said.

"I'm relieved to know it."

"As am I. I've seen you fight, Nicolaos, and your technique is appalling, more like a street thug than a soldier."

"Then that would be appropriate, King Pleistarchus, because that's where I fight," I said.

He laughed, and this time it was a happier sound. "I could wish that I were you and not me. I'm pleased you survived."

I nodded. I'd seen what a tough job it was to be a king of Sparta, and I'd rather be me, too.

He said, "You and that rather clever girl of yours stopped a war. Sparta owes you both a debt."

"Not all your fellows agree."

"I'll keep them in line. Tell Pericles that Athens must curb her ambitions. Tell him that the Hellenes are like a chariot pulled by two horses. If one horse gets ahead of the other, the whole thing overturns."

"I'll tell him."

He offered me a kingly nod of the head. "Farewell, Nicolaos, son of Sophroniscus. Usually I offer a wish to meet again, but in your case I suspect it would mean bad news for both of us."

Diotima emerged from Gorgo's tent, carrying the old, broken pieces of wood. She looked somewhat stunned. "I'm ready to go, Nico."

As we left the Spartan camp, three men stepped in front of me, three of the five whom Markos and I had beaten.

"What now, Skarithos," I said. I was tired. I was hungry. "It's all over. Everything's done."

Skarithos sneered, "This time you don't have Markos to protect you."

"No, instead I have King Pleistarchus. He just thanked me."

"What Pleistarchus thinks isn't what I think. We have kings to serve us, not rule us. We Spartans think Athens needs taking down, and if you're in the front rank of your army when that happens, Athenian, then all the better. I want to meet you on a battlefield."

I was already on my battlefield, fighting a war few men even realized existed. Pleistarchus had his work cut out for him if he thought he could keep this lot on a leash. Perhaps Pericles was right, perhaps war was inevitable.

Skarithos looked over my shoulder. I didn't bother to turn; I knew he could see his king watch us depart. Skarithos stepped aside.

"I'll be seeing you, Athenian," he hissed as we shouldered our way past.

"Not if I see you first," I said. It wasn't the most witty reply, but I really was tired. All I wanted was to go home.

We walked out of the Spartan camp for the last time, down the path that would take us back to the Athenians. Diotima was unusually subdued. She trudged along beside me with her head down and concentrated on stepping as delicately as she could through the mud. After five days, and thousands of men and women walking back and forth, the ground was churned up like the aftermath of a war.

"What did you talk about in there with Queen Gorgo?" I asked.

"Woman talk. You wouldn't be interested," she said. "But one thing I'll tell you. Gorgo is dying."

I wasn't surprised. The Dowager Queen of Sparta looked thin enough to be dead already.

Parked along the road, out of the worst of the mud, was a long line of racing chariots. Their horses snorted and pranced.

The easiest way to take a chariot home is to drive it. The chariots from all the cities traveled in convoy because they made such an attractive target for brigands. Besides, it was the perfect opportunity to do a bit of road racing.

Coming up the path from the Athenian camp was a bunch of men. They waved sticks, and I could hear their angry voices from more than a hundred paces away.

When they saw Diotima and me, they stopped. I walked another five paces before I realized they waited for me.

"Stop, honey." I grabbed Diotima's arm. "Come with me." I turned her around, and we walked the other way at a brisk pace, only to see behind us a mob of Spartans with hard eyes and harder clubs. At their head was Skarithos, who only moments ago had threatened me.

The Spartans stopped when I turned toward them.

I looked over my shoulder. The Athenians stood at the other end with arms crossed and grim expressions.

It occurred to me that I'd angered a lot of people. The Spartans had insisted an Athenian killed Arakos. Instead, I'd proven it was one of their own. Pericles had insisted the Athenians were innocent. Instead, I'd proven an Athenian had cheated at the Nemean Games, and tried again at the Olympics. Both Sparta and Athens were in bad odor with the other cities, and it was all my fault.

At the very least, I was about to take a beating.

Diotima was safe. Hellenes wouldn't harm a woman for what her husband had done. What was about to happen would be painful for her to watch, but not as painful as it would be for me.

Diotima saw the problem, but my brave girl wasn't scared, merely perplexed. There was no other path and no building in sight in which we could hide.

"We could run cross-country," she suggested.

"Outrun trained soldiers?"

"Nico! Nico!" It was Pindar. He ran down the street past the Spartans—he didn't even notice them—waving a sheet of papyrus in his right hand and holding his lyre in his left. "Listen to this, you're going to love it," he said.

"I'm sorry, Pindar, I don't have time to talk," I said.

"I've written your praise song, Nicolaos. I didn't even use one of the prepared ones. You get an authentic Pindar original composition, my boy. One of my better efforts, too, if I say so myself." He began to tune his lyre.

At that instant, both mobs advanced.

"I'll listen some other time, Pindar. I *really have to go*."

"But this is your Olympic victory song, lad! They'll remember your name forever. There are men who would die for one of these."

"I know. Send your bill to One-Eye. He owes me."

I jumped onto the nearest chariot and snatched the reins from a slave. He protested, but I ignored him. The chariot was rigged for two horses and ready to go.

I held out my hand. "Come with me, Diotima."

Diotima's eyes shone. "Father will be furious with you again."

"No, he won't," I said. "We're going to Athens, for the official marriage we promised our fathers."

Diotima smiled and stepped up onto the chariot. "Let's go."

I whipped the horses, and the chariot lurched off across the open country, with Diotima at my side, pursued by an angry mob of Spartans and Athenians, and Pindar, waving his music.

AUTHOR'S NOTE

THIS AUTHOR'S NOTE talks about the real history behind the story, interesting facts that I couldn't squeeze into the plot, and trivia to do with the characters. Which means it's full of spoilers. If you haven't read the book yet, this would be an excellent time to avert your eyes and turn to the front!

The pankration was the most brutal sport in Olympic history, probably the most lethal too. So it will come as no surprise that pankration had a huge fan base, even more so than chariot racing. A pankratist who won at the Olympics was treated like a rock star. Pankratists were the highest-paid athletes in ancient Greece. It was normal for a winner to be voted honors by his home city; he'd receive some special reward, typically free food for life—more valuable than you might think in chronically hungry ancient Greece—and he could expect his statue to be raised in his city's agora.

Pankration is virtually unknown today. In 393 AD the Christian Emperor Theodosius banned the Olympic Games and all other pagan festivals, and that killed pankration. Which is a pity because if it had survived, pankration would be Europe's answer to the Asian martial arts phenomenon.

From the many surviving pictures on vases, it appears pankration was vaguely similar to judo, only a judo in which punching, kicking, and choking your opponent to death were perfectly legal. If you're interested, there's a modern revival of the sport; I assume the rules have been toned down slightly.

Despite the violence, there was a great deal of science to pankration. Like all martial artists, a top practitioner could face a better-armed man and have the skills to win. In the time of Alexander the Great, for example, the best pankratist in the world was a certain Dioxippus of Athens. Dioxippus, in a challenge, took on a fully armed and armored Macedonian soldier. That means the Macedonian wore bronze armor and a helmet, and carried a sharp-edged sword. Dioxippus not only won, but did so with such contempt for his opponent that he didn't even bother to hurt him, merely subduing the Macedonian in an irresistible lock. The Macedonians were ashamed that Dioxippus had beaten one of their best so handily. In revenge they framed him for a major theft and he, feeling his honor destroyed, took his own life.

But the most dramatic event in Olympic history—both ancient and modern—occurred with another pankratist. There once was a man named Arrachion who won the pankration at three Olympiads in succession! To win this fighting sport once was amazing; to do so three times in a row implies an almost supernatural ability to hurt people. Arrachion clearly was not someone you would wish to annoy.

Here is how Arrachion won his third Olympic crown. This excerpt is from the ancient writer Philostratus, in his book *Imagines*. We take up the fight with our hero in big trouble:

Arrachion's opponent, having already a grip around his waist, thought to kill him and put an arm around his neck to choke off his breath. At the same time he slipped his legs through Arrachion's and wound his feet inside Arrachion's knees, pulling back until the sleep of death began to creep over Arrachion's senses.

But Arrachion was not done yet, for as his opponent began to relax the pressure of his legs, Arrachion kicked away his own right foot and fell heavily to the left, holding his opponent at the groin, with his left knee still holding his opponent's foot firmly in place.

So violent was the fall that the opponent's left ankle was wrenched from his socket. The man strangling Arrachion signaled with his hand that he gave up.

Thus Arrachion became a three-time Olympic victor at the moment of his death. His corpse received the victory crown.

His corpse received the victory crown.

Arrachion had been at the top of his sport for twelve years. He certainly knew the consequences of what he was doing, and yet he knowingly sent himself to his death, because Olympic victory was more important than life itself.

This historically true scene provided me with the inspiration for Timo's self-sacrifice in Sacred Games. In the book it might read like one of the less believable pieces of melodrama, but the essence of that incredible event actually happened.

TIMODEMUS OF ATHENS was a real athlete of the ancient world. He came from one of those sporting families that seem to throw up great athletes in every generation. Between them, the family of the *genos* Timonidae won four victories at the Pythian Games, eight at the Isthmian Games, and seven at the Nemean Games, one of which Timo collected himself.

After the Nemean victory, Pindar wrote a praise song in which he predicted that Timo would win at the Olympics, which he duly did.

Pindar was the most famous praise singer of his day. They were poets-for-hire, who for a fee would create a poem or song to honor a man whose deeds made him worthy of praise. Pindar really did write a praise song for Timodemus, which is known today as *Nemean 2*. This book begins with my own, very loose, translation of the first stanza. This is the one and only time that I've used my own translation of an ancient Greek text rather than rely on an academic version. To make it more accessible to modern readers, I cut some words and changed the meter. I hope Pindar's *psyche* will forgive me.

Pindar *might* be the author of the most famous epitaph ever written:

Stranger, go tell the Spartans that here,
According to their laws, we lie.

Those lines were chiseled into the funeral stone for the 300 who held the pass at Thermopylae. No one knows who wrote them.

After the war, Pindar and Simonides, the great praise singer of the previous generation, were sent on a mission to raise funeral stones and write epitaphs for all the fallen. Since they were the world's two greatest living poets, the Greeks were emphatically sending their A team.

It's known which poet wrote many of the surviving epitaphs, but no one ever claimed credit for the greatest. Most people assume it was Simonides, because the lines are more in his style. The problem with that is, the historian Herodotus listed all the epitaphs written by Simonides, and he specifically does *not* list the epitaph for the Three Hundred. Which leaves Pindar next in line for the authorship.

Pindar never does get to sing Nico's victory song. I can't let him! Pindar's collected works are one of the most complete sets of poems from the ancient world; if Pindar sang Nico's song, I'd have to explain how come it doesn't appear in the extant collections.

WOMEN WERE FORBIDDEN to watch the Games. We know this for sure because the ancient travel writer Pausanias tells us so. He also tells us what the penalty was. I copied it for the sentence passed on Timodemus. Pausanias said:

As you go from Scillus along the road to Olympia, before you cross the Alpheius, there is a mountain with high, precipitous cliffs. It is called

Mount Typaeum. It is a law of Elis to cast down it any women who are caught present at the Olympic Games, or even on the other side of the Alpheius, on the days prohibited to women.

It must be added that, to the best of my knowledge, not once did the Greeks ever enact this terrible penalty, not even in the one famous case in which a woman was caught red-handed. This woman was discovered not only inside the stadion, but inside the box from which the coaches of the athletes watched.

The story goes that a lady by the name of Callipateira was the widow of a strong athlete, and that her son also was a fine runner. When her husband died, Callipateira took over the job coaching their son, to the point at which he qualified for the Olympics. Determined to see him compete, Callipateira disguised herself as a man and joined the other coaches in their box. Her son won! Callipateira was the first woman in history to train an Olympic victor. She was so excited that she gave herself away. The judges were entirely unwilling to punish such a remarkable lady, so they told her not to do it again, and then they changed the rules so that no other woman could ever pull the same trick. That is why from that day on, the coaches at the Olympics were required to watch the Games stark naked.

Oddly, the law forbidding women uses the ancient Greek word for *married* women. As a result it's become a standard meme on the Internet that unmarried virgins were permitted to watch the Olympics. This is helped by Pausanias making a vague statement about seeing virgin girls at the Games.

Let's think about that. We have a stadion filled with thousands of drunken, sports-crazed men, and in among them are a bunch of teenage virgins.

I don't think so.

What is very likely is that fathers brought along unmarried daughters to matchmake them with eligible bachelors from other cities. In fact, I consider it certain that the Olympics was a major matchmaking event. But there's no way teenage girls were in the stadion when the contests were held. It's just a recipe for disaster.

There must have been a women's camp, and it must have been on the other side of the river, given the rule as stated by Pausanias. The placement and the layout is the work of my imagination.

Though women couldn't compete at the Olympics, they did have their own Games. The Heraea Games were held in honor of Hera, queen of the Gods, just as the Olympic Games were in honor of her husband, Zeus. The women's Games were severely underreported, in much the same fashion that women's sport doesn't get the same attention these days.

WHEN TIMODEMUS SAYS that he'll wait until he's thirty, and then ask his father to find him a fourteen-year-old virgin, he's following the standard system of the times. It was practically illegal for a man to remain unmarried after thirty, but most men waited until the last moment before getting hitched. The men of ancient Greece were notorious commitment-phobes. Probably some modern women are reading this and thinking not much has changed.

Marriage between citizens was always negotiated by the fathers. That's the source of the problem that Nico and Diotima experience. Given human nature, they can't have been the first young couple to arrange matters for themselves and then expect their fathers to make it official. This is why Nico is confused about whether Diotima is his wife or his fiancée. The circumstances that led to their predicament are related in *The Ionia Sanction*.

THE WORDS OF the ancient Olympic Oath have been lost. The modern oath, with its high ideals and fine values, is unlikely to bear much resemblance to the original. The ancient Olympic Oath appears to have been an anti-cheating device, to which extent it had more in common with the modern oath one takes when giving evidence in court.

To a people who truly believed in the power of the Gods, it was more than lip service to swear by Zeus. The Greeks believed very much in the concept of luck. Except to them, luck was supplied by the Gods. A man who forswore an oath to Zeus could expect very bad luck indeed. The statue of Zeus before which the oath was taken really did show a wrathful god holding a lightning bolt in each hand; I'm not making that up at all.

Despite the oath, cheating certainly did occur. There are known, documented cases, and nearly all of them involve bribery. This is why an athlete's relatives also had to swear not to cheat.

Anyone who was caught was fined a huge sum, which was used to install a zane—a statue of Zeus—in a public place at Olympia, with the name of the cheater prominently displayed for everyone to see for generations to come. It was a name-and-shame strategy.

WITCHCRAFT WAS THE elephant in the room when it came to cheating in the ancient Olympics, just as drugs are a major problem in the modern Games. *We* know that witchcraft doesn't work, but *they* didn't.

The Greeks believed in witchcraft—a very different witchcraft to the modern version, but witchcraft all the same. The Greeks wrote curse tablets by inscribing their curse into a thin sheet of lead and then tossing it down a well. Hundreds of these curse tablets have been recovered, some are on display in museums, and they're all very malicious.

There's no record of anyone using hemlock to cheat. That part of the story is the product of my own demented imagination. Yet the ancient Greeks certainly knew enough to try it. Hemlock had been the poison of choice for a gentle self-exit for centuries. Indeed on some islands, notably Keos, it was the custom for men when they reached sixty years to take hemlock to make room for the next generation.

Hemlock was prescribed as a folk medicine to treat arthritis and tremors right up until relatively recently. Don't try this at home. Hemlock is unbelievably deadly, and as Heraclides points out in the book, the line between a medicinal and a fatal dose is very slim.

HERACLIDES DISPLAYS AN unusual degree of skill for the primitive state of ancient Greek medicine, but I think we may reasonably expect high ability from the father of Hippocrates. After all, Heraclides taught his son.

Hippocrates is the most famous doctor in all of history. To this day the word "Hippocratic" is synonymous with the very best in medical practice. Doctors still swear the Hippocratic Oath. Hippocrates wasn't the world's first doctor, but he was the first to record the effects of his treatments, and to apply the principle of doing what he saw worked, and refrain from repeating what didn't. Today we'd call it evidence-based medicine. Hippocrates invented it.

At the time of this story, the man destined to become the world's greatest doctor is one year old. The name of his father really was Heraclides. In those days, doctors learned their trade by apprenticeship to their fathers.

Such was Hippocrates's skill that the Greeks in his own lifetime called him Hippocrates the Great. Despite which, there is only one contemporary mention of him in surviving books. I know this seems almost too good to be true, but the only contemporary reference to Hippocrates comes from none other than Socrates!

It happens in a book called *Protagoras*, written by Plato, in which Socrates refers to Hippocrates of Kos in a familiar way that makes it clear the two men were acquainted: yet another amazing proof that the men and women who founded our civilization all knew one another.

Socrates and Hippocrates almost certainly met about forty years after the time of this story, on the occasion when Hippocrates visited Athens, which the great doctor did at the invitation of Pericles. Which means that at one point in history, Pericles, Socrates, and Hippocrates were in the same room together. One wonders what the world's greatest statesman, the world's greatest philosopher, and the world's greatest doctor said to one another. Alas, we'll never know.

IN NICO'S TIME, the latest fad in sports science was the all-meat diet. It's easy to see why. The usual Greek diet was almost entirely seafood, vegetables and fruit. All very healthy! Red meat was extremely expensive and hard to obtain. But meat, and the fat that goes with it, is high-energy food, just the thing for a top athlete. After several meat-eating athletes won famous victories, the all-meat regimen became mandatory for any serious competitor. It must have cost their fathers a small fortune.

THE BUTCHER OF the Games is a job I invented, but I think that there must have been such a position, because there were so many sacrifices held at the Olympics.

We think of the Olympics as a sporting event, but to the Greeks, the Sacred Games were first and foremost a religious festival, and no religious ceremony was complete without a sacrifice.

The everyday, typical Greek sacrifice was *always* eaten. That was how poor families got their only meat meals, and since the sacrifices were supplied by rich men, it was as much as anything a charity system to get some quality food to the poor.

The sacrifice of the hundred white oxen at the Olympics was the largest such event of the ancient world. Though they might be a supersized meal, they were a typical sacrifice and therefore could be eaten.

This is the equivalent of holding a sausage sizzle after a Sunday church service. These days we don't tend to think about how the meat got inside the sausage, but you need only go back a few generations, to, say, the early 1900s, for the roast pig on the spit outside the community church to be very recently deceased. In a world without refrigeration the healthiest way for the meat to get to the barbecue was for it to walk there on its own four feet.

The Olympic Oath was almost certainly sworn over sacrificed meat. An oath sworn over a sacrifice was particularly powerful, and the meat of such might not be eaten. But that was by far the exception.

OF ALL THE events described in this book, the most ridiculous is the ox made of bread. So needless to say, it really happened. This is one of those cases of real life being sillier than anything a writer could get away with.

The philosopher Empedocles believed in reincarnation; he declared that he himself had once been a fish and a bird, and that therefore we should not kill our fellow beings. All of which is remarkably Buddhist for an ancient Greek of the fifth century BC. Pythagoras too had taught reincarnation in the century before. It's interesting to speculate how differently Europe might have developed had their teaching caught on.

But Empedocles is better known for his other doctrine: that everything in the world is made up of four elements: earth, water, fire and air. Previous philosophers had had a go at answering this very important question: what was everything made of? Thales, the world's first true scientist, had held that all matter was simply different forms of water. His student Anaximenes opted for air. Xenophanes liked earth. Heraclitus, who gets a mention in *The Ionia Sanction*, declared that fire was the basic element. Empedocles covered all the bases by declaring that all four of these made up the basic elements. This idea caught on big time!

In fact, it caught on all too well and never let go. To this day, the four elements of Empedocles are central to the theories of alchemists who haven't quite caught up with the latest developments, with astrologers and practitioners of magic in the Western tradition.

———

FEW THINGS CAN destroy your confidence in the accuracy of historical dating as completely as the detailed study of who won what at the Olympics, and in which Olympiad. Every Greek city ran its own calendar, with its own years; the only thing everyone had in common was the Olympics. So the Greeks used the Olympiads to synchronize their calendars, and when writing about a given world event, would refer to the year it happened by its closest Olympiad. The typical logic would go: "World Event X happened in the same year that So-and-So won the Such-and-Such event at the Nth Olympics." The Greeks expected everyone to know the winner lists for every Games.

The only problem was, it was by no means certain in which Olympiad So-and-So competed. There are some astounding contradictions, even in the ancient sources, due to fallible human memory. For example it was commonly stated, even in ancient times, and you'll find it repeated all over the internet, that King Alexander I of Macedon competed in the stadion (sprint) event at the 80th Olympiad, which happens to be the Olympics when this book is set. Herodotus mentions it, and there's even a fragment of a praise song written by Pindar. But Alexander doesn't appear in *Sacred Games* because it would be unusual for a man in his fifties to be sprinting! The date is simply wrong. If Alexander did compete at the Olympics, and it's by no means certain that he did, then it must have been thirty years before.

In the book I have the heralds argue over which Olympiad Dromeus won in. Their inability to agree is all too accurate. The most comprehensive winner list—and that's not saying much—was compiled by a fellow named Eusebius. Eusebius lived much later, but wrote chronologies for all sorts of things, and one of them was a "complete" list of winners of the Olympic stadion event. Even so, he must certainly have missed some winners, and he must surely have been relying ultimately on the fallible memories of men such as the heralds, who passed on the list by oral tradition. You don't have to miss too many entries before the dating of the winners is out by twenty years or more.

DROMEUS IS NEEDLED mercilessly for having won an Olympic crown without having to compete. This actually happened.

The story goes that in the Olympics at which Dromeus competed, there were only two contenders for the pankration: Dromeus and a man named Theagenes. Theagenes had also entered for the boxing, which he won.

Dromeus then stood up to compete for the pankration, but Theagenes refused. He declared that he was too tired to compete. The judges were furious, and they fined Theagenes heavily, but they couldn't force him to fight. There was no choice but to declare Dromeus the winner as he was ready and willing to compete. Dromeus thus became the first person in history to win at the Olympics without doing a thing. It was no fault of his own, but it surely must have weighed on him.

Dromeus really did come from the city of Mantinea, and the real Diotima also came from Mantinea. The connection was too good to pass by: I made up the bit about them being related.

BELIEVE IT OR not, the mortality rate in this book is probably low compared to the reality. The pankratists and the boxers really were absolved of murder before the contest began. The chariots were as dangerous as they looked.

There was a famous chariot race held a few years before the Olympics of this book, at the Pythian Games, in which no fewer than *forty* chariots crashed out. Pindar wrote a praise song for the winner, who was probably very relieved to be still alive.

No one was in the least bothered by the deaths. Quite the opposite, in fact. The degree of danger they faced enhanced the virtue of the sportsmen. This is by no means only an ancient attitude. The demand for safety in sport is a very recent attitude indeed. Back in the 1960s and 1970s, not long ago at all, a Formula 1 racecar driver had a 1 in 3 chance of surviving a five-year career.

THE STARTING STALL system used for chariots at the Olympics was a fascinating mechanical device. Pausanias describes its operation, and I slavishly copied his description for the book.

The *hippaphesis* provided for a staggered start, controlled by gates that opened in sequence, with the teams on the outside starting first and from behind, but given a running start, whereas the teams in the more advantageous center line had to go from a standing start. It was obviously very complex.

People don't normally associate advanced mechanics with ancient Greece, and we might doubt today if this device actually existed, but for one astounding fact: a statue made by the inventor has been discovered.

Pausanias tells us that the *hippaphesis* was invented by an Athenian architect, one Kleoitas son of Aristokles. Modern archaeologists have discovered a statue in Athens, into which these words are inscribed:

He who first invented the horses' aphesis at Olympia,
Kleoitas son of Aristokles made me.

Which means we've discovered an artifact that was personally made by someone mentioned by name, in a text that's 2,500 years old! What are the odds of that happening?

IF YOU THINK there's a lot of sex happening in this book, consider this: at the Beijing Olympics, they supplied 70,000 condoms to the athletes at the Olympic Village.

They ran out of condoms. They had to send in another 20,000.

Every Olympics Village of the last few decades has set similar remarkable records. There's no reason to think the ancient Games were any different.

IN ANCIENT GREEK religion, someone who touched a dead body was considered ritually unclean. They had to restore themselves by washing their hands in seawater. Back in Athens or any other city, a bereaved family would place a bowl of seawater outside their door, so that those who came to pay their last respects could wash on their way out.

The custom clearly has its origin in basic hygiene. Nico is punctilious about washing, which is why, after he's touched the body of Arakos, he asks where in landlocked Olympia he might find some seawater. I think it certain that in those parts of Greece that were away from the sea, the local residents would have decided the largest available river was the place to go.

THE SACRED TRUCE was a for-real system. A couple of months before the Games were due to begin, three runners were sent from Elis to crisscross Greece, shouting as they went that the truce had begun. The moment you heard that, you were legally and spiritually obliged to give even your worst enemy safe passage across your land, as long as the sole intent was to attend the Games. Once at Olympia, you and your enemy could pitch your tents side by side, secure in the knowledge that bad things would happen to anyone who broke the rules.

You're probably wondering if anyone ever broke the Sacred Truce, and the answer is yes. Exactly forty years after this book, Sparta happened to be at war with Elis, the Olympic hosts. A tricky situation, but not an impossible one given the system. Except then the Spartans attacked an Elisian fort during the Truce. The Judges were not impressed, to put it mildly, and nor were the other cities. The Judges fined the Spartans two hundred thousand drachmae. To put that in perspective, it was enough money to feed a family for about five hundred years.

The Spartans refused to pay the fine, so the Judges of the Games banned Sparta from attending the Olympics. In like manner, Exelon threatens to ban Athens over the death of Arakos.

I'M SURE THAT the Sacred Truce didn't extend to fights breaking out between spectators from opposing cities. Incidents like this happen in football stadiums around the world every day. Getting caught up in such a skirmish usually requires either a low IQ or a high blood-alcohol reading. The ancient Olympic Games were well supplied for both conditions, so I assume that at every Games there was a certain amount of drunken brawling.

GORGO IS ONE of the few women mentioned by name in the Greek histories, and one of even fewer to have had a powerful influence in Greek politics.

Gorgo began her career in international diplomacy at the tender age of eight. That seems almost unbelievable, but the story is told by Herodotus that when she was eight she advised her father the king not to aid an insurrection in Persia. The influence that Gorgo wielded within Sparta was well known to the other Greek states. Her intelligence was extraordinarily high. The story that she deduced the existence of the secret message that warned of the Persian attack is true.

The death of Gorgo's father, King Cleomenes, really was as bizarre and gruesome as she relates in the book. At the time, the official cause of death was suicide, but even back then people were whispering the word *murder*. If true, the killers would certainly have been from the Spartan leadership. That the krypteia may have done the deed on orders is my speculation, but not impossible.

Gorgo was totally bought into the Spartan ethic. The question that I put into Diotima's mouth, "How is that you Spartan women are the only ones who can rule men?" was in fact asked by an unknown woman from Athens. Gorgo's answer was, "It's because we're the only ones who give birth to real men." The same quote is used in the movie *300*, in which Gorgo appears as a character, somewhat scantily clad.

Gorgo of Sparta, Diotima of Mantinea, and a third lady, Aspasia of Miletus, stood high among the intellectual elite of the fifth century BC, which is saying a great deal since there would not be another century to match it until the Renaissance, 2,000 years later. There's no reason to believe that the real Gorgo and the real Diotima ever met, but there was no way I was going to let this series run without these two brilliant women getting to say hello to each other.

YOU HAVE TO feel sorry for King Pleistarchus of Sparta. When your father's one of the most revered warriors in all of human history, and your mother's the most intelligent woman on the planet, you've got a tough act to follow. He seems to have acquitted himself well.

At the time of this story Pleistarchus must have been in his mid-thirties. He was underage at the time his father died in 480 BC, which we know because a regent ruled in his name for the first few years. I assume that his mother, Queen Gorgo, put considerable effort into making sure her son was ready to rule, and given her background, I suspect she was demanding.

The forces of progressive politics in Sparta—to the extent that there were any in that most unusual of cities—came oddly enough from within the two royal families. It was the common Spartans who were the ultraconservatives. The reason for this is the one that Gorgo gives in the book: that a king knows his descendants will be ruling the city for hundreds of years to come, and therefore takes the long view. The common Spartan was very, very reactionary.

The political order was as the book gives: two hereditary lines of kings who ruled simultaneously, with a council of elders to advise them, and an elected council of ephors with power of veto.

THE STORY OF the krypteia ritual looks like something I must have made up, but it was for real. The krypteia was nothing short of training and field practice in the art of assassination. The ancient biographer Plutarch says this of the krypteia ritual, from his *Life of Lycurgus*:

> *The so-called* KRYPTEIA . . . *is as follows: The magistrates from time to time sent out into the countryside at large the most discreet of the young men, equipped only with daggers and necessary supplies. During the day they scattered into obscure and out-of-the-way places, where they hid themselves and lay quiet. But in the night, they came down to the roads and killed every helot whom they caught. Often, too, they actually made their way across fields where the helots were working and killed the sturdiest and best of them.*

Aristotle has a word on the subject too. He says that the ephors, as soon as they came into office, made formal declaration of war upon their own helot slaves, so that there might be no impiety in slaying them.

WHAT MADE WAR *inevitable was the growth of Athenian power, and the fear which this caused in Sparta.*

So said Thucydides in his great history of the Peloponnesian War, and in that one sentence he pretty much sums up why everything went so horribly wrong. If you studied ancient history at school then your stomach is probably churning at the sight of it, because it's almost impossible to get through any ancient history course without writing a long essay about that sentence!

The Olympic Games of 460 BC was the first after Athens became a full democracy, and the last before the First Peloponnesian War began. *Sacred Games* plays out, in the microcosm of the Olympics, the hideously complex intercity politics unfolding across Greece.

This book takes place almost exactly twenty years after the Persian Wars. In the face of the Persian onslaught, the Greeks had united for the first time (sort of . . . mostly . . . even then there were major arguments). But once the Persian War was over, it didn't take long for the alliance to fracture.

The interweb of alliances and enmities between the Greek city-states was at least as complex as the diplomatic situation in Europe prior to World War I, and just as liable to explode. So when my fictitious Arakos the Spartan is murdered at Olympia, that could be all that was needed to send Greece into a general conflagration.

In the author's note to *The Pericles Commission*, I described Athens as a deer caught between two wolves: Sparta and Persia. Now we're up to book three, and it's not getting any better for our heroes. Athens has started a war in Egypt; it's a strategic diversion to force the Persians to send their army there rather than back into Europe. But it's a huge commitment. If Sparta joins in, things are going to get tricky. Now it looks like Sparta wants to play.

Athens, a city of not more than 250,000 people, barely larger than a modern town, is prosecuting wars on three continents. And right now, they're winning every one of them.

NICO AND DIOTIMA have had a busy year. Which is only fair because the Athenian year spanning 461 to 460 BC was one of the most momentous in human history. Things can get hectic when you're inventing western civilization.

In *The Pericles Commission*, Nico and Diotima dealt with internal political threats to the new democracy. In *The Ionia Sanction*, they dealt with threats from Persia in the east. Now in *Sacred Games* they've seen off danger from Sparta in the west. I think they deserve a holiday.

They're going home to be married. I'm sure nothing can go wrong there.

EVENTS AND WINNERS OF THE 460 BC OLYMPICS

NICO ONLY GETS to see three events, but of course while he's busy investigating, there's a real Olympic Games going on in the background. For what it's worth, here are my notes on who won what at the real Olympics of 460 BC. I've included Nico's efforts so you can see where he fits in. If you've read the author's note, then you'll know how dodgy the winner lists can be. It's possible for a winner to be misplaced by sixteen or twenty years. In the great majority of cases we have no idea who won, but where there's a likely winner, I've named him.

I find it hard to believe that every Olympics was run to the same strict timetable. There were a few scheduled items that had to be fixed in stone—such as the opening and closing ceremonies, and the sacrifice of the oxen on Day Three—but beyond that the Greeks probably didn't care exactly when the events began and ended.

The judges were free to add extra competitions around the edges of the core events. We know for example that this Olympics was one of only fourteen to include a mule race. And of course at these Olympics they added the unique event of murder investigation.

Day 1 – Morning

The Olympic Oath

Competition for the Heralds

The boys' events: running, wrestling and boxing

A lad by the name of Kyniskos won the boys' boxing, which we know because a statue was made of him by the sculptor Polykleitos. The winner of the boys' wrestling was a certain Alcimedon, who was praised by Pindar in a song now known as *Olympian 8*. (Which goes to show that Pindar was present at these Games, and that he managed to get some work!)

Day 1 - Afternoon

The afternoon of Day 1 was free time. Fathers looking to find husbands for their daughters would be checking out the prospects. Old friends from different cities would be catching up.

Day 2 - Morning

Nico and Markos take an extra special Olympic Oath.

Chariot Races

there were four:
2-horse chariot race for colts
2-horse chariot race for older horses
4-horse chariot race for colts
4-horse chariot race for older horses

For my own dramatic purposes I had the 4-horse race for older horses run first. Nico and Markos miss the other events.

Horse races

there were three:
Race for stallions
Race for colts
Race for mares

The mule race probably came after the horse races, no doubt for comic relief.

Day 2 - Afternoon

The Pentathlon:
Running
Wrestling
Long Jump
Discus
Javelin

Day 3 - Morning

The sacrifice of the oxen. This was *the* event of the Games for the ancient Greeks.

Day 3 - Afternoon

First up was the *dolichos*, which was the long distance race. The winner in 460 BC was the famous Ladas of Argos. He was known as a runner so very light on the ground that his feet never left an imprint. It's said that he died on his way home from these Olympics, and that a memorial was built by the roadside where he collapsed.

Next came the *stadion*, which was the sprint event. Needless to say, it was one length of the stadion. The winner is listed as Torymmas of Thessaly. More than any other event, to win the stadion race was to win immortality, because most Olympics were uniquely named by the stadion winner.

Then came the *diaulos*, which was two lengths of the stadion. Winner unknown.

In the evening a massive barbecue feast was held of the ox meat and, at this particular Olympics, also the bread ox of Empedocles. (Yes, that really happened.)

Day 4

Wrestling

The winner of the wrestling was Amesinas of Barce, who trained by wrestling with a bull while he tended his cattle. He even brought the bull with him for extra practice.

Boxing
winner unknown

Judging of the Murder Investigation event
The winner is listed as Nicolaos, son of Sophroniscus.

Pankration
The winner was Timodemus, son of Timonous.

The *hoplitodromos*: the race in armor
winner unknown

For the *hoplitodromos*, competitors ran two lengths of the stadion in standard soldier kit. Nico misses this event, of course, because at that moment he has Timo slung over his shoulders and is racing for the aid station.

Day 5

Closing Ceremony

GLOSSARY

Agora. The marketplace. Every city had its agora, and so too must have Olympia during the Games.

Amphora. The standard container of the ancient world. Amphorae come in many sizes. An amphora vaguely resembles a worm caught in the act of eating far too big a mouthful: wide at the top, tapering to a pointy bottom. Amphorae are used to hold wine, oil, water, olives, you name it. Tens of thousands of ancient amphorae have survived to this day.

Attica. The area of southern Greece controlled by Athens. Most of Attica is rural, very hilly, farmland. When Gorgo says she would cheer on her men as they laid waste to Attica, she means to the farmland that fed Athens. It was a common strategy in those days to destroy the enemy's food production.

Aulos Pipes. A recorder-like musical instrument, but with two pipes which form a V at the mouthpiece. Music was played during some Olympic events, such as the long jump.

Bouleterion. Council house. Boule means council. Olympia had a bouleterion, which was the administration center during the Games.

Chaire! "Rejoice!" Friends who met each other on the street would call out, "Chaire! I rejoice to see you!" In the Bible—clearly at a much later date—*chaire* is the first word spoken to Mary by the angels.

Chiton. The chiton is the usual garment of a wealthy citizen. The chiton is a large rectangular sheet, or two sheets pinned together, wrapped around the body from the right, wide enough to cover the arms when outstretched and fall to the ankles. The sheet is pinned over both shoulders and down the left side. Greek clothing is neither cut nor shaped; there's a lot of spare material below the arms. The chiton is belted at the waist so the extra material doesn't flop around. The chiton is worn with a **himation**, a bit like a stole, across the shoulders. The chiton is for men with no need to labor. A middle class artisan might wear an **exomis**.

Deme. A deme is like a combination of suburb and sub-tribe. All of **Attica** is broken up into demes. When an Athenian introduces himself to a stranger, he always gives his name, his father's name, and the deme in which he lives. Hence, "Timodemus, son of Timonous, of the deme Archarnae of Athens," or, "Nicolaos, son of Sophroniscus, of the deme Alopece of Athens."

The patronymics and the demes I used above are totally correct. This was the standard way of naming. Even in writing, there are many real people mentioned in classical sources about whom we know almost nothing, except who their father was, and where to find their house. A man took the same deme as his father.

Demeter. The goddess of the harvest. She's also the goddess of fertility, which makes it so appropriate that Klymene is her priestess. No one knows why the priestess of Demeter had to observe the Sacred Games; not even the ancient Greeks could remember the reason, and that makes the tradition very old indeed. Some scholars have speculated that, because of this rule, the Sacred Games might have begun as funeral games to celebrate death and rebirth.

Drachma. The standard coin of Greece. The average workman earned about a drachma a day. One drachma is worth six **obols**. Every city minted their own coins, which created the need for moneychangers and exchange rates. At an event like Olympia, every coin imaginable changed hands in trade. It must have been chaos for the stallholders (and for the **pornoi** too!).

Exomis. The exomis is the standard wear of middle class artisans. The exomis is a sheet of linen wrapping around from the right, slightly wider than the shoulders of the wearer and falling to knee length. The corners are tied over the left shoulder, which is all that prevents the exomis from falling off. This leaves both arms and legs free to move without hindrance.

Sophroniscus wears an exomis every day when he sculpts, and therefore feels uncomfortable in the more restrictive **chiton**. Pericles, on the other hand, wouldn't be seen dead in an exomis. He always wears a chiton and drapes around him a **himation** of fine wool.

Genos. A family bloodline. It's the same as *gens* in Latin, and the origin of the word genus in English. The genos Timonidae was a family in ancient Athens who produced sports stars over many generations. Timodemus and Timonous were both members of the genos Timonidae.

Gymnasium. Gymnasium is a very Greek word. I've used the Latin form for familiarity. The Greek is **gymnasion**. The gymnasium at Olympia is Roman. In Nico's day there were very few permanent buildings, and there's no known gym from that date. I consider that impossible, so I've placed a temporary wooden structure where the Roman gymnasium was later built.

To the Greeks, the gymnasium was not only a place to exercise, but also a social center and where boys went to school. Both meanings survive to the present day. In German, a gymnasium is a high school.

Hellanodikai. The Judges of the **Hellenes**. Dikai means judges. The hellanodikai were men of outstanding integrity who were selected to run the Olympic Games and adjudicate disputes. Considering how desperate everyone was to win, I don't envy them the job.

Hellenes. The Greeks. They never called themselves Greek. They called themselves Hellenes. To this day, in their own language, the word for Greece is Hellas.

Hetaera. A courtesan. Diotima might not be pleased about her mother's salacious past, but the hetaerae were high class, well educated, and capable of holding their own at the highest levels of society.

Himation. A stole or cloak worn with a **chiton**. The himation is made of wool and worn across the shoulders and down an arm.

Hydria. A ceramic jar used to store water. Whence all the modern words beginning *hydro*, such as hydroelectric.

Hippaphesis. It means horse-starter. The hippaphesis at Olympia was the world's first starting gate for horse races. It worked as Nico describes in the book—a V-shaped device that enforced a staggered start, with the outer wings of the V going first and the apex of the V last. The hippaphesis was invented by an Athenian named Kleotas.

Hippeis. Knights. Not quite the same as medieval knights in shining armor, but it's the same basic idea. Every city had its knights, which meant citizens wealthy enough to provide a horse when they fought in the army. The term is very ancient because by classical times everyone was fighting on foot, even the now misnamed hippeis. Some cities formalized the hippeis system, Sparta being one of those.

The Spartan hippeis were elite troops. It's hard to imagine just how good you'd have to be, to be considered elite at Sparta. The modern SAS or Green Berets might be a reasonable equivalent. In battle, the hippeis fought in the place of honor, on the right flank, and appear to have provided a bodyguard to the kings.

The hippeis were more than that, though, because they also had powers of arrest. Herodotus and Xenophon both describe cases in which members of the hippeis were sent to bring in men accused of crimes against the state. In both cases the crime was treason. From this it's reasonable to assume the hippeis had a role in state security.

Hippodrome. It means simply horse arena. The hippodrome is where the chariot races were held. The hippodrome at Olympia was entirely lost during major floods in medieval times, but when you look at a map of the ruins there's an empty space in the bottom right corner where it is fairly obviously the hippodrome must have been.

Iatrion. In modern Greek it means hospital. In ancient Greek, it was more like an aid station or a doctor's surgery. Given the state of medicine in ancient Greece, it was a good place to avoid. There was an iatrion set up at Olympia during each Games—very wise, considering the casualty rate—but it's not known where it was. I've assumed it was in the most sensible spot: halfway between the **stadion** and the **hippodrome**.

Kalimera. Good morning. A polite usage between anyone. The more intimate **chaire** would be used between friends.

Krater. A large bowl which sits on the ground and is used to mix wine and water.

Krypteia. Krypteia means secrets, and is the origin of the English words crypt, cryptology, cryptic, etc. The bizarre Spartan coming-of-age rite called the krypteia sounds like something from epic fantasy, but it was quite real and is described by the ancient biographer Plutarch in his *Life of Lycurgus*.

Krypteia was also the name of a kind of secret police, or a black operations group. The first mention of the krypteia as an organization comes in Plutarch's *Life of Cleomenes III*. At the battle of Sellasia in 221 BC, 239 years after the time of this story, a man named Damoteles is described as the head of the krypteia. Damoteles is ordered to do some reconnaissance on the flanks, but instead he promptly betrays his own king. The Cleomenes III of this tale is a descendant of the Cleomenes who was father of Gorgo.

The Spartans weren't the most literary of people, even at the best of times, let alone in reference to a dark organization of secret state assassins, so virtually nothing was ever written about the krypteia. Once you've read this glossary entry, you'll be as knowledgeable as anyone alive today. Speculation about the krypteia is wild and highly variable. It's my own idea, but I think very reasonable, to assume the best performers from the rite of passage were selected for assassin duty.

From this it seems both the **hippeis** and the krypteia were involved in state security, which might sound odd at first, but no one who lives in the modern world should be surprised at the idea of two competing intelligence organizations within a single state.

Kynodesme. We had such fun trying to think of a modern name for this thing. It means literally "dog leash." *Kyno*—dog. *Desme*—leash. The kynodesme was a leather cord that tied around the tip of the penis and then wrapped around the scrotum, to stop bits from jiggling while the athletes competed. It was the *only* thing athletes were allowed to wear. There are surviving pottery pieces on display in museums, decorated with images of athletes, that show them wearing a kynodesme.

Megaron. Back in the bronze age, before classical architecture had been invented, palaces and great houses consisted of a large hall—like a small version of the Great Hall of an English castle—with a front porch and a central fireplace, and a hole in the roof to let out the smoke. Such buildings were called a megaron, which means, in fact, great hall. *Mega*—great. *Ron*—hall. There were several very ancient bronze age ruins at Olympia. The classical Greeks had no idea what they really were, but took the largest of them to be the megaron of the ancient king Oinomaos. For all we know, they might even be right.

Metic. A resident alien in Athens. Metics run businesses and they pay taxes, but have no say in public affairs. A modern equivalent would be residents of the USA with green cards. Diotima is a metic. There was something of a prejudice against marriage between citizens and metics.

Naos. The large, central room of a Greek temple. Whenever you see a picture of the inside of a Greek temple, you're looking at the naos. This was the room that held the cult statue. After you walk up the temple steps you come to a small vestibule called the **pronaos**, and the pronaos leads on to the naos.

Nemean Games. There were four major sports meetings in

ancient Greece: the Olympic Games, the Nemean Games, the Isthmian Games, and the Pythian Games.

The games alternated in a complex pattern. The Olympics were held every four years in summer. Everyone knows that one! The Pythian Games were also held every four years, at Delphi, at the midpoint in the calendar between each Olympics. In effect the Olympic and Pythian Games took turns being held every second year. The Isthmian Games were held every two years, the same years as the Olympic and the Pythian Games, at the isthmus that connects the Peloponnesian Peninsula with the rest of mainland Greece. The Nemean Games were held at Nemea, every two years, alternating with the Isthmian Games. So the whole thing went: Olympic and Isthmian Games—Nemean Games—Pythian and Isthmian Games—Nemean Games, and then the cycle repeats.

Olympic victors won a crown of olive branches, winners at the Pythian Games received a crown of laurel, a crown of pine branches for the winners at the Isthmus, and Nemean victors won a crown of wild celery. Anyone who could pick up four victories in a row was declared to be a **paradoxos**.

Obol. A small coin. Six obols make a **drachma**. Most items in the agora cost an obol or two. When you die, it's an obol that they place under your tongue, to pay the ferryman to take you to Hades.

Opithodomos. A covered porch at the opposite end of a temple to its entrance. A good place to meet friends and hang out.

Ostrakon. An ostrakon is a pottery shard. Ostraka—that's the plural—were the Post-It notes of the ancient world. There was always a plentiful supply because people were constantly dropping

amphorae. To send a friend a message, simply pick up the nearest ostrakon, scratch your message, and have your slave carry it. Thousands of ostraka have been recovered, because they were also used as voting slips in elections, and the used ostraka were then dumped as landfill.

Paradoxos. It means a marvel, and is the origin of our word paradox. A man might be referred to as *paradoxos* if he'd done something truly remarkable. In particular, anyone who won the **pankration** at all four major Games was named paradoxos. A modern equivalent might be winning, in a single year, all four Grand Slam events on the international tennis circuit: an almost impossible achievement.

Pankration. The martial art of the ancient Greeks. Gouging eyes and biting was forbidden; every other dirty trick you can think of was fair game. Clearly pankration was not for the faint of heart. Pankratists were the highest-paid sports stars of ancient Greece.

Pornê. A hooker. The word means *walker*, because like their modern colleagues, the pornoi walked the streets. Our word pornography comes straight from the ancient Greek for prostitutes, and taken literally, means *images of walkers*. Pornoi flocked to Olympia for the Games. They were housed in the women's camp. Since there was nowhere for them to walk, they declared their profession by hanging their sandals outside their tents. There was a world of difference between a pornê and the high-class **hetaera**. There are two plurals for pornê: *pornoi* for a mixed group of males and females, but *pornai* if you know they're all women. I've used the generic plural in all cases to avoid confusion in English.

Pelops. A hero-king from legend. His father was Tantalus, who killed his son Pelops to feed him to the Gods. The Gods resurrected Pelops just before dinnertime, though Demeter had already eaten his shoulder, so they gave him one of ivory. Pelops then won the hand of Hippodamia, as Libon relates in the book, in the process murdering his future father-in-law. Considering Pelops's father had previously killed him, and the happy couple had recently murdered the bride's father, seating at the wedding reception must have been tricky. There was a large mound in the middle of the **Sanctuary of Zeus**, which the classical Greeks believed to be the grave of Pelops. The Peloponnesian Peninsula is named for him.

Praise Singer. Praise singers were poets-for-hire, who sang their poems, and who for a fee would do a terrific marketing job to make you look great. It's difficult to think of a modern equivalent to the praise singer. If you can imagine a spin doctor with literary talent and the skills of a singer/songwriter you're probably not far off. The two most famous praise singers in history, head and shoulders above the rest for talent, were Simonides and Pindar. One of these two men almost certainly wrote the famous epitaph for the 300 Spartans who fell at Thermopylae, but neither ever claimed the credit.

Pronaos. The room before the **naos**. Many churches have a small vestibule before you enter the church proper. This is the same thing.

Psyche. A human spirit. When you die, your psyche descends to Hades. If the proper burial rituals aren't performed, a psyche can be trapped in the mortal world. The psyche of a groom murdered by Pelops was said to inhabit the **taraxippus**.

Sacred Games. The ancient name for the Olympics. The Sacred Games were dedicated to Zeus, king of the Gods. They were held at Olympia, hence the modern name for the event. There were four major Games in the Greek sporting calendar: the Olympic, Pythian, Isthmian, and the **Nemean Games**.

Sanctuary of Zeus. The center of Olympia was not the stadion, but the Sanctuary of Zeus. To the ancients, the Olympics was a religious observance first, and a sports event second. Within the sanctuary was the **Temple of Zeus**.

Skamma. These days we'd call it the long jump pit, but the ancient Greeks didn't use sand. They tilled the earth alongside one length of the **stadion** until it was soft and level and could take an imprint. Long jump in the Sacred Games was from a standing start—no run up allowed!—the athlete was allowed to swing weights held in his hands, and it was all done to music.

Stadion. No prizes for guessing this one. It means stadium. What's less well known is that stadion was originally a unit of length. The sports field at Olympia is one stadion long, hence its name. The sprint event at the Sacred Games was also called the stadion, since competitors ran one length of the field. The Olympic stadion is in the top right-hand corner of the map, and it's a lot smaller than you'd think, considering its vast reputation.

Strigil. A curved piece of bronze with a handle at one end, used to scrape down the skin. Classical Greece has soap, but no one wants to use it because it's made of goat fat and ashes. Instead, a slave rubs you down with olive oil, and then scrapes away the dirty oil and the dead outer layer of your skin with a strigil.

Taraxippus. The horse terror. *Tara*—terror. *Xippus*—horse. I know it's usually *hippos* for horse, but they haven't yet invented the dictionary and standardized spelling. The taraxippus was an altar outside the first turn of the chariot race track at the **hippodrome**. Most crashes occurred on that turn, supposedly because a **psyche** trapped within the taraxippus induced great fear in the horses.

Temple of Zeus. The Temple of Zeus at Olympia is brand spanking new at the time of this story. It stunned the Greeks with its brilliance and was the greatest ever example of Doric architecture. The Temple of Zeus won't be completed for another three years, but it surely must have been open for inspection at these Olympics. The cult statue will not be installed for another thirty years. When it is, the Statue of Zeus at Olympia will become one of the Seven Wonders of the Ancient World.

ACKNOWLEDGMENTS

THAT THIS BOOK exists is thanks to the endless support from my wife, Helen, and my daughters, Catriona and Megan. Helen is my first reader, and also the last before each book releases, since she reads the final proofs with exquisite care. Sometimes I open a manuscript file to find that Catriona has been reading through it, which I know because of the notes left behind in red, telling me what I did wrong, how to fix it, and with firm instructions on the fate of her favorite characters. More often than not, I take her advice.

Janet Reid is my amazing literary agent. People who aren't involved in the process don't quite understand how difficult a job agenting can be. How Janet manages to remain sane I don't quite understand.

Juliet Grames is my patient editor at Soho Press. She's astoundingly thorough! Thanks to her editing, I understand my own writing better than ever before.

Anneke Klein and Bill Kirton read early versions of *Sacred Games*, as they have every book I've ever written. As always, they provided invaluable comments.

And finally, a big thank-you to you! Every time I receive fan mail, or see a reader review online, I know a book that I've written has touched someone enough that they took the time to say something about it, which is very cool indeed.